Revolt at the Beach

Revolt at the Beach

More Twisp Family Chronicles

Book VIII

Youth in Venice

C.D. Payne

Aivia Press

ISBN-13: 978-1882647064

ISBN-10: 1882647068

To: David Permut, Bob Weinstein,
and the late Mickey Freiberg

A NOTE ON THE SERIES:
Youth in Revolt contains Books 1, 2, and 3
Revolting Youth is Book 4
Young and Revolting is Book 5
Revoltingly Young is Book 6
Son of Youth in Revolt is Book 7
Revolt at the Beach is Book 8
Cut to the Twisp contains text deleted from the post-1994 U.S. and
U.K. editions of *Youth in Revolt,* plus additional short pieces.

Warm thanks again to Till Hack for his editorial assistance.

Principal characters

The Twisps

Nick Twisp: Married to Dr. Ada Olson. Father of Scott Twisp. Also father of Miren and Nerea Lurrieta by Sheeni Saunders.

Scott Twisp: Son of Nick Twisp and Ada Olson.

Jake Twisp: Nick's younger brother. Originally named Noel Wescott. Married to Lillian Twisp.

Joan Twisp: Nick's older sister. Married to Bill Tibble.

Tyler Twisp: Joan's son and Nick's nephew. Married to Uma Spurletti.

Miren Ohlmann: Daughter of Nick and Sheeni. Married to Ryder Ohlmann.

Estelle and George F. Twisp: Parents of Nick, Joan, and Jake.

The Saunders

Sheeni Saunders: Nick's first girlfriend. Married to François Durrance, a French wine wholesaler. Mother by him of François Durrance II and Marthe Durrance.

Paul Saunders: Sheeni's older brother. Father of Veeva Saunders. Married to second wife Reyna Vesely.

Connie Saunders: Paul's first wife and mother of Veeva Saunders.

Veeva Saunders: Sheeni's niece and long-time friend of Jake and Tyler Twisp. Married to author Desmond Upton, who writes under the pen name Miles North. Mother of Xenia and Marty Upton.

Other characters

Trent Preston: Former boyfriend of Sheeni Saunders. Married to Apurva Joshi. Father (with Violet Barnes) of Azura Preston.

Azura Preston: Daughter of Trent Preston. Girlfriend of Scott Twisp.

Mary Moran: Mother of Lauren and Megan Moran.

Brenda Blatt: Associate of Mary Moran.

Roland Pacalac: Associate of Nick Twisp.

Leonard and Kerri Davidson: Parents of Nick Davidson.

Valerie and Harvey Haseltine: Sibling friends of Nick Davidson.

Esmee Carstann: Friend of Valerie Haseltine.

Lefty: Boyhood pal of Nick.

Marcus Swandon: Former NFL player and Tyler's live-in bodyguard.

MAY

THURSDAY, May 14 – Google screwed up my life.

My dad in a moment of idleness at work (he has many) decided to Google our respective blood types. He discovered that it was scientifically impossible for him to have fathered yours truly. (Him: type AB, me: type O.) He reacted not well to this news. I wasn't there, but apparently he had some super huge fight with my mother. His panicked secretary came close to dialing 911. When I got home from school, Mom seemed pretty upset. She said he has packed his bags and bailed. He's checked into one of those extended-stay motels out by the cloverleaf.

Why this could be bad news for me: My mother is something of a giant for a chick, being a towering six-one. My newly announced non-dad is nearly six-four. Having just turned 15, I stand a mere five feet, five inches tall. I'd always assumed that any day now I'd be commencing some phenomenal growth spurt. Now this is seriously in doubt. What if my actual father was some sort of dwarfish fellow, and I'm destined to remain sized forever like a Hobbit?

I'd ask Mom who the DNA donor was, but she seems too upset to broach the topic. Or to make dinner.

The good news is I'm no longer related to Mr. Leonard S. Davidson, one of the notable jerks of our time. As a tot I kind of liked the guy, but since about age eight he's been creeping me out. That loser was never in the running for any father of the year awards. An ego a mile high and a temper to match. He was always right and I was always wrong–with a swat every now and then to remind me. So it turns out he wasn't my dad, he was my evil stepfather. That explains a lot.

They'd met in Las Vegas; Mom was a showgirl and he was a card dealer. She doesn't know it, but I've found the photos she keeps hidden of her in her costumes. Super glamorous makeup and hair so you'd hardly recognize her. Lots of sequins and feathers and not a stitch covering her boobs. Good thing I'd seen plenty of internet porn so it wasn't such a shock. Still it's a bit weird knowing your mother used to parade around half-naked being ogled by throngs of drunken gamblers.

So how did we wind up in Terre Haute, garden spot of the Midwest? One Christmas Eve a drunk driver wiped out my non-grandparents in their Cadillac. So their only son had to move his family (Mom and me) back to Indiana to manage the business. He inherited a chain of dry cleaners. Not a giant chain like McDonalds or Pizza Hut. He started with a chain of seven locations and has grown the business into a chain of four locations. He blames the decline on those coin-op dry-cleaning machines they started installing in laundromats. That's why he likes to sneak into them when no one is around and squeeze Super Glue into the coin slots. He's the Big Boss and my mom works in his office part-time as Personnel Manager. Mostly it's her job to keep the black ladies showing up for work despite the miserable toil, toxic chemicals, and crummy wages.

The phone rang, so I listened in over the handset in my room. More rants from my ex-dad. One highlight and I quote: "I'm not going to spend another dime supporting some bastard's bastard!"

Fine with me, Dad. I'll happily remain an impoverished midget if it means not being related to you.

SATURDAY, May 16. A budget motel near the Texas-Oklahoma border. Mom decided to bail big time on her marriage. She's always been kind of impulsive. We're heading back to Las Vegas. She gave me two hours to pack and call up my friends to say goodbye. We're traveling light, so I had to leave my computer and 99 percent of my stuff. Electronically, I'm making do with just my laptop and phone–about on par with kids in Bangladesh. I could only think of one friend who might conceivably miss me. I phoned Jayden and gave him the news. He said exiting Indiana could only be a smart move. I promised to text him with details of my trip.

I was born in Las Vegas, but left there when I was three, so I have no memory of the burg. It's in the desert and is supposed to be quite hot with temps over 115 degrees some days. People go there to gamble, raise hell, and hook up with hookers. They wake up with raging hangovers in trashed motel rooms. That could be fun to try, but I don't suppose they let kids my age do it. Mom did say it's too late for me to start school there, so I get an early start on summer vacation. No final exams! That's good, but I'll still have to face all those hostile stares at some new school in the fall. Where I won't know a soul and will be shunned by all the cool kids. That sucks, but I'm trying not to think about it.

Mom just phoned my non-dad to tell him where we are. As if he cares! Then we had to delay going to dinner at the diner down the road while she had a cry in the bathroom.

We're back from dinner. Mom had four gin fizzes to drown her sorrows, so I had to take command of the car keys. First time I ever drove a car. Piece of cake. Too bad it was less than a mile back to our motel.

We're sharing a room, which is kind of unnerving. Mom's paying for everything with cash (even gas), which leads me to believe my ex-dad has canceled her credit cards. What a bastard. I'm trying to look on the bright side. He'd been making noises about my working all summer at the dry cleaners nearest our house. Thank God, I dodged that bullet. His bread and butter is helpless bachelors and career gals who get ALL their laundry dry cleaned. That means I'd have been handling strangers' smelly socks and underwear. All for way less than the legal minimum wage. Too nightmarish to contemplate.

SUNDAY, May 17. An Indian casino in the middle of nowhere. We're on the seventh floor; Mom finagled a discount on the room since she used to be in the business. View out the window of endless tracks of Arizona wasteland. A big change from Indiana scenery. Does it never rain here?

Dinner in the Golden Eagle room. No actual eagle on the menu. I had a steak, which was not bad. Husbanding her funds, Mom had only one cocktail. The farther away she gets from Indiana, the more depressed she seems, whereas just the opposite is true for me. I think travel gets you out of your rut—even if poverty, homelessness, and sleeping in your car may await down the road. If you're really poor, I think the government gives you surplus cheese so you don't starve. Good thing I like cheese, although a diet solely of cheese could be constipating (as are gross gas-station restrooms, I've discovered).

Mom just put on her bathing suit and went down to the indoor pool. I declined her invitation to come along. I'm using my swim trunks for sleeping attire and don't want to get them wet. At home I sleep in the buff–not having owned a pair of pajamas for years. I expect somewhere out there my future wife is also sleeping in the nude. You think about these things after hundreds of miles of staring out the window at boring scenery.

Perhaps Mom will meet some millionaire Indian down there and all our troubles will be over. I'll be adopted by the tribe and learn to ride like the wind on my own fleet pony. Every month I'll get a fat check as my share of the casino revenues. Probably not though.

MONDAY, May 18. Las Vegas, Nevada. We made it. No highway signs on the outskirts yet proclaiming it the birthplace of Nicholas F. Davidson. Could be there someday though. Mom scored us a modest comp room at the Normandie, where she used to work. It's this casino in the shape of an ocean liner that also tries to look like a ship on the inside. We're way down in the depths of the "hull" and don't even have a porthole to look out of. The casino used to have a section of artificial ocean in the front along the street, but they filled that in after too many drunken tourists were falling in and drowning. Now it has a white sand "beach" and some palm trees. There's also a stand that rents motor scooters, which I'd like to try, but as usual I'm too young. Being 15 is such a useless age.

I want to go explore, but Mom says we got in too late. She's tired from all that driving. So here I am in swinging Vegas and all we're going to do is go to bed.

TUESDAY, May 19. Sunny and hot. Not muggy though like Indiana. At breakfast in the budget buffet room I had to shake hands with all these people my mother used to work with. Several of them expressed the opinion that I soon would be taller than her. If only I had some hope of that. So far Mom's not saying word one about the midget whose adulterous impulses gathered me forth from the cosmic dust. And I bugged her all the way through New Mexico on that topic.

Mom gave me $10, smeared me with sunblock, and made me promise I wouldn't stray off the Strip (main drag lined with casinos). She suggested I check out Circus Circus which has free circus shows. That sounded major dull, so I toured the Bellagio, the Venetian, and New York-New York. What they don't tell you is these casinos are mostly just tarted-up shopping malls with attached gambling halls. At every turn they are endeavoring to suck dollars from your wallet.

As I was having a burger at McDonalds in faux Manhattan my phone rang. It was Avery Weston from Terre Haute, whose awareness of my existence I had long doubted.

"Hi, Nickie D.," she said. "What's this I hear about your blowing town?"

"Hi, Avery," I gasped. "Yeah, I've cleared out for good."

"So where are you?"

"In Vegas. I'm having a cheeseburger in the New York-New York casino. We're staying in a suite at the Normandie. That's the one that looks like a ship."

"So how come you just snuck out like a rat? How come you didn't say goodbye to anyone?"

"Uh, well my mom had to go into the Witness Protection Program really fast. That's all I can tell you. You'll have to promise me you won't tell anyone."

"Of course, Nick. That's amazing. Are you in trouble?"

"Not if we lay low for the next 20 years. The FBI changed all our identities. You're probably the last person who will ever address me as Nick."

"Wow, that's so awesome! What's your new name?"

"That's a total state secret. In fact, you might be in considerable danger if I told you. Speaking of which, now that I'll never see you again, I can say that I, uh, kind of liked you."

"Really? How come you were keeping it such a big secret?"

"Oh, I don't know. You always seemed pretty busy with other guys."

"I could never go out with you, Nick. Since you're shorter than I am."

"Yeah. That's what I figured."

"But I kind of liked you too."

"Really?"

"Yeah. You'd be totally hot if you grew a foot or two."

"Thanks. Both my parents are tall so I'm overdue for a growth spurt. Should I look you up someday when I'm playing pro basketball for the Pacers?"

"Please do. Well, have a nice life."

"Yeah. You too. Thanks for calling."

Wow, cute Avery Weston may be missing me slightly. That's sort of blowing my mind.

In case you're wondering, since there were three Nicks in my kindergarten class, Miss Reynolds started calling us Nickie S., Nickie P., and Nickie D. The names pretty much stuck, although my friend Nickie P. has moved on to his middle name Jayden. That reminds me, I've yet to send him a single text.

WEDNESDAY, May 20. Another bombshell from Mom at breakfast. One of her old Normandie colleagues made some calls and found her a job.

"Doing what?" I asked.

"Dancing on a cruise ship. It sails out of Miami. So pack your bags, honey. We're leaving today for Los Angeles."

"Uh, Mom, L.A. isn't really on the way to Miami."

"I know that. There's something I need to do there first."

Wow, we're going to live in Miami. That sounded fine with me. Miami's a balmy place that offers much more than bizarrely themed casinos. It has the ocean, beaches, and 50,000 girls in bikinis. Who knows, someday I might be able to muster up the courage to talk to one of them.

"Dancing, huh?" I said. "Do they know what you look like?"

"Don't you worry about that. I've still got the body for it. The rest of the magic I can do with makeup."

"Right. If you say so. When are we leaving?"

"In ten minutes. So get a move on."

Another long boring drive. California is supposed to be scenic, but you can't prove it by the drive from Las Vegas. Eventually we pulled up in front of a seedy-looking apartment building near the intersection of Vermont and Pico. In the distance to the east were the tall buildings of downtown L.A.

"Not such a classy neighborhood, but this is supposed to be the place," said Mom, parking in a red zone. She dialed a number, someone said "Hello," and she hung up. "OK, honey, here's what I want you to do. Take this letter up to apartment 22B and hand it to the person who answers the door."

"Who is it?"

"Just a friend of mine. It'll be fine. Don't you worry."

"Are you coming with me?"

"No, I have to stay in the car and guard our stuff."

"Why can't your friend come down and get the letter?"

"Just do it! OK? Do your mother a favor for once in your life. I'm totally stressed out here!"

"Oh, all right."

I grabbed the letter and exited the car. Apartment 22B was on the second floor. I knocked on the door and held out the letter to the old guy who answered.

"Who the hell are you?" he asked.

He looked like he needed a shave and possibly hospice care.

"I'm nobody. My mother wants you to read this letter. Don't ask me why."

"Are you trying to sell me something? Is this about Jesus?"

"None of the above, sir. Just take the letter, OK? We're in a hurry."

"All right. But you stay right where you are."

The guy read the letter and turned very pale.

"This is totally preposterous," he gasped. "Where's your mother?"

"Waiting down in the car."

He grabbed his keys off a table beside the door. "We'll see about this. She can't do this to me!"

But my mother wasn't waiting in the car. The car was nowhere to be seen. And stashed in a corner of the apartment lobby were my bags.

Now it was my turn to go white. I felt the blood drain out of my brain and I started to tremble all over.

"Are those your bags?" he demanded.

"Fraid so," I said, forcing back tears.

"What's your mother's goddam phone number?"

I mumbled the number, he dialed it on his cellphone, got her message and bellowed, "Are you crazy, Kerri? You get right back here! I mean it! This is totally ridiculous! This is the most irresponsible act I've ever heard of! I want you back here right now!"

We waited a tense 20 minutes, but Mom didn't show. He sighed and looked at me. "Your mother is totally crazy. Did you know that?"

"Not really. But I'm beginning to think you may be right."

"I'm going to call the police. That's what I'm going to do. They'll put a bulletin out for her car. This is child abandonment!"

"Yeah. It kind of feels like that."

We hauled my bags up to his apartment, but he didn't call the police. He sat in a recliner and stared at the ceiling. I stood by my bags and tried not to look at him. I was beginning to think I had seen the dude somewhere before.

"What's your name, kid?" he said at last.

"Nicholas F. Davidson."

"She named you Nick. I might have known. What does the F stand for?"

"Frank."

"Well, that's no surprise either."

"And you are?" I asked.

He sighed. "Nick Twisp."

I'd heard that name before.

"As in 'Nick Twisp's Double Juggle?'" I asked.

He sighed again. "That's me."

"Right. My mom used to watch your TV show."

"Yes, well, that's nice I guess. I suppose you thought it was stupid and inane."

"It was OK. I thought Azura Preston was pretty hot. I liked it when you played the black dude."

"Everybody liked that part except the N.A.A.C.P. That's why I got nominated for Emmys but never won."

"Right."

Long silence in the room.

"So why am I here?" I asked.

"Why are you here! Don't you know?"

"Not at all. Can you clue me in?"

"Your mother appears to be under the impression that I'm your father."

The second major shock of the day. Well, that explains my height impairment. The guy couldn't have been over five-seven. Even more ominous, his hairline had marched back a few inches. My ex-dad may have been a world-class dork, but he still had all of his hair.

So I told him about the cataclysmic Google discovery and our fast trip west.

"I remember Leonard Davidson," he said. "He was tall and good-looking and full of himself."

"Now he's only tall and full of himself."

"He's completely in the wrong here. If you were an infant, the state might care about paternity. But at this late date he's legally on the hook for you. No way can he escape his parental obligations."

"Well, I think he intends to try."

"The man's an idiot. So how old are you, Nick?"

"Fifteen."

I could see he was doing some mental calculations.

"When's your birthday?"

"April 23."

More mental calculations; I don't think he liked the result. Probably all that subtraction landed him right back in bed with Mom. Nor was he too pleased to hear that she was now bound for Miami.

Eventually I asked him if dinner would be served. I told him that it had been a long drive from Vegas and we hadn't stopped for lunch.

"Do you cook?" he asked.

"I can make a grilled cheese sandwich," I admitted.

"Good. I'll have mine with bacon and tomatoes."

I went into his kitchen to scrounge up some food. When I opened a cupboard door, a bug dropped down and shot across the counter.

"What was that?" I said, startled.

"You must have lived a sheltered life, Nick. That was a cockroach."

"That's gross. Can't you spray?"

"Wouldn't do any good. The whole building's infested with them. I'm just thankful we don't have bedbugs."

"I thought you were some big-shot TV star."

"I used to be. The show ran for six seasons, which is a miracle considering our ratings. Fortunately, the network liked what we were doing. We did some funny shows."

"So—what? You blew all your money on drugs?"

He laughed. "Not hardly. I'm doing OK. I have a nice house in Pacific Palisades. That's on the west side north of Santa Monica."

"So why aren't you living there?" I asked, putting the bacon on to fry.

"My wife kicked me out. On Valentine's Day. I rent this furnished apartment by the month. It's only temporary."

"Why did she kick you out?"

"Oh, she didn't like my attitude. She says I'm too much of a wet blanket to live with."

"Are you getting divorced?"

"Could be. Who knows? It's all up in the air. I don't want to run down marriage for you, kid, but I think there's only a finite number of times you can eat breakfast with someone. Or have sex with them. Or listen to their cares and complaints. You reach your limit and that's that."

"I think it would be great if my parents got divorced. My mom deserves someone better than the creep she married. She might have trouble finding someone though, being so tall."

"As I recall she was amazingly statuesque. I'm surprised you're not taller."

"That makes two of us. Should I thank your DNA?"

"That's very much not decided, Nick. Even if I were your father, it doesn't follow that we'd be connected in any way."

"Oh. OK."

I went back to slicing a tomato with his dull knife.

"Hey, kid, I shouldn't have said that. I shouldn't be giving you 'don't exist' messages."

"What kind of messages?"

"'Don't exist' messages. I used to get them all the time from my parents when I was your age. It's very bad. You internalize them and start taking them to heart. Pretty soon you're thinking suicide sounds like an idea worth exploring. So, I'm glad you exist, Nick—no matter who your father is. I just have to get over the shock of your turning up here out of the blue."

"Yeah, it surprised me too."

I wonder if Mom ditching me with some stranger qualifies as a "don't exist" message?

We had potato chips with the sandwiches and ate at the little round table in the kitchen. I liked them OK with the tomato slices and crispy bacon inside. It was a new take on grilled cheese. I tried not to think of the roaches that may have been crawling over the bread.

"So how old are you, Mr. Twisp?" I asked.

"Fifty-three."

Wow, I would have said he was older than that. More bad news for my DNA. I could tell he was my dad. We had pretty much exactly the same eyes. The noses and jaws weren't far off either.

"You can call me, uh, Nick I guess," he said.

"Is Twisp your stage name? It sounds too silly to be a real name."

"No, I come from a long and undistinguished line of Twisps. It's our actual name."

More bad news for me. No way I would ever be changing my name to Twisp–even if the guy was totally hot to adopt me.

After dinner I said I felt like taking a walk.

"People don't do much walking in L.A.," he pointed out. "And this neighborhood isn't that safe after dark."

"It's not dark yet. And wouldn't it be safer with two people?"

So we went for a walk. Before we left he dialed a number and left another irate message for Mom. Probably neither of us expected her to call back.

We walked a few blocks south to a place called Exposition Park and passed by a giant stadium where U.S.C. plays football. I asked him what he was doing these days besides hiding out from his pissed-off wife.

"I'm writing my memoirs–or supposed to be. My agent's trying to get me acting work."

"No more juggling gigs?"

"Nah, I've lost my edge. Too old. People don't pay money to see some aging comic drop his balls."

"Right."

"I was quite remarkable in my prime. Arguably the best juggler in the past 500 years."

"Really? That's impressive."

"Well, it's kind of a dying art. If you read the literature, there were jugglers in ancient India, Persia, and China who could do quite extraordinary feats. But who knows if the descriptions were accurate? The accounts could be highly exaggerated. So I may be the best juggler of all time, but I'm only claiming the past half-millennium."

"I saw some of your juggling on your TV show. I assumed you had help from special effects."

"A common misconception, alas. No, that was just my hands and a zillion hours of practice."

"Sounds kind of boring."

"My memoirs?"

"No, practicing juggling."

"I didn't mind it. It's good to have some discipline in your life. I wish I could bring the same intensity to my memoirs. I kept a journal when I was kid. For quite a few years. Pretty juvenile stuff that I'm trying to edit. I don't think readers want to know how many times I had to retire to my bedroom to relieve my sexual tensions."

So he kept a journal like I do. I suppose my literary inclinations come from him. His diaries sound remarkably jejune. I bet I'm a much better writer than he is.

"Do you have a girlfriend, Nick?" he asked.

"Uh, no. I'm pretty reserved around girls."

"That's OK. It's perfectly fine if you don't get around to girls until you're older. I don't know if you're a Twisp, but they tend to be emotionally vulnerable at your age. We're inclined to take these things far too seriously."

"Like how?"

"Like falling hopelessly in love with the first pretty girl we meet. Like going totally off the deep end–with disastrous consequences for all."

"You did that?"

"Did I ever. You can read all about it in my memoirs someday."

I had trouble imagining the guy as some horndog teen. And it certainly would be a gross-out having to read about his ancient love life.

Fortunately, his apartment had two bedrooms so I had a place to sleep that night. Only one bathroom though. Back in Terre Haute I never had to share a bath. He gave me my own personal towel which looked semi-clean. I asked him if the cockroaches ever visited a person in bed.

"No, Nick, they generally prefer moist dark places like kitchens and bathrooms."

"How many are there do you suppose?"

"Could be several thousand at least in the building. Probably not a million."

Damn! If I had his bankroll no way would I spend five more minutes in this pit. I was beginning to suspect he was a tightwad like my ex-dad.

I said goodnight and settled into the sagging double bed. I hoped the previous tenants weren't scabies-infected heroin junkies or meth-abusers. I heard him getting into bed on the other side of the wall. Then I heard his phone ring and he had a long conversation. Probably not with my Mom or his pissed-off wife, since he sounded pretty lovey. I mostly couldn't make out the words, except a couple of times I heard him say, "In English, please." So it could be that my new dad has some foreign GF. Then I fell asleep.

THURSDAY, May 21 – My mom called me early in the morning while I was still in bed. I told her she was a goddam traitor.

"I had to do it, honey," she insisted. "I wanted you to spend time with your dad and get to know him. I knew he wouldn't have had anything to do with you if I hadn't left like that."

"You could have given me a warning."

"No, I don't think so. You wouldn't have agreed. How's he treating you?"

"OK. He said he was going to call the cops, but I don't think he did."

"Of course not, honey. He knows you're his son. You've always looked like him. And even more so lately."

"Where are you?" I asked.

"A rest stop in New Mexico. Don't tell him I called."

"OK, if you say so."

"I love you, Nick honey. You mean everything to me. We'll be together soon. I promise."

"OK, if you say so."

"You take care. I'll send you money when I can."

"OK. Drive safely. Don't fall asleep and hit a tree."

"Thanks. I feel fine so far. I'm really looking forward to this new job."

"Right."

Then she told me she loved me a few more times and finally rang off. I was still pissed at her, but I guess she canceled out some of yesterday's "don't exist" message.

I took a shower and dressed. My "roommate" was still snoring. I looked in his cupboard for cereal. Just old guys' Grape Nuts and something made with "nuggets of flax." Not even the roaches were touching that. So I made some toast and stared out the window until he got up.

"How does breakfast in Beverly Hills sound?" he asked.

"OK."

His car was parked in the garage under the building. I was expecting a tightwad's ratty Toyota, but it was an old guy's silver Lincoln Town Car. Pretty pristine with a plush leather interior. The radio was tuned to NPR playing classical music. Boring, but I didn't touch the dial.

The restaurant was in a pink stucco hotel hidden behind a forest of palm trees. We sat outside on a terrace near a pool. Too early for swimmers. Just a Mexican guy in a fancy uniform skimming out leaves with a long pole. My new dad ordered coffee and old codger's oatmeal; I had a fancy omelet with avocado and a cheese I never heard of.

"Anything on your agenda, Nick?" he asked, spooning four raisins onto his oatmeal.

Like what? I thought. I'd been abandoned by my parents, I'm bunking with a stranger, yet I'm supposed to have something on my social calendar?

"I wouldn't mind seeing the ocean," I replied. "I've never seen it before."

"You haven't seen the ocean!"

"No. Just Lake Michigan. It kind of looks like an ocean."

"Lake Michigan is no ocean. OK, we can go to Venice today."

"Venice, Italy?" I asked, startled.

"No, we have one here too. Quite a bit less historic than the Italian version. How's your omelet?"

"Fine."

"After breakfast I'm going to call my lawyer," he announced. "Shelly's an entertainment lawyer, but he should be able to refer me to someone competent in family law. Your Mr. Davidson is a businessman, a man of property. He just needs to be reminded of his legal obligations. There's no way he can duck his responsibility for providing you with a home."

"But I don't want to live with him, Mr. Twisp. The man is a major jerk. Plus, he'd be even meaner toward me now that he knows I'm not his son."

"Well, Nick, there may not be any alternative. I don't see how you can live with your mother. If as you say, she intends to work on a cruise ship, you'd be on your own and unsupervised for long periods in Miami."

"What's wrong with that? I can take care of myself. I'm no baby."

"You're only 15, Nick. You're legally a minor. You need an adult guardian in your life."

"So how about you?" I said. "I'd be quiet. I'd stay out of your hair."

"I did that already, Nick. I raised a teenage son. For that they should be handing out medals. Thank God Scott's 22 now and doing fine. Thankfully he didn't quite drive me fully nuts. But I'm not ready for another trip down that highway to hell."

"He was on your TV show, right?"

"Yes, he played my son. Now he's in the cast of that cable show 'Wildcatter' about oil drillers. He likes it even if he does spend much of his time on location in Bakersfield."

"Is that where he lives?"

"No, he has an apartment in Brentwood. Not far from here. He's living with Azura Preston, but I don't think that's going well."

"If he breaks up with her, maybe I could go live with him," I suggested. "He is my half-brother after all."

"That point is not at all decided, Nick. And he wouldn't be competent to supervise you. I doubt I'd trust him with a small dog. It wouldn't be that bad, Nick–returning to Indiana. It would only be for three years. Then you'd be 18 and going off to college."

"Right. When you were my age, would you have been OK with that? Would you have gone back to live for years with a man who despises you?"

He blushed and looked down at his oatmeal.

"When I was your age, Nick, I was out of control. That's what landed me in juvenile custody all those years. I'm no model for what anyone should do at age 15."

"Then you know what I'm going through. What I'm facing."

"Yeah, Nick. That I do. That I do indeed."

More diners showed up, and twice these old guys (friends

of his) came over to say hello. Both inquired if I was his son or grandson. Both times he stammered out unconvincing denials. So maybe he's the deadbeat who should be talking to a lawyer about accepting his parental responsibilities.

We didn't go to the ocean. His agent called and said a producer wished to meet with him. We zoomed back to his apartment so he could shave and change his clothes. As usual he left his phone on the table beside the door with his keys. While he was busy in the bedroom, I touched my phone to his, established a link, and uploaded his phone directory. It took less than 30 seconds employing an app that Jayden had scored on his favorite pirate website.

He looked a little less grizzled when he emerged. Also the hair had been combed to reduce the shiny forehead acreage. I asked him for $50.

He recoiled, but not as badly as my ex-dad, who used to react to money requests like I'd demanded a kidney and most of his liver. He took out his wallet and fished out a single twenty.

"This should tide you over until we decide what to do with you," he said.

I thanked him and asked for a door key.

Another crisis for my new dad. He hemmed and hawed, then scrounged up a key from a kitchen drawer.

"Are you going somewhere?" he asked.

"I thought I'd check out downtown. It looks walkable."

"OK, but stick to the main streets. Call me if you get lost. I shouldn't be gone too long."

"Right."

Our first parting. He looked like he was considering giving me a hug, but then didn't. After he left I gave the apartment a thorough snoop, but found not much of interest. It was like he moved in with two suitcases of clothes and that was it. The guy was living here like Mr. Anonymous. In his closet was a big duffle bag stuffed with unopened letters. Fan mail? Quite a few of them appeared to be from Portugal.

I switched on his laptop, but access was blocked by a password request. Too bad. I wouldn't mind having a peek at the journals of his law-breaking years.

I looked through his phone directory. Quite a few Hollywood

stars were listed. I guess he is a big shot, although you wouldn't know it to look at him. He had listings for chicks in Argentina, France, Czech Republic, Japan, and Russia. Quite the international playboy. Under Scott Twisp he had also entered a number for "Azura," so I swallowed hard and dialed it. She answered on the second ring.

"Uh, hi," I said. "This is Scott Twisp's brother."

"Scott doesn't have a brother. Is this a crank call? How did you get my number?"

So I mumbled a halting summary of this week's improbable events.

"You're staying at that crummy apartment with all the roaches?" she asked.

"Uh, yes. Mr. Twisp, I mean my dad, just left to see some producer."

"OK, stay there! I'll be right over!"

Wow, Azura Preston is coming to see me. That's quite a frightening thought. She's total Hollywood royalty since her dad is like the most famous actor never to win an Oscar.

She knocked on the door 20 minutes later. Quite a bit more beautiful (and petite) than she looked on TV. Blue, blue eyes that were kind of blinding to look at. Am I jealous that my half-brother is cohabitating with this goddess? Does the Pope curse in Latin?

A total stranger, yet she gave me a big hug.

"I can see you're a Twisp," she said, looking me over. "You look a little like Scott, but you have nicer skin."

"My mother has flawless skin," I admitted.

"Good. It's always good to dilute those Twisp genes. I see you got the Twisp stature. You're not a race of giants."

"Am I as tall as Scott?"

"Not quite. I'd say he has an inch or two on you, but I expect you'll catch up. He's playing a brawny oil wildcatter. In real life, of course, he wouldn't last five minutes with one of those oil-drilling crews. They'd laugh his puny bod right off the rig."

"Mr. Twisp says you two might be breaking up."

"He wishes. He's never liked me being with his son. He thinks I'm flighty and I'm going to break Scott's heart. But I'm the one trying to make things work. Scott's the one up there right now entertaining the babes of Bakersfield."

"I doubt there's anyone in Bakersfield who compares to you."

"Thanks, Nick. That's sweet. I wish your dad thought that way. He really should thank me. Why do you think his show lasted all those seasons? People weren't tuning in to see him juggle and do his Amos 'n' Andy routine, that's for sure."

"You were why I watched the show," I confessed.

"Nice of you to say so."

"Are you in any TV shows now?"

"No, I'm trying to concentrate on film work. I was in that movie 'Zombie Debutantes.' I played one of the rich debs who lived."

"Right. I wanted to see it, but it didn't play very long at the mall back home."

"It didn't play very long anywhere, unfortunately. Next month I'm headed up to Bozeman to shoot a western."

"Really? They don't make many westerns anymore."

"I know. This is one of those new alternative takes on the genre. I play the schoolmarm, but instead of being sweet and virginal, I'm like the biggest slut in town. I take on everyone: cowboys, Indians, Mexicans, the guilt-wracked preacher, the town drunk, the lame and the infirm, you name it."

I couldn't help but wish she'd take on me too.

"That sounds, uh, challenging."

"It should be fun. Plus, I get to revive my horseback-riding skills. Well, let's grab your stuff and get going."

"Uh, where are we going?"

"Out of Roach Motel, that's for sure!"

I left a note on the kitchen table that I was OK and would call him. Azura helped me carry my bags down to her big black Lincoln SUV.

"Does everyone in L.A. drive Lincolns?" I asked.

"My dad bought this for me. He says you need as much metal as possible around you these days since everyone is driving while texting. That's how your granny got killed."

"My granny was texting?"

"No, she was crossing a street up in Oakland and got run down by a distracted driver."

Wow, my present and past grandparents were all traffic fatalities. Nevertheless, Azura constantly looked at her phone and sent texts at nearly every red light. Soon, having left all signs of grunginess behind, we entered a neighborhood of the conspicuously affluent. As we pulled up in front of a ritzy modern apartment building, her phone rang. She handed it to me.

"Er, hello," I said.

"Hey, bro!" boomed a hearty voice. "Zee's been sending me some amazing texts."

"Er, who's Zee?"

"That's the lovely blue-eyed miss who rescued you from our dingy dad. Strange dude, huh?"

"He seems OK. I just met him yesterday."

"I wish I could say the same. I've known him for 22 fun-filled years. So how did he come to father you?"

"I don't know. He hasn't said yet. My mother was a showgirl at the Normandie casino."

"Well there you have it. He worked there forever. And I guess it wasn't all work. So tell Zee I'm coming home. They can shoot around me tomorrow. I'll be there in a few hours. We'll get acquainted and compare notes."

"OK."

"Don't worry, bro'! Being a Twisp is not that bad!"

"If you say so."

He rang off.

"I think that was Scott," I said.

"Of course it was," she giggled. "He's very excited to meet you."

Their apartment was a posh two-story loft like something out of a magazine. In the center was a glassed-in atrium with a sunken hot tub and a mini-forest of potted ferns. Not at all like the rentals in Terre Haute. We dumped my bags and went around the block to a restaurant that Azura likes. I was still full from breakfast, so I followed her example and ordered the smoked-trout salad.

We talked about my trip west and the events of yesterday.

"Wow, your mom ditched you with a total stranger," she said. "That's got to hurt."

"She said he wouldn't have had anything to do with me otherwise."

"I guess she knows her man. You hold your fork just like Scott: with the handle between your index and middle finger."

"I think you have a more secure grip this way."

"Right. You're both so ready to resist when those fork-nabbers attack."

Not wanting to bore her with my life, I asked her about growing up with such a famous father. She told me about her childhood and the big disruption seven years ago when her dad left her mother and went back to his first wife.

"Do you hate her?" I asked.

"Hate Apurva? God, no. She's about the nicest person I've ever met. I can't believe my dad ever left her in the first place. If he'd had any sense at all back then, I wouldn't be here."

"Well, I'm glad you are."

"Uh-oh, you got that Twisp charm gene. I better watch out."

I haven't even met my half-brother and already I want to usurp his place in life.

Some people around us were giving us the eye; they must have recognized Azura. They were cool about it though and didn't bother her. She paid for my lunch, which was fortunate since my skimpy salad cost $26. When we returned to the apartment she left this message on my new dad's phone: "Hi, Uncle Nick. I stopped by your place to say hello and encountered your namesake Nick. I invited him back to our place. Scott's coming in tonight if you want to check in. Take care!"

"Is Nick Twisp really your uncle?" I asked.

"Not hardly. But I don't feel comfortable calling him Nick, and Mr. Twisp sounds too formal. So I call him uncle. He doesn't seem to mind."

Azura had a pilates class to go to; I stayed behind "to rest." Naturally, I used this alone time to snoop. Many framed photos in their bedroom of the cute couple and other handsome folks. All looking trim and affluent. Not like the motley donut-abusers in my ex-dad's family. Giant bed with drawers underneath. Book on the paleo diet on one night stand and a biography of Billy Wilder on the other. Two other bedrooms: one with workout machines and a pro-looking weight set. The other with bookshelves, two desks with computers, and a sofa-bed. The books seemed to fall into two categories: acting, actors, and the film business. Or diet, health, and exercise. Plus, there was one entire shelf of guidebooks to L.A. These guys must really know where to go and where to eat. Not to mention what to eat and how to work it off.

Scott showed up way before Azura expected him. He's a fast driver, but then he does pilot a red Porsche 928. He probably pays more for car insurance than I'll ever earn in my lifetime. He dropped his bag, kissed Azura, and gave me a brotherly hug. He looked like he did on TV, but way more bulked up. Not grossly over-developed like those bodybuilders, but more muscular than most guys his size.

"Wow," he said, looking me over. "There's another Nick Twisp in this world."

"Uh, I'm Nick Davidson," I said.

"Nice to meet you, Nick," he replied.

"Did you hear from your dad, honey?" asked Azura.

"I did, Zee. He's pissed. He wants my new kid brother back A.S.A.P. I told him no can do. I said we had to get to know him first. I think, Nick, he was hoping to get you on a bus back to Indiana before anybody found out about you."

"I have a feeling I'm not making his day," I admitted.

"Well, the cat is out of the bag," said Scott. "Do you want to go back to Indiana?"

"Not at all! Not ever!"

"Then you don't have to," said Scott. "There are no compulsory return to Indiana laws in this state."

There followed a 10-minute discussion of where we should go for dinner. At one point I admitted that I had never seen the ocean. That narrowed the choices down to Santa Monica or Venice. Eventually, they decided on a Mexican restaurant with a Korean chef one block from the beach in Santa Monica. Scott drove us in Azura's SUV. He totes his wallet and other essentials in a leather man's bag (purse), but I'm trying to overlook that.

People were waiting for tables at the restaurant, but we were seated right away. I guess people defer to celebrities like that, although I don't see why they should. A group of attractive women at a nearby table smiled at Scott and hissed and booed. He smiled back and waved.

"Why are they booing you?" I asked. "Is your acting that bad?"

"Looks like you haven't been tuning in to 'Wildcatter,'" he replied.

"Uh, no."

"I play the spoiled son of the owner of the company. I'm rather devious and scheming."

"He's a first-class shit," added Azura. "I think it's affecting his personality."

"I hope not," laughed Scott.

While we were waiting for our food, we discussed my boring life in Indiana. Scott asked if I had any siblings back there.

"Nope, there's just me."

"It could be that your mother figured out that her hubby was shooting blanks," said Scott. "So she hooked up with our dad because she wanted a kid."

"Could be," I conceded. "But why would she choose him?"

"Good question," he replied. "But there is a fairly rabid Nick Twisp Fan Club. And most of its members are chicks."

"He was a big-name star in Vegas for years," said Azura. "I'm sure there were many women who found him attractive."

I told them about his loving phone conversation yesterday with a possible foreign-speaking girlfriend.

"It could be a girlfriend," said Scott, "but it was probably our sister Nerea in Argentina."

"We have a sister?" I asked, surprised.

"We have twin sisters–well, half-sisters. They're 38, which means he was a papa at your age. Nerea runs a circus in Argentina. Miren is married to our cousin Tyler Twisp's half-brother Ryder Ohlmann. He used to own a big juice company, but he sold it and now does venture capital projects with Tyler."

"Is that Tyler Twisp, the one-legged billionaire who owns the Big Red football team?" I asked.

"The very same," confirmed Scott.

"He used to be the world's only one-legged billionaire," said Azura. "But a Russian oligarch offended the Kremlin and got kneecapped last year under mysterious circumstances. They had to chop off his leg too."

"You should know our dad dotes on his daughters," said Scott. "He calls them all the time. Too bad you weren't born a girl, Nick. I'm sure you'd have received a much warmer welcome. No way would he be trying to sneak you on a bus back to the Midwest."

My third restaurant meal of the day. The food was spicier than

I was used to, but I ate most of it to be polite. I asked them if they knew why Nick Twisp, a wealthy celebrity, chose to live in a roach-infested apartment in a sketchy part of L.A.

"I think he's trying to guilt-trip Scott's mom," said Azura. "But it's not working."

"Well, it may be working somewhat," added Scott. "But I'm not sure that's his reason. I discussed it with Tyler's wife Uma, who's a psychologist. Our grandfather was a drunk who finished out his days on skid row in downtown L.A. She thinks he may have made an unconscious decision to follow his father down that same path. People sometimes do that."

"Does he booze it up?" I asked.

"Not that we've noticed," said Scott. "But we don't see him that often. Was he drinking yesterday?"

"Not that I saw. And I didn't smell it on his breath or see any bottles around."

"Well, that's good to know," said Scott. "I think he's been at loose ends since the TV show ended."

"Plus he gave up juggling," said Azura. "And he's not in demand as an actor."

"Let's face it," said Scott. "What Dad needs is a new career."

"Or a new interest in his life," said Azura, pointing at me.

After dinner we walked to the Santa Monica pier to look at the ocean. It looked like Lake Michigan with slightly bigger waves. I took a picture of the setting sun with my cellphone to send to Jayden. Then Scott's phone rang and he handed it to me.

"Hello, Nick. This is Nick," said my new dad.

"Oh, hi."

"Are you planning to come back here tonight?"

"Uh, I think I'm staying at Scott's."

"Right. Well, I'll talk to you tomorrow."

"Uh, OK."

"Fine. Good night."

I handed back the phone.

"Was he pissed?" asked Scott.

"I don't know," I said. "He was kind of abrupt and subdued."

"Passive aggressive," said Scott. "Get used to it. You'll be seeing a lot of that from him."

FRIDAY, May 22 – I spent the night on Scott and Azura's sofa-bed. My ringing phone woke me up early. It was my ex-dad in Indiana calling to apologize. He said he was sorry for acting "so immature." And now he wants "my family back." He said he's been calling my mom, but hasn't been able to get through to her. Good thing while she was taking a shower in Vegas I had the foresight to block all his numbers on her phone.

"Sorry, Dad," I said. "She's hooked up again with my real father. I think they're engaged."

"How can that be?" he demanded. "She's still married to me!"

"Right. Well, they just left to talk to a lawyer about that."

"What! Who is this guy? What's his name?"

"Uh, I'm not allowed to say."

"Well, you tell her to call me as soon as she gets back."

"Uh, OK."

"Are you in Vegas? Where are you staying?"

"We're sort of near Las Vegas, but I'm not allowed to say where."

"OK, I'm coming out there. Tell your mother I'll see her this afternoon."

"Uh, Dad, I don't think she wants to see you. I wouldn't bother making the trip."

"I'm coming, Nick! I'm going to get this resolved. Don't you worry, boy, we'll have you back here in time for school on Monday."

As if I had any interest in that. I'm still too short to date Avery, plus there's a geometry final on Monday.

"Don't come, Dad! It won't do any good!"

But he had already hung up. So I dialed my mother's number. She answered sounding sleepy.

"Hi, honey," she said, "are you OK? Is something wrong?"

I told her that her husband had just phoned.

"What did he want?"

"He said he's added up all the money he spent on me. He's planning on suing you for the total amount plus interest."

"What a rat! I can't believe all the years I wasted living with that man."

"I get the feeling he's trying to track you down, Mom. Did you tell anyone at the Normandie where you were going?"

"A few people know. Should I phone them and ask them not to say anything if he calls?"

"I'd do that right away, Mom. Where are you?"

"A motel somewhere in Texas. All that driving was wearing me out."

"You might want to keep your cellphone off too. In case he tries to trace you that way."

"But how will we keep in touch, honey?"

"Get a new phone when you get to Miami. Or at least a new number."

"OK, I guess I could do that. And how are you getting along with Mr. Twisp?"

"Great," I lied. "I think he really likes me."

I don't see why after 15 years of raging jerkdom my ex-dad suddenly should start acting like Mr. Family Man. Inconsistent parental behavior can really mess with your head. Now my situation was even more precarious. Only one conclusion was possible: I would have to start being nicer to Nick Twisp.

I took a shower and installed a set of ZipPits that Scott gave me. These are thin electronic discs that clip to your armpit hair and are supposed to eliminate offensive odors. Scott is such a big-time ZipPits believer, he owns part of the company. In fact, he bought his Porsche at age 19 with dividends from his ZP stock.

After Azura made us a breakfast of organic free-range eggs and nitrate-free grass-fed bacon (no toast: too many carbs), I told them I should be getting back to "my dad's place."

"You don't have to go, Nick," said Scott. "I thought we could work out this morning on my machines."

"Scott works out every day," said Azura. "He's trying to look like a beer-swilling Texas redneck."

"Texas rednecks don't have abs like mine," he replied.

"You could abrade granite with Scott's abs," she said, sipping her herbal tea.

Yes, I would kill for Scott's abs, but I wouldn't stay to work out on his machines. So he gave me a lift back to the ghetto in the SUV (my bags wouldn't fit in his Porsche). My new dad was washing his breakfast dish when we let ourselves into his apartment. He seemed surprised to see us.

"Hi, Dad," said Scott. "Your son here was anxious to get back."

"He's not–," said Nick, stopping short. "He's not, uh, in time for breakfast."

Another near miss for me in the "don't exist" department.

"That's OK," said Scott, dropping my bag and flopping down in the recliner. "We already ate. I hear you had a meeting with a producer."

"Some producer," sighed my SDE (shortest dad ever). "He has no credits to his name and is about five minutes out of U.S.C. film school."

"What did he want you for?"

"Slasher movie. I'd be juggling knives right before stabbing the screaming sorority girls."

"What did you say?" asked Scott.

"I told him to call me back if he got his budget funded."

Azura was right. My new dad definitely needs a new career. Perhaps something healthy and not too demanding like delivering the mail. Or selling used Town Cars to fellow old folks.

"You boys want some coffee?" he asked. "I could make a fresh pot."

"Sure, OK," said Scott. "Are you working on your memoirs?"

"Trying to," said Nick, picking something suspicious out of the coffee-maker basket. "I'm not sure what to leave in and take out."

"Well, leave in the sex parts and the major law-breaking if you want to sell books," said Scott.

"I'll keep that in mind."

He poured three cups of coffee and put out a plate of mini sugared donuts. No roach tracks were seen, but I'm sure such confections are highly prized in the insect kingdom. Nevertheless, I grabbed a few.

"About my brother's mother," said Scott, "where did you meet her?"

Nick looked like he resented both Scott's question and his occupying the ratty recliner; he sat down next to me on the lumpy sofa.

"It's not like I made a practice of harassing the showgirls at the Normandie."

"I'm sure you didn't," said Scott.

"I got a summer engagement up at Lake Tahoe," he continued. "About 16 years ago. For two weeks. Suzy, my regular assistant, didn't want to go. She had scheduled a camping trip with one of her deadbeat boyfriends. Kerri Davidson had seen my show many times so she knew my routine. I hired her for the two-week engagement. Your mom and you couldn't go because she was busy with her practice."

"My mom's an oral surgeon," said Scott. "So it was just you and Kerri up there at Tahoe with two weeks to kill. Sounds pretty romantic."

"She was the one who came to my room. She said not to worry, that she was on the pill. It was just something that happened up there. We didn't see each other after that. I heard sometime later that she was out on maternity leave, but I never made the connection. Why should I? She was married."

"Sounds like she's married to a guy with fertility issues," said Scott. "So you got elected to do the deed."

"I got elected," he sighed. "No offense, boys, but I was never that keen on having kids. Now it appears that I've got four of them. And most of them came as a big surprise."

We all laughed.

"It's that Twisp DNA," he continued. "It has a fierce will to perpetuate itself. I suppose it has to be extra-virulent since it offers so little that appeals to most women. Both Tyler and your uncle Jake got their wives pregnant right away. I hope you're using protection, Scott."

"Always," he replied. "But I can't agree that all of us Twisps are unappealing to women. I can hardly go anywhere in Bakersfield without attracting a mob of crazed females."

"That hardly rebuts my argument."

"Why not, Dad?" asked Scott.

"Because that's Bakersfield. It doesn't count. It's never counted for anything."

Does running down your son's popularity in Bakersfield qualify as a "don't exist" message? I thought it might.

After Scott left, my new dad asked if I'd heard from my mother.

"Not a peep," I lied. "Have you?"

"Nothing. I'm astounded she could be so inconsiderate and irresponsible. You realize I have nothing here to entertain a teen-ager."

"I'm pretty good at entertaining myself. Would you like some help editing your memoirs?"

"I hardly think so, but thanks for the offer."

He had relocated to the recliner and was vigorously kneading a tennis ball. I had seen him do this before. I asked him what was up with that.

"Squeezing a tennis ball helps tone your hand muscles. And it's a good way to relieve stress."

I expect I was the guy stressing him out. Since I seemed to be making him uncomfortable, I retreated to the spare bedroom to catch up on my journal writing, sniff my armpits (gloriously springtime fresh), and mull over two mysteries:

1. If my mother needed a sperm donor, how come she didn't choose somebody taller and more attractive? Did she have no regard for the appearance and/or dating prospects of her future off-spring?

2. Why has my ex-dad suddenly changed his tune? Perhaps it has now dawned on the cad that he no longer has an outlet for sex. I don't think they were doing it much, but prolonged celibacy can be scary as I've learned all too poignantly. His secretary Gloria might be willing to help out in that department, but she'd probably expect a raise in her meager salary. He may want my mother back for sex and is willing to put up with me as the price he has to pay.

As to the first mystery, it could be that my mother thought she was breeding another talented juggler–with the expectation that jugglers always had a way of making a living. Guess she got that wrong on both counts.

Lunch was make-your-own-sandwiches; dinner was home-de-livered take-out Chinese. Nick Twisp, possible boozer, washed his down with one beer out of the can, but didn't touch the rest of the six-pack. I made do with water from the tap. While we forked in the garlicky repast, Nick asked me how I did in school.

"I do OK," I replied. "Mostly As and Bs."

"Are you planning on going to college?"

"Sure. I guess so. It's a ways off still."

He was probably wondering if I would be sticking him with massive college-tuition bills.

"Most Twisps don't really do college," he observed. "We tend to be autodidacts. I spent my college years in the custody of juvenile authorities. Scott got busy acting and skipped it altogether. Your uncle Jake had one semester of junior college, then gave it up to be czar of a salad bar–which he later ditched to go on the road with the Ken Kern Singers."

"My mother likes them."

"I know. I may have introduced her to them."

Wow, it's more than likely I was conceived to the swingin' sounds and close harmonies of the Ken Kern Singers. No wonder my musical tastes are so retro.

"So you don't think I should go to college?" I asked.

"No, of course you should go–if that's what interests you. Your cousin Tyler played football for U.S.C. I guess that counts as going to college, although quarterbacking the team was pretty much a full-time job. He got a full scholarship, of course."

"And now he's a billionaire."

"Right. But not from going to college. He's just naturally astute."

I got the message. My new dad wants me to take all manual-arts classes in high school and pursue a trade like welding. Sorry, he won't be getting off that easy.

After dinner we watched the latest episode of "Wildcatter" on Nick's big laptop. It's one of those shows with 10 different plots all going at once. One segment followed Scott as he tried to seduce a co-worker's busty girlfriend. It's supposed to be set in rural Texas, but all the chicks look like Hollywood starlets. Scott was affecting a Texas accent and being mucho devious. Hard to believe a half-brother of mine could be that slimy. His dad, I noticed, was watching him proudly.

When the show was over, I asked him what he thought of Scott's performance.

"I think he's the best thing on that show. That's why the producers keep featuring him more and more. He was originally supposed to be killed in a gas well explosion. But they canceled that and kept him on."

"Have you told him how much you like his work?"

"Sure, I guess so."

Hmm, that's not what I heard from Scott.

Nick closed his laptop and studied the ceiling. I can't see the fascination, but he does that a lot. He was also kneading his tennis ball. "Scott and I worked together for six years on my show. We had our artistic differences. He was fine starting out, but then he read too many of his reviews. He started to ham it up. I think comedy should be underplayed. I like subtlety; Scott was playing things way too broadly. But he's better in this show. He's holding back, he's being more real."

"I'll tell him you said so."

"Sure. You do that."

When I went to bed, I thought of my ex-dad now wandering around Las Vegas looking for Mom and me. I hope he does some gambling and takes in a show or two so his trip isn't a total bust. Perhaps he could hire a hooker to keep celibacy at bay. Meanwhile, on the other side of the wall my new dad was cooing over the phone with that mystery foreign-speaker.

SATURDAY, May 23 – I woke up in the middle of the night with something moving in my ear. It was goddam cockroach! I guess I must have yelled pretty loud because my new dad rushed in to investigate. His only comment: "That's not typical roach behavior."

So what did I get–the Marco Polo of roaches? The roach born to explore? I was about ready to call up my ex-dad and tell him to come get me. I could return to Indiana, watch taller dudes date Avery, take my final exams, and spend my summer sorting stinky laundry. I'd probably do it too except that last part sounds just slightly worse than roaches burrowing in to eat your brain.

I stuffed wadded-up toilet paper into my ears as bug shields and went back to bed. Took me a long time to get back to sleep after that monumental gross-out.

Another sunny day in southern California. Yes, the sun even shines in crummy neighborhoods. After breakfast I asked my new dad for another $50. I figured he owed me at least that much for last night's ear trauma.

"Fifty dollars seems to be a constant figure with you," he replied, recoiling. "That's quite a large sum of money to be handing out to teenagers."

"I thought I'd take a city bus to the beach. I see they run down Pico."

REVOLT AT THE BEACH

"City buses do not cost $50."

"Transportation, lunch, sightseeing, souvenirs–it all adds up.
And don't forget, you didn't pay a cent for my first 14 years."

He extracted two twenties from his wallet and handed them
to me. "Don't get into any trouble. And be back in time for dinner."

I kind of liked that. He was beginning to sound like a dad. I
asked him if he had a spare cellphone I could borrow.

"What happened to yours?"

"It died," I lied.

He dredged up a battered Samsung 4. Fairly ancient technology, but at least it was a smart phone. I returned to my room and
transferred all my data. Then I switched off my old cellphone and,
as an extra measure of security, extracted its battery. Call me paranoid, but I don't want my ex-dad showing up here to drag me off
to a life of laundry serfdom. I don't think my new dad's contacted
him either, since I would have heard about it. Nor has he mentioned any lawyers lately. I'm hoping my winning personality is
growing on him.

I took the bus to Santa Monica, then walked south along their
broad sandy beach. No Art Deco hotels like Miami Beach is supposed to have, but jammed with humanity–some in abbreviated
swim wear. Quite a few more Asian girls than you see in Indiana.
I may be destined to hook up with one of them someday, since
they're usually petite, often cute, and generally brainy. This is assuming I ever get up the nerve to talk to one. It's more than a drag
being shy and knowing no one my age in this entire state. A few
girls here and there gave me the eye. Perhaps they were thinking
I resembled that TV actor whose name they couldn't remember.
The one who did all that lame juggling.

In Venice there were vendors along the beach selling "art,"
handicrafts, and useful stuff like phone accessories and sunglasses. I looked but didn't buy. Quite a few people were gliding by on
bikes, skateboards, and roller blades. Even a few cops in shorts
on bikes. A much livelier scene than anything in Terre Haute. The
ocean looked kind of inviting too. I could see being a regular here
someday with my buddies and girlfriend (I wish).

When I got back, a black lady who lives across the hall stopped
me outside the door.

"Tell me, son, is that grouchy white man in your apartment who I think he is?"

"Who's that?" I asked.

"Nick Twisp, the juggler."

"Never heard of him. My dad's a professional embalmer."

"Oh. I guess Nick Twisp is too rich and famous to be living here."

"No doubt."

I found my "rich and famous" new dad in the bathroom. He was looking a bit spiffier than usual.

"Get dressed," he said. "We're going out to dinner with Trent Preston and his wife."

"You mean *the* Trent Preston?" I asked, impressed.

"Who else? I've known him since he was just a kid up in Ukiah."

Like I was supposed to have heard of that place. But I retired to my room and put on my best slacks and sport coat. Who knows? Hobnobbing with famous movie stars might be a way to raise my profile with chicks.

On the way there MBD (my baldest dad) warned me not to mention last night's ear incident. Guess he's ashamed we're living in a slum.

We met them at a fancy restaurant in West Hollywood. Azura's dad was tall, tanned, handsome, and either had all of his hair or a fabulous toupee. I don't see why he couldn't have been my father–except it might make it awkward if I ever won his daughter away from my brother. His wife was a comely older gal who appeared to be Indian. Her first name was Apurva, which seemed confusing similar to Azura. Both gave me warm hugs like they had known me forever. Even before we ordered they both expressed the opinion that I "looked just like your father."

"I suppose," replied Nick, who no longer was finding it tenable to weasel out of my paternity.

Apurva asked if I had any photos of my mother. So I whipped out my new (to me) phone and showed her a few shots from our Indiana days.

"She's lovely and quite tall," she commented. "And such a winsome figure. I can see why your father was attracted to her."

"It was all very brief," said Nick. "Just an accident of geography, circumstance, and proximity."

Another possible "don't exist" message, but who's counting?

I chowed down on my pricey steak and answered their questions about my previous 14 years of existence as Nick Twisp's unknown love child–all the while emphasizing what a jerk my ex-dad was and how happy I was to be away from him.

"He certainly sounds like a most disagreeable fellow," said Apurva. "How fortunate you are to have found your real father."

"I'm sure he's happy to have found you too," said Trent.

"Uh, right," said Nick, motioning to the waiter for another bottle of wine.

In the course of the meal several people came over to shake Trent's hand. Not star-struck fans, but people he knew in the movie business. Schmoozing in restaurants with stars is one of the perks of that biz. One ancient guy introduced his wife, a flashy blonde barely older than Azura.

When they left, Nick said, "Have I told you my theory on why you shouldn't look down on old farts with young trophy wives?"

"No," said Apurva, "but please do. This I'd like to hear."

"OK. It all comes down to genetics and the resources the male body commits to it."

"I believe he's talking about sperm," said Trent.

"Exactly," he said. "With every ejaculation you lose about 400 million of them."

That means I spilled 800 million already today–a fact I kept to myself.

My new dad went on, "Each one of those little guys requires two to three months of careful incubation. For this task the male body hangs a delicate sac outside the body in a very vulnerable location."

This brought a giggle from Apurva.

"She who has not received a kick in the balls should not laugh," said Nick. "Plus, let's not forget all the grief we get from the prostate."

"You too, huh?" said Trent. "I've got a stream like a dehydrated canary."

Way more information than I wanted.

"I get up two times a night," said Nick.

What a liar. He's forever shuffling in there to piddle.

Nick continued with his thesis: "So let's consider the guy who is going to all this effort and is married to a post-menopausal woman."

"Now you're getting personal," warned Apurva.

"No, think about it," insisted Nick. "He's discharging all this valuable sperm where it will do him absolutely no good genetically. Consciously he may not mind, but his DNA is saying, 'Hey, bub, what's up with that? Why are you wasting this precious resource?'"

"So he ditches wife number one to marry some young babe," said Apurva, "who will spend all of her child-bearing years on the pill because her aging husband doesn't want any more kids."

"Exactly so," said Nick. "And that is the animal nature of the mature male that will not be denied."

And why my new dad may be on the prowl for someone younger and prettier than his old wife.

"Well, I'm denying it," said Trent. "And very happy to be doing so. Is that why you've left Ada?"

Exactly the question I didn't dare ask.

"I didn't leave her," said Nick. "She left me."

"Well, I hope you're working to get back with her," said Apurva.

"It's complicated," he sighed.

"I don't see why," she replied. "Either you want Ada back or you don't."

"Uh, I don't think we should discuss this in front of the child."

He didn't say so, but I expect my presence is a new complication in his rocky marital life.

After that they discussed his moribund acting career. I got the impression my new dad was hinting strongly he'd like to be considered for a part in Trent's next picture. Perhaps he could help move the props or be a driver transporting stars to the various locations.

Eventually, there was an moderately vicious fight for the check. Apurva and I stayed out of it. Trent won in the end. I'm sure the bill made not the slightest dent in his fortune. He also insisted his bodyguard drive us home in Nick's Town Car. Trent is so famous he has to be shadowed by an enormous black dude named Franklin. Personally, I felt much safer being piloted back to the ghetto by Franklin than by my tipsy dad.

SUNDAY, May 24 – Normally a day to sleep in for the non-religious, but we had to get up early to breakfast at the palatial home of my billionaire cousin. Apparently, Tyler Twisp is famous for his Sunday brunches: hosting Presidents, senators, captains of industry, sports stars, media figures, and assorted Twisps. Today the guest list was family only. His mansion is in a lavishly landscaped hillside compound overlooking Santa Monica bay. I'm surprised we weren't frisked at the door to make sure we weren't harboring any stray insect vermin. In case you don't read the sports page, Tyler lost his leg in his first season as an NFL quarterback when he got sacked and fell wrong, giving him a compound fracture that got infected. The guy who tackled him, a large black man named Marcus, now works for him as head of his security detail.

Tyler is quite tall and distinguished-looking for a Twisp–as is his older half-brother Ryder (who is not a Twisp, but is married to my half-sister Miren). She's also quite attractive for her age and speaks with a slight Spanish accent. She seems nice and said she was very pleased to meet me. I also got introduced to Tyler's wife Uma (mucho shapely for a psychologist), my uncle Jake (much younger than my dad), his wife Lillian (pretty and friendly), and some chatty blond gal named Veeva Saunders, who I think is Miren's cousin. She was there with her taciturn husband, who writes violent action-thriller novels under the name Miles North.

A prolonged Twisp baby boom has been underway: the place was crawling with screaming little kids whose parentage I never sorted out. Some are my cousins and some are God knows what. My aunt Joan (Nick's sister and Tyler's mom) was invited, but she declined as usual because she still harbors a grudge against Marcus. So I had to talk to her for ten awkward minutes by telephone. She said she hoped I'd have an easier adolescence than her brother.

"Don't get married when you're 15," she warned.

"I'm not planning on it," I assured her.

Actually, I wouldn't mind commencing a trial marriage with some cute girl. I think the regular sex would do us both a world of good. Perhaps that's what my dad was thinking when he eloped to Mississippi with his pregnant GF. (I got the full story from Veeva.) The babies turned out to be my twin half-sisters, but Nick never found out about them until years later when Veeva and Jake tracked them down. They'd been adopted by a Basque family and were acrobats in a circus. All very interesting and all of which MSD (my secretive dad) hadn't mentioned to me. I wonder when he changed from Dangerous Youth to Mr. Dull?

I was talking with Scott and my uncle Jake (a high-paid comedy writer for TV shows), when Scott's mom Ada arrived. She'd come there especially to meet me, a fact which she expressed to her estranged husband, who seemed none too pleased to see her. He didn't make a scene though; Tyler doesn't permit rancor to disturb his brunch fests. When you're as rich as he is, not even your feuding relatives dare step out of line.

She seemed friendly enough considering I was incontrovertible proof of her husband's infidelity. She shook my hand and asked how I was getting on with "your new father."

I said, "OK so far."

I could tell she was checking out my teeth, but then she is an oral surgeon. She's an older blond lady who's way more attractive and less grizzled than her husband. He could do a lot worse, that's for sure. They've been married for over 20 years and should just suck it up, bury the hatchet, and be resigned that they're stuck with each other for life. Plus, I'm sure she's pulling in more coin these days than my deadbeat dad.

She appears to be best pals with Lillian, Jake's wife. They sat down with their plates on either side of me and extracted the full Nick Davidson story, such as it is. I wanted to go back to the lavish buffet for second helpings, but didn't feel it was polite to interrupt the interrogations.

"You mean your father expected you to work all summer in his dry cleaning shop for no pay?" asked Lillian at one point.

"Well, he was providing me with room and board," I replied. "Sometimes we even had hot meals."

"That's awful," said Ada. "And those dry-cleaning fluids are terribly toxic. You're well away from that man."

"He didn't hit me that often," I admitted.

"Your father beat you?" asked Lillian, appalled.

"Mostly when he'd been drinking, which was quite a bit lately. I have a few scars from his belt buckle and diamond pinky ring. And then there's my chipped tooth."

I pointed to a tooth I chipped while testing Jayden's experimentally motorized skateboard.

"That brute should be reported to the police!" said Lillian. "And arrested!"

"Oh, I'd just as soon steer clear of him," I said.

"I remember your mother, of course," said Ada. "I believe at one point I extracted her wisdom teeth."

Probably now she's wishing she skipped the anesthesia.

I assured her it wasn't a long-term affair, just a two-week fling at Lake Tahoe.

"Nick shouldn't have told you about that," said Ada. "You have no business knowing such details at your age."

I felt like telling her I was 15 not five, but kept my mouth shut. Then Uma sat down with us and I really clammed up. According to Veeva, she can peer into your innermost psyche like an X-ray machine.

Later Veeva took me aside and told me that after the Valentine Day bust-up Nick had asked to stay in one of Tyler's ritzy guest-houses, but my cousin refused, not wanting to take sides. Yes, we're living in Roach City so Nick can guilt-trip both his wife and Tyler. Bubbly Veeva is a font of information. (We swapped phone numbers so we could stay in touch.) She said Uma and Jake went to high school together in some remote Nevada town. Uma was Jake's first GF. Then she dumped him and later married a cancer doctor, who committed suicide when she hooked up with Tyler. They have two sons who Veeva says are by far the "most spoiled" and "worst behaved" of all the cousins. You couldn't prove it by me. I think the entire lot of them could benefit from a few months in juvenile hall.

After finally refilling my plate, I strolled out to the terrace and talked to Veeva's novelist husband. We discussed what sort of weaponry you'd need to pick off the passengers on a distant yacht sailing across Santa Monica bay. He said any decent sniper could do it with a L115A3 rifle firing 8.59 mm rounds. He also told me one of his books recently sold to the movies for $2 million. I said my new dad really, really needed a part in it.

"Your father, huh? In some ways he's rather remarkable."

"He's the best juggler in the past 500 years–or so he claims."

"I have a character who slurps a raw oyster, which turns out to be plastic explosive. His entire head explodes."

"My dad would be perfect for that. He ate a dozen oysters all by himself last night."

"OK, I'll talk to the producer about him."

Azura overheard this and asked him to keep her in mind too. Networking: it's how you get ahead in Hollywood.

Right before we left, I talked a bit with my billionaire cousin. I thanked him for breakfast and told him how much I enjoyed meeting my new relatives. I said that even in such a high-pressure social situation my new ZipPits were doing the job.

"Yes, it's one of our best-performing companies, Nick. We're always looking for confidential and trustworthy testers to try out new products. Are you interested?"

"Totally. You name it, I'll try it."

"Good. You remind me so much of Scott at your age. He gave me some very good advice over the years."

"Well, I'd like to be helpful any way I can," I said, hoping I didn't come across as too much of a suck-up.

I would have chatted longer, but was efficiently hustled toward the exit by Bergen, Tyler's all-business German secretary.

Sundays can be kind of a drag, but even more so when you go from dining with the one percent to staring at the stained popcorn ceiling in your ghetto crib with your pissed-off dad.

"I wouldn't have gone there if I'd known Ada had been invited," he said, drumming his fingers on the recliner's scarred vinyl. (I had hid his tennis ball; all that squeezing was starting to bug me.) "What was Tyler thinking?"

"I liked her," I replied. "I think you should send her roses, a nice card, and a two-pound box of chocolates. Mixed nuts and chews."

"Why would I do a thing like that?" he demanded.

"Because then you could move back to your nice house," I said. "And get some pussy which you so obviously need in the worst way."

That part I thought, but didn't say.

MONDAY, May 25 – We're moving! Kind Veeva took pity on me (only me, not my dad) and said both of us could crash at one of their places. They live in an estate above Beverly Hills, but also have a weekend house in Venice. Behind it is some sort of mother-in-law unit where we can stay. While we were packing, I asked my new dad who exactly this Veeva gal is.

"I had a girlfriend once named Sheeni Saunders," he replied, looking pensive. "She's the mother of your sisters."

"Right. And where is she?"

"France."

Oh, had to get far away from Nick. I can understand the impulse.

"Sheeni has an older brother named Paul, who was married to a woman named Connie. Their daughter is Veeva Saunders."

"And where does Paul live?"

"Paris, I think, or maybe Prague. He's married to a Czech gal now. Veeva was one of the producers of my TV show. She's a principal in Terra Ductile Films that makes those kiddie movies."

"Why doesn't she put you in one of her movies?"

"She says they haven't had a part yet that suits me. Most of their actors are under the age of 12."

It didn't take long to pack. All the food and kitchen stuff had to be left behind. Veeva was adamant with Nick on that point. She wanted none of our roaches making the trip toward a better life.

Veeva's place was a few blocks from the ocean along a murky canal. The front house was a shingled bungalow that had been remodeled. At the back of the small rear garden was an ultra-modern concrete and glass structure three stories high. The first level was a compact living room with galley kitchen. A staircase led up to a small bedroom and bath. Up another flight was a penthouse bedroom with a wall of glass doors facing west; these opened to a small balcony offering a sweeping view of the blue Pacific. Nick, of course, wanted to claim that room.

"Uh, gee," I said, "do you really want to go up and down those stairs all night?"

So I got the nice bedroom, and he and his balky prostate made do with the one that was convenient to the john.

The yard wasn't big enough for a regular pool, but they'd managed to squeeze in a long, narrow lap pool plus a hot tub. Everything was clean, spotless, and manicured. Virtually bug-free too. It was all a vast step up from our previous habitation. Now was the time to start living that Southern California dream lifestyle.

"This whole neighborhood used to be slum," said Nick, checking out the view from my balcony. "Then the Yuppies moved in and it got gentrified."

"It's quite nice," I said.

"Pacific Palisades is better. You're too close to your neighbors here. The lots are too small. I told Veeva she was nuts to sink all that money into this place."

Thank God she wisely ignored him.

"And they bought a place right next to a canal. You know what that means."

"Singing gondoliers disturbing your sleep?"

"Rats. Venice has always had a problem with rats along their canals. That's why most of them got filled in."

Let's hope the Yuppies have solved that problem.

"And I don't like that there's no covered parking for my car. You're in charge of keeping it clean."

I can do that, but it'll cost him: 50 bucks a wash!

Veeva herself arrived a few minutes later. She brought two bags of starter groceries, a bottle of wine, and the vital password for the WiFi. She told us the schedule for the gardener and pool cleaner, and showed us where a stacked washer and dryer were concealed behind a door. Now I can wash my grungy clothes.

"Any questions?" she asked.

"Are we allowed to use the pool?" I said.

"Of course. Make yourself at home. No peeing in the water though."

"Right."

"I hope your kids follow that rule," said Nick.

"We're beating it into them daily. I should warn you, the Gargoyle was making noises about dropping by to visit."

"I can handle that," said Nick.

"Who's the Gargoyle?" I asked.

"My mother," she replied. "Don't let her appearance frighten you. She went a little overboard on the plastic surgery."

For lunch we walked to a restaurant on Venice Boulevard a block up from the beach. (I think my grilled cheese sandwiches were beginning to pale.) For a guy who was on TV for six years and is alleged to be a noted Las Vegas entertainer, my new dad sure doesn't get many people recognizing him. I've yet to see anyone ask for his autograph. Our snotty waiter treated him little better than a bum off the street. Of course, we might get better service if he put a little more effort into his appearance. Scott told me our dad used to put on a show at restaurants juggling the silverware and dinner rolls, but I guess he's given that up.

There was a shiny black Mercedes parked in the driveway when we got back. Its owner was lounging on the slimmed-down sofa in our loaner living room.

"Hi, Connie," said Nick.

"Hello, Nick," she replied. "I've come to make the acquaintance of your latest outrage."

At first glance she looks like an old lady with too much make-up. Then you notice something is way wrong: like maybe she'd been in a bad fire and most of her facial features got scorched off.

I swallowed hard and shook her extended hand. She looked me over with her faded blue eyes–all that was left of her face that looked remotely real.

"So, there's another Nick Twisp on the planet," she said.

"Uh, the name's Davidson," I replied. "Nick Davidson."

"Naturally, you'll be dropping that pointless name soon enough. Your Twispian essence cannot be denied for long. Your father will be adopting you, and all the formalities will be observed."

"Nothing's been decided, Connie," Nick said. "What can I get you?"

"Nothing, thanks. I want to be able to drive home without making three pit stops along the way. Nick dear, forgive me for being so direct, but your life has gone off the rails."

Thankfully, she was addressing that remark to the other Nick.

"I'm doing OK," he replied.

"Nonsense! You are becalmed, adrift, your boat is in irons to belabor the nautical metaphor. You have no work and you are sleeping on someone's borrowed sofa."

"No, we've got proper beds here," he said.

"What's happening with your wife?" she demanded.

"I'm waiting for Ada to file for divorce."

"And your career?"

"My agent is working on acting jobs for me. I met with a noted producer last week."

"In short, you are merely *waiting* for something to happen. In Hollywood very little comes to those who wait. If you are fin-

ished with your wife, you should divorce her. And forget this acting business. It's not happening."

"But I'm a performer, Connie. That's what I do."

"That's what you did, you mean. Now you have to find other
work–such as behind the camera. You directed some episodes of
your TV show, so why not be a director?"

"I doubt anyone would hire me, Connie–especially at my
age."

"So hire yourself. Start a project. Get the ball rolling. Direct
your own feature."

"And what would I do for financing?"

"Hit up your wealthy friends, what else? I could use a good tax
write-off. And you don't need $20 million. You could produce a
nice little movie for $2 million or less. People do it all the time."

"I'd need a story and actors. And a film crew. And locations.
And post production. And a distributor. It's a huge undertaking,
Connie."

"So get off your butt, Nick. You're turning into a loser. And
Twisps make especially repellent losers."

"Why's that?" I asked, intrigued.

"Because, young man, even in the best of circumstances you
Twisps are not that popular or appealing. That is why you must
always try harder. The world won't come knocking on your door
bearing riches as it does for Trent Preston and his like."

"You can't make a movie without a decent story," said Nick.
"That's why most low-budget films go nowhere. Bad stories make
tedious movies."

"Look to your past, Nick. Your own youth, although improbable in its particulars, was highly cinematic. It offers a wealth of
incidents that could translate to the screen."

"I'd need kid actors for that, Connie. You know how hard it is
to find anyone competent."

"Your star is right here, Nick."

It appeared she was pointing at me.

"Him?" sneered my new and not-that-loving dad.

"Who else?" said Connie. "All Twisps are natural actors. That's
what makes them such effective liars. Deceit is an inborn trait. Tell
me a lie, Nick."

"Uh, well," I stammered. "I'm very happy to meet you."

"See?" she said. "See how he simulates sincerity. Here's your Nick Twisp. He was born for the part. The zits can be added with makeup. Now all you need is your Sheeni Saunders and a few other bit players. Also someone stunningly beautiful to play my younger self."

"I'd need a producer, Connie. I can't carry the ball all by myself. I'd get swamped in details. Do you think Veeva would be interested?"

"I doubt it, Nick. She's got her own movies, two impossible kids, a lazy housekeeper with immigration issues, and that increasingly bizarre husband. You'll have to look elsewhere."

"Are you interested?" he asked.

"Sorry, Nick. Too much work, and God knows, I don't need the frown lines. You should find someone young and hungry and resourceful."

"That sounds like a recruitment job for you, Connie."

"OK, I'll ask around. I'll have a name by the end of the week. On one condition."

"What's that?"

"You file for divorce, start couples counseling, or do *something* to end the impasse with your wife."

"Oh, OK."

"And start shaving. You look like a bum."

"Stubble's the new look, Connie. Everyone's doing it. It's considered sexy and masculine."

"On Ryan Gosling, maybe," she replied. "On you it looks like you're grooming to panhandle for quarters."

Wow, I've been in this town for less than a week and already I'm being considered for a starring part in a major movie. The film may be low-budget, but I'm one actor who won't be working for peanuts.

TUESDAY, May 26 – I slept last night with the door to my balcony open. You can't hear the surf much during the day, but it comes through clearly at night. Kind of relaxing. A nice change from the boom-boom cars blasting through in our old neighborhood.

No calls lately from my mother, although I emailed her my new phone number a few days ago. I tried calling her, but got a message that her phone has been disconnected. We are both ducking you-know-who.

I took my cereal upstairs to eat on the balcony. As I was crunching down I heard a voice call out, "Stop looking at me!"

I put down my spoon, peered over the railing and saw a girl staring up at me from a neighbor's yard. She had light brown hair and appeared to be somewhere between 15 and 25. It's hard to tell for sure with chicks, especially cute ones.

"You're not talking to me are you?" I said.

"Who else?" she replied. "You're not allowed to look down here."

"Why not?"

"Because we hate your guts."

"That's odd. You don't even know me."

"We hate that you've built that monstrous tower. It's horrible and it's blocking our view of the ocean."

"Wasn't me. We're just guests here."

"You could do the world a favor and set it on fire."

"Not likely. Then we'd be homeless. And jailed for arson."

"That doesn't follow. If you were in jail, you wouldn't be homeless. What's your name anyway?"

"Nick. What's yours?"

"I don't think that's any of your business."

"OK. Shouldn't you be in school?"

"I go to private school. I'm home this week finishing my end-of-term honors project."

"Which is?"

"Undecided as of yet. I'm procrastinating desperately. Why aren't you in school?"

"My school year ended early."

"I expect you were expelled. For some heinous misdemeanor."

"No, I moved suddenly. I used to live in Indiana."

"I bet you miss those placid banks of the Wabash."

"Not particularly. Want to come over and have some breakfast?"

"I already ate. It's practically lunchtime or are you still on Midwest time?"

"No. I've been here a week. Perhaps I could help you with your project."

"Not likely. I need a decent grade. Some of us are going to college."

REVOLT AT THE BEACH

"I was an honor student back in Indiana."

"You wouldn't last five minutes at my school. It's gruelingly competitive."

"I may be smarter than I look."

"I hope so—for your sake. Well, I can't waste any more time talking to you, Nick."

"When you need a study break, come out and give me a whistle. Or we can take a walk to the beach. Oh, I forgot. I can't today. I'm going to the beach with Azura Preston."

"In your dreams, liar."

"No, she lives in Brentwood with my brother Scott Twisp. He's in 'Wildcatter.'"

"I know who those people are. And they have no connection to you."

"Suit yourself. I better get back to my cereal. It's getting soggy."

"Goodbye, Nick. And stop looking down here."

"Goodbye, whoever you are. Keep me in mind for your next excursion to the beach."

"Hah! Not likely!"

She went back into her house. That could be the longest conversation I've ever had with a cute girl in my life. Naturally, I had to phone Veeva to ask who she was.

"That would be Miss Valerie Haseltine. Her father's the biggest busybody in the neighborhood. A real Mr. Not in My Backyard. He almost cost us our building permit. Fortunately, we have deeper pockets than he does. Our lawyer squashed his lawyer like a bug. His daughter impresses me as something of a chip off the old block, but I suppose you're infatuated with her."

"Not at all," I lied. "I just wondered who she was."

"My advice is to steer clear of her. So I heard the Gargoyle read the riot act to your old man yesterday."

"Yes, and he shaved this morning. And has been banging away on his laptop for hours. And we're going to dinner tomorrow at his wife's house."

"Good. There may be hope for the man yet. The world would be a different place if everyone got goosed periodically by my mother. Well, keep me posted on developments there. And try not to fall for Valerie. That girl screams trouble."

Could be, but I think Veeva may be tarring the daughter un-fairly for the troubles she's had with the father.

Azura showed up only 45 minutes late, which is fairly on time for a celebrity. She was wearing a big floppy hat and oversized sunglasses to help conceal her identity. She said I made an ideal beach companion for helping keep the paparazzi at bay, since I didn't look like anyone Azura Preston would be associating with. I tried not to take that personally.

We walked to the beach and settled into a private spot on the sand. Not too crowded today since it was a weekday. Azura removed her blouse, but kept on her shorts. Yes, she was wear-ing a bikini top. Quite the perfect shape that made me even more jealous of my brother than usual. After I stripped down to my bathing suit, she looked me over and said she was grateful that I'd removed my ZipPits.

"Scott leaves his on at the beach. He says it's wonderful free advertising. He doesn't care how much he embarrasses me."

"That's pretty bold," I admitted, though I might do the same if I owned part of a lucrative company.

Azura continued to check me out; I was hoping she liked what she was seeing. She commented that all male Twisps my age re-semble famine victims.

"I've been trying to bulk up," I admitted. "But it's not work-ing."

"I think it's a strategy to seduce girls by making them feel sorry for you. Scott was the skinniest and horniest guy on the planet back in our teen years. I suppose you inherited that syn-drome also."

I confessed that I probably had.

"Scott was always after me for sex. It's not really all that flatter-ing. After a while you feel like merely a tool to relieve someone's lust."

"But you're still together," I pointed out.

"I love the guy. Things are better now that he's calmed down. I hope we can survive this separation. I tried going on location with him a few times, but I felt so useless. You don't really want to be in Bakersfield with nothing to do. It's very damaging to one's self-esteem."

"Are you going to marry him?"

"I don't know. We've talked about it. We'll see how I feel when I come back from Montana."

I took out my cellphone and snapped some selfies of us sitting arm-in-arm on the sand. These I intend to show to a certain skeptical neighbor when I get the chance.

I told Azura about my possible acting job. She said acting was much harder than people assume. She said the camera is an infallible eye that always knows when you're faking it. She also said that of all the directors over the years on the "Double Juggle" TV show my new dad was by far the worst.

"Why's that?" I asked.

"He was picky and not that communicative. It was like he expected you to read his mind. Plus, he made these grimaces that just sucked out all your self-confidence. It wasn't only me either. All the actors felt like we were floundering when he was directing. Scotty had the worst time with him. I don't think their relationship ever quite recovered–not that it was that great to begin with. I hope he does better with you."

"Well, so far he's an improvement over my first dad."

"Good, Nick. That's promising."

We got our feet wet in the surf, but the water was too chilly for swimming. We walked along the beach and got a smoothie from a stand. Azura told me all about the paleo diet, which is based on what cavemen ate. I told her I could probably never embrace a diet that banned cake, pie, and donuts. Not to mention ice cream. Hell, it even frowns on the bun in your hamburger. And wasn't the average caveman in 10,000 B.C. dying around age 19? How healthy was that?

Then she got recognized, and people started snapping photos of us with their cellphones, so we beat it back to my place. My new dad invited Azura to cook our dinner, but she politely declined. So he phoned out for pizza after she left. I asked him how the movie script was going.

"Not bad," he replied. "Perhaps all the pain from my childhood can start paying me back at the box office."

I told him that Azura had been giving me some acting tips.

"I wouldn't get your hopes up," he replied. "You shouldn't put much faith in Connie's opinion. I expect we'll have to go with professional actors in all the parts. We need kids with experience."

"But how do I get experience if I don't get any acting jobs?"

"You're too late. A lot of these kids starting acting in commercials at age two. By age five they were pros."

"Azura says I could be the greatest actor to come out of Indiana since James Dean."

"Right. Well, we'll give you a test. I'll give you a shot. I'd rather deal with you than some egotistical teenager's shark of an agent demanding my left nut on a stick."

Something I may need to demand in my contract as well. Plus a kidney as a bonus clause in the event I win an Oscar.

WEDNESDAY, May 27 – More morning cereal crunching on the balcony. As before this activity lured my cute neighbor from her den.

"Why are you still here?" she demanded.

"I live here, Valerie."

"Who told you my name?"

"I made some enquiries."

"You're a horrible prying spy. I should dial 911 and report you."

"Please don't. I'm trying to eat my breakfast. How's your project going?"

"It's ruining my life, Nick. My parents say I'm too young for writer's block, but I've always been precocious."

"You could swipe something off the Web."

"All papers we turn in are analyzed by computer for just such deceptive intent. I'd be expelled and wind up working on the assembly line next to you."

"I'm not going in for factory work; my family are all actors."

"Don't you mean liars?"

"Come over here, and I'll show you some photos I took yesterday with Azura Preston."

"I could never step foot onto that despoiled property."

"How about I come over there?"

"My father would shoot you for trespassing–with my zealous encouragement, of course."

"OK. How about we meet on neutral territory? Say on the corner in five minutes?"

"Well, all right. But expect to be humiliated when your pretensions are punctured."

She was even cuter up close. Amazing eyes that were some-where between gray and blue. Petite, but curving most provoca-tively under a frayed jersey borrowed from some giant. I showed her my cellphone photos.

"OK, you know Azura Preston. I'm terribly, terribly, terribly impressed. Are you satisfied?"

"Uh, I'm getting there. Now do you believe that my father is Nick Twisp, the juggler?"

"And who are you, Nick Twisp Junior?"

"No, my name is Davidson, but it's kind of a long story. I could buy you a coffee and tell you about it."

"All right. As long as I'm blocked, I might as well be bored too."

We walked a half-dozen blocks to her favorite coffee hangout. She ordered some improbable concoction involving soy milk and herbal tea that cost over $5. I had a small black coffee and a pump-kin muffin. We sat at a metal table on their outdoor patio.

"You could stick a derrick on that muffin and pump out enough oil to power L.A. for a week," she commented, sipping her tea.

"Are you always so hostile, or just around me?"

"Don't flatter yourself that I'm any way around you. Last night I prayed that an earthquake would send you and your tower crash-ing to the ground."

"Not very smart. It could tip right over and flatten your house."

"At least then I wouldn't have to turn in my project on Fri-day."

"Let's not think about that. Shall I tell you about the sudden transformation of my life?"

"OK, as long as it doesn't involve magical powers or Jesus."

I told her about growing up in Indiana and the events of last week.

"Your mother abandoned you with some stranger," she said. "That's got to suck big time."

"It was way bad the first few days, but I'm kind of used to him now. I like that he might put me in this movie he's making. It's about his teen years. He was quite out of control. He fathered twin daughters when he was only 15. He missed out on college because he was in prison for shooting some guy."

"Are you lying, Nick? Your credibility is very much in doubt."

"Honest, Valerie, it's all true. That and much more. I've only heard a little about him so far from my new relatives."

"You should know I hate the name Valerie."

"OK. What should I call you?"

"My friends call me Cal."

"Because you live in California?"

"No. When I was younger, I was quite skinny. Sort of like you. Kids called me Valerie the Calorie. That got shortened to Cal."

"You're not skinny anymore," I observed.

"Yes, and if you don't keep your eyes elevated, I'll call 911 to report a pervert."

"You must keep the emergency operators busy."

"I phone them constantly. We're all on a first-name basis now."

I told her how I came to be called Nickie D.

"Well, I won't be calling you that. It's much too juvenile."

I like that this implied that our contact would be continuing. Right before she finished her tea I manned up and asked for her cellphone number and contact info. She turned them over without a struggle and even requested mine.

Walking back to our block, we crossed a bridge over the canal. I asked her if she'd ever seen any rats.

"Only the ones who moved in next door. Have you ever met that writer dude?"

I said I'd met him at Tyler Twisp's Sunday brunch, and he seemed very nice.

"You should read one of his books. Everyone thinks he's totally sick and twisted. That's why my father called off his lawyer. He didn't want the guy going crazy and shooting up the neighborhood."

"Just because he writes violent books doesn't mean he's violent personally."

"How perceptive of you to notice. Desmond's the only one I respect. His wife's a total cow and his kids are little screaming monsters. My dad says the whole family is a menace to society."

"Right. Well, I don't know them that well. I just met them a few days ago. They are being nice and letting us stay in their guesthouse for free."

"That's only because their conditional use permit says it can't be a rental. Otherwise, she'd be charging you big bucks."

I could see in the future I'd have to tiptoe around the topic of Veeva Saunders and her family. We parted on our neutral corner. She thanked me for the tea and told me to eat more. I replied it wouldn't do any good and said I hoped we'd see each other again. She said, "That very much remains to be seen," and strolled off toward her house. Not to be sexist, but she looked just as good from behind.

Driving to dinner that evening my new dad asked me who that girl was he'd seen me talking to. I said she was just a neighbor who wasn't very friendly.

"How does she look?" he asked.

"She looks, uh, OK."

"Not gorgeous?"

"Some might call her that. I try not to be overtly sexist in my attitudes."

"Right. Like every other 15-year-old boy. Well, don't get too emotionally involved with her."

"OK, I'll make a note of that."

"I mean it, Nick. Very few guys wind up with the chicks they meet at your age. Learn something from your dad's mistakes."

"And by 'dad' you mean who . . . ? You?"

"That seems to be the consensus these days. Plus, you look just like me."

"Nice of you to notice."

"And always use protection. Let me know if you need any condoms."

"I just met the girl. Geez!"

"Well, it pays to be prepared. One slip-up and you can have people addressing you as dad for the rest of your life."

"That reminds me," I said. "I need another $50."

"And they'll be making financial demands on you too."

"So here's a question for you, Dad."

He didn't flinch when I tried out that experimental salutation.

"OK, shoot."

"That girl Sheeni Saunders whom you fell in love with at age 15."

"What about her?"

"If she showed up here tomorrow and wanted to get back together, what would you say to her?"

Very long pause. So long I thought he was going to duck the question.

"I can't really say," he said at last. "We'd have to talk about it. I'd have to take a measure of her sincerity."

Just as I thought. The guy fell in love with a chick when he was my age and 38 years later was still stuck on her. This is supposed to prove that the emotions of a 15-year-old don't count for beans? I think not.

His house in Pacific Palisades was even ritzier than I expected. Probably cost several million dollars at least. Big garden in back landscaped like some tropical paradise with a full-size pool shimmering in the fading light. Ada (my stepmother?) had set a table for three out on the stone terrace and was grilling seafood kabobs at her outdoor kitchen. MED (my exiled dad) extracted a bottle of wine from the outdoor wine cooler and checked out the label.

"Where did you get this French Chardonnay?" he asked.

"A friend of mine gave me a case of it," she replied.

"A friend, huh? Anyone I know?"

"No."

"Never marry a woman of mystery, Nick."

"OK, Dad. Say, that smells good," I said, hoping to break the tension.

"Thanks, Nick," she said, stirring grilled mushrooms into the rice. "Would you like milk, sparkling water, or mango juice?"

"I'll take a Coke if you've got one."

"Sorry, sodas are not something anyone should be drinking. How about some fresh mango juice?"

"OK, that sounds fine."

It was a yellow liquid that tasted not bad. Probably be better with some rum in it. Dad poured two glasses of wine and we sat down at the table. No toasts were proposed, no glasses were clinked. We dug in.

"I've signed you up for a service that delivers dinners," she announced. "From what I heard, Nick, what you two have been eating could be construed as child abuse."

"We do OK," he lied. "It's gourmet every night."

"I bet. Nick, when's the last time you had a fresh salad?"

That query was directed at me.

"Uh, last week I think."

My dad flashed me a look of sharp rebuke.

"A proper diet could put some meat on your bones," she said.

"All Twisps are thin at his age," Dad declared. "Our DNA is devoting most of its efforts to mental development."

"And skipping the emotional maturity entirely," she added. "Another kabob, Nick?"

"Sure. Thanks," I said, keeping my head down to stay out of the crossfire.

Eventually, she sat back in her chair, sipped her wine, and remarked that she really liked the house.

"It's yours," Dad replied.

"We'll subtract half its value from my share of the assets," she replied.

"OK, if you insist. Anything monthly required?"

"Not by me. How about you?"

"Of course not. We'll have to amend the trust."

"I expect it will be dissolved."

"Yeah, you're right. Anything else?"

"That about covers it."

"I'll hear from your lawyer?"

"In a few days. You want to tell Scott or should I?"

"You tell him. He always liked you better."

"I put more effort into it than you did."

"So you always told me."

I'm not sure, but I think they just worked out the terms of their divorce.

Dessert was strawberry shortcake with whipped cream. My best meal ever in California. Personally, I'd think twice before divorcing someone who could cook like that. After dinner I got a tour of the house that I'll never live in. Too bad. It's quite the posh place.

He was pretty quiet on the drive back except to say that he had just eaten the most expensive meal of his life.

THURSDAY, May 28 – Not even the birds were awake when my phone rang this morning.

"Yeah," I yawned.

"Was I hallucinating or did you say you'd help me with my project?"

Instant adrenalin rush.

"Oh, hi, Cal. Sure I'll help. What would you like me to do?"

"Call me back at a decent hour. It's much too early to talk."

I called her back later after I'd taken my shower, but before I'd crunched through my cereal. We agree to meet at our neutral corner and proceed to a restaurant on the beach for breakfast. Good thing I'd squeezed more cash last night out of my despondent dad. I haven't yet got the full fifty, but he crossed my palm with $35.

I ordered something called "twice-grilled" French toast and she went with poached eggs on toast. Mine arrived all dressed up with blackened grill marks and real maple syrup. Hers came with a giant chunk of pineapple on the side.

"What am I supposed to do with this?" she asked, pointing to her chunk. "Gnaw on it like a goat?"

"Good thing my dad isn't here. He'd juggle that for sure."

A faint peppering of freckles across her nose. I hadn't noticed that before. Also a small scar on her forehead from some childhood mishap. No makeup at all that I could see. She didn't need any. It wasn't that scary sitting across from her and eating. Just pleasant and comfortable.

"OK, here's my idea, Nick. My project doesn't have to be written. It just has to be creative and interesting."

"Right."

"For example, it could be a video."

"OK."

"So how about I interview you in a video?"

"Sounds way boring."

"No, here's the thing. It'd be about what we discussed yesterday. You know, your abandonment by your mom and your discovering your new family."

"I don't know, Cal. That's kind of personal."

"But it's of compelling human interest!"

"But I'm hiding out, Cal. I don't want my stepdad to find me and drag me back to Indiana."

"Well, nobody would see it except my teacher."

"You wouldn't be showing it to your friends so they could laugh at me?"

"God, Nick, you're kind of paranoid. Of course, I wouldn't show it to anyone–not if you didn't want me to. I'd totally respect your privacy."

I thought it over. I could see that saying no to her would be difficult.

"All right. I guess we could do that."

"Great, Nickie D.! You're a lifesaver!"

"OK, but if your video gets an F, don't blame me."

I wound up eating her pineapple chunk; I sneaked a steak knife from the waiters' station and went at it.

"Where should we do the video?" I asked, carving away.

"It needs to be someplace private where we won't be interrupted."

Many venues were considered, but the only one that seemed workable was my private balcony in the sky. She said she hated the idea of crossing into "enemy territory," but could see no alternative.

"Shall we use your cellphone?" I asked.

"No, I'll borrow my brother's camcorder."

"You have a brother?"

"Yes, unfortunately. Harvey's 15 and my parents' gravest mistake."

"And how old are you?" I asked, casually.

"Sixteen, Nick. And you are?"

"Uh, 16 also," I lied.

"Really? I would have said you were somewhat younger than that."

"No, I'm just, uh, short for my age."

I waited on the corner while she got the camcorder and other equipment. I liked the idea of hanging with her, but I was still dubious about this video scheme. She returned carrying a camera bag, and we walked toward Veeva's house. She halted by the driveway.

"Something the matter?" I asked.

"Nick, I need you to grab my shirt and drag me. I don't want to feel that I've entered here of my own free will."

I paused for a moment to process that statement. Perhaps to a chick it made sense.

"Not a problem," I said, grabbing what I hoped was a non-intimate area of her shirt near her left shoulder. I gave a tug and she reluctantly followed me up the driveway. I dragged her into our living room and encountered my new dad, who was drinking coffee and reading the *Los Angeles Times.* His eyebrows shot up when he saw us. I released my grip on her shirt.

"Hi, Dad," I said. "This is my friend Cal."

"I see. Nice to meet you, Cal."

"Hi, Mr. Twisp. I didn't watch your TV show because Veeva Saunders was a producer on it. My father was suing her at the time."

"I understand. That's OK."

We headed toward the stairs.

"And you are going where?" he asked. "To your bedroom?"

God, the man has a dirty mind. I blushed.

"Uh, no. We're going out on the balcony. To make a video."

"A video, OK. Have fun. And let me know if you need anything."

That last part he said with a wink. I blushed again.

"Your father doesn't look much like a celebrity," she whispered as we trooped up the second flight of stairs.

"That's why he had to do all that juggling: to distract the customers from his looks."

We both walked by my neatly made single bed without looking at it. Needless to say, it was the first time I'd ever had a girl in my room.

"Out here's the balcony," I said, leading the way.

She put down the camera bag and looked out over the railing.

"Wow, you've got a great view up here, Nick. This whole place is much nicer than I expected. It's almost like you're sleeping in a tree house."

"I know. It's just the sky and the ocean and the birds up here."

"Uh-oh, you can see right into my bedroom window. I'll have to make sure I keep my blinds closed."

I had her point out the window in question so I'd be sure not to look in that direction.

She mounted the camcorder on a mini tripod and set it on

the table. She clipped a little microphone to my shirt, attached its mate to her shirt, then plugged the cord into the camcorder. I liked that we were now linked together, if only electronically. She did a test to adjust the focus and sound level, then said, "OK, Nick, are you ready?"

"I'm ready, Oprah."

"This is serious, Nick! My grade depends on it. No joking around."

"Right."

So we did the interview. This time she was a lot more probing in her questions than yesterday in the coffee shop. She got me to open up candidly about my old dad, my home life in Indiana, my mother's previous career as a topless showgirl, my new dad, his initial reaction to me, and how I had discovered him unemployed and wallowing in roaches in a slummy part of L.A. She even got me to 'fess up about the brain-devouring roach that had invaded my ear. All in all, I put 42 minutes of my intimate life story down on high-def video.

"Good, Nick," she said, clicking off her machine. "You're fairly articulate for a boy. Not too many hems and haws."

"Thanks. What should we do now?"

"I have to go home and record a commentary. You know, to bring it all into perspective."

"Oh. Shall we get together later when you're done?"

"I'm going to be pretty busy. I'll talk to you soon."

A few seconds later we were untethered and she was gone. Damn, not even a thank you hug.

Dad was banging away on his laptop in his bedroom when I came down the stairs.

"That was one spicy tomato," he said.

"Uh, I guess so."

"You appeared to be dragging her here against her will. I hope we don't need to have a conversation about date rape."

"She asked me to drag her. She had issues about stepping onto Veeva's property. If my age ever comes up around Cal, I'm 16."

"I get it. You're a mature fellow."

"Right. And I need another $50."

"What?"

"Yeah, I bought her breakfast this morning. This dating business is expensive."

"Here's a news flash, kid: women are liberated these days. They can pay their own way."

Nevertheless, he came across with $40, but made me wash his lousy Town Car. It wasn't even that dirty. Then I went for a swim in Veeva's pool. Totally great, although I'd prefer a full-size pool. Then I chatted up the Mexican gardener, who came to trim the bushes and blow leaves into Cal's yard.

Dad came out later all spiffed up and looking at his watch. I knew something was up. So this van pulls into the driveway and three foreigners get out. No, it wasn't a drug deal. They (two guys, one chick) were from some TV station in Lisbon, Portugal. Dad's old TV show is being shown there and it's a giant hit. It seems Portugal is the one place in the world where they really dig juggling and white guys pretending to be black.

The men set up their camera (much more impressive-looking than Cal's) in our living room and conducted the second Twisp interview of the day. Dad told the foxy gal with the microphone that he lived in nearby Pacific Palisades, but preferred to "do my writing at my beach house." Guess he didn't want to 'fess up that we were homeless and living off Veeva's charity. I got introduced (off camera) as Dad's "nephew." They interviewed him for over an hour, then all four of them left in the van for a late lunch. The nephew wasn't invited.

Hours later another van pulled in and a hippie-looking dude delivered our new meals on wheels. The name of the company is Gazelle Gourmet, although the main dish appeared to be chicken not gazelle. Dad still hadn't returned, so I had a lonely dinner for one. I'd rate the food better than my junior high school cafeteria, but not as good as McDonalds. The leftovers I put in the frig for Portugal's most celebrated TV star, should he decide to return.

No call from Cal, so I texted her that I'd love to see the final version of her video.

11:32 p.m. Still no reply from Cal and no sign of my partying dad. Nothing happening in Cal's window either. So it's off to bed for me.

FRIDAY, May 29 – Having been built for the ages from solid concrete, this place is pretty soundproof. I didn't hear Dad return last night, nor did I hear any subsequent activities. Therefore I was surprised to come downstairs this morning and find Miss Foxy Lisbon Media Personality making coffee in our compact kitchen. She was dressed in the same chic gray suit she had on yesterday.

"Hello, my name is Jacinta," she said in her charming accent. "You are, of course, his son and not his nephew."

"Yeah, I don't know what that gambit was about."

"Great men often wish to be thought bachelors. Is he really getting a divorce?"

"Yeah, that part's true. Have you been talking to him at night on the phone?"

"No, darling. I just met him yesterday. Then he has another girlfriend?"

"I don't know. He hasn't said."

"No matter. We are leaving today. That's life. Your father is a genius, you know."

"So I hear. Would you like some toast? Or I could fry you an egg."

"That would be nice."

We were eating breakfast when the great man himself shuffled down the stairs.

"Oh, hi, Jacinta," he said. "I thought you had an early flight to catch."

"Not so early. Your son has cooked for me a delicious omelet."

"That's odd. He's never cooked one for me. I was under the impression his cookery stopped at grilled cheese sandwiches."

I figured they might want to hurl themselves at each other again, so I excused myself and went up to hang out on my balcony. I was hoping to lure out Cal again, but she didn't show. I expect she's gone off to school with my revelatory video. Later I saw the van pull in, and Jacinta left with her two scandalized compatriots. I went downstairs, and Dad felt the need to apologize.

"I don't usually do things like that, Nick. I guess I was still upset from my divorce. It's my first, you know."

"How can it be your first if you also got married at 15 in Mississippi?"

"Well, that one really didn't count. We lied about our ages and used false names. I felt married, but Sheeni sure didn't. Some scandal-mongers tried to make out like I was a bigamist a few years back, but it didn't stick. Nobody cared."

"Why didn't Sheeni feel married if you had the ceremony?"

"I don't know. I guess she wasn't ready to commit. She was pregnant at the time. It could have been the hormones."

"Is she married now?"

"She was. To some cheatin' Frog. But she ditched him for good in February."

The same month my dad's marriage unraveled. How odd. By "cheatin' Frog" I assume he's referring to a Frenchman and not a reptile.

A busy morning. I got three phone calls in quick succession. The first was from my mother, who has made it to Miami, is rooming with some co-dancers in their waterfront condo, and is busy rehearsing. She was pleased that we'd moved out of the ghetto and was surprised about my new dad's pending divorce.

"You could come here and make a play for him, Mom," I suggested. "You appear to be sexually compatible."

"I have no interest in marrying your father, Nick. And I'm sure he's not regarding me very favorably these days. Is he treating you OK?"

"Pretty good. He makes me wash his car though, when I ask him for money."

She noted my address and promised to send me a check soon. We also exchanged phone numbers. Then she told me she loved me about 12 times before I managed at last to hang up.

Next call was from my brother, who was on his way back from Bakersfield. I asked him how fast he was driving.

"Traffic's fairly light so I'm holding it steady at 90."

"Do you get many tickets?"

"I have the latest radar detector. And that phone app that scouts out cops. But quite a few of the highway patrol guys watch 'Wildcatter.' They usually only pull me over to ask if Azura Preston is as hot as she looks."

I felt like asking the same question, but managed to stifle the impulse.

Scott said he heard about the divorce and was wondering how our dad was doing. I told him about last night's visitation by Jacinta.

"That sounds like him. Does he know about Brent?"

"Who?"

"My mom's new boyfriend."

"I think he suspects something, but I don't think he knows the details."

"Good, let's keep him in the dark. I know we're popular in Portugal because I'm Facebook friends with umpteen thousand girls from there."

"Have any of them showed up in L.A. looking for you?"

"Not yet. Let's hope they wait until Zee leaves for Montana. Hey, I'll talk to her and we'll make a time to get together. Maybe go for a run on the beach or get in a workout."

"Uh, right."

Is that what brothers do? Build their muscles together? I'm clueless as to how one relates to a brother.

The last call was from Cal. She was phoning from the girls' restroom at school over a friend's cellphone.

"There's been a bit of a disaster, Nick," she said. "I asked Harvey for some help with the titles on my video. The traitor blabbed about us to my parents. They're furious that I was associating with a houseguest of Veeva Saunders. They really do despise her. My father confiscated my cellphone."

"That's awful!"

"I know. No one can function socially without their phone. Naturally, I couldn't remember your phone number."

"But you managed to call."

"My friend Esmee hypnotized me and got me to recall the digits."

"You have a friend who can hypnotize people?"

"Yes, her father is Carstann, the famous mentalist. She's been doing it since she was four. She likes to hypnotize boys and get them to do stupid things. Not such a great feat, since they're always doing that anyway."

"Your parents don't want you to see me again?"

"No, and they're quite irrationally firm on that point. They told me to regard the line between our properties like the border between Israel and Gaza."

"Will they give you your phone back?"

"In a few days probably. No one can endure living with me for very long when I'm being hateful. In the meantime we can communicate by signs."

"Signs?"

"Yes, I'll place a sign in my bedroom window. And you can hang one on your balcony."

"Right, I get it."

"I handed in my video, Nick. Philip says he's looking forward to viewing it."

"Who's Philip?"

"My teacher. He's 26 and quite a simpatico spirit. Esmee is dying to hypnotize him and find out if he's gay."

"Why do you suspect that?"

"I don't know. Anyone that handsome and together and hip has got to be gay. Otherwise, there'd be women congregating outside his classroom door and drooling on the glass."

I heard a bell ring and Cal said she had to go. I thanked her for calling and said I looked forward to seeing her again. I think it's most unfair of her parents to involve me in their neighborhood wars. What did I ever do to them?

Then Connie Saunders showed up to take us to lunch. I said I was fine eating Gazelle leftovers here, but got dragged along anyway. She appears to be unnaturally fascinated by all things Twisp, including me. Despite being immensely wealthy, she doesn't like expensive restaurants. So we went to a place on Wilshire that specializes in soup. Now soup is OK if you're female, sick as a dog, or elderly, but it's a pretty meager lunch for a kid like me devoting so much energy to mental and sexual development (I wish). So I had to supplement my soup with three desserts.

Connie was glad to hear that Dad got his divorce rolling at last. She said she liked Ada, but never saw the connection between teeth repair and comic juggling. Of course, if Dad restricted his dating to chicks in his field, he'd be a bachelor for life. He reminded her that she was the one who advised him to marry Ada.

"You needed a wife at the time," said Connie. "And she seemed the likeliest prospect. I don't think you Twisps do well unattached."

I certainly think I'd do better attached to someone cute and sexually liberated.

Connie also said she has scrounged up a producer for his

movie. I wasn't paying much attention, but apparently it's a gal named Mary Moran, who has made quite a few films. She's the youngest daughter of a gent named Colm Moran, who also made movies back in ancient times like the 1970s and '80s. He produced his movies in between running a bathing suit company in Ukiah.

At that point I brought the conversation to a screeching halt and demanded to know what was this burg Ukiah I kept hearing about.

Dad said it was a small town about 100 miles north of San Francisco that used to be big in lumbering. It's the home town of Trent and Sheeni, and where Dad accidentally (he claims) shot Sheeni's father. He lived, but has since passed on (though not from the lingering effects of a gunshot wound).

Dad said he'd be "delighted" to meet with Mary, especially since they had Ukiah in common. I hadn't heard of most of her movies, but I remember seeing one of them last year. Based on her family's business, it was titled "The Incredible Shrinking Bathing Suit." Jayden and I were there the day it opened at the mall, but were kind of disappointed because most of the chicks in the movie were old and fat. Plus, the bathing suits didn't keep shrinking (as the title promised), but were mostly just standard old bikinis. All in all, it was pretty much a gyp.

When we got back, I checked Cal's window, but no signs were observed. I wasn't sure when she returned from school, so I went out and loitered on our neutral corner. Eventually, this kid strolled by and told me I was an idiot.

"What?" I said, startled.

"I watched your dumb video," he replied. "You're a fool to reveal so much to my sister."

"You must be Harvey, the snitch."

He was a little taller than me and remarkably good looking. I felt like disfiguring his face with my fist, but am not much of a brawler.

"Here's a tip, Nick. Never believe anything that my sister tells you."

"Er, why's that?"

"Because she's a pathological liar."

"I doubt that. I think you're the person with the problem."

"Well, don't say I didn't warn you."

He started to walk away, but I had a question to ask him: "Say, Harvey, do you know if your sister has a boyfriend?"

"My sister doesn't do boyfriends, Nick. She does zombie slaves instead. She's had quite a few of those. And you, for example, also appear to be infected."

The guy was creeping me out. I told him he was a weirdo, and he should butt out of his sister's life.

"Fine, Nick. I look forward to watching you suffer."

It seems to me that all the Haseltines–except for lovely Cal– were more than a little strange.

I made this sign: "C U?" and taped it to my balcony. I hoped it would get the message across, but be sufficiently cryptic to Cal's spying parents. Every five minutes I ran back up there to see if she had responded, but her window remained blank.

Tonight's Gazelle Gourmet was some sort of beef concoction. Dad took a tentative bite and said if that was gourmet, he was the "ghost of Mae West." Nevertheless, we both ate it. I observed that it was a good reminder of why one should try to retain mothers and wives in one's life.

"My mother was a lousy cook," he replied. "She once served me cow's liver 17 nights in a row."

God, no wonder he ran away from home.

I told him about Cal's parents' arbitrary decision to ban me from her life, and asked if he could intervene with them.

"Wouldn't do any good, Nick. Parents instinctively dislike me. They always have for some reason. Parents take one look at us Twisps and always think the worst."

"But they've never even met me!"

"Doesn't matter. Just the rumor of a Twisp in the neighborhood is enough to spook them. My advice is to give their cute daughter a pass."

Easy for him to say. He just spent the night with a foxy chick half his age. I've never even had so much as a platonic girlfriend.

While I was loading the dishwasher, Veeva pulled into the drive with her family. (They are spending the weekend in the front house.) She popped in briefly to invite us to breakfast tomorrow.

I spent the rest of the night until bedtime waiting forlornly on my balcony for signs of life from you know where. After a while I was beginning to feel like someone's zombie slave.

REVOLT AT THE BEACH

SATURDAY, May 30 – Although Veeva is not Mexican, she made huevos rancheros for breakfast. Dad addressed her husband as "Desmond" even though there's some dispute whether that is his real name. His last name is alleged to be Upton. Their kids are Marty (six) and Xenia (four). Both are named after characters who got offed creatively in Desmond's novels. I don't think that's creepy, but Veeva said it was "very inflaming" to the Gargoyle.

Xenia poured syrup on her eggs, got sticky all over, and insisted on crawling onto my lap. Marty announced loudly that I "wasn't allowed" in their yard or pool. When his mother contradicted him, he kicked me hard under the table. Since we're house guests, I pretended not to notice.

After breakfast we got a tour of their house, which Veeva says is an "airplane bungalow." That means it has large roof overhangs and a small upper floor. Formerly, this space was two dinky bedrooms, but it got made over into a large office for Desmond–all soundproofed to muffle distracting kid noises. In the center of the room was a regulation-size, intricately carved pool table to keep him occupied while awaiting inspiration. As it was too massive to come up the narrow stairs, the roof had been lifted off so it could be hoisted in by crane. Must be nice to have unlimited funds for such necessities.

"And how did your neighbor react to the truck crane?" asked Dad.

"Not at all well," said Desmond. "I thought we'd be treated to an exploding brain aneurism. He certainly turned red enough. But, alas, all his arteries held. I have a nice view of their house up here. His lovely daughter has a bit of a wild streak."

"Why do you say that?" I asked.

"She likes to undress in front of her window with the blinds open. You can read a description of her nubile body in my novel *Strangled Strangers*."

Not the greatest news, but a book I would certainly have to read.

We lingered in their kitchen after Trent Preston arrived with donuts. Apparently, he and my Dad meet at least monthly for mutual donut-dunking. Dad told him about his new movie project. Trent asked to be kept in mind for the role of Sheeni's dad. When at last I got away, I rushed up to my balcony and I spotted this sign in Cal's window: "L 5 M."

What did that mean? Was it Roman numerals? Did "L" stand for "love?" Or possibly "hell?" Finally, it came to me: the "L" was a graphic representation of a corner. Her message was: "Corner in five minutes."

I hurried to our corner, but she was long gone. No doubt pissed off by my failure to show. Damn! So I took a chance and headed off at a brisk trot in the direction of her favorite coffee shop. I was relieved when I spotted her at an outdoor table with another girl.

"There you are, Nick," she said. "I was beginning to give you up for dead. This is my friend Esmee."

We exchanged hellos and I sat down. She was one of those short girls with too much hair, makeup, jewelry, and chest. Very top-heavy, but kind of pretty. The torn (intentionally?) neckline of her shirt revealed a tanned shoulder and an overloaded bra strap.

"I loved your video, Nick," she said.

"Uh, thanks," I said, looking questioningly at Cal.

"I had to let Esmee see it, Nick," she said. "We have no secrets. Besides, she can blackmail me mercilessly to get her way."

"You have something to hide?" I asked.

"God, I should hope so at my age. I hear you were talking to my loathsome brother."

"Loathsome but cute," added Esmee.

"He warned me to stay away from you. He said you were a pathological liar and worse. I felt like punching him."

"And why didn't you? Violence is the only way to deal with my brother. I should warn you that, though scrawny, Harvey has had years of training in diverse martial arts. No doubt he was trying to provoke you."

"He provokes me," leered Esmee. "He provokes me in a big way."

"Esmee can't see past my brother's exterior to the vileness that lurks within."

"I'm appropriately shallow for my age," she replied. "I only dig cute guys. Nature doesn't equip us to look for inner qualities at age 16."

"Do you agree, Nick?" asked Cal. "Are we only interested in superficialities?"

"Uh, not me. I consider the whole person."

"Good. We'll fix you up with Barb Flixsnoff."

"Who's that?" I asked.

"She's the plainest girl in our school, Nick," said Esmee. "But extremely nice. You'll love her."

"We shouldn't tease darling Nick," said Cal. "He's only just arrived here from the Midwest."

I liked that she was now calling me that.

"He's lost and out of his depth," Cal continued. "Do help him, Esmee."

Esmee leaned toward me, placed a warm hand on the back of my neck, drew me close, looked into my eyes, and spoke to me earnestly. I immediately went limp as if someone suddenly had severed all my tendons. I felt far removed from the scene and completely at peace.

"You are having a beautiful day, Nick," said Esmee, soothingly.

"Beautiful day," I agreed.

"Doing what I say pleases you greatly," she added. "I have terrific news. You are now our zombie slave."

A wave of happiness cascaded over me from that glorious news.

"Test him," ordered Cal.

Esmee rummaged around in her purse and produced a safety pin.

"What are you going to do with that?" I asked, mildly curious.

Esmee smiled. "You will feel absolutely no pain, Nick." She stabbed me in the back of my hand with her pin.

A small bubble of blood oozed from the pinprick, but I felt no pain.

"No pain reaction," observed Cal. "That's good."

"What shall we have him do, Cal?" she asked.

"Every time he sees Veeva Saunders he's to tell her that she's a big fat cow."

"Big fat cow," I repeated. "When I see Veeva Saunders."

"*Every* time you see her," Esmee stressed.

"Every time. Right," I said.

"What else, Cal?" asked Esmee.

"When he hears the word 'dinner,' he will say, 'Pardon me, I farted.'"

"Pardon me, I farted," I said.

Both girls laughed. Their jolly laughter was most delightful to my ears.

"What else, Cal?" asked Esmee.

"You will remember who told you to do these things, Nick darling, but you won't tell anyone in the world. It's our own precious secret."

"Our secret. Right."

"One more thing, Nick sweetheart," said Cal. "When you say 'Pardon me, I farted,' you will, of course, do your best at that time to squeeze out a toot."

"Squeeze one out. Right."

Esmee gave my neck another gentle squeeze and said, "You will now wake up, Nick. And you will have a wonderful day!"

My muscle control returned, and I felt supremely happy to be alive. Plus, it was nice to be sharing that private secret with Cal. How fortunate I was to have met her!

JUNE

MONDAY, June 1 – Confined to my room. I'm being punished. I'm not sure why. Yesterday was something of a disaster. I saw Veeva lounging beside their lap pool and told her she was a big fat cow.

She raised her sunglasses and peered up at me.

"What did you say, Nick dear?"

"I said you were a big fat cow."

"That's what I thought you said. Have I offended you in some way?"

"Er, no."

"Then you should know that I go to the gym daily. I have a body fat index lower than those gaunt fellows in India walking around with begging bowls. The last bite of chocolate that passed my lips was in December, 2009. So would you like to withdraw that statement?"

"Certainly not."

"OK, I see. Well, one expects a certain degree of eccentricity from Twisps, so let me ask you this: Have you been diagnosed with Tourette syndrome?"

"Uh, not to my knowledge."

"Then I suggest you apologize."

"For what?"

"For calling me a big fat cow."

"But you are one."

She shook her head and told me to go away.

Later she told my dad she was canceling our invitation to dinner. She wouldn't tell him why, but he got pretty upset. Then when we sat down to our Gazelle Gourmet (ham paired nastily with brussel sprouts), I repeatedly tried to fart while apologizing for it. This got him extremely annoyed. Then Veeva showed up to have a "small conference" with Dad, and I called her a "big fat cow" again.

So now I'm confined to my room, and Dad has made an emergency appointment tomorrow with Uma (cousin Tyler's psychologist wife) for me to discuss my "attitude." Even worse, I haven't seen or heard from Cal in over 24 hours and miss her desperately. Nothing is happening in her window, not even any partial disrobing.

Only one positive side to being grounded: I missed out on a fraternal bodybuilding session with Scott.

To pass the time I downloaded the e-book version of *Strangled Strangers* and have been reading it on my phone. I noted this passage on page 86:

> The window glowed golden above the swaying palm tree. Stricker raised his rifle and peered through the telescopic sight. He smiled. That was not the bedroom of the Russian. Centered in the cross-hairs was a girl–a naked girl with nothing better to do than to stand in front of her open window on a warm summer night. She brushed her fingertips across her full breasts, then smoothed the dark triangle between her legs. Her hand lingered there as two fingers pressed in deeper. She was young, probably no older than 16 or 17. Her body was perfect–untouched by the depredations of age, rich living, or bad choices in men. She was as desirable as she would ever be, and somehow Stricker sensed that she knew it.

So there you have it. Did it really happen? Or was it just a product of Desmond's twisted imagination? I'm hoping for the latter.

TUESDAY, June 2 – I had my session with Uma. Very unnerving. We met in her office on the second floor of Tyler's mansion. Lots of framed diplomas on the walls to reassure the victim that she was not a quack. Probably be easier to talk to her, though, if she wasn't so beautiful, fashionably garbed, and stacked. Plus, she's married to a guy who has more money than God. All very intimidating. She did her best to put me at ease, emphasizing that I wasn't in any sort of trouble. She said she was there to help me "learn more about yourself."

"Right," I said, taking a seat in a chair facing her.

After some idle chitchat, she got down to brass tacks.

"Your father tells me you persist in saying to Veeva Saunders that she's a big fat cow."

"Well, she is."

Uma stifled a smile.

"And why do you think that?"

"I'm just being honest."

"Do you detect some hostile feelings directed at you from Veeva?"

"Mostly when I tell her that she's a big fat cow."

"You know Veeva's one of my oldest friends. We went to Princeton together."

"I thought that college was for guys only."

"No, it's accepted women since 1969. Veeva is a complicated person. I sometimes feel that she does not approach me entirely from a position of goodwill. Do you feel that as well?"

"Uh, not really."

"On more than a few occasions she has hinted strongly that she does not approve of my approach to child-rearing."

"She should talk. Her kids are little monsters."

"Exactly. Is that why you think she's a fat cow?"

"No."

"OK. Moving on, do you resent her husband?"

I did, but I certainly wasn't going to say so.

"Uh, no. I think he's nice."

"You're not disturbed by the violence and mayhem portrayed in his novels?"

"Well, I don't think dull stories about nice people would sell many books."

"Alas, probably not. Do you think less of Veeva for marrying a man who writes such books?"

I gave it some thought. I figured I should say yes to something just to get her off my back.

"That could be true," I nodded.

Uma smiled; I had said the right thing. She jotted a note on her pad.

"Now, about your difficulties with the word dinner."

"Pardon me, I farted," I said, squeezing out a loud and juicy one.

"Remarkable," she observed.

Yes, it was one of my better efforts. Rather smelly too.

"Dinner," she said.

"Pardon me, I farted."

That one barely qualified as a toot.

"Dinner," she repeated.

"Pardon me, I farted."

Not even a squeak that time.

"It appears, Nick, that you have issues around food. Recently your mother left you in the care of a person unknown to you. That had to be stressful for you."

"A bit, I suppose," I conceded.

"Do you miss your mother?"

"Uh, not so much. She calls me sometimes."

"And what does she say to you?"

"She tells me what she's doing. She tells me she loves me."

"Do you believe that?"

"Sure, why not?"

"You say you don't miss your mother that much. Tell me about that."

"Well, she was married to this jerk–my previous dad. I wasn't too happy living with them."

"So you blame your mother for bringing this man into your life?"

"I guess so. Maybe."

"And when you ate din–I mean your evening meal with them, did you feel comfortable? Did you feel nurtured?"

"I guess not."

Uma smiled and made another note on her pad.

"Compulsive behavior can be scary, don't you think, Nick?"

"I guess it could be."

"How many times a day do you wash your hands?"

"I don't know, it depends. Maybe two or three times. Probably more if I were doing something dirty like rebuilding a Harley or sorting coal."

"Do you ever feel the need to walk around a chair multiple times before you sit down in it?"

"Er, no. Should I?"

"Do you make your bed in the morning?"

"Sure."

"Why's that?"

"Well, it only takes a few seconds. And it makes for a neater room."

"You like your bedroom to be neat?"

"Uh, yeah."

Possibly a misstep as she wrote something and underlined it.

"Is there any other activity that you do more than say the average person?"

I think she was referring to masturbation. I'd heard that psychologists zero in on that pretty fast. No way I was going to open that can of worms.

"I can't think of any," I said, trying to look sincere and keeping my hands well away from my crotch.

We talked quite a bit more about my mother, what kind of cook she was (not the greatest), my ex-dad, the foul odors I encountered in his dry cleaning shops, and what farting meant to me. Kind of an embarrassing subject, but I have to hand it to her, she really tried to explore it in depth. Then my hour was up, and I went out to sit on their terrace while she conferred with my dad. A maid came out to ask if I wanted any refreshments, then brought me a warm scone and a glass of milk.

Dad gave me the verdict on the drive home. I have a classic obsessive compulsive disorder brought about by the recent traumatic upheavals in my life.

"That sounds bad," I said. "Is there something I can take for that?"

"I wish, kid. Apparently, there's a history of it in our family. She thinks your uncle Jake has a touch of it too. No, she says we have two choices: either reunite you with your mother or start intensive therapy with Uma."

Bad news both ways. Uma was way too prying, and no way did I want an entire continent between me and Cal. I had to stay in Venice!

"I think I'll be OK, Dad, if we just substitute the word 'supper' for you know what."

"And what about your calling Veeva names?"

"I think she should just understand that I mean 'big fat cow' in a very loving way."

"That may be a stretch for her, Nick. No, you're doing therapy with Uma. Three times a week, starting tomorrow. She thinks you're a very interesting case."

Fuck!

WEDNESDAY, June 3 – Since I'm psychologically disturbed and not a delinquent, my grounding has been lifted. Fat good that's doing me. Cal has disappeared off planet Earth, and I'm now at liberty to be dragged kicking and screaming to sessions with Uma. Who gave that nosy woman the right to probe into my innermost recesses? So today I clammed up and was much less forthcoming than before. I answered mostly in monosyllables or tried to change the subject. She sensed my resistance and dug in her heels just as hard.

We were back on the topic of Veeva Saunders, alleged "big fat cow."

"Do you feel that Veeva Saunders reminds you of your mother?" she asked.

"Hardly. Veeva's just average height. My mother is six-one and used to be a glamorous showgirl in Las Vegas."

Big, big mistake. My interrogator honed in on that like a laser-guided missile.

"Showgirls usually wear very skimpy costumes. How do you feel about that, Nick?"

"I'm too young to get into those shows."

"How do you feel about your mother performing partially nude in public?"

"I hear your husband's football team got some good prospects in the spring draft. Do you think Big Red will have a chance of making the playoffs this year?"

Somehow the hour lurched to a close and I made my escape. Today I had to take the bus back as Dad had a meeting with Mary Moran, his wannabe movie producer. Riding down Lincoln Boulevard, I spotted a suspicious store and got off at the next stop. I strolled into "Haseltine's Pet Shop" and came face-to-face with Harvey, wearing a long gray apron and a plastic name badge that identified him as "Harv."

"Look who's here," he said, "my sister's zombie slave."

"Hi, Harv. I take it your family is in the pet store business."

"Your powers of deduction are certainly impressive. I can't talk to you unless you buy something."

"OK. What's the cheapest thing you sell?"

"We have live crickets for 39 cents each."

"You mean people buy crickets for pets?"

"No, moron. They feed them to their animals, chiefly reptiles."

"OK, I'll take one."

He put a despondent cricket in a small ventilated plastic bag and rang up my purchase.

"That's 44 cents with tax."

I fished out two quarters and told him to keep the change.

"Say, Harv," I said, casually. "I haven't seen your sister lately."

"You should count your blessings, Nick."

"What has she been doing?"

"Hanging with her wretched friends, I expect. Certainly ignoring your stupid balcony messages."

"Do you know if school is out for her yet?"

"Nope. She goes until Friday, but my last day was Monday."

As if I cared that he was now free to slave in his family's store.

"Then she's probably busy with end-of-term activities," I said. "Is your father here?"

"He's in the back room taking inventory."

"Any chance I could introduce myself to him?"

"I wouldn't advise it, Nick. He keeps a loaded handgun under the counter."

"I don't see the relevance."

"Your balcony signs, Nick. He sees them and he knows what you're after. He's expressed a desire to strangle you with his bare hands."

"I see. Well, some other time then."

I got out of there fast. Down the block, I opened the bag and gave Jiminy his freedom. Stunned by this unexpected reprieve, the little guy just sat there and looked at me. I told him to scram before some bird nabbed him.

When I got back, Dad was in the living room showing something on his laptop to an older woman. Probably late 40s. Nicely dressed and not bad looking for her age group. She was obliged to introduce herself since I could tell Dad was pissed.

"Hello, Nick," she said, extending her hand. "I'm Mary Moran."

"Hi," I said, giving it a weak squeeze.

"I just got an irate call from Uma," he said. "What's this I hear about your not cooperating?"

"Geez, Dad, the woman asks the most embarrassing and personal questions."

"That's what therapy is about, kid. What did you expect?"

"She has like no boundaries at all!"

"Get over it, Nick. You're going to have to open up to her. Hash out all your problems. I need Uma on our side. I hope to get her husband to invest in our movie. He won't if you're pissing off his wife."

Great. I have to sit there three times a week and get reamed out by some prying shrink so my dad can make his stupid movie. I guess that's life in Hollywood for you.

I asked him for $50 for "lunch money." Bad tactical move. Instead of parting with the cash, he dragged me off to lunch with him and Mary. We went to a seafood restaurant she likes in Marina del Rey (where rich people in L.A. park their yachts). We sat outside on their dockside deck. A listless gang of dissolute seagulls had congregated there to stare at the one-percenters eating fish they regard as their own.

Mostly boring movie talk, but Mary did say one thing of interest: her father back in Ukiah was once briefly engaged to Trent Preston's mother. I guess if that had worked out, Dad would have been competing with some other stud for Sheeni Saunders's attentions. Mary said she has two brothers who are much older. She came along nearly two decades later and was a "big surprise" to all concerned.

"That happened to Dad too," I commented.

"Not quite," said Dad. "Mary was an unplanned pregnancy, whereas you were the product of premeditated and diabolical female scheming."

"That sounds like another 'don't exist' message, Dad. I may have to bring that up on Friday with Uma."

"You do that, Nick."

Mary has two kids and a former husband who's a big-shot at Fox. He ditched her a few years back to run off with his intern. I thought Dad would launch into his spiel about the genetic burden of males and why they need young trophy wives, but for some reason he didn't.

Dad gasped audibly when the check arrived. It would have been cheaper for him just to have handed me the requested $50. My appetizer, entree, beverage, and two desserts totaled nearly a hundred bucks.

THURSDAY, June 4 – My phone rang this morning as I was getting out of the shower. To my amazement, it was Cal. She has wheedled her phone back from her father.

"Hi, Nick," she said. "Did you enjoy last night's dinner?"

"Pardon me, I farted," I said, doing so loudly.

"Good work, Nick. It's nice to know you're still following orders. How are you getting on with your hostess Veeva?"

"Not so well, Cal. I've been calling her a big fat cow. My dad is making me go to a therapist, who has concluded that I have an obsessive compulsive disorder."

"No doubt an astute diagnosis, Nick. I can see you're in good hands."

"You haven't been responding to my balcony signs."

"Nice of you to notice that. Well, I'm free this afternoon after school. Want to join Esmee and me for coffee?"

"That sounds great."

"And try not to be late this time, Nick. Tardiness is not a quality I admire."

The day crawled by. I used the idle hours to finish *Strangled Strangers*. Curiously, none of the victims in the book were strangled nor were any of them strangers. The naked girl in the window turned out to be both the Russian gangster's granddaughter and mistress, which was way too kinky for me. By my count the hero Jack Stricker killed 11 people, three of them with his bare hands. His preferred technique is to grab the head and give it a violent twist, neatly severing the spinal cord. I'll have to remember that stratagem in case I ever come to blows with Harvey.

It looks like Mary Moran got hired because she was here again today. This time she had ramped up the makeup and splashed on a floral perfume. She's very well packaged for a gal her age and not at all matronly. Dad could do a lot worse than her, although I suppose he'll be fishing in younger streams. Let's hope my example discourages his genes from pursuing further reproductive success.

They were conferring on scenes and possible locations. Mary

wants him to have a finished screenplay for her to read by Monday. He says that is doable since he's just "cutting and pasting" from his juvenile journals. I guess at some point those ancient texts were transcribed into his computer from the original papyrus.

I cooled my heels on the coffee shop's patio for at least an hour before the girls showed up. They seemed pleased to see me, and Cal almost gave me a kiss. She leaned over as if intending to plant one (nice view down her neckline), but proceeded on past my eager lips to borrow a sip from my coffee cup. Oh well, I enjoyed the proximity anyway–not to mention the touch of her hand resting lightly on my shoulder.

When they returned with their drinks, Esmee did her thing with the warm hand to the back of my neck. Instant total relaxation as before. She does have some sort of magic touch.

"You've been a very good subject, Nick," she said. "And you will continue to follow our instructions exactly as we say."

"Yes, I will," I assured her.

"I have some good news for you, sweetheart," said Cal. "You no longer regard Veeva Saunders as a big fat cow."

"She's not a big fat cow," I repeated.

"In fact, you now find her immensely attractive. Even more attractive than me."

"Really?" I asked, doubtfully.

"Yes, indeed, Nick. Veeva Saunders is the most attractive girl in the world. You will not be able to keep your hands off her. You will not be discouraged if she resists, because you know in your heart that she finds you just as desirable as you do her."

I smiled at this wonderful news. Could it be that I would soon be getting laid? I did think of one obstacle though.

"But, Cal, what about her husband?" I said.

"He likes you so much, Nick. Of course, he wants you to have sex with his wife. Because he knows that you two are the ideal loving couple. But here's the thing, Nick honey: Veeva will be very angry if you don't have sex with her as soon as possible. The longer you wait, the angrier she will become."

"That sounds bad," I said.

"You betcha," said Esmee. "So don't be a wallflower, Nick. Get in there and go for it!"

"Right," I smiled. "Go for it!"

"You will also continue to say 'Pardon me, I farted'," said Cal, "when people mention the word d-i-n-n-e-r."

"They don't say it much now," I pointed out. "Mostly they've switched over to supper."

"Well, that won't do. OK, you will now say it when people mention the word lunch. I don't think there are any substitutes for that word."

"Well, there's brunch," said Esmee. "And déjeuner."

"Not anything we need concern ourselves with," said Cal.

Esmee did her thing again; I was no longer so relaxed, but still felt really jazzed. I hoped it wasn't just the caffeine from the three refills I'd drunk while waiting.

I asked Cal if she would be working in her family's store this summer.

"How do you know about the store?" she demanded. "Have you been spying on me again?"

I explained how I had spotted it innocently while riding the bus.

"My father tried me for a weekend once in his boring store," said Cal. "I cured him forever of the thought of employing me in any capacity. My sap of a brother works there to save up for college."

"You're not saving for college?" I asked.

"I leave that to my parents, Nick. After all, that is what parents are for."

Cal and I walked back to our block and parted at the corner. She said I was not to phone or text her, but should await her call.

"Why's that?" I asked.

"Because, Nick honey, my parents are on full alert. And I don't dare risk having my phone confiscated again. My life nearly ground to a halt without it."

"I see. By the way, have you received a grade yet on your video?"

"Didn't I tell you? Of course it got an A. Unfortunately, Philip commented that he found it deeply moving."

"Why is that unfortunate?"

"Because finding your story moving is so very, very gay."

FRIDAY, June 5 – Dad was in a bad mood today. He had to

drive me to my session with Uma then continue on to his lawyer's office to discuss his divorce impoverishment. I hope Ada leaves him with enough of a bankroll to send me to an elite college. Extracting cash from his wallet may become even more onerous. As I exited his Town Car at Tyler's I requested my usual $50 for "bus fare and incidentals." He forked over a measly $5 bill. I don't know if he's paying Uma some high hourly rate to torture me or she's just doing it for the glory.

Today we got around to the dreaded M word. She asked me what I thought about when I masturbated. I guess she just assumed I did the deed, which is probably a safe bet for most guys my age. Since I was under an edict of compulsory candidness, I said I usually thought about attractive girls I know with their clothes off.

"Do you ever think about your mother?" she inquired.

"No, because you really can't masturbate without an erection."

"Do you specifically try not to think about your mother?"

"No, she just doesn't come to mind. You might want to Google 'incest taboo' if you're unclear on that concept."

"Sarcasm is a way of not confronting your real issues, Nick."

"Sorry."

"In an average week how many times do you masturbate?"

In a good week I could probably hit 25 or 30, but I played it safe and said "four to six."

"When you masturbate do you ever think about passing gas?"

"No."

"Do you find passing gas to be as erotic as masturbating?"

"Not in the least."

"Do you sometimes get an erection when passing gas?"

"Not that I can recall."

"Dinner."

"Uh, is that a question?"

"We've made a breakthrough here, Nick. You didn't vocalize compulsively to the stimulus as you were doing before."

"Yeah, I guess you're right."

"See, Nick. There's some benefit to working on these issues with me."

"Yeah, that could be true."

"I think that's enough for today. I'm meeting someone for lunch."

"Pardon me, I farted," I said, passing an impressively loud and toxic cloud.

There was no one around when I got back. So I took some of my dwindling cash reserves and had pizza at the beach for my midday meal. Another sunny, warm day which seems to be the norm for Southern California. A question: why do people live in places like Terre Haute, Indiana and Fairbanks, Alaska when they could live here? It beats me.

Dad was upstairs slaving on his script when I returned. His film crew is multiplying. I got introduced to a fat gal named Brenda Blatt, who is to function as his combo location manager, property master, and line producer, whatever that is. If her job is to produce long lines at the box office for his movie, I'd say she's got her work cut out for her. She looked to be in her mid-twenties and was built like a professional wrestler. She's worked with Mary on other movies. Her special expertise is doing stuff on the cheap. She certainly dressed like she knew her way around thrift stores. No makeup except for a smear of lipstick that was somewhere between pink and orange. Not at all like some fat gals who you think might be pretty if they slimmed down. Brenda was not going to be a beauty at any weight. She shook my hand heartily when Mary made the introduction.

"Hi, Nick. I hear you might be the star of our movie."

"I don't know. I've never acted before."

"Neither had the shark in 'Jaws,' but that movie made millions. Did you hear? We're offering $5 for a catchy title."

"I'll give it some thought."

"I suggested 'Prelude to a Juggler,' but that went nowhere."

"How about 'Gunning for My Father-in-Law?'" I suggested.

"Not bad," she laughed. "I'll add it to the list."

"Or 'Outlaw Teens Get Married.'"

"Another possible winner, Nick. Keep 'em coming."

Mary and Brenda left hastily when Veeva arrived to complain that too many cars were clogging the driveway. The Saunders/Uptons were here for another weekend, and wow, was she looking good. My heart beat madly as I smiled and shyly said hello.

"Oh, hi, Nick," Veeva answered, eyeing me warily.

"You're looking especially gorgeous today."

"OK, if you say so."

"I've been giving it some thought. You know, Veeva, there isn't that much difference between our ages."

"I think you need a refresher math class, Nick."

"No, think about it. When you're 75, I'll be 52. And when you're 90, I'll be an old man of 67."

"Please don't rush me into my grave, Nick. I still have a few years left."

"I'm free all weekend," I said with a wink. "I think we need to find some private time to be alone together."

"I think you need a few more sessions with Uma, Nick. Or pick someone else to be the target of your humor, which frankly I'm not getting at all."

I was assuring her of my absolute sincerity when she abruptly left. Wow, so sexy from the back too. And an ass to drive a guy wild.

Later I was standing on a stepladder and peering into her kitchen window, when Dad came out to say that we were going to Uncle Jake's house "for supper."

"I can't leave now," I protested. "Veeva's here."

"You leave Veeva alone, Nick. She's not interested in hearing your opinions of her. And what are you doing up on that ladder?"

"Uh, trying to see where she is."

"Well get down! And let's go! I mean it, Nick. You can't tell her any more that she's a big fat cow. You'll get us thrown out of here!"

"Oh, I don't think that any more, Dad."

"Good. Then I guess Uma's been helping. And try not to insult Lillian either. I hope to get my brother to invest in my movie."

Uncle Jake and Aunt Lillian live in a big old house in the Adams district of L.A. (that is, old by Los Angeles standards, which means 1920s). They have three little kids (two girls, one boy), who seem slightly less riot-prone than their hoodlum Twisp cousins. All were safely salted away in bed by 7:30, so we got to eat our supper in peace. Lillian wisely employs a cook, whose succulent grilled swordfish steaks were a nice change from Gazelle Gourmet. I gulped mine down in record time and was ready to go home, but dad wanted to linger.

I think Dad may be a bit jealous of his baby brother, who's the head writer on a hit TV show called "One-way Rocket." It's a comedy about a mixed crew of guys and gals on a rocket ship bound for Mars. The trip takes three years and there's no return. They'll be stuck on Mars as colonists forever. They're still on year one of the trip, and quite a few are having second thoughts about being marooned on Mars. Some are agitating to turn back, alliances are shifting, and the bed-hopping is non-stop. Lillian turns up now and again on the show as the captain's former girlfriend on Earth who is always sending him videos of what he's missing back home. Naturally, Dad wants to guest-star on the show, but Uncle Jake isn't coming up with any parts.

"How about Dad as the first Martian they encounter?" I suggested. "He could be juggling the shrunken heads of previous Mars explorers."

"Not bad, Nick," said Jake, opening another bottle of wine. "I could see him in a loincloth and gold body paint. Or we could have him in black face again."

"Not likely," said Dad. "Hey, I need a title for my movie. Something short and snappy."

"Sort of like you were at that age," said Jake. "How about 'Arsonist in Love?'"

"Wow, that's not bad," said Dad. "Nick, write that down."

I took out my phone and noted it electronically. I also noted the time.

"Isn't it time to go, Dad?" I asked.

"Hell, kid," he said, "we just got here. What's the rush?"

"Yeah, Nick," said Jake. "Do you have a heavy date or something?"

I couldn't tell them that lovely Veeva awaited my kisses back in Venice and was growing angrier by the minute. To make a long story short, we didn't make it back until nearly midnight. By then no lights were visible in the front house. Darling Veeva had gone to bed!

Nor was there any disrobing going on in Cal's window. I've checked frequently every night and seen nothing but a boring window shade.

SATURDAY, June 6 – My phone rang pretty early. I was hoping it was Veeva or Cal, but it turned out to be my brother.

"Hi, Nick," said Scott. "Got a minute?"

"Sure. All I was doing was sleeping."

"I thought we should discuss this Veeva thing of yours."

"OK."

"When I was your age, Veeva was a great friend of mine. She still is. She's really on our side. I don't understand why you're insulting her."

"I'm not any more, Scott. I think she's totally hot."

"Well, good. That's a relief. And what's with this farting business? I know we Twisps can be devious at times. I'm trying to figure out what this farting ploy is all about. What are you trying to accomplish?"

"I don't know, Scott. I just do it. Uma says it's an obsessive compulsive disorder."

"So you're not faking that? You're not just doing it to annoy Dad?"

"Nope. I'm not."

"Did you do this kind of thing back in Indiana?"

"No, never. Do you think it could be related to smog?"

"I don't know, Nick. The air is pretty clean in Venice. You're right next to the ocean."

"Well, I'm not faking it. I'd stop if I could."

"You do it whenever someone mentions dinner?"

"No, I've switched to the midday meal."

"You mean lunch?"

"Pardon me, I farted."

Loud discharge and fearsome smell.

"Damn, Nick. That's the strangest thing."

"I know, Scott. I was fairly normal until I found out I was a Twisp."

Since I was awake, I showered and dressed, then crept stealthily outside and through our hosts' unlocked back door. I found Desmond alone reading the newspaper in his kitchen.

"Hi, Nick," he said. "You're up early."

"Uh, where's Veeva?"

"She went to her mother's with the kids."

Instant monumental panic.

"For good?" I gasped.

He laughed. "No, just for the day."

"Is she angry and upset?"

"No, I think she's mostly forgiven you for those slurs."

"Why did she go there?"

"She has to be nice to her mother occasionally. She's compet-ing with her two brothers for favorable treatment in the will."

"Oh."

I was totally at a loss for what to do.

"Is there something you need, Nick?"

"Uh, no. I read your book *Strangled Strangers*."

"How did you like it?"

"It was, uh, good. Can you really kill someone by twisting their neck like that?"

"Certainly. All such details in my books are based on facts. Navy Seals are trained in that technique for when they need to dispense with someone silently."

"All details are true, huh? You mean there are girls sleeping with their grandpas?"

He laughed again. "Probably more examples than you imag-ine. The human race at its fringes is quite perverse. Would you like me to sign your book?"

"That's OK. I read the pirated e-book version."

"Right. When your generation comes of age, all us writers will be starving."

Technology moves on, I thought. Get over it, dude.

"Do you know what time Veeva's coming back?"

"I couldn't say, Nick. But I'll tell her that you're looking for her."

He seemed pretty casual about it. I guess it's true that he doesn't mind my having glorious sex with his wife.

Dad also was reading the paper. Guess they haven't heard that you can now get the news via your phone. Or perhaps they just like to murder trees. He asked me to fix him an omelet. I said I would do it for $50 and five condoms.

"Why do you need condoms?" he asked.

"The usual reason, Dad. I'm not intending to make water bal-loons out of them."

"You're making progress with that honey next door?"

"You could say that."

Veeva was certainly a honey and often next door.

We settled on five condoms and $30. Plus, I had to wash his lousy, stinking Lincoln again.

After I did those onerous tasks, I hoofed it fast to Cal's coffee place, but saw no sign of her. No phone call from her either. It's a good thing I wasn't relying on her for sexual relief. I ordered a large coffee and an oil-filled muffin, then dialed Veeva's number. No one answered, so I left this sultry message: "Hi, sweetheart. This is Nick, your dream lover. Sorry I didn't make it back last night in time for our rendezvous. I hope you weren't too upset. I can assure you I was just as sexually frustrated. I scored some condoms, so I'm totally prepared. I know you wouldn't want to risk having any more obnoxious children. Two are plenty, I'm sure. I think the best plan is for you to sneak up to my bedroom tonight. All that concrete makes it very soundproof. I've got something pretty good-sized and very hard with your name on it. I know we'll both have a great time. I think you're so hot and I'm longing for your lips—not to mention those sexy other parts! Call me as soon as you can! 'Bye for now. Let's make this a weekend neither of us will ever forget!"

If that message doesn't turn her on, then I don't know women.

Having some hours to kill, I took a long walk on the beach. I spent some time studying girls in bikinis. Yes, I would soon be getting up close and personal with those alluring female curves. I strongly suspected that touching was considerably more satisfying than looking. Best of all, I would be doing it with a fairly mature gal who was quite familiar with all the ins and outs. It wouldn't be a case of two neophytes fumbling in the dark. And sticking it God knows where from desperate inexperience.

I had a late midday meal at a Mexican restaurant on the beach, then headed back home. I was surprised to see a large black Escalade SUV parked in the drive. I hoped it wasn't Dad doing a major drug deal to finance his movie. I walked in the door, and there were Tyler, Uma, and Dad all looking at me quite severely.

"There you are, Nick," said Dad. "Uma's been assisting me in making some arrangements for you."

"Are you getting a hotel room for me and Veeva?" I asked, amazed that everyone was being so enlightened about our not-so-secret love.

"Veeva alerted us about the message you left on her phone, Nick," said Uma. "And your conversation with her yesterday. I'm afraid that your condition is far more serious than I first assumed."

"I love her and she loves me," I said. "The age difference doesn't matter!"

"Veeva doesn't love you, Nick," said Uma. "She loves her husband. You're in a delusional state, Nick. We feel you're at risk of harming yourself or others."

"I'm OK," I replied. "I feel fine. I think I'll go to my room now."

"Stop right there!" commanded Tyler.

I froze.

"We've found a good place for you, Nick," said Dad. "It's a private clinic that deals with troubled youth. You'll like it there."

A horrible realization dawned. They were proposing to stick me in a loony bin!

"This is all a misunderstanding, Dad. I'm not a wacko. I'll be fine if everyone just refers to it as the midday meal."

"Sorry, Nick," he said. "It's gone beyond compulsive farting. Way beyond that. You need help. Psychological help."

"I can't go away, Dad! Not now. Veeva will be pissed. She'll be getting angrier by the minute!"

"Veeva is fine, Nick," said Uma, soothingly. "She's not angry. I talked to her at length. She agrees with us. She wants you to get the help that you need."

"I've already packed a bag for you, Nick," said Dad. "They're expecting us at the clinic. We're leaving now."

"I'm not going anywhere!"

"Yes, you are, son," said a deep male voice.

I turned around and saw a tall figure looming in the doorway. It was Marcus, Tyler's bulked-up bodyguard.

SUNDAY, June 7 – Wow, you fall in love outside your age bracket, and the next thing you know you're locked up in a place that smells like pee (and vomit) with a lot of mental cases. I'm not exactly sure where I am, but it was a long freeway drive from Venice. My traitor Dad signed a bunch of papers, then I got led away by two scary dudes in white coats. They took me into a little room and made me turn over my phone, belt, wallet, comb, and

ZipPits. Next I had a truly wretched meal in the cafeteria from hell, then got assigned a room–complete with oddball roommate. He's a skinny blond kid named Luther. Of course, the first thing he did was ask me what I did to get locked up.

"I fell in love with a 38-year-old married woman," I said.

"Like you read about in the tabloids? Has she been molesting you?"

"I wish. She called my shrink and said I was too scary to remain on the streets. Is the food here always that crummy?"

"Depends. They have a different cook on the a.m. shift. Usually the best meal is lunch."

"Pardon me, I farted."

Loud blast and noxious aroma.

"Looks like you might have other problems too," observed Luther, waving the smell back at me.

"I have an obsessive compulsive disorder. So you might want to substitute midday meal for that trigger word."

"I'll be remembering that for sure. Any other words set you off?"

"That's the only one I know about. What are you in for?"

"I hear the Vienna Boys Choir in my head. Right now they're singing Sur le pont d' Avignon."

"What's that?"

"A Provençal folk song. They mostly sing Christmas songs–all year round. It gets a little tiresome. I used to be a boy soprano, then I grew hair on my balls. Want to see?"

"Uh, no. I'll take your word for it."

I got introduced to our "lodge leader," a guy named Ken, who's a psych major at Cal State Northridge. He sleeps here every other night, alternating with a dude named Mike. We're in Lodge B, although it doesn't look much like a lodge. It looks like a cheap stucco building borrowed from some budget motel. Luther says I may be assigned to another lodge after the shrinks evaluate how nuts I am. That doesn't happen on weekends. Ken asked me to promise that I wouldn't hurt myself or anyone around me. I said "OK." The person I really want to hurt is my new dad for sticking me in here.

We watched TV in a grim room with some other (obviously disturbed) guys, then it was time for lights out. A narrow aisle separated our austere iron cots. Thin mattress, bottom sheet only, and one skimpy blanket. My pillow smelled like armpits. Could prison be any worse? Luther offered to give me a blow job, but I said I wasn't into guys. He said he wasn't really either, but only offered because we might be locked away from chicks forever.

Very scary news. I asked him why he thought that.

"This is a private mental hospital, Nick. Our parents pay big bucks for us to be here. The staff has no incentive for us to get better. The longer we stay, the more money they make. If you try to run away, they bring you back and lock you up even tighter. You may never see your 38-year-old molester ever again."

Truly dire news. Hell, why didn't I stay in Indiana and work in my ex-dad's dry cleaners? Suddenly, sorting stinky laundry seemed like the all-time dream job.

"She, she wasn't a molester," I stammered, fighting back tears.

"Too bad. Next time you should try getting some pussy before you get locked away for life."

I could see only one faint possibility for hope: If Ada grabbed all of Dad's money in the divorce settlement, he wouldn't be able to afford to keep me here for long. But, damn, what if he borrows the money from Tyler? How long could I be here before the fees totaled a billion dollars? Probably several centuries at least.

I lay awake for hours, stewing about my situation. I thought if I could somehow call my mom, she might be able to do something. But I didn't have my phone and I couldn't remember her new phone number. If only someone could hypnotize me to excavate it from my brain. Yeah, and then loan me their phone. I finally dropped off sometime after the birds began chirping and got a few hours of restless sleep.

Breakfast this morning wasn't bad: corn fritters with maple syrup and bacon. First time I ever had corn fritters. I may spend the rest of my life locked in a nut house, but at least I've experienced a tasty new breakfast food.

Some guys were playing basketball, but I didn't join in. I'm not that good at sports and I was still minus my belt. I have no hips and not much butt, so I had nothing to keep up my pants except my two hands. In my present state, the only game I conceivably could play is soccer.

I took a walk around the grounds to try to keep from going nuts. High chain-link fences all around. Escape could be a challenge. If I could somehow get out, I could hitchhike back to Terre Haute and give my ex-dad a big warm hug. Or head to Miami and see if I could find my mom. Maybe I could lie about my age and get a job on her cruise ship.

I got sleepy after our midday meal and took a long nap. Sundays are kind of boring anyway–even in the loony bin. When I woke up Luther was humming along to the song in his head. He does that a lot. He warned me that the staff shrinks will be getting their claws into me tomorrow. He said if I hear voices, I should keep that under my hat. He said kids with voices in their heads always get labeled schizophrenics. Then you're mired forever in the "mental industrial complex."

"I'm OK," I said. "I don't hear any voices."

"Well, stick around here long enough, pal, and you'll start."

Then it was another bad dinner, more TV, and lights out. I went to sleep thinking about sexy Veeva Saunders. Despite banishing me to the crazy ward, she still rated number one in my heart. Just slightly ahead of Cal Haseltine, who's probably desperate with worry now because I'm not answering my phone.

MONDAY, June 8 – A ray of hope. I had just taken a seat in the office of the head shrink, when my despised dad showed up with that fat gal Brenda Blatt. He demanded to see me at once, pissing off Dr. Patel, who was all set to probe my inner psyche. He said this interruption "could only upset the boy," but finally allotted Dad five minutes for "a brief chat."

"How are they treating you, Nick?" he asked.

"Just die, OK?" I replied. "I hate you more than I can say. I wish I never met you!"

I was giving him the clearest "don't exist" message I could manage.

"Brenda," he said. "Tell Nick what you told me."

"Hi, Nick," she said. "I went to a funky girls' school for a few years up in Stockton. I had a good friend there who was very resourceful. One of the things she did was teach herself hypnotism out of a book. She liked to hypnotize our enemies to have some yucks at their expense. She got them to do all kinds of goofy stuff."

"Brenda thinks you might have been hypnotized, Nick," said Dad. "Were you?"

"I can't tell you," I replied. "It's a secret."

"Did they instruct you not to say anything about it, Nick?" asked Brenda.

"It's a secret," I repeated. "It's all a big secret."

"Who was it, Nick?" asked Dad. "Was it someone you met on the beach? Was it that girl next door you were hanging out with?"

I clamped my lips tight and shook my head. They could interrogate me until the end of time, but I wasn't going to spill.

"Brenda, you stay here with Nick," said Dad. "I'm going to make some calls. And tell that Dr. Patel to leave him alone until I get back."

"Right," she said. "We'll sit here, and Nick can tell me all about this babe next door. What's her name?"

"Valerie, but her friends call her Cal."

"Is she cute?"

"Very."

"Yeah, those kind can be the most trouble. So how did you meet her?"

Dr. Patel returned, and Brenda told him to leave us alone until "our father" returned.

"And who are you?" he demanded.

"I'm Brenda Twisp, Nick's sister. I'm an attorney with Benchley, Portis, and Waugh. You are not to interrupt our consultation until his father returns."

"This is most irregular!" Dr. Patel exclaimed, exiting in a huff.

"Here's a tip, Nick. If you say you're an attorney, most people won't mess with you."

"I'm too young to say that."

"Well, file it away for when you're older."

I was telling Brenda about Cal and the video we did together when Dad rang her. He said he was "making progress" and would return in an hour or two. Brenda said she would hold down the fort and keep all the shrinks at bay.

I asked her what sort of things they got their hypnotized enemies to do.

"OK, Nick, some background: the cool kids at my school were the Arcadians. Our enemies were the Delphians. They were a bunch of thieves, skanks, freaks, sluts, and general lowlifes. Clubs were officially banned, but we existed in defiance of the rules and were constantly at war. You had to do something at that dreary school to combat the tedium. My friend Chloe would contrive to separate a Delphian from the herd, which was hard 'cause they traveled in packs for protection. She'd get one alone behind a building or in a restroom and do her magic. First she'd turn the girl into our spy so we'd get advance warning of what those slime-balls were up to. Then she'd plant a time-delay fuse in her. So the next time they served meatballs in the cafeteria the girl would stand up, heave a meatball at the headmistress, and scream, 'I've had it with this swill!' Or if a teacher mentioned 'Holy Roman Empire,' the girl would rip off her panties and yell, 'Holy Jesus! I need somebody roamin' over me!' It was pretty juvenile stuff, but–what the hell–we were teenagers. And naturally Chloe always told the girls they could never say who put them up to it. Hypno-sis can be powerful. I'd love to learn it to use on cute guys and temperamental actors."

"Have you studied it?"

"I read Chloe's book, but it didn't stick with me. I guess you have to have the knack. Chloe was a master at it. There are prob-ably still girls today tossing their food whenever they see a stray meatball for lunch."

"Pardon me, I farted."

Not that loud, but smelly.

"Yes, Nick, I'd say some master has been at work on you."

"It's a secret."

"Right. So you say. First they had you tell Veeva she was a big fat cow, then planted the idea that she was hot for your bod. I'd say the mastermind of this crime was someone who had it in for Veeva."

"It's a secret."

"Right, Nick. I'm just thinking out loud here. So I heard some neighbors had quite a feud going with Veeva over certain building disputes. Is your girlfriend a member of that family?"

"Uh, well, yes."

"Right. You know, Nick, there are some girls who are mean by nature. They are natural-born Delphians."

"Cal isn't mean. She's great."

"I'm sure she's greatly stimulated your hormones. We'll have to see if she's entirely innocent here."

Dr. Patel returned and she shooed him away.

"You sure have him intimidated," I commented.

"When you're fat, Nick, you have to assert your dominance right away. Otherwise, people assume you're some low-status peon they can walk all over. My life improved greatly when I figured that out."

"Are you dieting?" I asked.

"Constantly. Otherwise, I'd have to hire my own forklift to cart me around."

A bell rang.

"What was that?" she asked.

"The bell for the midday meal."

"Well, Nick, I don't want you to think I'm Pavlov's dog, but I could do with a light snack. How about you?"

She opened her giant purse and removed a large bag of cheese curls and six Heath bars–three of which she handed to me. We snacked on her stash while out in the hallway troubled youths shuffled toward the cafeteria.

"Well, Nick, you sign on to do a movie and you never know quite what's in store next. How are you holding up?"

"Fine. I wish Dad would get back."

"That makes two of us."

It was after one p.m. when he finally showed. He said he'd talked to "the responsible parties" and they'd be here soon. A few minutes later Esmee walked in with her father. You'd expect a mentalist to have a turban and a long beard, but he looked like any other harassed dad. His daughter was avoiding eye contact by staring at her painted toenails on display in her flip-flops.

"Esmerelda, you will apologize to this boy," Mr. Carstann said sternly.

"Hi, Nick," she said. "Sorry. It was just a little joke."

"Some joke!" said my dad. "Do you realize the trouble you've caused?"

"Sorry," she muttered again. "I can fix it, but you have to leave me alone with Nick."

"I'm not going anywhere," said Dad.

"I'm afraid you have to," said Mr. Carstann. "We're too much of a distraction."

They filed out and Esmee shut the door.

"Did you blab about me, Nick?" she demanded.

"I didn't say a word. I said it was a secret. Brenda figured it out on her own."

"The fat interfering cow. Well, let's get this over with."

She grabbed the back of my neck, pulled me close, and did her relaxation thing. She told me I was no longer hot for Veeva, who didn't have a thing for me either. She said I was not to react as before to the word "lunch." She said some other stuff, then said at the count of three I was to wake feeling great and harboring no ill will toward her or Cal. She did her count, then opened the door and said, "OK, he's back to normal."

"I certainly hope so," said Dad.

"Lunch," said Brenda.

"Yeah," I replied, not farting, "I could use some."

Brenda handed me a large brown envelope. "I liberated this from Dr. Patel."

Inside the envelope were my phone, wallet, comb, ZipPits, and vital belt.

"Let's blow this joint," said Dad. "It's giving me the creeps."

"What about my stuff back in the room?" I asked.

"Forget it, Nick," he said. "All that can be replaced."

Esmee's father held out his hand to me. "I apologize, Nick, for my daughter's deplorable conduct. I'll make sure it won't happen again."

"That's OK," I said, shaking his hand. "No hard feelings."

I asked him what exactly a mentalist did. He told me to take a dollar bill out of my wallet and look at the last five digits of the serial number.

"Are the digits 65816 followed by a B?" he asked.

"They are! How did you know that?"

"Mentalism," he replied, tapping the side of his head.

Brenda and I wanted to find a nearby restaurant for lunch, but Dad said we had to beat the traffic back home before the commuter rush started. So Brenda raided the "deepest reserves" of her purse, and passed out more Heath bars. Dad spent the first ten miles apologizing over and over again for sticking me in that nut house. I told him it was OK, and I didn't hate him anymore. He said he blamed Uma for the whole debacle.

"She painted such a dire picture of the state you were in, Nick. She had me completely panicked."

"You can't blame Uma for reacting like a psychologist," said Brenda. "She sees aberrant behavior and interprets it as mental illness. I see it, and think drugs, booze, male stupidity, or someone making mischief."

"I'm just thankful Brenda was on the scene," I said. "I could have been locked up there for years."

Dad apologized yet again. He added that Veeva was "totally upset" and was threatening to sue the Haseltines.

"Ah, everybody should just forget about it," I said.

"Well, I hope you'll be steering clear of that coy temptress and her creepy friends," he said.

That reminded me: I hadn't checked my phone for Cal's urgent messages. I did so and came up blank. What's with that standoffish chick?

TUESDAY, June 9 – It was great waking up in my own bed, even if it was borrowed from Veeva, who would not be showing me the ins and outs of sexual delights. That was an entrancing illusion while it lasted. Now I was back to being a horny teen with five condoms that will be moldering away from disuse.

Last night I received phone apologies from Veeva, Uma, Tyler, Scott, and Mary Moran. I'm not sure why Mary was so apologetic. Perhaps she felt tainted from her association with Dad. Uma offered to meet with me to "work out any issues stemming from this traumatic incident," but I politely declined. Tyler asked what he could do to help. I suggested he add corn fritters to his brunch menu. He said he would talk to his chef about it. Even Azura called from Montana to apologize for not saying goodbye before she left.

"I wanted to phone," she said. "But Scott said you were having a mental breakdown."

"Just a misunderstanding," I assured her. "I'm back to normal now."

Everyone was apologetic except Cal when I encountered her at the coffee place this morning. I was sipping my tepid brew on the patio when she arrived.

"Are you following me, Nick?" she demanded.

"How can I be following you when I was here first? Where's Esmee?"

"Grounded for three weeks, thanks to you. And right at the start of summer vacation!"

"Did you hear I got locked up in a mental hospital?"

"Yes, I heard. I got yelled at by my parents for associating with you. They made me write a letter of apology to that big fat cow Veeva Saunders. I only hope she can read between the lines to perceive my deep insincerity and withering sarcasm."

"How come you guys did that to me? I thought we were friends!"

"It was a practical joke, Nick. That's all. You pull practical jokes on your friends or your enemies. So it was a nice combo package for you. Anyway, I'm beginning to think my initial impression of you was correct: you're not very bright."

"Why do you say that?" I asked, offended.

"Because I warned you about Esmee. Right off I told you she liked to hypnotize boys and get them to do stupid things. I was totally up-front about it. But there you were being taken in by her."

"You could have alerted me to be on my guard. I take it your parents haven't grounded you."

"No, instead they cancelled my enrollment at math camp."

"Is that bad?"

"Do you have to ask? When I was 12, I had a very brief infatuation with calculus. I think it had to do with developing breasts and calculating the area under the curve. Ever since then they've been signing me up for summer math camp. As if I want to hang out in a dank tent with a bunch of greasy math nerds. So every year about this time I have to misbehave in a major way to get that treat taken away."

"I might have been locked away in that nut house for years!"

"I'd have gotten you out, Nick. Jesus, do you think I'm that heartless?"

"Oh. Well, I didn't know that."

"Esmee was formulating a plan to hypnotize the guard at the gate when your irate father tracked her down. We thought you had snitched on us."

"I never did!"

"So it appears. Well, no harm done. You're back and looking not much the worse for wear."

"My therapist thinks I may be scarred for life."

"I appreciate your efforts at guilt-tripping me, Nick. But you're wasting your breath. I'm immune to such ploys."

"Gee, Cal, I hope you're not a sociopath."

"Goodness, Nick. You do say the most charming things!"

Since we weren't supposed to be associating with each other, we parted at the café and walked back separately. Despite disrupting my life and proving less than sympathetic to my subsequent travails, I still liked her. She had gnawed her way into my heart and was proving a difficult squatter to evict.

Big excitement back at Twisp Central. Dad finished his screenplay. By sharing pages, Mary and Brenda were reading it simultaneously. I claimed dibs after Brenda, but Dad said I was not on his list of approved readers. So I got a short summary from Brenda. She said my dad may have been the biggest hormone case in the history of Oakland, California. He went bonkers for Sheeni Saunders and all hell broke loose. He was like an out-of-control missile or the Titanic freed from its moorings. Part of the time he was disguised as a chick and working as an attendant in a girls' locker room. I can only pray I'm on hand when they film that scene.

His title kind of sucks though: "Nick Twisp's Mayhem for Love."

Everyone hates it except the auteur himself.

WEDNESDAY, June 10 – My bag of stuff got delivered today. With it was a nasty note from Dr. Patel and a shockingly large bill.

Dad asked me if I got any high-priced psychotherapy while I was there. I said all I got was a request by a college kid not to off myself or strangle anyone.

"So all they did was provide room and board for two days," said Dad. "I don't see how that's worth 12 grand."

"The eats were pretty lousy too," I added. "Although not as bad as the meals here."

"I'm doing my best, kid. I'm trying to make a major motion picture here. Give me a break."

"Sorry, Dad. And by the way, I need another $50."

For the first time ever, he forked over the full amount without complaint. It took a month, but I think I may finally have him trained.

Then Mary and Brenda arrived to go over his script scene-by-scene. Brenda wondered how they were going to send a car and a travel trailer rolling down a hill, crashing into a building, igniting a giant fireball, and incinerating several city blocks on their puny budget.

"That's your job to figure out," said Dad, helpfully.

"What do you think, Mary?" said Brenda. "Should we look into doing it with miniatures?"

"No miniatures!" said Dad. "They always look fake. I want real cars, a real trailer, and real fire. It's the biggest scene in my movie. Hell, I still have P.T.S.D. from that nightmare."

"What's that?" I asked.

"Post-traumatic stress disorder," said Brenda.

"Oh, right," I said. "I have that from my recent incarceration in the loony bin."

"You can switch off those violins, Nick," said Dad. "That vein of sympathy has run dry."

I think he may be a bit of a sociopath too.

Brenda went on with her notes: "And there's this Chevy Nova in a living room. Very few houses have a door big enough to admit a car."

"That has to be a real car too," said Dad. "My mother had that car in her living room for years. She rearranged her furniture around it. She used to lounge in it with her obnoxious boyfriends and neck to Elvis on the car radio."

That woman was my biological grandmother. No wonder I'm a refugee from a sanitarium.

"And you have Sheeni residing in a two-story trailer," said Brenda. "Those are pretty hard to come by. Can we make it a double-wide mobile home instead?"

"Certainly not," said Dad. "They are not at all the same. A two-story trailer implies her parents had higher aspirations. A double-wide just connotes they're poor white trash—which the Saunders definitely were not."

"And will audiences grasp that distinction?" asked Mary.

"Discerning audiences will," said Dad. "And they'll appreciate that we went the extra mile to be authentic."

Dad gave me six pages of the script to study for my screen test, which is set for tomorrow afternoon. Casting calls for the various roles are going out next week.

Here is the question: Do I want to be a movie star?

I'm kind of a shy kid fresh off the boat from Indiana.

Major film stardom is a pretty big step for me.

Do I have what it takes, or should I gracefully bow out and watch from the sidelines?

THURSDAY, June 11 – I was sipping my second refill when Cal arrived at our coffee shop.

"Where were you yesterday?" she demanded, taking a seat and poking a delicate finger into the remains of my oil-laden muffin.

"Trying not to associate with you as instructed by my dad."

"Oh, daddy's boy, huh?"

"Hardly. How would you like to do me a favor?"

"I take a dim view of favors, Nick. What do you want?"

"My big screen test is today. Perhaps you could help me go over my lines. You read the lines for Sheeni, and I'll read the ones for Nick."

Cal grabbed my script pages and looked them over. "Who's this Sheeni Saunders person? Some relative of Veeva?"

"Her aunt, I think. Dad went nuts for her when they were our age. She was beautiful, but rather difficult."

"Not at all like me," sighed Cal, "but I'll give it a shot. What's this scene about?"

"I'm carrying your watermelon back from a store, and you're telling me about your vastly superior boyfriend."

"I've never had one of those, Nick, but I guess I can fake it."

So we practiced that scene and another one where we're hiking in the woods and kiss for the first time. Since it was L.A., the people around us on the patio were cool about it and pretended not to notice. For the second scene we did everything except the actual kissing. I was willing, but Cal refused. She said she would only kiss me if she were being paid SAG rates.

"What's SAG?" I asked.

"Screen Actors Guild, Nick. Where have you been living–under a rock?"

"How would you rate my acting?" I asked.

"On a scale of one to ten, I'd give you a solid minus two."

"What am I doing wrong?"

"You're reading the lines like you're reading them, not living them. Think about the sense of the words you're saying. Say them like you're in an actual conversation."

We tried the scenes again. She said I was better, but still not convincing.

"What should I do?" I asked.

"When I say my lines, listen to what I'm saying. Don't think about what you're going to say next. Be a part of the conversation. It's OK if you don't say the words exactly as written."

I tried that the next time and the scenes played much better. A woman two tables away even laughed. I was really getting into it and nearly brushed my lips against Cal's before she turned away.

When I'm with her, I do feel a rather overwhelming urge to press my lips against hers. I can't say I ever felt that way toward anyone else before. I had never paid much attention to my lips, except when I was a kid and trying to learn to whistle.

I was too nervous to eat much of my Gazelle Gourmet leftovers for lunch. Then Brenda arrived to set up a camcorder on a tripod, and Mary handed me new script pages.

"What's this?" I asked.

"Revised pages, Nick. We're changing Sheeni's name to Shona so we don't get sued by the actual person."

"But won't everyone know we're talking about Sheeni since she's the one who lived in a two-story trailer and had Dad's babies?"

"My reasoning too," said Dad, "but our lawyers insist on the change."

"Can I say Sheeni in my test?" I asked. "That's what I rehearsed."

"OK," sighed Dad. "But inflexibility in actors is not a trait I admire."

I got ready, Dad said "action," Brenda read Sheeni's first line, and I launched into the scene. And was really, really terrible.

"Thanks, Nick," said Dad, switching off the camera. "We'll, uh, let you know."

"I know that was bad, Dad," I said. "But I know a way I can do better."

"How's that?" he asked. "Cease being a cardboard cutout? Go to acting school for ten years?"

"Let me call Cal to come over and play Sheeni. That's who I rehearsed with."

"You're not supposed to be associating with that girl, Nick."

"I'm not, Dad. We happened to run into each other at the coffee shop this morning."

"And why do you need her for your test?" he asked.

"No offense, but Brenda as Sheeni isn't really providing the motivation I need."

"OK, Marlon," sighed Dad. "Call her!"

Cal was extremely reluctant to participate. I had to meet her at the property line, grab her shirt as before, and drag her into the guesthouse. Dad and the others greeted her coolly.

"I just received a bill, Miss Haseltine," said Dad, "for $12,419 for emergency mental health services for my son."

"It wasn't Cal's doing!" I insisted. "It was all Esmee's fault!"

"Is that true?" asked Dad.

"Not really," she replied. "I have a vendetta against certain parties."

"Well, at least you're being honest. OK, let's get this over with."

We did the test again. I tuned out the camera and all the others except Cal. I hardly looked at the script. I listened to her and reacted to what she said. In the second scene our lips nearly met.

Dad switched off the camera.

"Wow, that was, uh, much improved."

"Should we try it again?" I asked. "I flubbed that one line."

"OK," he said. "And this time try to be more disturbed by her description of Trent. And, Valerie, cut back a bit on the coquetry. Sheeni is nothing if not subtle. And, Nick, let's see a real kiss this time."

We played the two scenes again. This time our lips actually touched: wildly stimulating to the nervous system as I suspected it might be. Then Dad had us turn to various angles and look up and down as the camera rolled.

"That's fine," he said, switching off the camera. "You were good. You, uh, both were. Have you done much acting, Miss Haseltine?"

"A bit."

"Right. Well, thank you for helping Nick with his test."

"That's OK," she said. "See you around, Nick."

"Want me drag you back to the sidewalk?" I asked.

"No, I'm fine on my own going that direction."

Cal left and I asked Dad if I got the part.

"We'll let you know, kid. Don't call us, we'll call you."

"Should I study some more of the script?" I asked hopefully.

"No. Right now I need you to wash my car. We're going to Mary's house tonight for dinner, and I want to show up in a clean car."

Damn!

Mary lived in a neighborhood of meandering streets near U.C.L.A. called Westwood. Her house was nice but not grand. Fairly cramped lot and no pool. Her two daughters joined us at the table. Megan is 19 and a star volleyball player at Brown, which is a college back east somewhere. I should have shoulder muscles like her. Lauren is my age and kind of pretty if you can overlook the braces. Her mouth when she smiles resembles the front end of a 1958 Cadillac. She told me that women with narrow faces like her mother should never marry Armenian men with wide jaws.

"Divorce is inevitable," she said. "Plus, their kids have to go through hell at the orthodontist's."

"Your braces don't look bad," I lied.

"Right. You can always pick out my boyfriend in a crowd. He's the dude with the bleeding lips."

"When do you get them off?"

"Not for a year at least! Assuming I don't kill myself first."

"Don't bore Nick with braces talk," said her sister, passing the salad. "I had them and I lived."

Lauren leaned over to whisper in my ear: "She lived, but she's still a virgin."

"I heard that and it's not . . . any of your business," said Megan.

Dad and Mary talked about Ukiah and people they knew in common. One of her brothers, for example, had been on the high-school swim team with Trent Preston. Dad mentioned that he once worked as a part-time "filing and typing slave" for Trent's father.

"Did you know that Mr. Preston invented a version of the string bikini more than a decade before it became popular in the U.S.?" asked Mary.

"That's hard to believe," said Dad.

"My father manufactured it briefly," she said. "They were all ahead of their time."

Lauren turned to me. "Do you like string bikinis, Nick?" she asked.

"I suppose, but only if they're shockingly tiny."

Mary asked me to spill about how I came to be dropped down out of a cloud with a new dad in California.

"Oh we know all about that," said Lauren. "We saw Nick's video."

"Uh, what video? I asked, alarmed.

"The one on YouTube," she replied. "You're being interviewed by some girl."

"You're kidding? It's on YouTube!"

"I think that's where I saw it, Nick. A friend sent the link to my phone."

I wanted to go check it out right then, but Dad made me wait until the meal was over. So I sat there stewing while they discussed his dumb movie. And tried to talk him into juggling stuff. (He refused.) Then they wanted to hear all about my getting hypnotized and being misdiagnosed as a delusional obsessive compulsive. Dessert was a luscious chocolate torte (Mary is quite the baker), but I hardly touched my piece.

Finally, Lauren and I got excused and went up to her room to check out the video on her computer. Yep, there I was on the balcony spilling my guts out. Over 60,000 hits so far and lots of snarky comments. Someone (possibly Avery?) wrote, "Hey, Nickie D., I thought you were hiding out with a new identity!" A bunch of trolls were calling me loser, momma's boy, whiner, etc.

"Don't pay attention to those creeps," said Lauren. "I think your story is totally sweet."

"Yeah, right."

The user name of the fiend who posted the video was Harvs-Pets. He had 11 other videos, all on topics like how to tell if your iguana is sick, how to clean a guinea pig's ears, and what fish to get that won't eat each other in saltwater aquariums. He was on camera in those.

"God, that boy is cute," said Lauren. "Do you know him?"

"I know him. And you'll be seeing him soon on the local news–with his head twisted off."

FRIDAY, June 12 – I was waiting impatiently at the coffee shop this morning when Cal finally showed.

"Don't start on me, Nick," she said before I had uttered a word. "I heard all about it from Esmee."

"You promised me that video would be kept private!"

"My brother is a sneak and a snake. Take it up with my poor parents. They gave birth to the reptile."

"Can't they get him to take it down?"

"Why should they? A video that annoys Veeva's houseguests is something they'd applaud."

"But if my ex-dad sees it, he'll drag me back to Indiana!"

"That's the least of your worries, Nick. You weren't very complimentary about your new dad. If any of those Hollywood gossip websites hear about it, they'll play it up big. They love stories about former TV stars now down and out in some slum."

"Fuck!"

"Next time, Nick, you should downplay the roaches. Are you skipping your greasy muffin today?"

"I wasn't hungry. You've got to help me, Cal!"

"Have you complained to YouTube?"

"Yeah, and I got an automatic reply saying they'd investigate."

"That could take some time, and they might not find anything objectionable. Too bad you weren't flaunting any nudity in the video."

"Don't you have any leverage over your brother, Cal? I'm desperate!"

"There is one Harvean misstep I'm aware of, but I've been holding it in reserve for my own needs."

"Tell me, Cal! Have a heart!"

"I could tell you, Nick. But then you'll owe me an impossibly huge favor to be collected any time I want in the future."

"Fine. It's a deal."

"You're sure?"

"You can have my first-born son! He's yours!"

"I'm sure I'd have no use for that disgusting infant. OK, phone Harvey and say Cooper at camp."

"Cooper at camp?"

"Yes, those three words may do the trick."

I did as she said and delivered that three-word message. Audible gasp from Harvey. I repeated the message. Long silence, then he said, "OK, you win. I'll take it down."

"Right now!" I insisted.

"Yeah, OK. Right now."

I clicked off and smiled at her. "Cal, you're a wonder. I could kiss you."

"Not that, please! I haven't yet recovered from yesterday's slobber."

Of course, I asked her about the significance of "Cooper at camp," but she refused to say anything more. Therefore, I can only speculate that Harvey and Cooper had been up to no good at camp. Their transgression must have been very serious indeed.

I kept a low profile at home this afternoon. Veeva was back with her family for the weekend, and I didn't want to run into her. If you could die from embarrassment, Dad would be shopping for my coffin right now. I called her names. I left her a phone message referring to my erection and her private parts. So for the rest of my life I'll have to slither away whenever I see her. Too bad because I kind of liked her.

After lunch I asked Dad if he'd like me to go through his big bag of mail.

"It's a Sisyphean task," he sighed. "I'm sure more sacks of the stuff have accumulated at the studio."

"Aren't you interested in what people think of you?" I asked.

"Not really. Applause is welcome, but one-on-one the public can be hard to take. I'll let you in on a secret, kid: performers as a rule dislike their fans. But read it if you want. Let me know if any attractive women have included nude photos of themselves."

"They do that?"

"It's been known to happen."

Wow, yet another reason for me to star in Dad's movie.

So I spent the afternoon reading his fan mail. All I can say is these people have swallowed massive quantities of the Nick Twisp Kool Aid. They love him! Imagine writing to some stranger you've only seen on TV. He's like their best friend in the world. Quite a few wrote that when they're sad they think about him and he cheers them up. Am I missing something? Most of the time he has the opposite effect on me. I thought he only appealed to old folks, but he got letters from all ages down to little kids. Admittedly, most of these junior correspondents were from Portugal. They also love him in Brazil. I'm beginning to think that the people dubbing the show in Portuguese are punching up the jokes.

There was one letter I had to ask him about.

"Hey, Dad, do you know some guy who used to live in Oakland named Lefty?"

"Sure. I wrote Lefty into my movie."

"He's working in a Chinese restaurant on Pico. He said he'll give you a free meal if you drop by some time."

"That's odd. Lefty's not Chinese, although if you put him close to a dog he'll swell up and look vaguely Asian."

"You want to go see him?"

"Nah, I'm sure we'd have nothing in common now."

That was his initial response, but tonight's Gazelle Gourmet (stinky chicken livers over mushy pasta) changed his mind. We headed off to that address on Pico. It turned out Lefty wasn't a waiter as we had supposed. He was back in the kitchen flailing away with woks, spatulas, and cleavers. Not washing them; he was the cook. He came out briefly to shake hands, present Dad a bottle of chilled plum wine, drink a toast, and offer us his deluxe banquet for two. We got served about eight exotic dishes—all quite tasty. The leftovers should last us a week. We lingered in the booth until Lefty could join us. I guess he was Dad's age, but he looked younger. He had more hair, a bigger gut, and more tattoos. Also a sparkly diamond in one ear.

"I never thought you'd turn out to be a famous juggler, Nick," he said. "Damn, that was a shock."

"It surprised me too, Lefty. And I never pegged you to be a Chinese chef."

"Yeah, I picked up that trade in the merchant marine. The Pacific's one big ocean. To keep from getting bored while off-duty, I'd hang out in the galley and pester the cooks."

"What do you hear from Millie Filbert?" Dad asked.

"Not a thing. I guess she got married and changed her name to what I don't know. Probably somebody's grandma now. She still ranks as the best pair ever. Like baseballs they were. You ever hear from that Frenchy babe of yours?"

"Once in a while. She lives in France."

"Yeah, I figured that's where she'd wind up. That chick had a brain like Einstein on speed. Nice tits too. I read in the paper about your divorce. Sorry about your parents splitting up, Nick."

"She's not my mother," I replied. "I was a recent surprise arrival."

"A woman briefly in my act," said Dad. "She said she was on the pill."

"Guess you learned your lesson there," laughed Lefty.

"So, how's your dick?" asked Dad.

"Still stubby, thanks to you. The arsenic should be kicking in any minute. Sorry to have to take out your son too."

Thankfully, Lefty was kidding. It seems my dad talked him into getting a penile operation that left his erect member considerably abbreviated. Lefty said he's "put it to good use" anyway over the years, but he wasn't currently attached.

Dad said we were "three lonely bachelors" with nothing to comfort us "except our memories."

And I don't even have that.

SATURDAY, June 13 – Compulsory breakfast next door. Veeva gave me a hug and said "not to worry about anything." I said OK, but spent most of my time there staring down at my frittata and fending off her sticky kid Xenia. She's a manic sugarholic and only eats things drenched in syrup, which she regards as prime finger food. Xenia's hostile brother continues to regard me as a trespasser in his life. Perhaps he's heard I'd been after his mom.

Veeva was amazed at the progress in Dad's movie. Mary has lined up most of the crew and casting starts next week.

"What about sets and costumes?" she asked.

"No sets," said Dad. "We're shooting everything on location. No costumes either. It's come as you are for the actors."

"You can't skimp on wardrobe, Nick," she said. "That establishes the whole look of your movie."

"The look of my movie is thrift-shop eclectic. That's what it was when I was growing up."

And still is from the looks of him. I notice he only shaves on days when he's meeting with Mary. If he marries her, it could be awkward living in the same house with Lauren. I might start regarding metal-clad mouths as extremely sexy. Or does the incest taboo kick in with stepsisters? I may ask Uma to clarify that the next time I see her.

I was all set to head to Cal's coffee spot, but Scott arrived to drag me off to his place. This time there was no escaping that long-delayed fraternal workout. He showed me what to do on each machine and we went at it. After nearly an hour of sweaty labor my abs looked exactly the same (as in non-existent).

Scott said no actor in Hollywood would dream of taking off his shirt in front of a camera these days unless he had washboard abs.

"It was different in the old days," he said, pumping away. "Actors like Kirk Douglas and Robert Mitchum and Burt Lancaster would strip to the waist and look like normal guys. They ate in the studio commissary and had steak five nights a week at Ciro's. They'd play a round of golf or toss a medicine ball back and forth. That was their workout. Hell, they regarded getting a rubdown as exercise. Now you have to be totally buff or some tabloid will be running a photo of your sagging gut."

Bad news for me since I think Dad's script calls for a scene on a beach. I don't have a gut, but the only way to spot a muscle on me would be to dissect my corpse.

Scott said our dad was very upset when I was having my mental breakdown.

"He really cares about you, Nick," he said.

"You think so?"

"Sure, but don't expect him to show it much. I think you've been good for him. I don't think he does well living on his own."

"How come he's so, uh . . ."

"Strange? Weird?"

"Yeah, how come?"

"I think it was our flaky grandparents, Nick. They totally messed him up. Then that chick Sheeni Saunders came along and finished the job. Is he still having those mystery phone conversations at night?"

"I don't know. Our new place is too soundproof to hear anything."

I told him about my video and its unauthorized appearance on the Web.

Scott asked if I had considered the possibility that "your girlfriend" might have conspired with her brother to put the video on YouTube in order to extract a major favor from me. I like California, but I think the paranoia level in this state is much higher than Indiana.

As we were getting ready to go out for lunch, Scott's phone rang and he excused himself to take the call. It sounded like a very friendly chat, and I don't think it was with Azura up in Bozeman. Could he be cheating on that goddess? Dumb! Then again, our dad just split with a woman who seemed perfectly fine in every respect. Plus, she provided free dental care. Is it the destiny of all Twisp men to be stupid about love?

SUNDAY, June 14 – I protested vociferously, but got dragged to brunch at cousin Tyler's. Naturally, I ducked Uma as much as possible. Once you've discussed your masturbatory habits and philosophy of farting with someone, you're pretty much done with that person. The buffet featured a large platter of corn fritters, but the chef had added fiery hot peppers and cilantro to the batter, rendering them inedible to people from Indiana. Was this a deliberate snub from cousin Tyler for annoying his wife?

I sat out on the terrace with my sister Miren. I asked her why we hadn't seen much of her. She said she's invited us twice for dinner, but our dad declined both times.

"I guess he's busy with his movie," I pointed out.

"I don't think he likes my husband," she confessed.

"Really? Your husband is tall, handsome, affable, successful, and rich. He's also good with his kids. What's not to like?"

"Ryder was something of a playboy like Tyler. I think Papa is afraid he won't be able to resist all those women who find him so attractive."

"He should talk."

"I know. But I trust Ryder. He's quite devoted."

"Guys are programmed to spread their seed widely. Dad thinks chicks should make allowances for that."

"That's very self-serving. So why should he hold Ryder to a higher standard?"

"Beats me. It could be that short homely guys have trouble warming up to tall handsome ones."

"Our papa is not homely, Nick. He's very handsome. And so are you."

Perhaps I could get her to point that out to Cal sometime. Miren told me something else of interest. Dad had been planning to go to Argentina and work as a clown with her twin sister Nerea's circus. He ditched those plans after I showed up.

Those little kids in Argentina should thank me. If Dad ever became a clown, I'm sure he'd scare the hell out of them.

Later, walking back from a lonely excursion to the beach, I spotted Cal standing on our neutral corner. I was about to wave to her when a familiar car drove up, she climbed in, and it disappeared from view around the corner. The driver was Desmond, Veeva's oddball hubby.

MONDAY, June 15 – Dad fired Gazelle Gourmet. He told them to take their chicken livers and stuff 'em where the sun don't shine. He has hired Lefty as a full-time cook and domestic slave. I'm hoping he'll also be in charge of washing the Town Car. Lefty was amenable to being wooed because he was working 12-hour shifts with no overtime pay or days off. He'd been living above the restaurant, so he's now crashing (temporarily, I hope) on our sofa. I'm not sure Dad has cleared this arrangement with Veeva. His original plan was to have Lefty bunk with me, but I threatened an emergency call to Child Protective Services.

Lefty arrived just in time to watch over me, since Dad, Mary, and Brenda are busy all this week holding cast auditions at a rehearsal hall in Studio City. No, Dad hasn't said whether I got the part.

Lefty asked me what I liked to eat. I said pretty much everything except asparagus, liver, chicken dark meat, and jalapeño peppers.

"Guess you're not up for my spicy chicken thighs with asparagus, topped with a calves' liver flambeau," he said.

"No, you'd be cleaning that dish off the walls."

"Want to go to the market with me?"

"Not really."

"Will you raise hell if I leave you on your own?"

"I doubt it."

"Your dad raised a lot of hell when he was your age. The FBI was hunting for him. And cops from all over."

"I don't have those tendencies."

"Any girlfriends I should be worried about?"

"Uh, no. I'm kind of grimly dull and boring."

"Good, Nick. Let's keep it that way."

After he drove off in his rattletrap Jeep, I hoofed it to the coffee shop. Cal arrived a few minutes later.

"Aren't you the stranger," she said, taking a seat at my table.

"I get invited to lots of brunches on weekends. How was your date with Desmond?"

"Who?"

"Desmond Upton, the best-selling novelist, middle-aged fogey, and father of two."

"He gave me a ride to downtown Santa Monica. Not that it's any of your business."

"How did you arrange that?"

"I didn't. He saw me on the street and offered me a lift. I noticed you down the block spying on me."

"I wasn't spying. I was walking home. He told me he watches you in your window undressing at night."

"Anything's possible, I suppose."

"Your blind has always been down since I've been there."

"Sorry to disappoint you. How's your acting career?"

"Still in limbo. Dad hasn't said if I got the part. They're doing casting all this week. Do you have a thing for Desmond? Or do you flirt with him to get back at Veeva?"

"Why should I answer your nosy questions?"

"Because I would sincerely like to know."

"That's hardly a reason."

We sipped our coffee in silence. I was finding her a very frustrating person to know. I'd met three girls my age in California. One hypnotized me with disastrous consequences, one has bad dental feng shui, and the last one was driving me insane.

"Do you like me at all, Cal?" I asked.

She thought about it.

"Not really, Nick. Was I supposed to?"

"I guess not. Then why are we hanging out together?"

"We're not. I come here for coffee and you stalk me."

Very disheartening assessment, but probably true.

I shuffled back home, then moped beside the pool all day. Dinner was Lefty's excellent southern-fried catfish. Only two of us at the table because Dad was working late. Too bad I didn't have much of an appetite.

"Something wrong with the eats, Nick?" asked Lefty.

"Not at all. Everything's excellent. I'm not very hungry."

"Girl trouble?"

"Yeah, I asked this girl if she liked me. Her answer was no."

"Sometimes girls mean exactly what they say. And sometimes they mean just the opposite."

"So how can you tell which it is?"

"Usually you can't. That's what makes chicks so tricky."

"So it's possible she does like me?"

"Could be, Nick. It's not usually a good idea to ask such a direct question. Girls can get skittish if you put them on the spot."

"What should I do instead?"

"Ask her out on a date. If she's not interested in you, she'll say no. End of story."

"How come you're not married, Lefty?"

"Just lucky I guess. The ladies I wanted to marry wouldn't have me. And the ones who wanted to hang the yoke on me scared me off for one reason or another. I think it's a miracle anyone ties the knot these days."

TUESDAY, June 16 – Early a.m. phone call from my long-lost mother. She's been talking to my ex-dad!

"He wants us to get back together, Nick. He's promising to change. He says everything will be better."

"And you believe those lies?"

"That's what my friends on the ship say. A tiger can't change his spots."

"Tigers have stripes, Mom. Leopards have spots."

"Well he has both. And they aren't changing. But I miss you so much. We could all be together again in Indiana."

"Bad idea, Mom. In a week we'd both be miserable. Besides, I like it here. I'm getting to know my brother and sister. And my real dad too."

"You deserve a proper family life, Nick. I do know that."

"Did you tell him where I am?"

"He knows, Nick. He saw some sort of online video you made."

Damn!

"What did he say?"

"He's angry about your dad. I think he's jealous of his success and position. He's threatening to get a lawyer to try and regain custody of you."

"He can't do that! We're not even related!"

"I guess he's still your father in the eyes of the law. He says he won't do that if I come back to Indiana."

"So he's claiming he changed, but now he's blackmailing you?"

"That's the situation, dear."

"If you go back home, do I get to stay in California?"

"Probably. He doesn't really want you back. But I don't want to go to Indiana without you. And right now I can't afford a lawyer to fight him on the custody issue. I don't know what to do. Should I talk to your dad?"

I thought about that. Dad was busy with his movie. Did he want to hire a lawyer to fight to keep me or would he be happy putting me on the next bus to Terre Haute?

"Uh, let's hold off on that, Mom. That creep you married may be too cheap to go through with his threat to hire a lawyer. Those guys charge hundreds of bucks an hour."

"That's true, Nick. He'd have to wash a huge pile of socks to pay for that."

Yes, a vast and smelly pile. All in all, a lousy way to start the day. And yet another reason to wring that traitor Harvey Haseltine's scrawny neck.

Lefty made chocolate-orange French toast for breakfast. Dad had five big pieces, plus seconds of the sausage. I hope his arteries can take Lefty's cuisine. He reports their auditions are going well. They found actresses to play his mother and Aunt Joanie. Dad, of course, will be playing his own funky father George F. Twisp. Today they've scheduled auditions for Sheeni and Trent Preston. No mention of Nick Twisp auditions, which I'm taking as a good sign.

I didn't greet Cal at the coffee place this morning in case she wanted to sit at another table. But she sat at mine.

"Where's your death muffin?" she asked.

"Dad got a new cook. I'm stuffed."

"That derelict in the old Jeep is your cook?"

Now who was doing the spying?

"Dad knew him when they were kids. Lefty's quite handy with a fry pan."

"I suppose he's left-handed like me."

"No, that's kind of odd. He's right-handed."

I told her about my ex-dad seeing her video and threatening to drag me back to Indiana.

"All you have to do, Nick, is get cast in your dad's film. He won't let you go back if it means reshooting his movie."

"That's true, isn't it? How can I make sure he selects me?"

"You could learn to act. Too bad you got Esmee grounded. We could get her to hypnotize your dad into thinking you were the next Lawrence Olivier."

"I'm not messing with hypnosis, Cal. Not ever!"

"Suit yourself, Hoosier boy. Did you enjoy my show last night?"

"What show?"

"I undressed with my blinds open."

"Damn! I missed it. I was watching a dumb TV show with Lefty. Any chance of a repeat performance tonight?"

"Sorry, I only do it when the mood strikes me–which is once in a blue moon."

I manned up and asked if she wanted to take in a movie with me Friday night. She checked her schedule on her phone and said she might be able to accommodate me, but would have to lie to her parents about it.

"Is that a problem?" I asked.

"Not in the least."

So Cal is willing to lie to her parents in order to see me. That seems to imply that she doesn't find me entirely repulsive.

Later that afternoon I ran into her despised brother on the street. I told him my ex-dad had seen the video and was threatening to wreck my life. Harvey backed away.

"Don't try anything, Nick. In less than a second I can kick out your front teeth. When you bend over to pick up the bloody bits, I'll deliver a karate chop to your hypoglossal nerve that will subtract 20 points from your I.Q.–permanently. I don't think you can afford to lose those."

"Don't even think about that, Harvey. I'll grab your head and give it such a violent twist, it will snap your spinal cord like a toothpick. You'll spend the rest of the day on a hospital table having your organs harvested."

"I very much doubt you'd get anywhere near my head before my foot would propel your testicles violently up into your abdomen, rendering you permanently incapable of impregnating my sister–although I suspect you're pretty far down on her list for that job."

"Too bad for you I have been trained to deflect such kicks,

while employing your own forward momentum to rip both of your ears out by the roots. You'll be living in a world of silence and studying lip-reading in your spare time."

"Not likely, Nick. The only thing you have a black belt in is bullshit. I suggest you back off now before I reboot your life to the permanently disabled."

All senses poised for combat, we stood there glaring at each other.

"So tell me, Harvey," I said. "What's up with your sister and Desmond?"

"She gets in his car, Nick, and they go places. I think even you can figure out what they're up to."

"Really? You think they're hooking up?"

"They're not going to the park to feed the pigeons, dumb shit."

"But she's under age!"

"Did that stop Humbert Humbert?"

"Who?"

"Read a book sometime, Nick. Don't be a moron all your life."

Later I Googled Humbert Humbert. He wasn't a real person, just some character in a smutty novel.

WEDNESDAY, June 17 – No nudity last night in neighboring windows. I don't know if Cal is hooking up with Desmond, or her brother is messing with my head. It's a good thing for him I don't have access to a gun. I've pretty much decided that hand-to-hand combat with Harvey is off the table. A guy who claims he can target your hypoglossal nerve is probably not bluffing.

Dad reports they found an actor to play Trent Preston, but Sheeni is proving harder to cast. They need someone young, beautiful, and capable of projecting prodigious intelligence. Mary likes this blond singer who's all over YouTube, but Dad thinks she looks like "trailer trash." Of course, he first met Sheeni in a trailer park, but apparently that's not the look he's after. Brenda agrees the singer could be a big draw at the box office, but Dad says he's not making a musical so she's out. While he was upstairs getting ready to go, I copied his list of girls who had passed the first cut.

At the coffee place Cal and I checked them out on our phones. Like every actor in Hollywood, they all had professional-looking websites with head shots, acting credits, and sample videos.

"What's with these brunettes?" said Cal. "I thought your dad's GF was a blonde?"

"She had chestnut hair, kind of like you. I guess they'd have to dye her hair. Dad is insisting on authenticity."

"As if anyone cares except him. Well, Nick, which one would you most like to screw?"

"What?"

"Isn't that what this is all about? Finding the most desirable girl for the part?"

"I think it's more complicated than that, Cal. There's more to love than sexual attraction."

"I'm not sure that message has reached Hollywood."

"I kind of like this girl Lila."

Cal found her webpage and checked it out.

"I can see why you like her, Nick. She's cross-eyed and has an overbite."

"She's not cross-eyed. Her eyes just wander charmingly sometimes. Her teeth are fine."

"Her ample breasts appear more rigidly spherical than typically found in nature."

"I'm surprised Brenda didn't veto her. She hates fake boobs."

"She would."

"Brenda's OK. She told me she's turned down three proposals of marriage so far."

"Sure, Nick. All from the same deranged guy."

"No, Cal. She has a very active dating life. Nearly as active as yours."

"I heard you've been interrogating my brother on that subject. You should join the CIA, Nick. Spying is your forte."

"I thought you and Harvey didn't speak."

"We break that rule, Nick, when the topic is you."

"Harvey seems to think you're hooking up with Desmond."

"That makes two of you, I suppose. You guys have so much in common. Have you ever considered asking him out instead of me?"

As usual I got no useful information out of her. Too bad her teeth are so perfect. If she were clamped into braces like Lauren, I might not be so far gone on her.

Dad had to interrupt his auditions this afternoon to haul his junk out of Ada's house. He tried to put her off, but she said it would all be going to the dump if he didn't act promptly. Sounds like she wants all vestiges of him out of her life. Chicks don't get sentimental about this, despite having had sex with the dude a couple thousand times. I tagged along to help out and snoop. Brenda also showed up with two burly movers and a big truck. The guys did the heavy lifting. Tall filing cabinets jammed with Nick Twisp memorabilia got wheeled out on dollies as Brenda and I packed clothes into cardboard moving boxes.

Meanwhile Dad and Ada went through rooms putting little colored tags on stuff that was going. Fairly amicable division of spoils except for some framed artwork in the library: a watercolor, two oil paintings, and some artsy photographs. Not by anybody I'd ever heard of, but apparently worth grappling over. Dad claimed they were his, Ada said they were "acquired jointly," and voices began to be raised. Things were threatening to get ugly, when Brenda suggested they delay their decision until an art appraiser could be called in to provide an evaluation. Dad grudgingly agreed, but said he wasn't willing to be "taken to the cleaners just because Brent is an art connoisseur."

I guess he heard about Ada's new beau.

Dad told me to photograph the disputed art with my phone in case any of them "mysteriously walked away."

Ada stood by tightlipped as Dad had the movers haul off several dozen cases from the wine cellar. Looks like 'ol Brent will be buying his own wine. He can probably afford it, since I hear he's a lawyer.

The whole enterprise took hours, and the truck was nearly full when the last paperclip was loaded and the big door rolled down. Dad wrote them a hefty check, and they drove off to Westchester to unload everything in a garage-sized storage locker he's renting. Before they left he told them to make sure the wine was stored close to the door (for accessibility), and not to help themselves to any bottles as they were all carefully inventoried. Probably a lie, but they pretended to believe him.

I was floating in the lap pool after dinner when a man came out next door to clip some roses off a bush. He looked like a much older and slightly taller version of Harvey.

"Hi," I said. I figured I should be polite since I might be fathering his future grandkids.

"You shouldn't swim by yourself," he replied. "You could get a cramp and drown."

"It's only four feet deep, sir. All I'd have to do is stand up."

"Well, I warned you."

"Right, thanks."

"My daughter can be trouble. I heard about the incident involving you. She does things like that. I don't know why."

"Oh, no harm done."

"I'd stay away from her if I were you."

"Thank you for the warning."

"I watched your video. You sounded like a sincere young man."

"Uh, I try to be, sir."

For a video that was supposed to be secret it's attracting an ever-broader audience.

"You're out of your depth with my daughter, Nick. It's the culture of L.A. I guess. My wife blames it on peer pressure. Valerie was quite a sweet little girl when she was five."

"I'm having more trouble with your son. He warned me not to mention Cooper at camp."

"Cooper at camp, huh? I'll check into that."

"Please do, sir."

Not as satisfying as twisting off Harvey's head, but it would do for a start.

THURSDAY, June 18 – Tomorrow's date movie has been agreed upon: "Diet of Death" starring Tom Cruise. It's playing nearby in Culver City. Lefty has agreed to drive us there in his Jeep. Very inconvenient not having a driver's license and access to a car. A big handicap for dating. My competition (Desmond) has both, but then I'm not encumbered with a wife and children. Since kids are maturing faster these days, it would be helpful if they lowered the legal age for driving to 13.

When we met for coffee, Cal was surprised to hear that Dad has found a likely prospect for Sheeni. Her name is Tiara Diamond and she's a blue-eyed, chestnut-haired beauty with a long list of acting credits. Years ago she was a semi-regular on that Disney show "Skateboard Park." I never watched it because even the goofy fat kid on the show was more adept on a skateboard than I was.

"Tiara Diamond has got to be the most pretentious name in the history of Hollywood," commented Cal, viewing a sample video on her phone.

"You'll notice her eyes don't cross and she has no overbite," I replied. "And her figure looks untouched by surgical hands."

"I expect it's been well pawed-over by other hands. No doubt she's inflaming your libido."

"She's OK, I guess. It's all up to my dad, Cal. I have no input. The girl he picks has to conform to his vision of Sheeni."

"If you Google Sheeni Saunders, you can see what she looks like these days."

I did just that. There was a recent photo of her at an academic conference in Paris. OK-looking for a gal in her 50s, but no better than the wife my dad just shed. And not at all in the same class as Uma or Trent's wife Apurva.

"Well, she's nothing special," I said.

"Are you kidding, Nick? She has fantastic bone structure. And look at her luminous eyes. I'm sure she was fatally beautiful when your dad first knew her."

"OK, if you say so."

I knew better than to argue such issues with a chick. I decided to stick my neck out.

"I think you're prettier than all these girls, Cal."

"What do you know, Nick? You're just a hick from Indiana."

Lefty was vacuuming when I got back. He told me to get out in the sunshine and "make some friends." Easier said than done. I walked to the beach and checked to see if the ocean was still there. It was. I was walking north toward Santa Monica when my phone rang. It was Azura Preston calling from distant Montana.

"Hi, Azura. How's the movie going?"

"Good so far, Nick. I like the director and the DP is mucho cute. The pace is so much slower than TV work. We sit around for hours while they set up lights and move scrims around. Now I know why so many actors take up knitting. Or bridge. Or drinking. What are you up to?"

I told her about my hot date tomorrow night.

"Sounds like fun, Nick. But try to keep it casual. We don't

want you two sneaking off to Mississippi to get married."

"You don't have to worry about that," I lied.

(I've decided to keep my options open in that department.)

"Have you heard from your hunky brother?" she asked.

"Scott calls me every couple of days or so. I'm keeping him informed about Dad's movie. They've cast quite a few of the parts."

"Remind your dad I'm available to play his sister Joan."

"I don't think she was beautiful like you."

"Aren't you sweet, Nick? But I'm plain as a post without my makeup."

"I doubt that."

"So I have to go now. Remind your brother there's a girl named Zee who likes him a lot. And she'd appreciate it if he'd return her calls once in a while."

"I sure will, Azura. You take care."

"You too, Nick."

Damn, my idiot brother is so blowing it with that chick.

I walked back home via Lincoln Boulevard, which was a mistake. As I was passing a certain pet store someone sneaked up behind me and put something down my shirt. Something alive!

"What the–!"

"Don't panic, Nick," said a voice that sounded like Harvey's. "It's only the world's deadliest spider."

Buttons shot away like bullets as I ripped off my shirt. I tried to pull off my t-shirt, but the fiend behind me held it down as something big squirmed and wiggled against my skin. Terrified, I leaped about like a wild man. I gave a final monumental heave, Harvey let go, and my shredded t-shirt flew out into the street, where it was run over by a passing bus.

"Did it bite? Did it bite me?" I screamed.

"Relax, moron," said my tormentor. "It was only a cricket. God, what a baby you are. So how come you snitched on me? I took down your stupid video."

"Some good that did. My ex-dad saw it. Now he knows where I live."

"So?"

"So he's threatening to get a lawyer and drag me back to Indiana!"

"Big deal."

"You owe me a new shirt, asshole! And t-shirt!"

"Good luck collecting that. Well, I got a customer. See you, Nick. You scream just like a girl."

So will he when I get his scrotum clamped in a vise. And I'm attaching the electrodes to his puny dick.

FRIDAY, June 19 – I had an unsettling thought while waiting outside the bathroom this morning. What if Cal has it in for Veeva because she's in love with Desmond? That would kind of explain roping me into that harassment caper. But why would a cute 16-year-old girl fall for some near-ancient writer who's not that handsome and drives a boring Volvo? OK, he's rich, but so's my family (I assume). All in all an unlikely scenario that I've decided to dismiss.

I was expecting Dad or Lefty to emerge from the bathroom, but it turned out to be Mary Moran dressed only in my towel. She smiled and said, "Sorry, Nick, I think I used all the hot water."

She had too. Also my toothbrush was suspiciously moist. Gross!

Looks like she and Dad have reached a new plateau in their relationship. I wish I could say the same. Four people and one bathroom is a ratio that's likely to produce friction. Let's hope Lefty doesn't start dragging gals back here too.

Mary and Dad were pretty lovey at breakfast. Are love affairs always that sickening to the people around them? At least I'm not all weirded out that she's trying to supplant my mother, since Mom was never in the picture anyway. I do like Mary, I guess, and she's always been super-friendly toward me. She has a nice body too. I wouldn't have minded if that towel had slipped a bit this morning. I should censor those thoughts until such time as the appropriate incest taboo kicks in.

Since Dad's brain presumably was flooded with endorphins, I hit him up for $50.

"What do you need that for?" he asked.

"Incidentals. It's expensive being a kid in L.A."

"It's even more expensive being a parent. You should try it sometime."

Mary silently shook her head.

"No wait, Nick," added Dad. "You should definitely *not* try that."

He took out his wallet, examined its contents, and said to Mary, "This lad has me confused with an ATM machine."

Nevertheless, he forked over the full $50.

Inspired by my example, Lefty asked, "Is Friday payday around here?"

"Next Friday is," said Dad. "You will be paid next Friday for this week's work."

"It's hell being a wage slave," grumbled Lefty, slapping another pancake on my plate.

At the coffee place this morning I asked Cal if she was excited about our impending date tonight.

"I have to pinch myself every five minutes to make sure I'm not dreaming," she replied.

Probably sarcasm, but perhaps interlarded with a pinch of sincerity.

"Any news on the movie front?" she asked.

"Dad's sister called him to invite us to their annual Father's Day blowout on Sunday. She told him she wants no mention of her in his movie. And especially no mention that she gave birth to Tyler out of wedlock."

"Is he rewriting the script?"

"No, he's ignoring her as usual. He is dragging me to her house though. I guess I should buy him a card."

"We'll buy our cards together, Nick. We'll pick out the ugliest ones on the rack."

"I kind of like my dad, Cal. He's a big improvement over my previous one. Father's Day back in Indiana was always an exercise in hypocrisy."

"It still is for me, Nick. Exceeded only by that annual horror known as Mother's Day."

"I'm sure your children will love it though."

Cal shuddered. "Sometimes, Nick, you say the most sickening things."

We bought our cards at a drugstore on Lincoln Boulevard. Mine featured a bewildered looking pug surrounded by about a dozen puppies. The printed message inside: "Hey Dad! Thanks for being doggedly frisky!"

"Very, very tacky," commented Cal, approvingly.

Cal's card showed Prince Charming kissing a sleeping Snow

REVOLT AT THE BEACH

White. The inside was blank, so Cal wrote: "I hope it wasn't date rape. Your loving daughter, V.H."

"Should I get him a box of chocolates?" I asked. "They're on sale."

"You probably should, Nick. Brown-nosing on Father's Day might help you get the part in his movie."

I splurged and bought the two-pound box for $8.95. It was a prestige brand imported from Bulgaria.

The rest of the day crawled by until it was time to pick up Cal on our neutral corner. She sat next to me on the hard pad that was passing for a back seat in Lefty's Jeep. She had daubed on an incendiary perfume that contrasted nicely with the old vinyl and motor-oil smells of the Jeep.

"Where to, Mr. Trump?" asked Lefty.

"Culver City, James. And step on it."

It turns out the movie, "Diet of Death," was based on a novel by Desmond Upton. A bit unsettling, since it was mostly Cal's pick. That giant menace-to-evildoers Jack Stricker (described in the novels as six-six and over 250 pounds of rippling muscle) was played by Tom Cruise, a guy who can only dream of being five-nine. He did his usual competent job though. Mostly he shot people, but he did kill one guy in a new way that I'll have to try out on Harvey. You grab them by the back of the head with both hands, then pull forward as you kick up with your knee. When your knee impacts their chin, you hear a very satisfying crunch as assorted neck bones shatter. Plus, there's a good chance they'll bite off their tongue.

Lefty was waiting by the curb to take us to our next destination: an all-night diner done in 1950s style. He grabbed a burger at the counter while we dined in a booth in the back. Vintage Doo wop groups were doo-wopping on the sound system.

"How's your strawberry shake?" I asked Cal.

"Very artificially strawberry. How are your french fries with gravy?"

"Kind of different. I think I prefer ketchup. Should I order more nachos?"

"Please don't. I don't think I'd handle obesity well. You have to admit Desmond is a genius."

"Uh, in what way?"

"He's turned our culture's fascination with violence into a machine to print money."

"I suppose. If you go for that sort of thing."

"It's every writer's dream to have someone like Tom Cruise play their hero. It's like they themselves are stepping into the shoes of a world-famous sex symbol."

"He's getting a bit long in the tooth, ol' Tom is. Don't you think?"

"That is entirely immaterial. This is the realm of myth here, Nick, not grubby reality."

"Reality can never be grubby with you in it, Cal."

"Keep that up, guy, and you will soon be wearing a lapful of my semi-digested nachos."

I invited her in when we got back, but she said she had to go. Lefty in the front seat pretended to look at his phone as I planted a very awkward kiss in the general vicinity of her inviting lips.

My first ever date with a girl. I'd give it at least a B+.

SATURDAY, June 20 – Mary didn't sleep over last night. (Alas, neither did Cal.) It could be that Dad was a total failure in the sack. Let's hope not, considering his heavy contribution to my genetic makeup. Or perhaps she felt she couldn't stay out two nights in a row for fear her daughters would be running wild in the streets. So I got a shower that was hot, unlike the retired juggler who shuffled in next. I think our water heater is sized for one mother-in-law only.

Lefty was making coffee when Veeva called to invite us all over for breakfast. She said she had a "petite surprise."

I was praying it wasn't an eviction notice as the three of us trooped across the yard to the front house. It wasn't. Sitting at the breakfast bar and buttering a croissant was Ukiah's most diehard Francophile Ms. Sheeni Saunders.

"Bonjour," she said, smiling.

"Sheeni!" gasped Dad. "I thought you were in France."

"Soon to be a common misconception, mon chéri."

They embraced rather more enthusiastically than Mary would have liked had she been here. Then Dad introduced Lefty and me.

"I remember you," she said, shaking Lefty's hand. "You took care of my darling dog Albert and swelled up like a blimp. We passed you off as a Cambodian exchange student."

"Yeah, that was me," Lefty admitted.

"It was Burma, Sheeni," said Dad. "He was Leff Ti, a devout Burmese."

"No, I'm sure it was Cambodia, Nick," she replied. "I remember it distinctly."

"Nope, it was Burma."

"It couldn't have been Burma, dear. They don't even call it that anymore."

Having debated that point to a draw, Sheeni turned to me.

"And yet another young Twisp to charm the ladies," she said, giving my clammy hand a squeeze. "And so like your father too."

"I'm hoping to burn down a major neighborhood soon," I joked.

"Arson was a favorite avocation of your father," she confirmed.

"Not exactly," said Dad.

Then Lefty got introduced to Veeva and Desmond, and we all filled our plates at the buffet and sat at the big oak table in the dining room.

"Hey, Veeva," said Dad, "where are your brats?"

"Exiled for the morning to the Gargoyle's," she replied.

"Veeva is so kind," said Sheeni. "She knows I don't do small children."

Must have been tough on her kids when they were little. I had to admit she looked quite a bit better than the photo of her on the Web. And dressed like something out of a fashion magazine. Big diamond flashing on her hand, but the wrong finger for a wedding ring.

"How long are you staying, Sheeni?" asked Dad.

"Haven't you heard, Nick? I'm here for good. France is a pleasant place to visit, but I wouldn't want to live there."

"But you lived there for nearly 40 years!" he pointed out.

"I've resigned from the institute. I sold my house. I packed my bags. All my children are in the U.S. except for poor Marie in Argentina. My son François was born in Lyon, educated in Paris, and now runs a winery in Hopland, which is just down the road from Ukiah, if you can believe that. It seems there's no escaping this country."

"And where will you live?" Dad asked.

"Who knows? I'm a vagabond. L.A., San Francisco, possibly New York. We'll have to see, won't we? For the time being I'm subletting a furnished condo in Westwood. I'm on the 14th floor and can observe the snarled traffic 24 hours a day."

Perhaps to prove she was a graduate of Princeton, Veeva then had a conversation with her aunt in French. I turned to Desmond and told him I'd seen his movie "Diet of Death."

"It's not really my movie, Nick. I just cashed the massive check. I think the screenwriter was using my book as a toast rack for all of its contents that made it onto the screen."

"Was killing a guy by a knee to the chin in your book?" I asked.

"Could be. After a time I tend to lose track of how I've dispatched folks. Readers get annoyed if I don't keep coming up with new and novel techniques. Right now I'm trying to concoct a way to render a wedgie lethal. I'm thinking a baseball bat inserted down the waistband and through a leg opening, then twisted until all blood to the torso is cut off."

"You mean like the ultimate tighty whitey?" I asked.

"Exactly. I'm just worried readers will carp that the cotton would tear before asphyxiation is achieved."

I told Desmond I was willing to test it on him, but he declined.

I heard Sheeni tell Dad it was fine for him to use her real name in the movie. In fact, she wants to help out.

"I have a sharp eye for detail, Nickie," she said. "I could be your script girl and do continuity."

"We call them script supervisors now, Sheeni. I do need one. It's too bad you got Cambodia wrong. It's little details like that which we can't mess up."

I left as that debate resumed; I can see now why it didn't work out with those two.

I found out later from Lefty that Brenda showed up there looking for Dad. She was annoyed that he wasn't answering his phone. She's discovered an abandoned building in Azusa that's condemned. It's at the bottom of a long hill. The fire department was planning to burn it as a training exercise on Monday, but she talked them into delaying it until Wednesday. So Dad had to interrupt his reunion brunch to go check it out. Also tagging along was wannabe script girl Sheeni Saunders.

Cal at the coffee place was intrigued to hear of Sheeni's return.

"Of course, she's up to something," she said.

"You think so?"

"Women don't contrive to surprise former boyfriends at breakfast just to be friendly."

"They don't?"

"Certainly not, Nick. Don't be naive. There's always a motive."

"Really? And what is your motive for having coffee with me?"

"Summer ennui, I suppose. One must do something to fill these idle hours. Was your father happy to see her?"

"I guess. He gave her a hug."

"Perfunctory or a tight clinch?"

"Pretty tight. Like those stone walls at Machu Picchu."

"So he's still in love with her. Well, that's interesting."

"But he's sleeping with Mary Moran. I wonder if Sheeni knows that?"

"Of course, she does, Nick. She probably knew about it before it happened."

"Does she want my dad back?"

"She wants something, Nick. She has an agenda. That I'm sure of. But right now we don't know what she wants."

"I know what I want, Cal," I said, placing my hand on hers.

"You want what every boy your age wants, Nick. And it's all too hideous to contemplate."

I asked Cal if she wanted to go to the beach with me today, but she declined. She said she was "busy." Doing what she didn't say. Cal is not very forthcoming about her daily activities. I have no idea what she does the 23 hours out of the day that I don't see her.

Later, Veeva came out for a chat as I was lounging beside the lap pool. I turned red and found it hard to look at her. I wish she would seduce me so I could get over that terminal embarrassment.

"So, Nick, what's up with your dad and Mary Moran?"

"Is this for your information, or are you reporting to Sheeni?"

"I'm just curious. I don't spy for Sheeni."

"All I know is that Mary spent the night here. Not last night, the night before. She used my towel and toothbrush."

"A considerate gentleman would provide those for guests. They seem well-suited, don't you think?"

"I guess. What's Sheeni's interest in him?"

"If I knew that, I'd tell you. She was quite eager to be invited to brunch this morning."

"Is she after Desmond? He's rich and sort of famous."

"He's definitely famous, Nick. But I get the feeling Sheeni thinks my husband is more than a little absurd. She may have been targeting Trent Preston at one point, but he's happy with Apurva. So you are persisting in seeing your tormentor next door?"

"How did you know that?"

"Very little escapes my attention, Nick."

"I like her, but I'm on guard against treachery."

"I hope so, Nick. I really don't see Valerie having sex with you, if that's what you're after."

More blushing on my part.

"I'm fine just being her friend," I lied.

"Let's keep in touch, Nick. Call me anytime. You have my number."

"Right."

If only she'd said that back when I was clamoring to have sex with her.

Dad missed both lunch and dinner. He came home late, alone, and excited. He said the building in Azusa was perfect for their needs. Already Mary has carpenters at work making it look like a Berkeley shopping street. Tomorrow she's interviewing special effects experts about staging the runaway cars and explosions.

"We need three things at this point," said Dad. "A white slab-sided Lincoln convertible from the 1960s, a decrepit travel trailer, and an actor to play Nick, since he's in the scene."

"Er, right," I said.

"We're trying to do it on the cheap, Nick, but we could have $5 million sunk into this project before we're done."

Dad's phone rang. It was Brenda.

"No, Brenda, I don't want a 1962 white Cadillac convertible. I don't care that it's a good deal. It has to be a Lincoln!"

He rang off and looked at me.

"Where was I" he asked.

"Five million dollars."

"Right. So if we consider you for this part, I have to know you'll approach it seriously. A lot will be depending on you."

"I'm serious about it, Dad. One thing though: will you be paying me?"

"Of course. We can discuss that later."

"So do I have the part?"

"I can't say yet. Tiara knows this young actor with a lot of experience she wants us to see."

I hadn't met Ms. Tiara Diamond yet, but already I hated her.

SUNDAY, June 21 – Dad tried to weasel out of Father's Day at Aunt Joanie's, but she put the screws to him. She said if he didn't show up, she'd tell her billionaire son not to invest in his movie. We picked up Scott in Brentwood on the way to Simi Valley. Like me he had a card and a gift. I asked him why he hadn't been returning Azura's phone calls.

"Been busy, Nick. I'll talk to you about that later."

Something was up with that guy. I could tell.

Simi Valley was way off in the deepest suburbs. I got a big hug from Aunt Joanie and a friendly handshake from her husband Bill. He used to restore old cars, but hurt his back hoisting too many bumpers. Now he goes around to garage sales with his wife and scores bargains that they hawk on eBay. At least they claim they sell them. Inventory seemed to be stacking up to the ceiling in all the rooms of their big, rambling house. They could open their own junk store right there. Joan might have been OK-looking once, but now she was scoring just a notch above the Gargoyle. Not actively scary yet, but showing tendencies in that direction.

We were the last to arrive. Already lounging on the patio were Tyler, Uma, Bergen (Tyler's German secretary), Uncle Jake, Aunt Lillian, my sister Miren, her husband Ryder, and all the rampaging cousins. None of the kids was allowed in the house for fear of breakage, so they were busy trampling the landscaping.

Tyler, resting his stump on a hassock and sipping a beer, told Bergen to get estimates for painting his mother's house. It needed it. The siding had weathered and paint was peeling off the window frames, reminding me of our house back in Terre Haute. (My ex-dad got many estimates, but always was too cheap to commit.)

I grabbed a Coke and dragged my brother off to look at Bill's workshop.

"OK, Scott," I said. "What's up with you and Azura?"

"It's looking bad, Nick. I've met someone."

"Who?"

"First promise me you won't say a word about this to anyone—especially Zee."

"Oh, OK. I promise."

"Brenda Blatt wanted to meet me. So I had drinks with her last week."

"What!? You're in love with Brenda!"

Truly, my mind was boggled.

"No, Nick, but she's really a great person. And very competent in her work. It's always good to network with talented people in this business."

"So who do you like?"

"Brenda invited a friend of hers along to meet me. A gal named Chloe Ptucha. We really hit it off."

"Chloe, huh? And how did Brenda come to know this person?"

"They're old school buddies. They went to some elite girls' academy up in Stockton."

"Damn, Scott. You're not in love. You've been hypnotized!"

"What?"

"Brenda told me all about this Chloe girl. She's a master at hypnosis. She used to pull all kinds of stunts on her enemies at that school."

"I haven't been hypnotized, Nick. Chloe is smart, gorgeous, and utterly captivating."

"Yeah, as in let me brainwash you, honey."

"Not true, Nick. Nothing like that is going on. I can assure you of that."

"Right, Scott. That's what I thought back when I was farting like a trained chicken and trying to rape Veeva. So are you going to break up with Azura?"

"I don't know what I'm going to do. But I want to get to know Chloe better."

"In the meantime, Scott, try calling Azura. It's not fair to leave her dangling."

"I know. I feel bad about that."

"And consult a deprogrammer, bro'. Before it's too late!"

Lunch was burgers grilled by Bill and big pans of rubbery macaroni and cheese. I managed to sit well away from Uma, who kept trying to engage me in conversation. Fortunately, Uncle Jake was always butting in, thus distracting her from my case. He may still be stuck on her, although I'd take Lillian in a heartbeat.

Scott gave Dad a biography of John Cassavetes, an actor who started making his own low-budget movies. I never heard of any of them, so they must have not been setting any box-office records.

My candy got passed around; only Bill and I sampled a piece. Despite their clamoring, the kids were strictly forbidden to touch it. I'm not sure what happened to the box. It didn't make it into the Town Car for the drive home. I wouldn't be surprised if it shows up on eBay tomorrow with two pieces missing.

MONDAY, June 22 – Summer is officially here, although you can't really tell the difference in Los Angeles. It's always pleasant here. And the air is mostly breathable where the affluent classes live.

Latest movie news: Mary told Dad they can't hire Sheeni as script supervisor. She said it was too important a job to "leave to amateurs." He was grumbling about this when he returned for Lefty's breakfast, having spent the night elsewhere.

"Were you at Mary's?" I asked, casually.

"I may have been," he replied.

I hate it when a parent tries to act mysterious. That is so inappropriate.

I managed to extract the name of the kid actor (presumably balling Tiara) who is up for my part: Denny Turnbull. I Googled him on my phone. He was that fat goofy kid from "Skateboard Park." Only Denny had been hitting the gym (and puberty) with favorable results. He had morphed into a muscular stud with wavy blond hair and smoke-blue bedroom eyes.

Cal at the coffee shop expressed the opinion that I didn't stand a chance against such a hunk.

"It was a nice dream while it lasted, Nick. Welcome to Hollywood heartbreak."

"Denny may not be what my dad is looking for. And I'd probably work cheaper too."

"No doubt. Did Tiara Zirconia get the part of Sheeni?"

"It's not clear yet. They're still talking to her agent. Shall we have another date on Friday?"

"So soon, Nick? Shouldn't dates be a special treat like Christmas or Halley's Comet?"

"Some people go out several times a week, Cal."

"They're called swingers, Nick. You're not one of them."

Nevertheless, she agreed to mull it over and get back to me. I asked what they did for Father's Day.

"Dad closed the store early, and we went to a fish fry at the V.F.W. lodge."

"Really? That sounds like something people do back in Indiana."

"All too true, Nick. Had they been serving steak, there might have been sharp knives at the table. I'd have slashed my wrists for sure."

"Did your dad like your card?"

"He was flabbergasted that I even bothered to get one. I told him it was your idea. He may be warming up to you, God help me."

"Is Harvey still in the doghouse?"

"He seemed to be. The turd sulked all through dinner. It was very gratifying to observe."

I told her about our excursion to Simi Valley and my brother cheating on Azura while possibly hypnotized.

"Let's Google her and find her photo, Nick. If she looks like Brenda, we'll know he's been tampered with."

"Good plan, Cal, except I've forgotten Chloe's last name. I only recall it sounds something like a sneeze. Could we get Esmee to undo the trance?"

"I doubt it, Nick. Usually they can only be reversed by the person who did it."

"My brother may dump Azura Preston for a girl who's seized control of his mind!"

"Relax, Nick. That's usually how it works anyway."

Hectic preparations back home for the shoot on Wednesday. I got introduced to the new DP (director of photography), a chubby guy named Roland Pacalac. He made the movie "Store Rage" a few years back that was a monster hit: all these people at a self-storage facility being offed in novel ways. Jayden and I used to debate endlessly whether a falling metal sign actually could decapitate someone. Brenda says he made that movie on a shoestring. It did so well a major studio shoveled tons of money at him for his next feature about racial strife in Cleveland. It was a total bomb, wrecking his career. Not even the ushers at theaters would watch it. U.S.C. Film School screened it for free as part of their Meet the Director series and nobody showed up. Now he's trying to make a comeback by working as cinematographer on indie productions.

Roland brushed donut crumbs off his grubby shirt and stuck out a paw. "Hi, Nick. I hear you may be our Rock Hudson to Tiara Diamond's Liz Taylor."

I shook his hand, which was even stickier than little Xenia's. "Yeah," I replied. "I guess I'm in the running."

"You need to grow a few oozing zits, Nick," he said. "Stop washing your face. Eat a couple dozen candy bars. Smear on a thick layer of lard as a cold cream at night. And beat off more or less continuously. Puberty is supposed to be a struggle, not a frolic in the park."

I certainly expect it was a struggle for him.

Brenda has found a trailer and a slab-sided 1963 Lincoln convertible, which is now being repainted white. Since both are going to be destroyed on Wednesday, she has to find duplicate vehicles for the other scenes. (Normally, the big destruction scene would be filmed last, but the schedule is reversed this time.) She also found a woman in Modesto who owns a 1950s two-story trailer. After its tires are replaced, it will be hauled 60 miles east to a RV park in the mountains where the trailer park scenes will be shot.

Brenda was busy making calls, but I managed to pull her aside for a private chat. I told her I didn't think it was right that her pal Chloe had hypnotized my brother.

"Didn't happen, Nick. I was right there and nothing amiss went on. Chloe doesn't have to hypnotize men, she's just naturally adorable. Hell, I almost signed up for Lesbianism 101 when I first met her."

"She couldn't be more attractive than Azura," I insisted.

"I tell you what, Nick. Next time she's free we'll all get together. You can judge for yourself."

"OK, but I'm not convinced. Scott couldn't have been swept off his feet this fast."

"Scott's a cute guy, Nick. I'm so addicted to 'Wildcatter.' He's so evil I could scream. If Chloe was fiddling with his brain, I'd have made sure he was falling for me, not her. When your brother slips a ring on my fat finger, that's when you should start getting suspicious."

"How do you spell her last name?"

"Ptucha. P-T-U-C-H-A."

I was right. I does sound like a sneeze.

TUESDAY, June 23 – Cal sipped her coffee and said it sounded more like the sliding movement of a bolt-action rifle.

"How do you know about that?" I asked.

"Desmond lent me some of his novels to read. Jack Stricker is always sliding cartridges into chambers. The imagery is very sexual, of course. But then, you wouldn't know about that."

"I know about sex, Cal."

"Uh-huh. I'm sure you've read all about it."

"The hard part of sex is getting any practical experience at it. I think it should be taught in school like gym. You'd get paired off and go at it. Then get graded on technique and number of orgasms achieved."

"Not happening in the good ol' Christian U.S.A., Nick. You should be burned at the stake for even suggesting it."

"You know how private my bedroom is, Cal. We could go there right now."

"No thanks. I'd prefer a swift prefrontal lobotomy to that."

Instead of sneaking back to my bedroom, we checked out Chloe's Facebook page. OK, she was not bad looking. Very blond and well packaged. I suppose she rated at least a 9.5. Right up there with Azura and Cal too.

"There goes your hypnotism theory, Nick. She's a beauty. And probably smart too."

"Why do you say that?"

"It says here she's a writer on that quiz show 'Beat a Genius.'"

"I never watch quiz shows."

"I'm sure you wouldn't watch this one. It caters to an audience of above-average intelligence. Each contestant is pitted against a panel of three brainy Ph.D.s in answering difficult questions on esoteric topics."

"I suppose you always shout out the answers first."

"Only 90 percent of the time. Harvey generally beats me on a few of them. I'm very weak on sports and geography."

"What was Mickey Mantle's lifetime batting average?"

"That would be .298 with 536 home runs, 2,415 hits, and 1,509 RBIs. I said I was weak, Nick, not hopeless."

When we parted, Cal said she was still making up her mind about our date on Friday. I told her I could do Saturday as an alternative. She said that was "totally out of the question."

Dad missed lunch, but returned with some major news. He decided that Denny Turnbull is too good-looking to play his younger self.

"There's no plot tension if a handsome guy is wooing a pretty girl," he reasoned. "Why should she resist him? Where's the suspense in that?"

"Uh, right, Dad."

If there's one thing I know about, it's rejection.

"So, Nick, we're going with you as Nick. You got the part, kid."

"Great, Dad. How much am I going to be paid?"

"You just had a big career breakthrough, Nick. You'll be starring in a major motion picture. And all you can think about is the money?"

"I appreciate the opportunity, Dad. I really do. But I've heard rumors that actors in movies get paid fairly well."

"Right–in some movies. You're getting SAG scale, of course. The payments will be deferred over several years to lessen your tax bite."

"You mean I have to pay taxes? But I'm a kid."

"You could be a tiny infant flogging baby food, and still the I.R.S. would be leaning over your crib to raid your wallet. You're also getting points."

"Great, Dad, but I'd rather have money."

"Points are money, kid. You're down for two percent of net profits. Don't worry, you're protected by the Coogan Act."

"What's that?"

"Jackie Coogan was this kid actor back in the silent movie era. He starred in 'The Kid' with Charlie Chaplin. Very cute kid that grew up to be a remarkably ugly man. That didn't stop Betty

Grable from marrying him. So he made a lot of movies and raked in millions. But when he turned 21, he discovered he was broke. His profligate parents had spent the whole wad. Fortunately, you don't have to worry. You're protected by that act. Your earnings will be going into a blind trust that even I can't touch."

All very promising, but I never did hear an actual dollar amount.

We were interrupted by a call from Ada. The appraiser has checked out their disputed art. The oil paintings are worth less than $1,000 each. The photographs are worth about as much as the frames they're displayed in. The watercolor could be a different story. It's a painting of a trolley rolling along a beach with a fisherman's shack in the distance. A label on the back reads: "Edward Hoffer, Charleston, 1929." The appraiser didn't think it had been matted professionally. He pried it out of the frame and discovered a signature along the bottom. The two Fs he said were in fact two Ps.

"Edward Hopper," said Dad. "Hey, haven't I heard of him?"

Ada said he was only one of the most famous American painters of the 20th Century. And he had been painting in Charleston, South Carolina in 1929. Comparatively few watercolors by him are known to exist.

"So what are we talking about?" asked Dad. "$5,000? $10,000?"

Apparently the appraiser felt it could go much higher than that. Perhaps as much as Jackie Coogan's missing bankroll. But it could also be a fake. He's recommending they send it to New York to have it examined by Hopper experts.

"That's very interesting," said Dad. "You know I bought that painting in Santa Fe years before I met you. Sorry, dear, it's not community property."

Loud expostulation on the phone by Ada. She remembered it as a wedding gift from her aunt Verna in Bridgeport.

More loud shouting by both parties and then he hung up.

"Damn," he said. "I could sell that painting and pay for most of my movie. I could tell my blood-sucking investors to drop dead. I'm sure I have a receipt for it somewhere."

"Where, Dad?" I asked.

"Probably in one of my filing cabinets. Which are now buried under tons of junk in my jam-packed storage locker."

"Wouldn't the gallery have a record of the sale?"

"It might, Nick. Assuming it's still in business. Assuming I could remember its name."

While he phoned his lawyer, I texted Cal that I got the part. She texted back: "Congrats. U must B bettr lookng than I thought." She added that our date was on for Friday.

Nothing like becoming a movie star to enhance one's appeal with the chicks.

WEDNESDAY, June 24 – Our big fire in Azusa made all the local TV news reports. It also snarled traffic on the 210 freeway, but Brenda says even a low-flying pigeon could do that. It was still dark outside when Dad dragged me out of bed. For some reason everyone has to get to movie locations at the crack of dawn. Our destination was clear across the traffic-clogged L.A. basin. Good thing Lefty was on the scene in Azusa serving coffee and snacks out of the back of his Jeep. Dad has added "movie set catering" to his job description.

The place was swarming with assistant directors, assistant cameramen, sound technicians, explosives experts, beefy guys hauling equipment out of a big truck, and a couple dozen firemen eager to see flames. Four rental cops were keeping curious Azusians at bay behind yellow caution tape strung around a two-block periphery. Bossy Roland was all over the place giving orders. At one point Dad had to take him aside and remind him who the director was. Mary was there with both daughters. Megan, the older one, was serving as apprentice script supervisor. Lauren, the metal-mouthed one, was overseeing the firemen's wives and kids, who had turned out to masquerade as "Berkeley pedestrians and shoppers."

I was nervously chewing my second donut when Scott showed up with three of his buddies. They had volunteered to drive the cars that will be dodging the runaway trailer and Lincoln.

"Big production, huh, Nick?" said Scott, pouring himself some coffee.

"I'm getting nervous," I replied. "I haven't read the script! I have no idea what I'm supposed to do!"

"Don't worry, Nick. I don't think you even have any dialogue today. It's all crashing cars and big explosions. You just have to look paralyzed with shock and fear."

That was a relief. No acting would be required for that.

Mary walked up, gave me a hug, and told me I was wanted in a motorhome parked nearby for "hair and wardrobe."

A friendly black gal named Felicity introduced herself and sat me down in a barber's chair.

"Your father has instructed me to give you a budget barber-college haircut, Nick," she said. "I hope you don't mind."

I told her it was OK. After she butchered my hair, she took photos of my head from all angles with her cellphone. She said it was so she could match the style and length in later shots. Then she applied a cheesy fake mustache to my upper lip and had me change into a t-shirt that read: I'M SINGLE, LET'S MINGLE. She said my pants were OK, but made me empty all my pockets. She took photos of my pants and shoes, and said I should be sure to wear them for all subsequent scenes that take place on that day in the script.

"Do people really notice things like that?" I asked.

"You'd be surprised, Nick. Quite a few people are making it their life's work."

I walked down the hill to inspect the doomed warehouse building, the front of which had been remade to look like three Berkeley storefronts. The center store was supposed to be a gourmet hotdog place called "Too Frank." It looked real from the outside, but inside you could see that it had been constructed of the thinnest materials. A network of ropes, fastened to hooks in the fake front, were connected to the bumper of a pickup truck. The truck would pull in the facade as the runaway trailer made impact. Lined up nearby were plastic barrels of a flammable gel that would feed the subsequent inferno. Wires taped to the barrels would trigger the igniters.

"Love your 'stache, Nick," said Brenda, giving me a hug. "I know you're going to do great."

"I hope so. I saw your friend Chloe's Facebook page. I guess maybe she's not hypnotizing my brother."

"Isn't she a doll? When they perfect DNA transplants, she's agreed to be my donor. I so want to be her twin! Oh, have you met Tiara?"

I turned around and my vision was enveloped in golden, radiant beauty.

"Hi, Nick," said a sweet voice that sounded like it was coming from a great distance. "I'm so looking forward to working with you."

I shook a cool, slender hand and stammered something.

"I'm not in today's scene, Nick, but I was too excited to miss it. I hope you don't mind."

"Uh, not at all. You, you don't look much like your photos."

"Nobody does, Nick. I hope you're not disappointed."

"Not at all!"

"If you've got a moment, we could grab some tea and get better acquainted."

"Uh, sure. OK."

She took my hand and led me uphill to Lefty's Jeep. I got yet another donut, and we retreated to a second parked motorhome. I sat on a gaucho couch and Tiara sat down right next to me. I noticed that up this close even her ears were endearingly lovely. She smelled like something rich and cinnamony baking in the oven.

"It's all turned out fine, Nick," she said, sipping her herbal tea. "They hired Denny to play Trent Preston."

"Is he your boyfriend?"

"No, just a friend. Since he lost all that weight, Denny's turned into something of a Lothario."

I made a mental note to look up that word later.

"Oh, is he?"

"I'm afraid so. I think your dad's a wonder, Nick. His script is so funny!"

"Is it? I haven't read it."

"You're in for a treat. My agent says this could be a breakthrough movie for us both."

"That would be, uh, terrific."

"I just have to get through it without falling in love with you. We're down for some fairly intimate scenes."

No wonder people became actors. It was all perfectly clear now!

I asked her if Tiara Diamond was her real name.

"Hardly, Nick. My mother cooked up that name when she started entering me in beauty contests at the age of four. You'd flee in horror if I told you my real name."

"Try me."

"OK, it's your funeral. Valdemara Vetugluin. Can you imagine that?"

I tried, but it totally didn't compute.

When she finished her tea, we went out to inspect the sacrificial Lincoln and trailer.

"Such a nice car," said Tiara. "What a shame. It survived all these decades, and now it's going to be wrecked."

"I bet you're a vegetarian," I said.

"How did you know?"

"Just a guess."

Then Trent Preston arrived with Sheeni Saunders. He was there representing his investment; she was there for what purpose–to bug Mary? I made the introductions.

Sheeni shook Tiara's hand. "So you'll be playing me? I can only wish I had been as lovely as you back then."

"I'm sure you were much prettier," said Tiara. "Wasn't she, Mr. Preston?"

"No gentleman could possibly answer such a question, Miss Diamond. Nick, what have they done to your hair?"

"Dad wanted a budget look. I guess he was too poor for decent haircuts back then."

"That's odd," said Sheeni. "He always had money for donuts. And condoms."

Finally, they were ready to shoot the first scene. Movies are shot out of sequence; we began in the middle of today's action. I was to stand outside of the Lincoln and try to keep it from rolling down hill. It really would be rolling, but there was a guy hidden on the floor of the front seat working the brake pedal.

"OK, Nick," said Dad. "Grab onto the car and kind of slide along with it. Try not to fall under it or get your foot run over. We can't afford to keep a medic on set. And remember to look panicked."

We shot about six takes of that. Not so hard. I did as instructed and looked really scared because I was. Roland was behind the camera and made a lot of suggestions, most of which Dad ignored.

Then I got excused while they shot cars dodging the runaway trailer, which was actually hitched to the Lincoln. (Roland framed the shots so you didn't see the car.) This went on until a catering van arrived with boxed lunches for everyone. I wanted to sit with Tiara, but the Gargoyle showed up and made me eat with her.

"I heard you embarrassed yourself trying to seduce my daughter," she said, inspecting her chicken-salad sandwich and bag of chips.

"It was just a misunderstanding, Mrs. Saunders."

"Call me Connie. Here's a hint, Nick: You Twisps are supposed to be entrancing the girls, not the other way around."

"Esmee has been punished by her parents and has promised not to do it again."

"A fairly worthless promise, if I know girls like her. And you're still hanging around with her co-conspirator."

"I had been, Connie. But I'm going to be busy making this movie."

"In which I have a sizeable investment. So no monkey business from you."

"Right."

"I see my former sister-in-law is gracing us with her presence. How unfortunate that France lost its allure. She's up to something."

"That seems to be the consensus."

"Naturally, I need to stay informed, Nick. Whatever Sheeni does, I need to hear about it from you. Capisce?"

"Totally."

"Good. And your brother Scott. What's he up to with Trent Preston's daughter?"

"They may be breaking up. He's fallen for a friend of Brenda's."

"He should tell me these things. I shouldn't be hearing about them second-hand. That goes double for you."

"You want to hear about my love life?" I asked, shocked.

"Of course. My assistance in these matters has been indispensable to you Twisps for generations. It is vital to the perpetuation of your clan. When he was your age, your brother used to have illicit liaisons at my house with his girlfriend."

"Azura?"

"No, Casey something. Very busty Italian girl. A relative of Tyler's wife as I recall."

"He never told me that."

"As a Twisp you should make it your business to know such things. So you like that Tiara girl?"

"Very much."

"I thought so. OK, I'll check her out for you. Now go see that wardrobe girl about getting your mustache back on straight."

After lunch I got to drive the Lincoln about 10 feet and then look on in horror as the trailer uncoupled from the hitch. Dad told me to imagine that I had seen my "favorite puppy" get run over. Instead, I imagined that Cal had just dumped me. We only needed three takes for that because my acting was so superb. I got a big thumbs up from Tiara after my third effort.

Then the demolition experts took over for the cataclysmic fire scene. Roland positioned four cameras around the street to record the action. Hooked to the back of the trailer was a long cable that extended down the hill to a powerful winch inside the building. The trailer appeared to be running free, but it was being pulled straight toward the building as our volunteer extras screamed and fled. (Carefully selected camera angles hid the cable from view.) Two seconds after the trailer impacted the building, explosions were triggered, while simultaneously a tech guy sent the Lincoln barreling down the hill via radio-controlled steering. More explosions were triggered when the car hit the flaming building. Then another charge ignited a trail of liquid fire that raced up the hill toward me. I stood there in the street doing my best impersonation of total disbelief and horror as Scott and his buddies–positioned off-camera–tossed blackened hotdogs and other "debris" at me. One-half second before I would have been burned to a crisp, Dad yelled, "Run!" I turned and ran like I was about to be immolated (which I was).

"Good job, Nick," called Dad. "I'm glad you waited for my signal."

"Right," I said, kicking off a shoe which I noticed was on fire.

After Roland recorded ten more minutes of flaming building, the Fire Chief blew his whistle and his crew turned on their fire hoses.

All in all, a very memorable start to my movie career.

THURSDAY, June 25 – Since Felicity had an ample stock of the custom t-shirts, I decided to wear mine to the coffee shop this morning.

"I'm single, let's mingle," said Cal, reading my shirt. "I don't get it."

"What don't you get?"

"What your being single has to do with anyone's desire to mingle with you. And what exactly do you mean by mingle?"

"It's a just t-shirt, Cal. Not a statement of philosophy. My dad used to wear one like this when he was my age."

"I think it's gross. I find it hard to believe that anyone like Sheeni would mingle with someone seen in that shirt."

"Well, it's incontrovertibly true that she did."

"I saw you on TV, Nick. You were sporting a bad haircut, missing a shoe, and holding hands with Tiara Diamond."

"No, Cal, she was holding my hand. I had just narrowly escaped a flaming death. She was comforting me."

"No doubt inspired by your shirt and manly mustache. So you like your new co-star?"

"She's OK. She says Denny Turnbull is a notorious Lothario. He's been signed to play Trent."

"So what is she like?" Cal persisted.

"Surprisingly nice," I admitted. "Not at all full of herself as you'd expect. She smells like cookies baking."

"Probably daubs vanilla behind her ears. The tease."

"No, it's more like cinnamon."

"She has got your number. That's clear to see."

I denied it, but not vociferously. I think it might be good for Cal to be aware that she now has some competition for my heart.

Interesting news when I got back. Dad said Roland's footage was "super great." He said we got a "big-budget Cinemascope look" at "Republic Studio prices." I guess that's good. He added that we're set to film a scene in a donut shop on Saturday.

"Shouldn't I read the script at some point?" I asked. "Or am I supposed to improvise the dialogue?"

"I'll give you those pages tomorrow, Nick. I don't like my actors to get stale and over-rehearsed. Besides, we're going to be busy today."

"Doing what?"

"Hunting down that missing receipt."

The storage place in Westchester was not unlike the facility in "Store Rage" where all those people met gruesome ends. We

didn't die, but got terminably bored sifting through Dad's decades of accumulated career detritus. Scott and Lefty did most of
the heavy lifting to clear a path to the filing cabinets stacked along
the back wall.

One highlight was when Scott uncovered a photo of Dad posing with Nancy and Ronald Reagan.

"Proof at last, Dad," said Scott, waving the photo. "You're a
Republican at heart!"

"They came to my show," Dad said, scrutinizing the photo.
"This was after he'd left the White House. Nancy was very complimentary; I'm not sure Ronnie knew what was going on."

"Did he ever?" asked Scott.

"He did quite well for a B-movie actor," said Dad. "Just goes
to show what you can do if you have a glib patter and a bunch
of wealthy white men behind you. There's another photo somewhere of me with George and Barbara Bush."

"Didn't you appeal to any Democrats?" asked Scott.

"Bill Clinton was supposed to attend once, but I think he got
lucky that night. The Secret Service called up and canceled.."

My stomach was rumbling when Sheeni Saunders arrived
with take-out burgers and fries. Also a couple bottles of her son's
pricey wine, some plastic cups, and a milkshake for the kid. They
all got pleasantly tipsy while I remained cold sober.

Sheeni wasn't much help in the search. She found a stash of
photo albums and spent hours slowing leafing through them. Lots
of photos of Dad with his arm around assorted babes. For a guy
who never looked much like Brad Pitt, he did OK in that department.

"This girlfriend of yours has extraordinary breasts," gasped
Sheeni. "They're quite enormous. Why didn't you marry her,
Nickie darling?"

Scott and I exchanged glances as if to say, "Nickie darling?
What was up with that?"

Dad checked out the photo.

"Good question," he replied. "If I think of her name, I'll give
her a call to see if she's still available."

Lefty was the one who found the receipt. It was from a gallery
in Santa Fe for $165.00. The picture was described as: "Old water-
color, framed. Winter scene in Taos."

"Fuck!" said Dad. "Ada was right. It must have been a goddam wedding gift!"

After dinner I got a friendly call from Tiara saying how much she was looking forward to working with me on Saturday. We didn't talk that long, but somehow an hour and 15 minutes ticked by on the clock. That girl's voice is like aural honey in your ear.

FRIDAY, June 26 – Scott phoned me early from L.A. Airport. He was on his way to Bozeman to spend the weekend with Azura.

"Are you going to break up with her?" I asked.

"I don't know, Nick. I'm just playing it by ear."

"You haven't known Chloe that long," I reminded him.

"I know, but I really like her."

"Are you sure you haven't been hypnotized?"

"I'm sure, Nick. I'm not as impressionable as you are. Where did Dad sleep last night?"

"I don't know. He was here when I went to bed."

"You've got to keep an eye on him, Nick. Sheeni might be trying to get her claws into him."

"Would that be so terrible?"

"I think so. That woman doesn't have a sincere bone in her body."

"She liked him well enough to have kids by him."

"Do we know that for sure? Do you think Miren looks like a Twisp?"

"It's hard to say. The only female Twisp I've met is Aunt Joanie. Miren sure doesn't look like her!"

"We don't know how much Trent Preston was still in the picture back then. From some angles, Miren looks to me a little like Zee."

"You think so? Wow."

Could my new family be shrinking already?

"And here's another thing, Nick. Sheeni was making a big play for Trent a few years back before he hooked up again with Apurva."

"So why is she after Dad now?"

"She's of that age, Nick. Her looks won't last forever. The clock is ticking. It's now or never for locking down another husband. If you ask me, the woman is looking for security."

Security and my dad? Could those two things ever possibly go together?

The good news is that five minutes later Dad shuffled solo out of the bathroom. I pestered him non-stop during breakfast for the script pages. Finally, he relented and handed me four precious pages of donut-shop dialogue.

"Don't over-prepare, Nick. It's not *Hamlet*, it's just a conversation about a mutt."

"Sure, OK."

I rehearsed the scene with Cal at the coffee place. Sheeni was trying to talk Nick into taking care of her dog, Albert, banished for chewing the family Bible. After two pages of flirtatious cajolery, he reluctantly agreed, but only if Sheeni would break up with Trent and consent to sleep with him.

"Your father drove a hard bargain," observed Cal.

"Is it so terrible wanting to sleep with the girl you love?" I asked, not at all rhetorically.

"It's not love at that age, Nick. It's vile, robotic lust."

"Why is it lust if he's still in love with her all these years later?"

"OK, you win. It's lust disguised as love. Shall we run through it again?"

"OK, but my dad doesn't want me to get over-rehearsed."

"I'm not sure that would be possible."

We rehearsed the scene four more times, emptying several nearby tables of customers.

"You're very good in the role of Sheeni," I said, as we were getting ready to leave.

"Thanks, Nick. You're semi-credible as a horny teenager."

"Are you looking forward to our date tonight?"

"I am. Just slightly more than a bad case of ebola."

I managed to plant the briefest of kisses on her lips anyway.

Connie Saunders (the Gargoyle) called me after lunch.

"I've been making inquiries into your Miss Vetugluin, a.k.a. Tiara Diamond."

"And what have you discovered?" I asked eagerly.

"She appears to be that curious anomaly: the neuroses-free actress. Nobody has a bad word to say about her. Indeed I might go so far as to say she is beloved by all who know her."

"That's promising, Connie."

"Is it? Do wish to meet the girl of your dreams at age 15?"

"Sure, why not?"

"It's too young! You will want to experience many other girls before you shackle yourself to one."

"There's something to be said for that, I suppose. But what if I fall in love with her?"

"Then your goose is cooked."

"It seems to me nature prepares us to fall in love at this age, but society makes it very hard for us to do anything about it."

"Yes, biology is out of step with civilization. That accounts for all the heartache in this world–not to mention the wars. Any Sheeni activities to report?"

"She's started addressing my dad as Nickie darling."

"Does he look incensed by that?"

"Not at all. The man is eating it up."

Later, Dad's soon-to-be-ex-wife phoned him. Ada said the painting had been rolled in a tube and is on its way to New York by private courier. In case the plane crashes, it's been insured for $1 million.

"I hope that's enough," said Dad. "I'm still looking for my receipt."

When he rang off, I asked him what that ploy was designed to accomplish.

"Just keeping her on her toes and my options open. Remember, Nick: Divorce is combat without the bullets."

Speaking of which, I decided to bite the bullet and pick up my date at her house. Mr. Haseltine answered my knock and did not slam the door in my face.

"Hello, Nick," he said. "We saw you on TV. So you're making a movie?"

"Yes, it's a comedy about my dad's awesome life."

"We'll be sure to see it," said an affable woman I took to be his wife. "Even if you do live in that monstrosity next door."

"Only as guests, Mrs. Haseltine," I assured her. "My dad dislikes the architecture as much as you do."

"It's so out of keeping with this historic neighborhood," she replied. "And it robs my garden of sunlight!"

"Er, right."

Then Cal arrived, followed by her repellent brother.

"Nick, you're so dreadfully punctual," she said, while behind her Harvey silently mouthed the words, "You're going to pay."

Pay for what? I fully expected to pay for the movie and the snacks afterwards.

We rode to Santa Monica in the back of Lefty's Jeep. Cal apologized for the existence of her parents. I said they seemed fine to me.

The movie (Cal's choice again) was a comedy (?) in Danish. Dialogue heavy with lots of subtitles to read. I didn't laugh once, but Cal said she thought it was "marvelously insightful." It certainly gave me the insight that I never want to live in Denmark.

As arranged previously with my absent chauffeur, we walked two blocks to a Japanese restaurant. Cal ordered a big bowl of chicken noodle soup. If I'd known she wanted that, we could have gone back to my place and opened a can of Campbell's. I had the salmon teriyaki, which the waiter assured me would arrive fully cooked. We were midway through the meal, when Cal dropped her mega H-bomb.

"Nick, you remember that enormous favor you owe me?" she asked.

"Right. My first-born son. Would you like to start practicing for his creation?"

"Definitely not. But I am ready to collect that favor."

"OK. What do you want?"

"I want the part of Sheeni in your dad's movie."

"What! You have to be kidding! That's impossible!"

"It's very much more than possible. You have your dad over a barrel. They have filmed the most expensive scene in his movie with you in it. They have to listen to you now."

"I doubt that, Cal. Dad likes Tiara. And she has lots of experience–unlike you."

"I'm not a complete neophyte, Nick. I've been going to acting class."

"Since when?"

"For nearly two years. That's where I go with Desmond. He's been underwriting my tuition."

"And why is he doing that?" I demanded.

"Because he's a nice guy. Because he thinks I have talent."

"And what do you do for him in return?"

"Virtually nothing worth mentioning. I brighten his dreary life. As I do for you."

"So who knows about these acting lessons?"

"Just Desmond. And now you."

"Why the big secret?"

"It's not done these days, Nick. Having aspirations is not cool. People with ambition get ridiculed. I saw no reason to blab it all over."

"Why didn't you say you were interested in the part before they signed Tiara?"

"I thought I did well in that screen test with you. I thought I impressed your dad. I thought he would follow up on it."

"My dad is pissed at you because of your hypnosis stunt with Esmee."

"I know. That was dumb. I did apologize to him for it."

"You sort of apologized. So how am I supposed to get him to give you the part?"

"Easy. You do really badly in the scene tomorrow with Tiara. You tell him you can't act with anyone playing Sheeni except me."

"Great! And how is Tiara going to feel about that?"

"She'll live. Actors are always getting replaced in movies. It's no big deal. It won't hurt her career."

"Right, except she'll never speak to me again!"

"It's the favor you owe me, Nick. That's what I want."

"But will your parents even let you act in a movie?"

"Leave my parents to me, Nick. I'll take care of them. You take care of your dad."

"Oh, shit. All right, Cal. You win. But I want something in return."

"What?"

"You agree to sleep with me. And stop treating me like I'm something disgusting on the bottom of your shoe."

"I don't treat you like that, Nick. I'm generally rather nice to you–for me. OK, we'll make a deal: I'll sleep with you when the movie is finished–assuming I get the part."

"Deal."

Kind of a wrenching development, but at least I now had the prospect of getting laid this summer. But it's likely this traumatic night has put me off Japanese food for good.

SATURDAY, June 27 – Brenda called Dad during breakfast and told him to look at his computer. A website called Hollywood-shovel.com ("Shoveling Prime Dirt on Major Players") was featuring a big expose on my video. Dad watched it and hit the ceiling. I've never seen him so angry.

"What the fuck did you think you were doing, you little shit?" he demanded.

"I was helping Cal with a school project. She said nobody would see it."

"Nobody except the whole damn world! So now everybody thinks I'm some sorry-ass has-been living with roaches."

"Sorry, Dad."

"You know what you did, kid? You damaged my brand. Image is everything in this town. There's a fine line between being a daring independent filmmaker and being a loser that nobody will hire. And you tossed me right over into that second category."

"I should have kept quiet, Dad. I can see that now."

"It's all the fault of that little bitch next door. What a schemer she is. I don't want you to see her again. I mean it, Nick. Not ever! You're done with that chick!"

Fuck! It was all Harvey's doing. Yes, he was making me pay. I should have strangled that foul toad when I had the chance.

In spite of Dad's major "don't exist" message, I didn't see any way I could avoid doing that favor for Cal. Getting her cast in the movie could be my only chance to see her again. And helping her become a major film star would be a good way to get back at her brother. But did I have the courage to disgrace myself in front of the entire film crew? And piss off Dad even more? And disappoint Tiara? Was this ugly predicament any better than sorting smelly socks back in Indiana? These questions were going through my mind as I rode in Dad's car to Brenda's favorite donut shop in Chatsworth.

"OK, Nick," sighed Dad, breaking the silence. "You'll have to put all this out of your head. We have a movie to make."

"Right, Dad. I'm really sorry."

"You were new in town, kid. You didn't know the ways of Hollywood. I'm sorry I yelled at you."

Good to hear, except I knew he'd probably be yelling at me again soon. I hoped his aging arteries could take the stress.

Our location was a building shaped like a giant donut. Suspended in the center of the donut hole was a circular sign: EL DORADO DONUTS. The sinuous letters radiated an ever-changing rainbow of colors. Amazingly, the sign appeared to be floating up there with no visible connection to the building. I asked Dad how they did that.

"Magnets," he replied.

"But how do they get the letters to light up? I don't see any wires."

"How should I know? Ask Brenda."

Brenda said the magic was accomplished by "electrical induction," whatever that it. She said their donuts were even more amazing than their sign.

"Oh, have you met my friend Chloe?" she asked.

I turned and Chloe Ptucha gave me a disarmingly warm hug. I had to admit she was quite beautiful and personable, but wondered if that was only an illusion. Had she seized control of my mind during our brief embrace?

"It's nice to meet you, Nick," she said. "I've heard a lot about you from Scott."

"Did he discuss me willingly, or did you put him in a trance to extract the information?"

She laughed. "You overestimate my powers, Nickie. Scott warned me about that. You should try one of these donuts. Brenda says they're the best in L.A."

Too stressed to eat, I skipped the donuts. My stomach felt like it could switch to barf mode at any time. Dad and Mary, I noticed, weren't having much to do with each other. I suspected a wedge had come between them, although that person was absent today. Since I would soon be stabbing Tiara in the back, I avoided her as much as possible and hung out with Chloe while the tech crew was setting up. I asked her how she liked her job.

"It's fun, but I'm looking around for something new. We have to concoct questions that are challenging for the contestants, but also interesting for the audience. I may soon exhaust my limited pool of knowledge. Scott thinks I should try acting."

"You could play my big sister in our movie," I suggested.

"Brenda says she's being written out of the script. Your aunt Joan got to Tyler and he put his foot down."

"His real one or his wooden one?" I asked.

"Oh, Nick, I can see you are one of those evil Twisps, just like Scott."

I wasn't feeling very evil. In fact I was beginning to wish Dad would write me out of the script too.

We did two run-throughs and three takes. Tiara was terrific, I was terrible. After the third take, Dad grabbed me by my shirt and dragged me into the back room by the donut fryer.

"OK, Nick, what the fuck's up with you?" he demanded, red-faced.

"I don't know, Dad. I was fine rehearsing the scene yesterday with Cal. I think she'd be great in the role of Sheeni. I found out she's been studying acting for years."

"Oh, so that's your game, is it? That little cock-tease has put you up to this. You think you have some leverage over me, but you're mistaken. I can make one call and get Denny Turnbull here in 10 minutes. And stick your butt on a bus back to Indiana."

"Please don't do that, Dad. I kind of promised her the part. Anyway, she says you can't replace me because it would be too expensive to reshoot that big fire."

"True, but I don't need to reshoot the whole fire. Just the three minor scenes you're in. I could do that in a couple hours with a skeleton crew."

Oops, there went my leverage; I decided on a different tack.

"Cal did great in my screen test, Dad. You have to admit that. She says Tiara is too sweet and too nice to play Sheeni. She says the camera never lies!"

Mary peeked in to ask what was causing the delay.

"Be there in a minute, Mary," said Dad. "I'm just strangling our star."

"Be patient with him, Nick," she cautioned. "Remember, it's his first time acting."

"Don't you worry, Mary. We're getting this all straightened out."

He waited until Mary left. "OK, dipshit, here's what we're going to do. You call that scheming girlfriend of yours and tell her to get her cute little ass over here. We'll shoot the scene again with Tiara. And then when she leaves, we'll try it with your girlfriend. And you'll do the best job you're capable of with both of them. No more sabotage. Is that clear?"

"Fine, Dad, but I'm not sure Cal has transportation. Can you send Lefty to pick her up?"

"All right," sighed Dad. "So call her. And make it snappy."

When I returned, Tiara smiled in sympathy and asked if I was OK.

"I'm fine. I was just getting some acting tips from my dad."

They must have worked, because I was much improved in the next two takes. I was even better after Tiara left and we tried the scene with Cal. By the third take we were really clicking.

"Where on earth did you come from, girl?" asked Roland, helping himself to yet another donut. "Until you showed up it felt like we were doing a remake of *Rebecca of Sunnybrook Farm.*"

"Do you have an agent, Miss Haseltine?" asked Dad.

"Not really, Mr. Twisp. But Desmond said I could use his."

"Yeah," sighed Dad. "He would."

SUNDAY, June 28 – I didn't sleep well last night. Too stressed. I flatly refused to get out of bed when Dad came up to drag me off to brunch at Tyler's. I hid under the covers until he gave up and left. Then I went back to sleep and snoozed through my usual time of meeting Cal for coffee. I was still in bed when Dad returned. By then I figured I had some momentum going, so I stayed put. Around three in the afternoon my phone rang, but I ignored it. It rang a few more times, so I switched it off. At 6:30 Lefty came up to ask me if I was sick. I said I was sick of the world and needed to be left alone. He asked me if I was hungry. I said no. After a while it started to get dark outside. No one was undressing in the window next door. I said the hell with it, and went back to bed.

MONDAY, June 29 – The world didn't seem quite so black this morning, so I got out of bed. At breakfast Dad asked me if I was feeling better. I said he could yell at me all he wanted, but I didn't need any more "don't exist" messages like threatening to send me back to Indiana. He apologized and said he could see my point. To make amends he said he would give me 10 percent of anything he makes off that painting. No big sacrifice, since it's probably a fake. He started to tell me what was happening with the movie, but I asked to eat my cornflakes in peace. Then I cut out and went to look at the ocean until it was time to meet Cal at the coffee shop.

She was late. I was on my second refill when she arrived.

"Did you hear the news?" she asked.

"You got the part?"

"Probably, if I can get my agent to behave. Your dad says if he gives him any trouble at all, he's sticking with Tiara. My brother, of course, is writhing in agony at my success. But that's not the news. Dailymail.com just broke a story claiming your brother has married Azura Preston."

I was skeptical. "How does an English newspaper know what's happening in Montana?"

"How else, Nick? They pay for scoops."

"Well, I hope it's true. I think she's great."

"Actors are always marrying actors, Nick. But it seldom works out. Too many ego clashes."

"Why do actors have such big egos?"

"Public adulation, Nick. It's a powerful drug that inflames one's perceived self-worth. The head swells artificially until no one on the planet can stand you—not even your agent."

"Well, it's not working for me. I'm acting in a movie and I couldn't even get out of bed yesterday. Too depressed."

"I wondered what happened to you. You weren't answering your phone either. I suppose you're tormented by the thought of never seeing Tiara Diamond again."

"Not at all, Cal. I'm just not sure all this wear and tear on my nerves is worth it."

"What you need, Nick, is a big thank-you kiss from your grateful co-star."

So she kissed me. This time with enthusiasm. She's right. After we unclinched, I did feel much better.

It's looking like my brother did get married. Dad was supposed to have a meeting with Brenda about Chevy Novas in living rooms, but she cancelled to be with her friend Chloe. Then he got calls from Ada and Trent asking what was up. Nobody's heard a word from the happy couple, and they're not answering their phones.

I got a scary call from Tiara Diamond asking if I knew anything about some other girl being considered for the part of Sheeni. I said I was too busy celebrating my brother's wedding to talk.

TUESDAY, June 30 – My mother phoned sometime far in advance of my natural waking hour.

"Hi, Mom," I yawned. "I hope this is important."

"I thought you should know, honey. I quit my job on the ship. I'm on my way back to Terre Haute."

"What! Why?"

"Oh, I'm kind of too old for that sort of work now. And Leonard did hire a lawyer. He was going to file some sort of motion with the court this week."

"That's awful, Mom."

"He's promising to change, Nick. So we'll see. I'm going to write a letter to your dad. I'm going to suggest that he adopt you. Leonard won't fight it if he wants me to stick around."

"I don't know if Dad would want to do that."

"Are you two not getting along?"

"We had a rough patch a few days ago, but things are better now. Do you really have to go back to Indiana, Mom?"

"I see no alternative, honey. But it's not so bad. I have lots of friends there."

"Can't you divorce him, Mom? My dad here is getting a divorce."

"I know. I read all about that. Is he taking it badly?"

"Not that I can see. He has a couple of girlfriends to distract him."

"That's Hollywood for you, I suppose. I saw your video. Did Nick object to it?"

"Not at all, Mom," I lied. "He was very supportive."

Then we entered the prolonged mushy part and I finally hung up. If I wasn't some ego-inflamed actor, I'd volunteer to go back to Indiana to be with my mother in her time of need.

Page two of the *L.A. Times* had an interview with a judge in Bozeman who claims he married the Twisp-Prestons late Sunday night at a gathering in the woods. All participants arrived in four-wheel-drive vehicles–their headlights illuminating the brief ceremony.

"Leave it to Scott to get married like Tarzan," observed Dad at the breakfast table. "It's all that bodybuilding and hanging out with those rednecks in Bakersfield."

"At least he picked a lovely girl," commented Lefty.

"We should get them a nice wedding gift," I suggested.

"Hah!" said Dad. "You want a gift? Invite me to your wedding! Or at least consult me first."

I'm not sure if Dad was really pissed, or if it was just a ploy to cheap out on a gift. In any case, I hit him up for $75.

"What's with the inflation, Nick?" he demanded. "Why am I not being extorted for your usual fifty?"

"Fifty bucks doesn't cut the mustard any more, Dad."

He sighed and handed over three twenties. "We're counting this as an advance on your film salary."

"An advance against what total amount?" I asked.

Dad looked at his watch. "We're late, Nick. We're due in Mar Vista to look at a house."

Mar Vista is a nearby neighborhood of modest houses just south of Santa Monica. We met Brenda and a realtor gal in front of a smallish bungalow with a FOR SALE sign posted in front. Though only two bedrooms and one bath in 900 square feet, the house's asking price was a lofty $679,000. Brenda was proposing to buy it herself (with the assistance of her rich granny) and rent it to Dad's film company. The floors would be braced from below, the side wall removed, and a giant forklift hired to insert an old Chevy Nova into the living room. When the shoot was over, the car would be extracted, the wall repaired, and Brenda would move in with her three cats. Dad said the street did remind him of his old Oakland neighborhood. The antsy realtor said they had about 10 minutes to make up their minds, because two offers had been received and more were expected–all well over the asking price.

While they were in the kitchen powwowing, my phone rang. Big shock. It was Scott, back in Bakersfield and not honeymooning with his new bride.

"I screwed up, Nick," he said. "Big time."

"How so?"

"I got carried away. Swept away in a wave of nostalgia for when I first met Zee. We were away from L.A. and all of our problems."

"You two have problems?"

"Yes, we do. So you know how the last step before breaking up is to get married?"

"I hadn't heard that."

"Well, it's true. So, that's what we did. Big mistake."

"You're breaking up?!"

"Yeah. I'm talking to a lawyer in 20 minutes about getting the marriage annulled."

"Don't you want to think it over first?"

"I've thought it over, Nick. Zee's totally great, but we're just not right for each other. You can't base a marriage on guzzling two bottles of wine, feeling nostalgic, and really digging the scenery of Montana. So can you give Dad the word?"

"You want to talk to him? He's right here."

"He's the last guy I want to talk to right now. Chloe's coming up tonight, and we're going to disappear for a few days. If you see Trent Preston, tell him your brother is sorry for being a jerk."

Wow, my brother had one of those Hollywood 19-hour marriages. I hope Cal and I can rack up more hours of connubial bliss than that.

I gave Dad the news on the ride to the real-estate office.

"Hmmph," he snorted. "I knew it would never work out with those two."

"Why's that?" I asked. "They lived together in apparent harmony all those years."

"Scott was always Azura's second choice, Nick. The guy she really loves is Sheeni's son François."

Leave it to that woman to mess up yet another Twisp.

JULY

WEDNESDAY, July 1 – Lots of news: The Scott-Azura debacle is all over the media. A Republican Senator from Oklahoma singled them out on Fox News as what is wrong with America. Trent Preston issued a statement saying they were "two nice young people" who "made a mistake." Dad had been fielding calls from reporters, but had to stop since they all wanted to ask about his "career setbacks" and "roach-filled" apartment. Looks like I made the "strictly private" video that will never die. Shouldn't I be getting royalties from all those views it's racking up? Hostile Ada dropped by to say she's attributing her son's marital disaster to his father setting a "consistently bad example." Dad replied that the last time he checked "divorce was a two-way street." I called Azura twice, but I guess she's not answering her phone.

Cal is now set as Sheeni, and Tiara has been retained as young Lefty's girlfriend Millie Filbert. Since Dad had to cut out the parts about his sister, he's been able to beef up the Lefty-Millie romance, which apparently was semi-sizzling despite Lefty's penile handicap (erect yes, straight no).

The house-sellers were big Nick Twisp fans, so they accepted Brenda's offer even though another offer topped it. Dad had to put it in writing on the sales agreement that they will be invited to the film premiere. Escrow has been accelerated wildly so Mary's carpenters can go to work chopping out the wall. Meanwhile, Brenda is scouring Craigslist and eBay for suitable Chevys and another Lincoln convertible. Dad wants her to find an especially cherry example of the latter, which he intends to keep. He's already reserved the license plate TWISPAN for it. I asked him if I'll get to drive the flashy convertible when I get my license. He said only if he developed "severe early-onset Alzheimer's." I'm keeping my fingers crossed that he goes downhill fast.

Since a rapprochement has been reached with the neighbors,

Cal came over after lunch to hang by our pool. She was searing the eyes (and my nervous system) in a torrid red bikini. Severely overstimulated, I had to sit hunched over most of the time. She swam about 57 laps in the pool, then got out and toweled off. She checked out my largely unclad body.

"You look like you were just liberated from a camp by General Patton's army," she commented.

"It's that Twisp DNA, Cal. We don't get tall and we don't bulk up."

"What do you do with all the calories you consume?"

"It all goes into mental development."

"Achieving a mental age of what now–12? Oh, did I tell you? I got an email from Denny Turnbull, my handsome co-star. He says he's extremely anxious to meet me."

"That guy is only interested in one thing."

"And I suppose you're not? Why are you all scrunched up in that unnatural posture? Come here and give me a kiss."

"Uh, I'd rather not at the moment, if you don't mind."

I was rescued by Harvey, who came sauntering out in his backyard.

"There's my poor, ostracized brother," said Cal loudly. "If he weren't so loathsome, he might be invited over for a refreshing swim."

"I put your video back on YouTube, Nick," he called. "And sent a link to all the gossip websites."

"I don't care, Harvey," I replied. "The damage has been done. It's so yesterday's news now. Everyone's moved on to my brother's marriage bust-up."

"If you come over here, Nick, I'll pick you up bodily and slam you into that prickly rose bush."

"If you come over here, Harvey, I'll bash your head against the concrete rim of the pool and hold it under water for a full 10 hours."

"Idiot! I'd drown in a couple of minutes."

"True, but with you I'd want to error on the side of caution."

"Before you made your first clumsy grab for me, Nick, I'd have you unconscious at the bottom of the pool."

"Not likely, old sport. Before that I'd have squirted sunblock in your eyes, and you'd be stumbling blindly into your dad's cactus patch."

"I sure hope that's not a boner you've got there, Nick," he taunted.

I glanced down. Damn, didn't thoughts of extreme violence override sexual stimuli? Apparently not in my brain.

"It's not a boner," said Cal, coming to my defense. "He's just extraordinarily well hung."

"I doubt that," said Harvey. "The dude is a shrimp in all departments–especially mentally."

The first time a girl ever referred to my private parts. How unfortunate that her statement so missed the mark. (Alas, I'm seldom the target of envious glances in locker rooms.) Still, I suppose we've broken the ice somewhat in that department.

THURSDAY, July 2 – First meeting of the entire cast. Not in a movie studio rehearsal room as you might expect. It was standing room only in our cramped living room (Dad shoved Lefty's stuff over in a corner). I met Estelle Twisp (my movie mother), an elderly gal cast as Mrs. Clarkelson (who it is rumored I will be showering with bare-ass naked), Sheeni's mom and pop (to be played by Trent Preston in *both* roles), a kid named Arvin playing Lefty, and the very-full-of-himself Denny Turnbull, playing the young and obnoxious Trent. The actor chosen to play beefy cop Lance Wescott got a better offer, so Lefty has been drafted for that part. Our chubby cameraman Roland will be playing Estelle's redneck trucker boyfriend Jerry. And the part of Mr. Ferguson, the neighbor, has been changed to Mrs. Ferguson, so Sheeni Saunders can make her acting debut. Last but not least, Cal and Tiara were successfully brought together without name-calling or hair-pulling, though a definite chill was observed.

Mary distributed copies of the script and shooting schedule. The last scene absolutely has to be in the can by August 15, when school starts for some cast members. (Truly a nightmarish thought.)

Dad felt the need to establish his directorial dominance. "OK, listen up, everyone," he called. "We've got a lot to do in not much time. So I need everyone to put your personal lives on hold until further notice. When we call for you, we need you there and prepared. Everyone on set will be addressed by your character's name. That's how I always run my shows. I suggest you do the same in conversing among yourselves. I'll be keeping rehearsals to a minimum. I like my actors to be fresh, willing to take direction, and letter-perfect on my scripted dialogue. Save your ad-libs for acting class. Any questions?"

Cal raised her hand. "Is the title really going to be 'Nick Twisp's Mayhem for Love?'"

Dad shrugged. "It's the best we've come up with so far."

She proposed an alternative: "Since the movie is about a rebellious youth, why not call it 'Youth in Rebellion?'"

Mary smiled. "I rather like that, Nick."

"It does have a certain je ne sais quoi," added Sheeni.

"OK, we'll add it to the list," he said without much enthusiasm.

Dad probably doesn't want *my* girlfriend naming *his* movie.

Denny Turnbull raised his odious hand. "I just want to say what a thrill it is for me to be cast in a film with the legendary Trent Preston. To play him as a young man is an honor I truly never expected."

I can certainly see why. What a brown-nosing, ass-kissing suck-up he is. And his golden tan looked as fake as the blond dye job on his hair.

Seven minutes later he had asked Cal for a date and been accepted for Saturday night. After the meeting ended and everyone left, I asked her why she agreed to go out with him.

"I did it for you, Nickie dear."

"Really? And how do you figure that, Cal?"

"You must call me Sheeni now. You'll recall that in the film you're supposed to be antagonistic toward Trent. My accepting Denny's invitation will assist you in preparing for that. It's called method acting."

"But I already was extremely antagonistic anyway."

"Well, this should help even more. Who knows? If I sleep with him, you might be so overwrought as to win the Oscar for Best Actor."

"More likely I'd be in jail charged with homicide."

"Keep those feelings bubbling, Nickie. Such intensity can really come across on camera."

FRIDAY, July 3 – I finally got to read Dad's script. It's funny I guess, but I don't know about the ending. Sheeni leaves him in the lurch. Of course, she did that in real life, but will audiences accept it? Seems like kind of a downer ending for a comedy. I think movies succeed when audiences can identify with the main character. But who wants to identify with getting abandoned by your love? I'd be totally bummed if Cal left me. This date of hers tomorrow with Denny is going to be very hard to swallow. I'm trying my best to blot it out of my mind.

Cal wasn't available for coffee this morning. Mary said Dad's "come as you are" wardrobe policy is acceptable for most of the characters, but she took Cal and Tiara out shopping for appropriate movie attire. Should be an interesting experience for all four of them, considering that Sheeni invited herself along too.

Stumped by Dad's love life, I phoned Mary's daughter Lauren to see if she knew what was up.

"Your dad is being a dick, Nick," she said.

"How so?"

"He's not telling my mom anything about what's going on. He says he likes her, but he's not sleeping over. Meanwhile, he's flirting non-stop with that French tart. Is he screwing her?"

"I don't know. I don't think so. He's been sleeping here most nights."

"You Twisps are all such bad news."

"Why's that?"

"Your brother dumped Azura Preston. And I've been waiting forever for you to ask me out."

"Uh, I'm kind of going with Cal Haseltine."

"That girl is going to break your balls, Nick. And probably your heart too. She's not to be trusted. You'd be better off with Tiara Diamond–or me."

"Thanks for the suggestion, Lauren. Let's keep in touch. Call me if my dad spends the night there."

"OK, Nick. And call me if the rat is fucking you know who."

Wow, Lauren likes me. Too bad I'm not a heavy metal fan. She did offer one good idea though. I dialed Tiara's cellphone. She answered sounding politely cool. I asked her what she was doing.

"I'm watching your pal Valerie try on an expensive tennis outfit. Is there a tennis scene in the movie?"

"Uh, not that I recall. How are Mary and Sheeni getting along?"

"Like America and Russia during the Cold War."

"I'm sorry you lost the part of Sheeni, Tiara."

"That's odd, since I heard you played a big part in it."

"Millie Filbert is still an important role."

"She has four scenes. Sheeni's in five times as many."

"Uh, right, but they're major scenes. And funny too."

"If you say so, Nick."

"Uhmm, I was thinking. Why don't we go out tomorrow night? I mean, if you're free."

"Right. You want to go out with me because Valerie has a date with Denny."

"Oh. You heard about that, huh?"

"So what time do you want to pick me up?"

"Great. Say seven o'clock?"

"Fine, Nick. See you then. I'm sure your dad has my address."

Tiara didn't sound exactly eager, but she did say yes. I'm going out with her to assist Cal in preparing for her movie role. It's the least I can do.

Later I phoned Cal to ask her how much they were paying her to be in the movie.

"My agent instructed me not to discuss that, Nick. He said such talk can sow dissension among the cast."

"Are you making more than $50,000?"

"Why? Are you?"

"I don't know how much I'm making, Cal. My dad hasn't said. I think I should make at least as much as you."

"Why? The whole film revolves around me, Nick. If I'm not credible as someone you could fall madly in love with, there goes your story."

"But I'm the central character, Cal. It's the story of my life!"

"Not really. It's just a few months in the life of your father. Face it, Nick. You're just the cipher being acted upon by events."

"Hardly that, Cal. Not when I adopt the dangerous persona of François Dillinger."

"Oh, right. I suppose that's true. What we need around here is less Nick Davidson and more François Dillinger."

She's right. It wouldn't kill me to start being more rebellious. I am a Twisp after all.

Speaking of which, I was going to tell her about my hot date with Tiara, but she rang off before I could bring up the topic.

SATURDAY, July 4 – Independence Day holiday. Kind of a big deal in Terre Haute, but L.A. seems much more blasé about it. Not many Revolutionary War battles in this area I guess. Fireworks are scheduled at the Santa Monica pier, but Tiara lives in distant Encino. Lefty's agreed to drive me, but says I should sleep over and take the bus back. In my dreams I'd ever get to do something like that.

I wasn't sure Cal would show for coffee, but she did. Too bad she dragged Esmee along. That girl is no longer grounded. I sat well away from her, ready at all times to deflect any grabs for my neck.

"Everybody has a hot date tonight except me," she whined.

"How did you hear about my date?" I asked.

"We all know about your tiresome date with Tiara, Nick," said Cal. "She was broadcasting it widely yesterday. She only said yes because Mary spent six times more on me than her. That girl has the worst taste in clothes."

"Don't let her kid you, Nick," said Esmee. "Cal's totally annoyed that you're going out with her. And I'm very impressed. I guess you're not the hopeless loser I thought you were."

"Esmee," said Cal, "please don't insult Nick. That's my job. Give me a kiss, Nickie."

I didn't feel much like it, but I leaned over and planted one on her welcoming lips.

"Esmee, I thought you liked Harvey," I said.

"Confidentially, I do, Nick, but he hates me because I'm BFF with his sister."

"He's working at the store today," I pointed out. "You could go there alone and work your magic on him."

"I can't, Nick. I promised my dad I'd drop that habit."

"But you'd be doing Harvey a favor," I said. "He's such a sourpuss. He might be a whole different dude if he had a girlfriend: a much nicer and happier guy."

"He's like totally hot," she said. "I have to admit that. But what if my dad finds out?"

"Why should he find out? You're an attractive girl. Why shouldn't you have a boyfriend without being suspected of playing tricks on him?"

"What do you think, Cal?" asked Esmee.

"I wouldn't wish my brother on Attila the Hun's ugliest sister, but go for it if you want. It might be a way to get him out of your system once and for all."

Remembering to address her as Sheeni, I kissed Cal again when we parted at the café.

"Don't do anything tonight, Sheeni dear, that I wouldn't do."

"God knows that's not excluding much," she replied. "And, Nickie, try not to have too much fun in Encino."

Can it be that she's just a tiny bit jealous?

This afternoon Veeva and Desmond hosted a holiday barbe-cue in our shared yard. Dad brought drinks. Lefty brought his famous fruity trifle (OK, but why not just bake a chocolate cake?). And I brought my sullen attitude.

Both Sheeni and the Gargoyle were there and making a point of ignoring each other. They used to be sisters-in-law, but seem not to have bonded. Scott was invited, but to everyone's surprise he actually showed up. He also brought a date: Chloe Ptucha, keeping her head down and trying not to look like a home wreck-er. Naturally, everyone felt the need to kid my brother about his momentary marriage. He took it like a man and said he hoped to do better "the next time."

Dad informed Scott that he has been drafted to play Paul Saunders, Sheeni's stoner older brother. Scott was agreeable if Chloe could play Lacey, the sexy hairdresser Paul wins away from Nick's dad.

"What do you know about acting, Miss Ptucha?" Dad asked.

"I know it's a lot harder than it looks, Mr. Twisp."

"Well, that's a start," said Dad. "I'll have you two read a scene later."

I asked Scott what he was planning to do about his apart-ment.

"I'm putting all my stuff in storage, Nick. I rented the locker next to Dad's. I'll be staying on weekends at Chloe's."

Lucky guy. Why couldn't I move in with my girlfriend too?

While Desmond was grilling the steaks, I asked his wife if she had known about his underwriting their neighbor's acting stud-ies.

"What can I say, Nick? The man is full of surprises."

"She's total jail bait, you know," I pointed out.

"He claims nothing is going on between them. I'm inclined to hope he wouldn't be that stupid. Can I rely on you to report any suspicious activities?"

"Of course. I think both of them should be kept on very short leashes."

"Good point, Nick, but I work long hours at my job. He's unsupervised most of the time."

"You could hire a private detective."

"No need, Nick. I've assigned the Gargoyle to his case."

Across the way Sheeni was leaning against my dad and rubbing his back with her hand.

"She's getting awfully touchy-feely," I observed.

"You may want to be nice to her, Nick. One of these days my aunt could be your new stepmother."

Could Dad want to trade free dental care for bonus French lessons? Not a swap I'd make.

My busy dating life: For being a semi-famous actress Tiara resides in a fairly modest ranch house. Her bedroom was no bigger than mine back in Terre Haute. (I got the brief tour of that room, not the extended stay.) Tiara said she had seen "all the current decent movies," so we went to an upscale mall in Sherman Oaks to "hang out." While we walked around and checked out the stores, Lefty took in a movie.

First we looked at a zillion shoes, then lipsticks, then purses. My date wasn't saying much, except to ask my opinion on these items–as if I had any. I told her that mall lighting, signage, snack-bar odors, background music, and pushy clerks tended to trigger a fight-or-flight response in me.

"You'll have to get over that, Nick. Malls are today's downtown, today's village green."

"I know. We have them in Indiana too. Are you going to buy that purse?"

"I don't know. What do you think?"

"Buy it, if you like it."

"Your friend Valerie would probably go for this. I can't say much for that girl's taste."

"That's odd. She said the same thing about you."

"Well, that's no surprise. But I suppose you still like her."

"I like you both," I said, trying to be diplomatic.

"I think Denny Turnbull is more her speed. I'm not surprised those two are hooking up."

I told her about Cal's selfless decision to go out with Denny to further my acting career.

"I suppose some people might believe that," she said, replacing the purse on the shelf.

Several of our fellow mallites recognized Tiara and asked for her autograph. She made me sign too, introducing me as the "upcoming film star Nick Davidson." Her fans looked me over doubtfully and did not appear pleased that some unknown wannabe had trespassed on their autograph pages.

Tiara glanced at my signature and said I should try to come up with one "a bit more distinguished." She signs "Tiara" boldly inside a diamond, then draws marks around it to suggest glittering radiance.

Still a vegetarian, Tiara nixed all the mall restaurants except Chipotle. We ordered and grabbed a table in the most remote corner. I asked her if she had a boyfriend. She said most boys found it intimidating to be with girls they'd seen on TV. Or they were only interested in her for the same reason.

"That's why acting is the lonely profession, Nick. It separates us from the rest of humanity. So we have to hang out with each other—until our egos clash and we wind up single and alone."

"So why be an actor, Millie, if it's like that?"

"Of all the girls' names in the world, Nick, you should know I hate Millie the most. It's so insipid!"

"Is Sheeni any better?"

"Only marginally," she conceded. "To answer your question, we act because that's what we do. We have a need to perform. We crave the applause. And the fame."

"I don't think I need any of that, Millie. I'm just doing it for the money."

"You say that now, Nick, but you'll change. After the movie comes out and you're in the spotlight, you'll be just like the rest of us. Hungry for more."

Sitting there chatting with her I could see how I might get hungry for more of her too. She was quite the beauty, and her perfume pushed all of my deepest buttons.

SUNDAY, July 5 – No Tyler brunch today; he's at his training camp in Oxnard whipping his football team into shape.

Dad at breakfast said that Mary was starting to think about publicity for the movie. He asked me how I wanted to be billed.

"You mean I have to pay for my own publicity?" I asked, aghast.

"No, kid. How do you want to be listed in the credits? What name do you want to use?"

"Oh, I see what you mean. I could change my name like John Wayne and Joan Crawford and Tom Hanks and those other movie stars."

"Actually, I think Tom's using his real name."

I thought it over. I liked the name Errol Flynn, but somebody had beaten me to it. "I guess Nick Davidson is OK," I said.

"Really? And what did Leonard Davidson ever do for you?"

Not much, that was for sure.

"He bought me my first tricycle. He got it at a yard sale for $2. It broke the first time I rode it."

"The skunk sounds like my dad. So here's another idea: you could be listed as Twisp. It's a respected name in Hollywood, despite your brother's efforts to be flayed alive in every tabloid."

"I don't know, Dad. Nick Twisp Junior isn't really cutting it for me. No offense."

"OK. So how about Nick Twisp II? That's classier."

I thought of the ugly car my mother drove for years: a Mustang II. No way was that runty compact a classy effort. But I could see he wanted me to sign on with the Twisps. I could join Uncle Jake, who had started out in life an inoffensive Wescott, but had made the leap to Twisp.

"OK, Dad. Nick Twisp II it is," I said, trying to sound enthusiastic.

I guess if you're stuck with the DNA, you might as well have the ludicrous name too.

Esmee was at the coffee place again this morning, but this time she was sitting several tables away with Harvey Haseltine.

I scowled at him and said, "Come over here, Harvey, and I'll throw my napkin over your nose and waterboard you with my scalding hot coffee."

He looked at me greatly shocked. "Why would you say such

a thing, Nick?" he demanded. "We've been best pals since kinder-garten!"

Cal sipped her coffee and said, "Esmee had to do some mental housekeeping after she and my brother decided to go steady."

"Just kidding, old chum," I called to Harvey. "How about buying me a muffin?"

"Sure thing, Nick," he replied. "What flavor?"

"Anything but banana. Thanks."

He bustled off to procure my treat.

"You'll be happy to know he's taken your video off YouTube again," said Cal.

"Good, Sheeni. I hope this infatuation lasts."

"I expect it will last longer than yours with Tiara. Or should I call her Millie? How was your so-called date?"

"Excellent. We went to a fancy mall and had organic vegetarian burritos. How was your ordeal with Denny?"

"You mean Trent? Fabulous. You'll be happy to know he's a much better kisser than you are."

Not great news. That guy works fast. It took me weeks to beg that first grudging kiss off her.

"I expect he's had more practice than me. I understand he begins every day with a prolonged make-out session with his bedroom mirror."

Harvey returned with my muffin.

"Oops," I said. "I can't do blueberry, Harv. Can you exchange it for something else?"

"Gladly," he said, traipsing off.

"Don't monopolize my man," warned Esmee. "Or I may have to amend his programming."

"Sorry," I replied. "I'm just so enchanted with the new and improved Harvey."

"He's the greatest," she agreed. "Now he has a winning personality to complement his good looks."

"We should have done that to Nick while we had the chance," said Cal. "Not that we could do much about his looks. Speaking of all things superficial, did you get a goodnight kiss from your date?"

"Certainly," I lied. "Several in fact."

"I suppose you felt her up as well?"

"Had the bra clean off and most of her underwear too."

"You are such a liar, Nick."

Harvey returned with an apricot-pecan scone. "Will this do, Nick?" he asked.

"Splendidly, old man. I owe you one."

"That's OK, Nick," he smiled. "Anything for a friend."

On the walk home I told Cal I was ditching the name Davidson.

"Was that your name, Nick? I'd forgotten."

"Now it's Twisp. Nick Twisp II."

"Well, that should make you stand out on Google, if not in life."

"Valerie Twisp wouldn't be such a bad name either," I ventured.

"Right. That might be a good one to lay on your mythical first-born son."

"That's not who I was thinking of laying it on."

"Oh? Are you thinking of getting a cat?"

Having at least planted the idea in her mind, I decided to drop the subject.

Like most Sundays on this planet the rest of the day was gruelingly boring. We went to Uncle Jake's house for dinner. Dad's special invited guest: Ms. Sheeni Saunders. All the adults raved about the wine she brought. Guess that's her strategy for winning the hearts and minds of Dad's relations. Meanwhile, she doesn't have much to say to me.

11:47 p.m. Ominous development: Dad left to take Sheeni back to her condo and has not returned.

MONDAY, July 6 – Early a.m. call from Ada. I had to confess that her soon-to-be-ex-husband was not on the premises.

"Do you know where he is?" she asked. "He's not answering his phone."

"He was last seen in the vicinity of Sheeni Saunders."

"Your dad was always blind to that woman's faults," she sighed.

"Shall I give him a message?"

"Tell him to call me when he has a moment. I have some news about the painting."

"Good news?" I asked, thinking of my alleged 10 percent.

"We'll have to see. Just have him call me."

Dad zoomed in a few minutes later. "We gotta go, Nick! We were due in Griffith Park 40 minutes ago!"

"I was ready, Dad. Where were you?"

"Uh, I was delayed at Sheeni's. Let's go!"

Probably the only thing delayed there was her orgasm.

He called Ada on the drive to the park. She reported that the experts have examined the painting. They tested the paint and the paper. Both are consistent with what Hopper was using in 1929. The signature appears genuine and the style is very similar to his other paintings of the period.

"What are you saying?" Dad asked. "That we hit the jackpot?"

Dad let out a blood-curdling yelp and nearly ran into a guard-rail. Apparently her reply was in the affirmative.

The experts' estimate of a likely auction price: $2-3 million, but "anything was possible."

I did a quick calculation using the low figure: 10 percent of half of $2 million = $100,000. A nice cash reserve for upgrading those dates with Cal (and Tiara).

As we were driving into the park Dad told me to keep the news about the painting "under your hat." Also, I wasn't to mention where he spent the night.

"So whom do you like, Dad?" I asked. "Sheeni or Mary?"

"I like both of them. A fellow my age is entitled to like two women, Nick."

Right. Especially if you're a Mormon, which he is not.

"OK, but you're pissing off one of them. Mary is wondering what's up with you."

"How do you know that?"

"I talked to her daughter."

"Right. You would. All this dating business was easier before everyone had spying kids."

"If you're planning to be with Sheeni, Dad, you should let Mary know."

"I can't, kid. She's too important to my movie."

I didn't say anything.

"I suppose you think I'm acting like a heel?" he said.

"No, I was thinking more like a dog."

We drove down a side road to a clearing where several vehicles were parked. Roland and Brenda were sitting on the tailgate of his SUV and snacking from an El Dorado Donuts bag.

"Bad traffic," lied Dad, hurrying up to them. "Is everyone ready?"

"We've been ready," said Roland, licking his fingers. "Nice of you to show up."

No rented motorhomes or big equipment trucks at the shoot today. It was to be a quick "run and gun" effort. That's because L.A. requires a permit to shoot in a park, and Dad was too cheap to buy one. Felicity had done her hair and makeup thing already on Tiara and Arvin, the guy playing Lefty. She worked on me while Dad and Roland conferred on camera angles and Eddie the sound tech taped a wireless mike under my shirt. He slid the thin transmitter into my back pocket.

No time for a rehearsal. As the camera rolled, Tiara and Arvin spread a blanket in a small clearing while up the hill I crouched behind some bushes. Then they sat down and drank Lefty's shoplifted champagne out of paper cups. They spoke a couple lines of dialogue, put down their cups, lay back, and started some serious necking. All the while, I was spying on them.

"Cut!" yelled Dad. "Cut! Lefty, what's with the damn boner? I can't have a boner in my movie! I'm going for a PG rating!"

Arvin removed a sweaty palm from Tiara's left breast. "Hey, you try kissing this chick and not getting excited," he said.

"Well, go off in the woods and deal with it. And make it snappy!"

Red-faced, Arvin slunk off to retire behind a tree and deal with his bulge. I don't know about him, but it would probably take me two or three manual sessions to remain sufficiently inert to shoot that scene with Tiara, who I noticed was not wearing a bra.

"How did I do, Nick?" she asked, straightening her shirt.

"You were great, Millie. Did you mind him pawing you like that?"

"No, he's supposed to. Apparently, in real life Lefty and Millie had stripped off everything. They were quite nude. I'm thankful I get to keep most of my clothes on."

Damn that ratings board! Too bad Dad wasn't going for an R rating–with me playing Lefty.

Eventually, Lefty returned looking wan and action resumed.

Roland filmed the make-out activity up close and also back at my location (a POV shot). Then it was my turn to get in on the action.

"OK, Nick," said Dad. "Now we need you to fall head-first over that bush."

I considered the bush. It was large, looked prickly, and the rocky ground fell away steeply beyond it.

"Uh, Dad, shouldn't a stuntman take over here?"

"We're doing our own stunts in this movie. Just fall forward. I'll be down below to break your fall. And give out a yell while you're falling. Don't worry, I did the same thing when I was a kid and I was fine. Except I tumbled all the way down the hill, through a big patch of poison oak."

I thought of the money (large piles of neatly stacked $100 bills), counted silently to three, then leaped forward. Yes, the bush was painfully prickly. And I accumulated considerable speed before I impacted the hard ground. And cowardly Dad dodged away at the last minute. Stunned, I gasped for breath as I felt something trickling into my eye.

"Good work, Nick," said Dad. "The blood is a nice touch."

Roland reviewed the monitor as I struggled to draw a breath. The wind had been knocked out of me.

"Looks good," he said, "but I'd really like to get it from another angle too."

"You ready to try that again, Nick?" asked Dad.

"Fuck you," I gasped, finally getting some air into my lungs. "And fuck your damn movie!"

They decided to forego the reshoot. Instead, they shot me landing downhill on the surprised couple: I fell forward on top of them, they screamed, Lefty hollered and cursed (using only PG-rated words), and indignant Millie kicked my supine body as I lay there groaning.

We had to shoot that scene three more times before Dad was satisfied that Millie looked sufficiently outraged and had kicked me with enough passion. I was a mass of throbbing pain as Roland shot the special effect of my falling down the hill. With the camera mounted on a long pole, he held the pole horizontally and rotated the camera as he walked down the hill while I grunted and gasped–thus capturing the tumble from my point of view (and sparing me from having to fall all the way down the hill).

Then Brenda and Felicity tended to my cuts and scratches as Lefty arrived in his Jeep with Cal and lunch.

"Great job on those abrasions," said Cal to Felicity. "They look almost real."

"They are real," I said. "And Dad will be hearing from my law-yer."

During lunch Dad apologized to Arvin for yelling at him. (That seems to be his pattern: yell first, apologize later.) He explained that rating issues aside, his boner wouldn't have worked in that scene because Lefty was supposed to be crooked, which Arvin obviously wasn't.

"Right," said Arvin staring at his sandwich. "Could we please drop this subject?"

After lunch we went to another part of the park and shot the scene where Nick catches Sheeni reading his diary and they share their first kiss. We did it in one take, which was good because a park ranger arrived on the scene wanting to know what was go-ing on.

"Just testing out this nifty new camera I got for my birthday," lied Dad. "But it's time to go if we hope to beat the traffic."

TUESDAY, July 7 – When I took my shower this morning, I discovered I was bruised down my entire left torso from Millie's kicks. I also had a scab on my scalp and a big bump on the back of my head. Chloe's right: acting is harder than it looks.

Even though she wasn't in today's scenes, Cal showed up at the Mar Vista house to observe the filming. We chatted while Aunt Joan and her husband Bill bustled in with more boxes of flea market finds that Brenda's using to decorate the rooms. In "my" room, for example, they've hung up a tacky poster of Frank Sinatra winking and pointing his finger at you. Way too spooky to live with in real life.

Cal had some interesting news: Esmee got Harvey alone in her bedroom, but nothing was consummated. He couldn't get it up.

"That's unprecedented," I said. "Guys our age can get it up to hump just about anything–alive or dead."

"I know," said Cal. "It's one of your more disgusting traits. I've seen Esmee with her clothes off. She's quite attractive too, if you don't mind rather large and pendulous breasts."

I felt a stirring down below and had to adjust my posture.

"Uh, what do you suppose the problem is?" I asked.

"We have two hypotheses, Nick. Either hypnosis blocks the normal libido processes or my brother is gay."

"He doesn't seem very gay," I pointed out.

"I know. Harvey's room is a mess and he dresses abominably. But he's never shown much interest in girls. And there's always Cooper at camp."

"What was that about?"

"I don't know. I just caught a bit of it. He was on the phone with someone. He said no one must find out about Cooper at camp. My parents may know what it means, but they're not saying. Esmee's going to put him under again and ask him about that."

"Good. Maybe being gay is what's making Harvey such an asshole."

"It's all very odd, Nick. I thought that gene was supposed to make you *nice*."

The first scene of the day involved three sailors bringing back the dead Chevy Nova and demanding their money back from Jerry (Estelle Twisp's trucker boyfriend). My character had to deal with the irate sailor (played by Uncle Jake) because Jerry was out of town. Two NFL linebackers donated by cousin Tyler provided the back-up muscle. They all looked spiffy in their white uniforms and trim caps.

We had to shoot the scene multiple times because Uncle Jake couldn't utter the words, "and we found evidence of a banana in the transmission" without getting the giggles. Once he started, they spread to me and the football players. Everyone was in stitches except Dad, who stood there unsmiling as a big red vein on his forehead began to swell and throb.

To forestall his stroke, we finally settled down and played the scene as written.

"I've got to use that line in a script for my show," said Uncle Jake. "It's inherently funny."

"Better not," warned Dad, "or I'll sue your ass."

"You wouldn't sue your own brother who's donating his services and investing in this claptrap production," said Jake.

"Just try me," replied Dad.

Brenda bought the rusty Nova locally in Compton, but was still searching for Dad's cherry Lincoln. She found one in Florida, but Dad wants the seller to pay the $1,200 shipping charge, since he'd have "the thrill" of seeing his former car in a movie. A flimsy argument that's not working so far.

Since there's lots of idle time on movie sets for gossip, I found out from Megan (Mary's daughter in charge of script continuity) that Roland asked Brenda out, but she declined. Good for her. Our DP is your slob's slob, plus I didn't appreciate his expecting me to take another suicidal leap over that bush. I noticed Lefty's been chatting up Brenda quite a bit, but he's got to be at least double her age. She shares her Heath bars with him though, which may signify some romantic interest.

After lunch Lefty donned his Oakland cop uniform, and we all moved to the kitchen to shoot the breakfast scene where Nick upbraids his mother for having Lance Wescott spend the night without consulting him. Estelle was impressively slatternly, and Lefty did OK as a moronic but hot-tempered cop. He had the advantage of having met the original Lance all those years ago. Uncle Jake spent part of his youth thinking that cretin was his dad, but discovered that his actual pop was noted drunk George F. Twisp (my grandfather). So Jake is a full-fledged Twisp and not an impostor. A bit like me and my clouded paternity. Fatherhood appears to be something that Twisps are inclined to duck if they can get away with it. Rather like those birds that lay their eggs in other birds' nests and expect them to raise their progeny.

Then we shot the scene where Lance and Estelle confront Nick with the evidence that he started the fire. She phones Nick's dad in Ukiah and tells him to "get his ass down here" because his son just "burned down half of Berkeley." Next up was the scene in my bedroom where Lance wallops me with his big thick cop belt. Actually, it was a sponge-rubber prop belt that Brenda dredged up, but it still stung a bit. No doubt a major star would have demanded a stuntman to absorb the blows.

The last scene had Nick in his bedroom resolving to spin off his evil impulses into that "atavistic sociopath" François Dillinger. This dangerous dude sports a mustache and a bad nicotine habit. Since excessive smoking can imperil your PG rating, Dad only shows François rolling his smokes, not puffing on them.

After we finished shooting, Mary's workmen started sawing the big hole in the living room wall and reinforcing the floor. They are doing this work without city building permits. Nor has Dad obtained any permits for filming on this street. He doesn't look much like an outlaw, but ol' François Dillinger may not have disappeared entirely from his life.

WEDNESDAY, July 8 – Feminine humming in the bathroom this morning. The tune sounded vaguely French, so you can imagine my surprise when the door opened, revealing steamy Mary Moran wrapped in my towel.

"Don't look so shocked, Nick," she said. "I'm not out of the running yet."

"Uh, right."

"Don't forget. I'm younger than she is."

"And prettier too."

"Thanks, Nick. And I haven't spent the last four decades breaking his heart."

"There's that too," I agreed.

Dad announced at breakfast that he and Mary were driving to Arizona today to look at another Lincoln that Brenda has found. This one is white (so it wouldn't have to be repainted) and allegedly was owned by a little old lady who just expired.

"But, Dad, what about the movie?" I asked.

"We can't do anything more until the Chevy is in the house, Nick. And Brenda can oversee that. We'll be back tomorrow. Lefty's in charge while I'm gone. Don't give him any trouble."

"OK, but I'll need another $75."

He forked over three twenties like they were being surgically removed from his own hide.

At the coffee shop Cal gave me the latest update on her impotent brother.

"Esmee pried the Cooper at camp story out of him," she said. "It seems there was a counselor who Harvey particularly disliked. So late one night my evil brother pushed his car into the lake. A kid named Cooper observed him sneaking out of the cabin. And because Cooper, like most sensible people, hated my brother, he snitched on him to the camp manager. So Harvey got in big trouble. They were going to call our parents, but Harvey said he would pay for the car, which was a battered old Honda. But the irate counselor claimed replacing it would cost him at least $2,000. So my brother had to write out a check for two grand, decimating his college savings fund."

"Well, that was dumb," I said. "But it doesn't sound very gay."

"Unfortunately not," she agreed.

"So why doesn't he want to make it with Esmee?"

"You want my theory, Nick? He's terrified of sex."

"Why? We're all genetically programmed to be gung-ho for the act."

"It could be those wires got crossed in Harvey. Along with lots of other ones."

"That's a possibility. And Esmee can be somewhat intimidating. I think she should play up to Harvey's interests."

"Which are what, Nick?"

"Look at his YouTube videos, Sheeni. They're all about animals."

"So Esmee should pretend to be an animal lover to seduce Harvey?"

"Exactly."

After lunch Cal came over to rehearse some of our upcoming scenes. Lefty asked if we wanted to go with him to watch the forklift maneuver the car through the hole. We declined.

"So I'm going," he said. "You guys will be OK on your own?"

"We'll be fine," I said.

"You'll stay out of trouble, Nick? You won't raise hell like your dad did when he was your age?"

"I'm much calmer than he was," I assured him. "You should realize that by now."

"I hope so. OK, see you."

He left and I looked at Cal.

"Don't even think about it, Nick."

"Why not?"

"Remember our agreement? You won't be collecting on that favor until the movie is finished."

"Harvey may not be the only Haseltine terrified of sex."

"I'm not terrified, Nick. I just think we should wait."

"Why exactly?" I asked, nuzzling her neck.

"Because sex makes guys too possessive. They get impossible to deal with."

"You've had some personal experience of this phenomenon?"

"We're not going there either, Nick. That's my business, not yours."

"OK, we don't have to go all the way. But have a heart. Let's try *something, anything*!"

So we made out on the sofa, and Cal let me put my hand under her bra. Quite tremendously stimulating, if you haven't tried that before. Whoever designed the female body was certainly a genius. Too bad the male body when placed in close contact with it gets so ready to take things further. The fastest sports car on Earth should have such acceleration, such drive to the finish line.

Eventually, Cal took pity on me.

"OK, Nick. You can pull down your pants and deal with it."

"Uh, what do you mean?"

"You can do it to yourself–with your hand."

"You mean right here? In front of you?"

"Sure. Why not? We're all friends."

"You won't be appalled?"

"Hardly."

So I undid my belt, and pulled down everything. There was my surprised erection, looking rather impressive if I do say so myself.

"Circumcised," commented Cal. "Too bad. You should sue. And those bruises are gross."

"Those are from Tiara kicking me about 300 times."

"You guys go for the kinky stuff, huh?"

"The kinkier the better," I lied. "Would you like to do the hand work?"

"That's OK, Nick. I expect you've had lots more practice."

It only took about four strokes. Talk about over-stimulation. My load soared overhead and splattered against the wall behind the sofa.

"That's why girls should never have unprotected sex," said Cal. "Especially with guys your age."

"Would you like me to do you now?" I asked, wiping up.

"I hardly think so, Nick. I may be off sex for good after the show you just put on."

Hey, she suggested it. I hope she's not traumatized for life.

Later Sheeni Saunders dropped by looking for dad. I said he had gone to Arizona with Mary Moran to inspect a car, adding that they would be "spending the night there."

She didn't lose her cool, but I could tell she was massively annoyed.

That night my mother phoned from our old house in Terre Haute. I asked her how she was doing.

"I'm OK, Nick."

"How's he treating you?"

"I'm fine, Nick. Things had been sliding in the office, so I'm busy trying to catch up."

"Is he helping you with that?"

"Let's talk about you and your movie, Nick. How do you like being a movie star?"

We talked about that for a while. She kept saying she was fine, but I'm not sure I believed her. I hope her husband isn't being a jerk as usual. I feel bad that I got away from the guy, but she's still stuck there with him. And let's not forget she only returned to him to save my sorry ass.

THURSDAY, July 9 – Lefty spent last night in Dad's bed. I expect the sofa is beginning to pale for him. If I were his age and living out of a couple duffle bags, I think I'd be worried. He seems pretty upbeat though. He says he takes life "one day, one dollar, and one chick at a time."

Lefty reports the forklift driver had "a hell of a time" getting the Chevy into Brenda's house. The driveway was too narrow to permit much maneuvering. Fortunately, about two dozen neighbors showed up to muscle the car through the hole and into place. Brenda promised them all tickets to the premiere.

A big object through a difficult hole. Is anyone else thinking of it like that, or is it just me and my dirty mind?

The owner of the coffee shop came out on the patio today and thanked us for our "loyal patronage."

After he left, Cal said, "Well, that's it. I'm never coming back here."

"Why's that?" I asked.

"I refuse to give my trade to a business that spies on me."

"How are they spying on you?"

"You heard him. He's been keeping track of how often we come here."

"He's not keeping track, Sheeni. He just recognizes our faces because we come here every day."

"We're not coming back, Nick. We'll go to that place on the beach."

"Where everything is twice the price. And it's hard to get a table. And those tourists from New York never wait their turn."

"That's a small price to pay for anonymity."

Esmee and Harvey arrived, the latter bearing another delicious scone for me.

"Thanks, Harv," I said. "You are the personification of the perfect pal."

"You're welcome, Nick. How I loved all the jolly times we had back in kindergarten."

"Those were the days," I agreed.

They didn't stay long. They had to get to the store so Esmee could help Harvey clean the cages and fish tanks. She said it's the least she can do for all "the wonderful animals."

Dad and Mary returned with his flashy new Lincoln convertible. Much nicer than the one that got incinerated. He likes everything about the car except its gas mileage. Its enormous V-8 engine (bigger than some cars) gets barely 10 mpg on the freeway. He'll be parking it at the Mar Vista house so as not to clog up Veeva's driveway.

We drove over there after lunch. The production crew had patched the hole and were painting the house exterior to match the paint scheme (slime brown with puke yellow trim) of Dad's old house in Oakland.

"Jesus, that's grim," commented Mary.

"Welcome to my youth," replied Dad.

Another derelict travel trailer was parked out front. Brenda said it was the perfect mate of the one that got wrecked except this one's two feet longer.

"You think people will notice?" she asked.

"Fuck 'em," said Dad. "Good job, Brenda."

Dad got misty-eyed when he saw the relocated Chevy, which occupied nearly the entire living room.

"Wow, it's deja vu all over again," he said. "But we need 'Pay Up or Die!!' spray-painted across the hood."

"That's on my list," said Brenda. "Anything else?"

"After you spray on the message, put a doily over it," said Dad. "And maybe a potted plant. That was my mother's solution."

Future ex-wife Ada dropped by a few minutes later. (Uncle Jake had clued her in to the location.)

"Very nice, Nick," she said, eyeing the Chevy. "You've created the ideal bachelor pad for yourself."

"Any news about my painting?" Dad asked.

"*Our* painting has been added to Sotheby's upcoming auction. Everyone there is very excited about it. They're putting it in a fancy frame. It's going to be the featured piece in the auction."

"I'm still looking for that receipt," said Dad.

"Good luck, dear. You'll be disappointed to know that I found a photo you took of all the wedding gifts. Right in the center is the painting. The photo is labeled 'our loot' in your handwriting."

"That doesn't prove anything," he replied.

"One more thing, dear," she said. "I discovered your friend Sheeni Saunders peering in my French doors yesterday. I'd appreciate it if you'd tell her to keep off my property."

FRIDAY, July 10 – A full day of filming at Mar Vista: from dawn until way past dark. We got through many, many pages. I'm beginning to think this movie actually may be happening.

Roland stepped from behind the camera to swagger around as Jerry, Estelle's other moronic boyfriend. Brenda strapped padding under his shirt to give him an even bigger beer gut. He was surprisingly good. The guy packs a lot of talent in a most unlikely package.

One highlight: I got to drive the Lincoln towing the trailer again. This time I made it all the way down the block. The script called for François to drive recklessly across the front yard, tearing up the landscaping. But Dad decided at the last minute he didn't want to bang up his nice vintage convertible.

"But we're losing some big laughs here," protested Mary.

"I don't care," said Dad. "That little old lady in Arizona would be rolling in her grave if we damaged her beautiful car."

The big news of the day: Dad fired Sheeni Saunders. He assured her that her acting was fine (which it wasn't), but Mr. Ferguson as a gal just wasn't working for him. So Dad handed the script to Joanie's husband and told him to "just be yourself, Bill." He took it in his stride, and came across on camera as a confused old duffer–which is just what Dad wanted.

Sheeni stuck around for five minutes pretending it was all a lark for her, then cut out. With any luck that may be the last we see of that woman.

SATURDAY, July 11 – Another early morning phone call. I thought it might be my mom, but it was the Gargoyle.

"Your brother certainly disgraced himself," she said, by way of a greeting. "Marriage is not something one does on the spur of the moment."

"Well, it might have worked out."

"You mean for longer than five minutes? I doubt it. But that's not why I called. What do you know about your jail-bait neighbor and my son-in-law?"

"Not much. He paid for some acting lessons for her."

"Why did he do that?"

"Because he's in the one percent like you. He has more money than he knows what to do with. He can only rip off his roof to hoist in so many pool tables."

"Let's have no class warfare here, Nick. So tell me, is he sleeping with that coy vixen?"

"Absolutely not, Connie. You can rest assured of that. In fact, she's scheduled to sleep with me next month."

"That sounds remarkably unspontaneous, but then your generation is a complete mystery to me. You must inform me immediately if she has any intercourse at all with my daughter's husband."

"OK."

"I've seen some dailies from your dad's movie. You're doing rather well, Nick. You remind me of a very, very young Anthony Perkins. Except you're short, not tall."

"Uh, thanks."

"What do you think of your performance?"

"I don't know. Dad doesn't let the actors see anything. He says it would just make us self-conscious and mannered."

"No doubt. That girlfriend of yours is quite good too. But it will not go down well for her if she's messing with Veeva's husband. You might give her that hint."

"OK."

I went down a flight and discovered Lefty asleep again in

Dad's bed. Guess my father spent the night elsewhere. He could keep us informed of his whereabouts in case Lefty has a massive heart attack or I need an emergency cash infusion.

We stood in line at the beach coffee place for six minutes, but Cal found the crush of weekend tourists intolerable. Many were displaced Manhattanites shouting for service. Very rude and such ugly accents too. So we hoofed it to our usual morning haunt (now called Spybucks by Cal), where we encountered Esmee and Harvey already settled in on the patio. We got our drinks and joined them. Harvey smiled and handed me a small bag.

"I did a bit of baking yesterday, Nick," he said. "I hope you like this muffin I made for you."

"You are such a pal, Harv. It looks delicious. I'll have it right now with my coffee."

I took a big bite, chewed briefly, and spewed out something horribly vile all across the table.

"What the fuck?" I gasped.

"The recipe called for raisins," said Harvey, "but I used cut-up pieces of soap instead."

"Harvey, dear, what's happening?" asked Esmee, alarmed.

"I'm not your dear, you fat cow," he replied. "Your tricks didn't work on me. I'm not some poor stupid pigeon like Nick."

"Harvey, you rat!" exclaimed Cal. "You were faking it! Esmee, didn't you give him the pin test?"

"I did! He didn't flinch! Not one muscle!"

"I fooled you!" said Harvey. "I fooled all of you! And, sister dear, I got your chubby friend to divulge some interesting tidbits about you."

"What did you tell him, Esmee?" demanded Cal.

"I, I, uh, I don't know what he's talking about!"

With that, Esmee dumped her iced coffee over Harvey's head and stomped away.

Dripping like he had just emerged from the Black Lagoon, Harvey smiled a diabolical smile and sauntered away in the opposite direction.

"That settles it, Nick," said Cal. "You've got to kill my brother."

"I'd like to, Sheeni. I really would. But I hadn't planned on spending my young adulthood on death row."

"You'd kill him if you really loved me."

"We have to get our revenge some other way, Sheeni."

"But how? God knows what falsehoods about me he's heard from that girl. Esmee's got a big mouth and loves to gossip. I can't believe I was ever her friend."

I felt a little sick. I hoped it was only soap Harvey put in that muffin and not other more lethal adulterants.

"We do know one thing now," I said, trying to drown the vile taste with my coffee.

"What?"

"That the Cooper at camp story Esmee got out of him was probably made up."

"You're right. So now we really need to find out the truth! Nickie, that will be your job."

"Why me?"

"Because you allege that you love me. And this will be your chance to prove it!"

When I got back Dad was on the phone with a reporter from *Time* magazine. They are planning a big feature story about the Hopper painting. Dad kept trying to steer the conversation around to his new movie, but Ms. Time mostly wanted to talk about Valuable Art. Dad admitted that they got it as a wedding present, so I guess he's given up lying about that. He said they might never have discovered its true value if they weren't splitting up–proving (in his words) that "divorce can bring some wonderful surprises." He also denied in the strongest terms that he had ever lived in any apartment with roaches or that his career was "in the toilet."

"There's a great deal of interest from distributors in my new film," lied Dad. "Semi-autobiographical, it is a moving and hilarious tale of a young rebel's first love. Our working title is 'Nick Twisp's Youth in Rebellion.'"

Not a bad title if he ditches the name he's tacked on.

I went up to my room and called the Gargoyle back. I told her I had warned Cal to leave poor Desmond alone. And I assured her that no hanky-panky had occurred between those two.

"Good, Nick," she replied. "If my son-in-law is to be incarcerated, I'd prefer it were for the contents of his books rather than for sex offences with minors."

I told her about Cal's deranged brother and asked if she could look into his "Cooper at camp" episode.

"And why are we interested in that topic, Nick?"

"It's very upsetting to Cal. It could detrimentally affect her performance in the film."

"I see. All right, I'll look into it. Anything else?"

"Dad's getting a big story in *Time*. It could be good publicity for the movie."

"Very good. Tell him I'm trying to get some of my friends to bid on his painting."

"Great. Mention that one expert has estimated it could go for $10 million or more."

"What expert was that?"

"Me."

SUNDAY, July 12 – On the road. We are car caravanning north on Highway 99 with most of the film company. Dad's driving his spiffy Lincoln convertible and towing the derelict trailer. We're getting some odd looks from passing motorists. Dad and Lefty are in the front seat; I'm in the back seat between Cal (heaven) and Denny (hell). Mary is behind us in her car with her daughters and Arvin. Brenda and Roland are somewhere behind her with assorted tech guys and actors. Felicity is bringing up the rear in a rented motorhome. Trent Preston will be flying up later in his private jet.

Our destination: the little town of Groveland in the foothills east of Modesto. Aunt Joanie and Uncle Bill are already there and camping in Bill's vintage teardrop trailer. I hope the place is more interesting than the current scenery. We're in something called the Central Valley which is boring in the extreme. Nothing but desolate flat lands and brown hills. Very hot too, and our car's aging A/C is barely functioning. Dad offered to put the top down, but Cal said she didn't want "to dry up like a prune." Someone's deodorant is failing big time. It isn't me because my ZipPits are on the job. I suspect it's the sweating pig to my right.

For the past hour he and Cal have been discussing what name he should use in the credits. Since he has "reached maturity" he no longer feels "Denny" is appropriate, but he dislikes his real name Dennis. Right now they're both leaning toward Denholm (a la the late English actor Denholm Elliott). He also likes Denzel, but doesn't want people to think he's black. I suggested Denweed, Denwish, Denzine, Dendumb, Denislav, and Deninski–all of which he rejected. I nearly had him talked into Denim, until I suggested Levis as a middle name.

One thing I've discovered about Denny Turnbull: his favorite subject of conversation is Denny Turnbull. He's also big on man-spreading his knees and crowding his smelly person into my personal space. Nevertheless, I shall always choose the middle seat so as to deny him any physical contact with Cal. These are the sacrifices one makes for love.

6:17 p.m. Groveland (population 601) at last. Not many groves to be seen. Just some old western-style buildings lined up along a couple of blocks of the main drag. Brenda reserved us a block of rooms in a motel on the outskirts of town. Arvin, Denny, and I were assigned a room with two double beds. Arvin suggested we draw straws or cut cards to see who had to sleep gay-style.

"I don't think so," I said. "I'm the star of this movie. I'm taking the bed by the door; you two can share the other one."

"You may be the star," said Denny. "But I have considerably more credits and acting experience than you."

"Good, Denzine," I replied. "Then you can act pleased to be sleeping with Arvin. Because your only other choice is the floor."

"You're supposed to call me Trent," he said, dumping his bag on my bed.

I tossed his bag across the room.

"You're really asking for it, Nick," he said, making a fist.

Right then Brenda arrived with a rollaway bed.

"OK, boys," said Brenda. "Let's all try to get along. And, Denny, nobody hits our star. Everybody clear on that?"

"Just tell the twink to back off," muttered Denny. "And, Brenda, you're supposed to call me Trent."

I think Dennis the Menace has an unhealthy wish to walk in the shoes of superstar Trent Preston.

"I'll sleep on the rollaway," said Arvin. "Hell, I can sleep on anything."

I dropped my bag and checked out the scene next door where Cal was bunking with Mary's daughters. Same bed situation, but the sisters were OK sleeping together since the incest taboo takes the edge off that controversy. I asked Cal how she liked her room.

"So far it's slightly ahead of math camp. Not much privacy, but at least the bathroom isn't in a shack down the trail. And no one is talking about equations. Are you and Denny sharing a bed?"

"Not hardly."

"Hi, Nickie!" called Lauren, braces flashing in the golden sunlight streaming in through the big window overlooking the parking lot. "We're going to have such fun this week!"

"And who are you again?" asked Cal.

"I told you twice already," she replied. "I'm Lauren, Mary's daughter."

"Right," said Cal. "And what are you doing here?"

"I'm, uh, helping out. I've assisted Mother on many of her productions."

"Good," said Cal. "You can go find out what we're doing for dinner. I'm famished."

It could be a celibate week for everyone. Dad is bunking with Lefty, and Mary is sharing a room with Brenda. A distinct marijuana aroma is wafting from the room where Roland is bunking with the tech guys. I think he'd rather be sharing the motorhome with Felicity. But our makeup/wardrobe gal (who is black) so far has been resisting his flabby ofay charms.

Dinner was in a rustic café down the block. All "us kids" sat together at a big round table. I sat between Lauren and Cal. I mostly talked to the former, since my love was being monopolized by Denny. I had the "hamburger steak" special, which would have gone down better if the whirling ceiling fan directly over Denny's head had suddenly let loose from its moorings.

MONDAY, July 13 – Yes, there is a God. My prayers have been answered. Denholm Turnbull awoke this morning with a nascent zit on the very tip of his chiseled nose. In case anyone missed it, Roland singled it out for comment during breakfast at the café.

"I hope that's not a zit!" he bellowed. "We can't have someone playing the great and godlike Trent Preston with a flaming crustacean on his nose!"

Right on the spot I decided to forgive Roland for all past and future transgressions against me. The man can do no wrong.

"It's not a zit," lied Denny, blushing. "I think it's a spider bite. Who chose that low-rent motel?"

"You should squeeze it before it gets too big," advised Lauren.

"Don't squeeze it," warned her sister. "Not until the pus pock-et forms."

"Do you mind?" I interjected. "I'm trying to eat here."

I turned to Cal, who was pointedly not looking at Denny. "How did you sleep, Sheeni dear?"

"Not bad considering the turmoil in the adjacent bed. It's so great to get away from my brother and that traitor Esmee."

We were far away, but I still found this text on my phone: "If u were here, Id dismembr u with a cleavr and sell ur parts from an ice chest at the farmrs' market as organic, grass-fed beef."

I wrote back: "If u were here, I'd roll u in hot asphalt and use u as a speed bump 2 slow the traffic 2 Yosemite."

After breakfast we drove to a nearby RV park where the trailer scenes were to be filmed. Aunt Joan and Uncle Bill were camped there in their tiny vintage teardrop. The interior is just big enough for a narrow double bed. Kind of like a coffin built for two. A hatch in the rear opens on a spartan exterior kitchen with two-burner range and ice chest. No bathroom, of course, but Bill had erected a tall, skinny tent nearby that enclosed a porta-potty. He towed the trailer with a fully restored 1938 Dodge pickup truck. A nice setup, I guess, but fairly primitive for the parents of a billionaire.

Right next door was the large but decrepit trailer Brenda had scored to house the Twisp vacationers in the movie. Aunt Joan and Uncle Bill spent yesterday decorating it with remarkably tacky religious art (the original trailer park had been run by a church). It's a good thing movies don't have Smell-O-Vision because that trailer smelled seriously foul on the inside.

"Jesus, let's get some windows open," said Brenda.

"Don't bother," said Dad. "I like the authentic aromas."

Yeah, he would.

The gal playing Estelle Twisp changed into shorts and a low-slung halter top that encased her goods just a few inches above her navel. I sure hope Cal doesn't droop like that in her old age. Roland again metamorphosized into Jerry the trucker (truly gross in shorts), and we shot the scenes where they first arrive in the Lincoln and where Estelle introduces Nick to Sheeni.

Some fellow campers stopped by to gawk, but most soon wandered away. Movie-making is terminally boring unless major buildings are being blown up.

My phone rang as we were eating box lunches provided by the café in town. It was the Gargoyle with news of her Cooper at camp investigations. After I hung up I reported to Cal what she had found.

"Veeva's mother called the camp. They said your brother was a model camper. He was involved in no incidents of misbehavior. They had one kid there named Cooper when your brother was attending. As far as they know they got along great."

"Then why were my parents punishing my brother?" she demanded.

"Uh, I don't know."

"Then call my father and ask him."

I phoned the pet store. Fortunately, Mr. Haseltine himself answered. He said he had checked into my Cooper at camp report, but had found nothing amiss. No, he had not punished Harvey for anything. He said Harvey was invaluable to the efficient operation of their store. I thanked him, said his daughter was doing great in the movie, and rang off.

"I don't get it," I said. "It could be your brother's playing mind games. You overheard his phone conversation?"

"Yes, just as I told you. I heard Harvey on the phone saying no one must find out about Cooper at camp."

"It could be he wanted you to hear that."

"My brother is devious, but not that devious. No, there's something he's hiding. And it's your job to find out what."

Damn. Maybe it would be easier just to kill him.

After lunch we shot the scene where I'm mooning about the trailer in love with Sheeni. (No acting required.) Then the scene where Mrs. Clarkelson (elderly religious fanatic) invites us to their church services, and Jerry asks her in "to sit on my face." The last shot of the day was Estelle and Jerry "flogging the mattress" in the rear bedroom while I was changing into swim trunks to meet Sheeni at the beach. For some reason Dad insisted on a shot of my bare ass from behind. Through some miracle I didn't embarrass myself when Felicity applied body makeup to my naked butt. I thought of the money (neat stacks of $500 bills) and did the scene in three takes.

On the drive back to the motel Denny handed me some written notes on my performance that I immediately crumpled into a ball and tossed out the window.

"I guess you don't want to improve your acting," he said.

"I think you should see a doctor, Denzine," I replied. "That disaster on your nose may be getting septic."

Surreptitious squeezing may have been going on. Probably a mistake.

Later, he showed up for dinner at the café with a Band-Aid over the eruption. Everyone at the table made a point of pretending not to look at it except me. I stared at it between every bite.

After dinner the six of us strolled around town to check it out. Arvin has been pairing off with Lauren (fine with me). Now if Denny hooks up with Megan, we could coexist as three happy couples. In front of an ice cream store a couple of local louts asked Denny if he was that dude on the skateboard TV show.

"Yes, that's me," Denny affirmed proudly.

"You nail that cute blond girl?" asked the creepier of the two.

"Yes, Denny," said Cal, "did you nail her?"

"I guess that's my business," said Denny, pushing past them.

The creepy guy's big pal stuck out a tattooed leg and tripped Denny. He stumbled forward, Arvin decked the big guy with one punch, Megan swiveled expertly and got the creep in a headlock. He squealed and squirmed. She released him, and both scurried off down an alley.

"Good job, Lefty," said Megan.

"You too," he replied, shaking her hand.

"Nick, how come you didn't punch anyone?" asked Cal.

"I was too busy guarding you," I replied.

That confirms it. If I'm going to be a famous actor, I'll have to sign up for some martial arts training.

TUESDAY, July 14 – Another hot and sunny day in the scenic foothills. After breakfast Brenda drove off with Denny to get his monstrous zit looked at. How unfortunate for his career if they have to amputate his nose. Apparently, Dad had a generous quota of zits as a kid, but I've been spared that plague so far. Now, if only I can also avoid his disfiguring baldness.

Today we commandeered one of the RV park's ladies' restrooms (they have several, so the campers didn't have to hold it) to film the notorious nude shower scene. Mrs. Clarkelson got to wear a flesh-colored body suit, but I had to perform buck naked. Dad seems to think he can showcase my bare butt multiple times without jeopardizing his PG rating. And why exactly does he want to do that? The whole thing seems kind of twisted to me.

Naturally, Lauren and Megan wanted to be on the set to observe, but I refused to disrobe until all were excluded. I found out later they had stuck around outside and watched the action on an external monitor.

I thought of the money (neatly stacked piles of $1,000 bills) and shed my robe upon command. The story had me surprising Mrs. Clarkelson in the shower under the mistaken impression that Sheeni occupied the stall. As the water poured down upon us my victim screamed in shock, shouted "Help! Rape!" and beat upon my chest with her bar of soap. Then Cal, dressed in a modest robe, hurried in to rescue me.

During this scene my back was to the camera, which meant my junk was fully exposed to Mrs. Clarkelson. She didn't seem to mind. In between the two takes she laughed and complimented me on my "nice manly package." Needless to say, with her in front of me in a dripping body suit I remained unrestrainedly limp. If fact, I was seriously wondering if I could ever get it up again.

Afterwards, Cal informed me that everyone outside had seen my willy.

"My back was to the camera," I pointed out.

"Not all the time."

"Well, it can't be helped. Besides, you've seen it before."

"Your Dad hopes to have his film released at Christmas."

"So?"

"So your bare ass will be his Christmas present to the world. And you'll be in school then. Everyone in your classes will have seen you stark naked."

"Only the ones with the price of a movie ticket. Anyway, I'm concentrating on the money. You have to be something of an exhibitionist to be an actor. Ewan McGregor has flashed his willy in numerous pictures."

"True enough, Nick. But he's not in high school."

Damn. She was starting to get me worried.

Brenda and Denny returned at lunch time. The latter had a big bandage over his nose. His boil had been professionally lanced and dressed. I sneaked a photo of his face, which I posted on my nearly moribund Facebook page. Not out of revenge, but to get some vital publicity for our movie.

After lunch we drove to a nearby lake called Mountain Fir or something. It was a private resort that Brenda had found. The water looked inviting, but we were there to Work. Cal and I changed into swim attire and reclined on a blanket on the sandy beach. We had a few lines of pretentious dialogue discussing our Intellectual Books, then Cal invited me to apply sun lotion to her "exposed areas." She lay back in her provocative new bikini and I went at it. The script called for me to get an erection, but Dad got annoyed when in fact I did.

"No boners, Nick. I told you, no boners in my movie."

"But, Dad, the script has Sheeni saying 'My, you get turned on easily.'"

"Right. We're suggesting boners, but we're not showing them. Go deal with that."

Like Arvin before me, I was obliged to make the walk of shame, this time to the men's restroom. But when I entered a stall, all was quiescent down there. Like midnight in the graveyard, nothing was stirring.

I returned to the beach for Take Two. We did the dialogue, I started with the lotion, and *sprong!* It happened again.

"Cut!" yelled Dad. "Hey, Nick. What's with you, kid?"

"I don't know, Dad. I think it has to do with 16 years of rigid, unceasing celibacy."

"Should I try to be less alluring, Mr. Twisp?" asked Cal.

"I don't think that's possible. You're doing fine, Sheeni. Hey, Felicity, take our star over to wardrobe and tape that pesky thing down."

I was spared some of that humiliation. In the motorhome, Felicity handed me a roll and told me to "tape it down good and tight."

Five minutes later my dick was mummified to my leg in about 30 feet of industrial tape. I limped back to the beach and we did three more takes without further interruptions. Then we got to jump in the water. We swam away from shore, and Cal pressed herself against me and kissed me.

"Better not do that," I said. "If I get turned on now, it will break off for sure."

WEDNESDAY, July 15 – Denny isn't shy about parading around in the buff after his morning shower. OK, he's got a big one. Ask me if I'm impressed. His abs are nothing to write home about, and he's still got a touch of fat kid's flabby tits. I think that's why he left his t-shirt on at the beach yesterday. He couldn't get his bandage wet, so he didn't go in the water. Too bad. He missed out on some excellent opportunities to drown.

The Gargoyle phoned as I was finishing my French toast at the café. She had done some more research and discovered that Harvey's Cooper lived in Sonora, a town just up the road from Groveland. She said his last name was Tucker, and gave me his address and phone number.

Cooper Tucker. One of those names that also works in reverse order: Tucker Cooper. Personally, I would not wish to have a name that rhymes with "super fucker," but that's just me.

"We must visit him," said Cal, excited. "We'll go there tonight!"

"How?" I asked. "We don't drive. And we don't have a car."

"Paltry details, Nick. I'm sure you'll work it out."

After breakfast we filmed the scenes in the script where Estelle, Jerry, Sheeni, and Nick go to a farm to buy Jerry's ill-fated trailer, and where Sheeni discovers her "darling dog" Albert (named after some dead French author). The dog (a black pug) was the ugliest one Brenda could find; the shifty-eyed farmer was played by the actual shifty-eyed coot whose farm it was.

When we got back to town, Scott and Chloe had checked into the motel and were waiting for us at the café.

"Did you talk to Mom?" Scott asked Dad.

"No. Why would I do that?"

"There's a been a hitch in the sale of your painting."

While Dad went outside to phone, Scott filled us in. Ada's cousin Nerva (daughter of Aunt Verna) read about the painting in *Time* and decided she was being cheated. She got an injunction to stop the sale, claiming her mother had been suffering from dementia when she gave them the painting as a wedding gift. Nerva claims her grandmother bought the painting and always intended that it should go to her.

"Does she have anything to that effect in writing?" asked Mary.

"I don't know," replied Scott. "My mom's boyfriend Brent thinks it's just a ploy to get a cut of the auction proceeds."

"No way," I said. "A gift is a gift. That greedhead must be quashed!"

Dad returned looking grim. "OK," he announced. "Everyone's per diem is being cut to $30. From now on, if you want dessert, you'll have to buy it yourself."

Loud boos from the movie company and the café staff. Even some of the local diners joined in.

Damn, no way I could skip dessert. I'd become semi-addicted to the cafe's excellent mixed-berry pie. Plus, I enjoyed eating it in front of Denny, who's deathly allergic to berries of all types.

Filming after lunch was delayed while Dad talked to his lawyer and to Brent. That must have been a fun conversation for him. I wonder if he hates Brent as much as I despise Denny. So I used the break to call Cooper and then arranged for Lefty to drive us to Sonora in Mary's car. We're claiming there's a Nicolas Cage movie playing there that we're dying to see. Cooper sounded amiable and said sure he'd like to meet friends of Harvey. His house is just a short walk from the shopping center where the theater is located.

Chloe was looking very fine. I think my brother agrees with her. I may be destined to be jealous of all of his girlfriends. Scott picked up the tab for the desserts at lunch. If I'd known he was going to be so generous, I'd have ordered two pieces of pie.

Eventually, we all got transported to the RV park, where we filmed the scene in which Nick first meets Paul (Sheeni's stoner brother) in front of the Saunders' two-story trailer. Dad wanted to have them sharing a joint, but since that automatically would get his movie stamped with the dreaded R rating, he had to substitute a regular filter-tip cigarette.

"I'm supposed to offer Nick a toke on my cigarette," said Scott. "And why would I do that?"

"Because you're stoned, Paul," replied Dad. "Your mind is so fried you don't realize it's not a joint."

"I get it," said Scott. "I'm like really, really stoned."

He played the part that way and was excellent. Somehow I suspected my brother knew his way around hallucinogenics. No actual smoking was shown, although in between takes I puffed on the Marlboro. I'm sure I could totally get hooked on nicotine if I tried. But who needs the expense and the cancer?

When we finished, Scott asked me if I'd heard from Zee.

"No," I replied. "Have you?"

"Only via her lawyer talking to my lawyer. I hear she's getting it on with the DP on that production. A guy named Tom, who filled in as the best man at our wedding."

I told him that probably smarted, but reminded him that he was the one who ditched Azura for Chloe.

"I know, Scott. I have no cause to complain–even if Tom is married with a couple of kids."

"So it's just a rebound fling, Scott. She probably won't be seeing him once they're done in Montana."

"Yeah, let's hope so if she's smart," he sighed.

After that we shot the scene where I lug a watermelon back for Sheeni and she shows me her upstairs trailer bedroom. This small space had been decorated all in white, with a big poster on the wall for an old French movie called "Breathless." Apparently, the original Sheeni had gone nuts over that flick and its star, some actor I never heard of. It was nice hanging out on the bed up there with Cal. It would have been even nicer without the film crew.

10:45 p.m. Sonora was a much bigger place than Groveland. It was a real town with busy stores and stop lights and city traffic. Of course, all the other kids wanted to tag along too.

"Why are we seeing this movie?" asked Lauren as we loaded up on snacks at the refreshments counter.

"Because Nick Cage is Nick's favorite actor," said Cal.

"He's my god," I affirmed. "I loved him in 'Godfather IV.'"

"They only made three Godfather movies," said Denny. "And Nicolas Cage was not in any of them."

"Perhaps not," I replied. "But he's certainly Italian."

After the movie started, Cal handed her popcorn to Denny. "Hold this," she said. "I need to go to the restroom."

One minute later I did the same with Lauren.

I met Cal in the lobby and together we sneaked out. We found Cooper's house and knocked on the door. The target of our quest answered.

First surprise: Cooper was exceeding handsome. He could be the best-looking kid since Rob Lowe was learning to shave.

Second surprise: Cooper couldn't admire his own beauty. He's blind.

REVOLT AT THE BEACH

"Blind since I got a virus when I was two," he confirmed, taking a seat on an old-fashioned glider on his front porch. "So I remember what colors look like, but I've always been kind of vague on purple."

"It's midway between blue and red," said Cal.

"I know that intellectually, but I can't quite picture it. So you're Harvey's sister."

"Unfortunately, I am," confirmed Cal. "Did he mention me?"

"He said you were pretty, but that was it for compliments. I read about your movie in our local paper. It sounds like fun."

I wondered how a blind person could read a newspaper, but didn't feel it was polite to ask.

"Parts of it are kind of fun," said Cal. "So tell me, Cooper, did you have some sort of contretemps at camp with my brother?"

Third surprise: Cooper totally likes Harvey. He thinks he's one of the nicest guys he ever met.

"Really?" said Cal. "Why's that?"

"Harvey was my bunk mate. He got the top bunk, I got the bottom. He was very good about taking me around until I got the lay of the land. I'm fine on my own once I get a place scoped out in my head. And in any crowd, you always get a few lowlifes who think it would be fun to tease the blind kid. You know like put a mop bucket in the middle of the room and watch me trip over it. Harvey quickly put a stop to those tricks. You're lucky to have such a cool brother."

Not what Cal wanted to hear. We discussed this odd development on the walk back to the theater.

"It could be that Cooper called Harvey after you made the appointment to see him," said Cal. "This could be more of my brother's mind games."

"But why would Cooper say he liked your brother if he didn't? So is that Harvey's deepest and darkest secret? The one that he wanted no one to find out. Is that what he's so ashamed of: that he was once really nice to a blind kid?"

"There's got to be some other explanation," said Cal. "And, Nickie, it's your job to find it."

When we returned, a sweaty Nick Cage was strangling some bulky Asian guy. Both Denny and Lauren had finished our popcorn.

"Where were you?" whispered Lauren. "Did you get the runs from all that pie?"

"Certainly not."

And even if I had, how was it any of her business?

THURSDAY, July 16 – Cal took me aside at breakfast to confide her latest theory.

"It all makes sense, Nick. I can't believe we missed it. Cooper is a very good-looking dude. And what do we know about such guys?"

"They're all stuck up unless they're blind," I ventured.

"No, Nick. Ninety-eight percent of them are gay."

"Really? Like you think, for example, Denny is gay?"

"No, because Denny is only temporarily good-looking. He's going to lose all of his hair and get fat again."

Best news I heard all week!

"Harvey's secret is that he's in love with a blind guy. Which means . . ."

"Your brother is gay!"

"Exactly. But we've got to confirm it. And I know just how to do it."

"Er, how?"

"Via Denny's nose. It isn't getting any better."

"I know, Sheeni. He's been sneaking into our bathroom at night and messing with it. Projectile squeezing is leaving a mess all over the mirror."

"Please, Nick, spare me the details. His nose is getting grosser by the minute. So we get your dad to fire Denny. And hire Cooper to take his place."

"But how can Cooper play Trent? He's blind."

"So we put him in some hip sunglasses. It's not that big of a part. All he has to do is look good and say a few lines of dialogue."

"I see. And while he's here, we get him to 'fess up about Harvey."

"Exactly. Now that we have a plan, it's your task to execute it."

Somehow that news didn't surprise me.

Being no dummy, I didn't go to Dad directly. I told Brenda we knew this totally handsome local kid who would be perfect as Trent. And what great publicity the movie would get for hiring a blind actor. Plus, he'd probably work way cheaper than Denny. She went to Dad, and 15 minutes later Denny was storming around the motel room like he was doing the mad beach scene from *King Lear*.

"I'm sorry you and your nose got fired, Denzine," I said. "I think you both would have been almost adequate as Trent."

Good thing I thought to duck because Denny swung violently at my nose. Then Arvin tripped him and held him down while I exited happily to begin the day's shooting.

"How did Denny take it?" asked Cal, as we rode in the Lincoln to the RV park.

"Not well. He threatened to get physical, but I put him in his place."

At that moment I got a text on my phone.

"It's from your brother," I said. "He says if I were there, he'd stick the business end of a shop vac over my nose and suck out my lungs and other superfluous organs."

"That imagery is very homoerotic, Nick."

"OK, if you say so."

"I know we're on the right track now with my brother."

I texted back that if he were here, I'd tie him by his ears to the trailer hitch of my dad's car and drag him over 20 miles of gravel roads.

Brenda was gone all morning. She went to Sonora to dump Denny at the bus station, find a copy of *Time* for Dad, and interview Cooper Tucker. Meanwhile, we filmed the scene where George F. Twisp (played by Dad) comes back from a business trip and discovers Paul making time with his live-in girlfriend Lacey (played by Chloe). We shot this in the RV park manager's modular home after Mary cleared out some of the tackier furniture and his extensive collection of Oakland Raiders football memorabilia. Chloe did fine, and Scott got to deck our dad with a single punch, if only in make believe. It looked fake in the replays, but Roland said it will come across as real when the Foley guys add the punch impact to the soundtrack.

We also did a bunch of miscellaneous scenes such as when I'm dressing for Thanksgiving and Estelle phones to warn that the Oakland cops are on their way. And the one where I return from Santa Cruz with Mr. Ferguson, who has rescued me after our swiped car runs out of gas. And the one where Dad and Lacey bring me back from Oakland after the fire, and George tells me to mow the grass, get a job, and butt out of his life. Dad's acting was very convincing in that scene.

Last scene of the day had George and Lacey catching me dancing around their bedroom in her bra and panties. Nearly as embarrassing to film as the shower scene. I'm trying not to imagine how that scene will be received by my future classmates. I may have to drop out of school for good and forget about college.

Brenda returned with six copies of *Time* and Cooper Tucker. He did great in his screen test, and his parents are thrilled he's going to be in a movie. They had never heard of Nick Twisp, but were longtime fans of Trent Preston. It turns out Cooper had some acting experience, starring last year as Algernon Moncrieff in a school production of *The Importance of Being Earnest*, which Cal is taking as another sign that he's gay. (Why exactly she didn't say.)

I showed him around our motel room, helped him unpack, then lent him a guiding arm when we walked to the café for dinner.

Being a welcome change from Denny's egotistical chatter and repulsive nose, Cooper was warmly received at the kids' table. All three girls competed for the two chairs beside him (Cal and Lauren won). They asked him so many questions, he could barely eat his shrimp quesadillas. Naturally, Lauren had to ask him if he had a girlfriend.

"Not at present," he admitted. "People find my situation intimidating."

"I know the feeling," said Lauren. "No one can look past my braces."

"That's absurd," said her sister. "Having braces and being blind are not at all comparable."

"I wasn't suggesting they were," said Lauren. "I'm just saying most people are very shallow when it comes to dating someone. Obviously, Megan, there are plenty of guys who are turned off by your rippling shoulder muscles."

"I don't see them standing in line to date wimps like you either!"

"Be nice, girls," said Cal. "Or we'll say this table is for actors only, and you can go eat with Roland and the rest of the crew."

"Who named you queen of this movie?" demanded Lauren.

"What exactly are braces?" asked Cooper, trying to keep the peace. "I've never been sure of that."

So Lauren took his hand and had him feel her imposing met-alwork. Possibly semi-erotic, but I'd rather do that sort of work under the bra.

"It's kind of like a fence," Cooper commented. "Like a metal fence around your teeth."

"Right," said Lauren. "A fence walling me off from guys."

"I'll go out with you, Lauren," said Arvin. "I'll buy you an ice cream cone after dinner."

"Too late, Arv," she replied. "I'm already stuck on Cooper. Want to tour the town with me, Cooper dear?"

"Sure," he said. "But first I need to try that berry pie that Nick was raving about."

He ordered dessert before me and scored the last piece in the place. I had to make do with boring apple pie.

While those three toured the town, Cal and I stayed behind and read the article in *Time*. I got mentioned in one sentence as the "co-star" of Nick Twisp's "home-produced" movie about his rebellious youth.

"Not very complimentary," said Cal. "If you read between the lines, they're making our movie sound like it's strictly from ama-teursville."

"Yeah, like a desperate attempt to revive his moribund ca-reer."

"Which it is, of course, but they didn't have to say so."

"It's that superior New York attitude, Sheeni. Dad says they're always looking down their noses at us West Coast types. He thinks it's because they're envious of our weather."

"It's not just the weather, Nick. It gnaws at them that the en-tire L.A. scene is so much hipper than they are. I suppose though the article is good publicity for the painting sale–if it ever hap-pens."

I thought of my elusive art profits and sighed.

"So what do you think of Cooper?" I asked.

"I think he's an absolute doll. If he's not gay, I so want to date him."

Great! Now I get to be jealous of a blind kid.

Later, as we were getting ready for bed, Cooper asked me who was prettier: Valerie or Lauren.

"Definitely Lauren," I lied. "She's absolutely gorgeous, even subtracting for the braces."

Cooper laughed. "That's what Arvin said you'd say. He says you're madly in love with Valerie."

"Uh, I do like her," I admitted.

"I expect so, Nick. It seems the sister is just as likable as the brother."

Wow. Could he just have admitted that he's in love with Harvey?

FRIDAY, July 17 – Cooper is a marvel. He showered, shaved, and dressed himself–all without assistance. He navigates around our crowded room like a sighted person. He's always cheerful and unlike Denny doesn't snore, belch, or fart. Even if he makes a play for Cal, he may be a difficult person to hate.

Dad was cheerier at breakfast. He got a call last night from Ada. She found a stash of post-wedding letters from her aunt Verna that do not read like the work of a demented person. Brent thinks they constitute legal proof that she had all her marbles when she gave them the painting.

"We're going to get Nerva and her lawsuit bounced right out of court," Dad declared.

"Great, Dad," I said. "Does that mean you're now paying for my desserts?"

"Not likely, Nick. I'm not going to pay to watch my stars get fat."

"I weigh 127 pounds, Dad. Cal thinks I look like I just got liberated from a Nazi P.O.W. camp."

"Sweets are bad for you, kid. They'll rot out your teeth. You can pay for your own dentist too."

"So how much am I making from this movie?" I asked.

"Plenty, Nick. A whole lot more than I had when I was your age."

That's a comfort. He just assured me that I'll be making more than 85 cents.

Tiara Diamond phoned as I was topping off my breakfast with

another piece of that teeth-rotting apple pie. She'd heard from Denny about his getting the ax.

"He wasn't very complimentary, Nick. He said you all were mean to him. He said you were making fun of his medical condition."

"Not true, Millie. We were as nice as anyone could be to that egomaniac. Anyway, it was hardly a medical condition. It was just a big ugly zit that he wouldn't leave alone. Our new Trent is so-o-o-o much better."

"I look forward to meeting him, Nick. Is he coming to L.A.?"

"Yeah, Cal just invited him to come back and stay with her family."

"I expect she intends to seduce him."

"Could be. I sincerely hope not."

"What do you hope not?" asked Cal, eavesdropping.

"I hope Denny wasn't traumatized for life from getting canned," I said.

Tiara overheard Cal and quickly terminated the conversation.

"Do you talk to that girl often?" asked Cal.

"She's always phoning me," I lied. "I think she must miss me."

"We used to think you were hot stuff, Nick," said Lauren. "And then we met Cooper."

Cooper smiled and dunked his toast exactly in the center of his sunny-side-up egg. I may have to devise a test for that guy to make sure he's actually blind.

Lauren asked Cooper what he wanted to do in life.

"I have a dream of being an actor. But my parents don't think that's very realistic."

"I don't see why not," she replied. "I bet a TV series about a cute blind guy would be a mega-hit."

"Nice of you to say so," laughed Cooper. "Know any Hollywood producers?"

"Yeah, I do. My mom and my dad!"

Wow. Could bunking with Harvey be the big break Cooper was waiting for?

Cal wants me to ask him if he's gay. But how do I bring up that subject? I'm from Indiana. Back home you could hang exclusively with guys, have a rainbow sticker on your car, have an iPod loaded with Elton John songs, and nobody would even broach the topic.

All of a sudden things got very, very exciting in Groveland. Having a movie company in town had caused only a minor stir. Then today Trent Preston arrived. Every female within 20 miles felt his awesome superstar vibe. They descended in swarms on our motel, where they had to make do with harassing former cable TV star Nick Twisp. (Trent and Apurva are staying out of town in what passes for a luxury B&B around here.) I guess they had a stowaway on their private jet, because Sheeni Saunders also showed up. She's checked into the last vacant room in our motel.

Sheeni invited herself along when we rode out to the RV park for today's shoot. She didn't think much of Brenda's two-story trailer. She said her family's trailer was a full two stories, whereas this one merely sports two small sleeping rooms upstairs.

"It was the best we could do on our budget," said Brenda. "I'd build one from scratch, but Steven Spielberg isn't producing this show."

Trent Preston arrived on set and made a major fuss over Cooper. Not to be catty, but snagging that virus at age two may have been a smart career move by him. Trent has promised to help him find acting work and wants Dad to beef up his part in our movie. Except isn't this supposed to be a biopic about Dad's youth, not Trent's?

Trent brought his own wardrobe and makeup people, who made him up first as Sheeni's ogre-like dad. His graying eyebrows, for example, were bushier than that shrub I vaulted over in the park. The scene had me knocking on their trailer door and telling him that I had come to take his daughter to the beach.

"Aha!" he bellowed, eyebrows flapping. "Then I trust, sir, that you are aware that in doing so, you have entered into an oral contract to perform *in loco parentis,* i.e., to provide for the safety and well-being of the aforementioned minor female."

I thought Trent was hamming it up excessively, but Dad wanted him to be even more over the top. The third take he imitated some long-dead actor named Charles Laughton. In the next one he did an impersonation of James Mason. Dad loved them both, but decided the Mason accent was funnier. No, the script won't be explaining why a trailer resident in rural California is speaking like an upper-class English actor.

The next scene had him answering the door and telling me

that I was banished from Sheeni's life "forever or for the next 1,000 years, whichever lasts longer." That line Trent ad-libbed.

Then we moved inside the trailer and they did a close shot of Trent acting stoned while examining the weave of the carpet. Next he changed into his Mrs. Saunders's disguise and pretended to be similarly fascinated by the rug. These shots were preliminaries to the big Thanksgiving banquet scene that we filmed after lunch. Trent tried his best to look like an old lady, but his granite-like movie-star jaw was hard to conceal. So they were trying to distract the eye with big jangling earrings and rhinestone-encrusted granny glasses.

When our boxed lunches were delivered, Trent and most of the cast gathered around Cooper to hear more of his inspiring life story. I sat apart from them because I was sort of getting annoyed by that budding star. I was surprised when Sheeni Saunders brought her lunch over and sat down beside me. She got right to the point.

"You don't like me do you?" she asked.

"I don't know. I guess I don't know you."

"Scott doesn't like me either. I can sort of understand that since he was perceiving me as a threat to his mother. I had nothing to do with your father's divorce, Nick."

One could debate that point, but I let it pass. "I guess not."

"They never seemed that happy together," she added. "Nick's a creative person and Ada's a dentist."

"Oral surgeon according to Scott."

"A minor quibble, Nick. She spends all day with her hands inside people's mouths."

She said that like she had had some painful experiences in a dentist's chair. Probably a root canal or two by some brute of a French dentist.

"So why are you here?" I asked.

"Trent invited me to come along, Nick."

"No, why are you here in America?"

"Oh, I don't know. I have lots of friends in France, Nick. I really do. But you know how it is: people get busy. They drift apart. You get a call instead of a visit. Then a text instead of a call. So sometimes you wind up dining alone in some médiocre bistro. With some Algerian waiter who thinks he has to flirt with you. But you know he's only doing it to relieve the tedium of his job. He's only going through the motions. So then you say what's the point of all this?"

"Sounds like a mid-life crisis."

"I suppose you could call it that. I knew I needed a change. I needed to be with people who cared for me. So I came to America to see my children and your father."

"You've hardly seen him at all for the past 40 years. You may not know what he's like these days."

"Oh, Nick doesn't change. I don't think any Twisps do. They hit age 15 and their personality freezes. Superficially, he's somewhat more mature. He thinks a bit before he acts. But he's essentially the same person I met all those years ago."

"So why do you want to hook up with some guy who's still kind of a teenager?"

"Because I'm so tired of the alternatives I've met. Look at most of the men his age. Would they be trying to make a movie with a bunch of amateurs in some trailer park in the middle of nowhere?"

"Trent Preston is no amateur. He's very big."

"I knew him as a first-grader, Nick. He was pretty charismatic even back then. It's sweet of him to be in your father's movie–even if he is making a travesty of my parents. Trent's participation should help your father get a distributor."

"Were you having phone conversations with my dad a couple months ago? Like regularly every night?"

"Wasn't me, Nick. Why?"

"Oh, just wondered."

She removed a brownie from her boxed lunch and handed it to me.

"So I hear you like your co-star."

"She's OK."

"Only OK?"

"No, quite a bit more than that."

"Then I'll tell you something rather frightening. In 40 years you will still be in love with her. You will think of her every day–even if you haven't seen her in years, even if she breaks your heart."

"Why would I do that?"

"Because you're a Twisp. Because you are your father's son."

She smiled and surprised me by giving me a kiss on the lips. She walked away, and I watched her join the crowd around Cooper.

Cal came over and tossed me the brownie from her boxed lunch.

"What was all that about?" she asked.

"I found out why Sheeni ditched France. She had a bad experience with an Algerian waiter there."

"She had an affair with him?"

"No, he was flirting with her, but only going through the motions."

"Ah, the curse of fading beauty. I hope I never get old."

"You want to die young?"

"No, Nick, I just want never to get old."

I ate three large brownies and felt a little sick. I wanted to take a nap, but we had to shoot the Thanksgiving dinner scene. This is the one where Paul and Lacey have drugged Sheeni's parents (with psychedelic mushrooms), and Trent arrives to nail Nick as the culprit who has been sedating Sheeni's roommate. Dad is praying that the ratings board will let this drug scene slide, since the only spoken reference is to "stuffed mushrooms."

It was a long afternoon. We did nine takes: five with Trent dressed as Mom and four as him dressed as Pop. (These will be inter-cut in the movie.) He ad-libbed differently in every take. The infection soon spread to Cooper, who also decided to improve on the script. I expected Dad to object, but apparently those two can do no wrong. Cooper was very good and didn't need any dark glasses. He looks in the direction of the person he's speaking to, so you can't really tell he's blind (if in fact he is.)

We shot a couple more scenes involving either Mr. or Mrs. Saunders. Then, as the sun was going down, we filmed the patio scene where Sheeni and I are making out and get interrupted by her mom. This was supposed to be fairly brief, but Trent decided to wing it, so I winged it along with him. The dialogue went something like this:

"Let's see this young heathen," croaked Trent.

"Hello, Mrs. Saunders," I said. "Nice to meet you."

"I doubt that very much. I've been discussing your case with Mrs. Clarklelson. Her reports are most unsettling. I fear for your immortal soul, young man."

"Nick's a very sweet boy, Mother," said Sheeni. "He's agreed to adopt Albert."

"That is no step toward spiritual redemption. That dog should be stabbed through the heart with a silver dagger one hour before the cock's crow on a moonless night."

Sheeni shook my hand. "Good night, Nick. Thank you for dinner. I'll see you tomorrow."

"Not so fast!" cackled Trent. "The inquisition has just begun!"

"Uh, my parents will be wondering where I am," I said.

"More likely they're wondering what they'll exhaust first: their beer supply or their sexual depravity."

"That's just idle gossip. My parents are quite respectable."

"Are they indeed? I've been informed by a reliable source that the knuckle-dragging oaf with the obscene convertible is not even married to your mother. They are fornicating out of wedlock!"

"I wouldn't know about that, Mrs. Saunders. I don't even know what that word means."

"Lord God in heaven! Smite this liar right where he stands!"

"No rain or lightning is in the forecast, Mrs. Saunders. So I guess I'm pretty safe."

"I curse you, Nick Twisp! You will go to France and sleep with camels. You will become a juggler with failing reflexes. You will marry a woman who will probe your gums with sharp instruments. You will have children who will arrive unexpectedly at awkward moments. You will violate my daughter, but she will torment you without mercy for all the years of your life!"

"Cut!" yelled Dad. "Good work, Mom. I think some of that may even be useable."

"Wasn't me, Nick," he replied. "I seemed to be speaking in someone else's voice. Someone from the grave. I think that may be her hovering up there above the trailer."

We all looked up. Perhaps it was only the last rays of the sun glinting off the aluminum, but there did seem to be some weird astral effect going on up there.

SATURDAY, July 18 – This morning's text from Harvey: "Ask my sistr about Pacific Palmetto in Malibu. Then choke and die." I put down my fork and showed it to her.

"I have no idea what that idiot is referring to, Nick. I have no association with the Pacific Palmetto Inn."

"Then how do you know it's an inn?"

"It's famous, Nick. Anyone who's been in L.A. for more than five minutes knows that."

At that moment Arvin and Cooper arrived at our table.

"Arvin," I said, "how long have you lived in L.A.?"

"All of my fabulous and glamorous life. Why?"

"So what is the Pacific Palmetto in Malibu?"

"Beats me. I never heard of it."

"That hardly proves anything," said Cal. "Arvin lives in Glendale. He couldn't be more out of it if he tried. My brother is just trying to stir up trouble and you're falling for it. You think I have some misdeeds associated with that place. Well let me tell you this: I don't give a damn what you think of me!"

With that she got up and abruptly left the café.

"Chicks," I sighed. "You can't win with them."

"Did you just figure that out?" said Arvin, ordering his usual egg-and-chorizo burrito.

"I know about that place," said Cooper. "It's an exclusive beach resort where wealthy people go to have discreet affairs."

"How do you know that?" I asked.

"Because someone extremely famous got discovered there with an under-age consort."

"Who?" demanded Arvin.

Cooper whispered something in his ear.

"Really?" said Arvin. "How come I never heard about that?"

"It all got hushed up. Large sums of money crossed palms."

"So how did you find out about it?" I asked.

"I have my ways, Nick."

Yeah, like maybe he was the precocious paramour.

"Cooper," I said, "there's a rumor going around that you're gay."

"That's odd, Nick. I heard the same thing about you."

Was that a denial? I can't tell.

After breakfast I phoned the Gargoyle and suggested she might want to find out if Desmond ever was seen at the Pacific Palmetto Inn in Malibu. Then I tracked down Cal and apologized abjectly for ever doubting her. She said we should try not to fall victim to her brother's mischief-making. She let me kiss her and use a bit of tongue. I'm not sure I liked that part. A bit too salivary if you ask me.

Dad decided to give everyone the morning off. We said good-bye to Scott and Chloe, who were driving back to L.A. Then Mary took us kids to the lake, while Dad and Sheeni went to have a gourmet lunch at Trent's fancy B&B. As we were reclining on the sand, Lefty showed up with Brenda and Felicity. The latter in her bikini was nubility on display, but Brenda in her vast one-piece suit was something of a visual assault. One's eyes were drawn to the scene, but didn't want to linger. Lefty in skimpy trunks was no more appealing.

Fortunately, as an antidote I had our three girls to gaze upon, plus Mary giving one hope for the sensual comforts of middle age. Lauren was all over Cooper like they were honeymooning at Waikiki. For being possibly gay, he wasn't doing much to discourage her attentions. She led him out to the deeper part of the lake for some aquatic snuggling. God knows what their hands were up to. Meanwhile, Arvin wasn't getting anywhere with Megan, and Cal was absorbed in her latest Desmond Upton novel.

"Want to go in the water again?" I asked.

"Not really," Cal replied, not looking up from her book. "They have some loaner paperbacks in the recreation hall. You could read."

"I don't want to read! I want to live!"

"Well, go live somewhere else. You're bothering me."

I opted to stay put and gaze down her bikini top. She has remarkably desirable breasts, but I may have mentioned that before.

"Cooper's acting rather straight today," I observed.

"He may just like the attention, Nick. I imagine being blind can be socially isolating."

"So can hanging out at the beach with you."

"Nick!! Please!!"

So Arvin and I walked around the lake. It was a hot and dusty trek, but it was something to do.

Dad called Mary and canceled the rest of the day's shoot. She said the wine appeared to be flowing so freely that he could no longer be concerned with anything "so mundane" as his movie.

He and Sheeni arrived back at the motel in the late afternoon. Dad had some news for me.

"We're all taking a haircut," he slurred.

"I've already had mine from Felicity," I replied. "If Cooper took up barbering, his clients would look like me."

"Ada twisted my arm, Nick. We're giving her greedy bastard of a cousin five percent. The bitch is lifting her injunction. I told Ada she's your damn relative, you pay her from your share. So we compromised. Three percent comes from Ada and two percent from me. So your share's being cut to five percent."

"That's not fair!" I protested. "You give up two percent and I give up five? That puts you three points ahead!"

"Hey, I'm the guy who was married to her all those years. I paid my dues, not you."

"If you cut my percentage, you can get another actor for your movie. I'm through!"

He threatened to strangle me, but with Sheeni's help we worked out a compromise: I'm back up to seven percent, which I made him put in writing. Sheeni signed as a witness. The skunk is still coming out ahead on the deal. Everyone got a haircut except him.

After dinner Lauren expelled Cal and Megan from their motel room so that she and Cooper "could have some privacy." For some reason this pissed off her sister, who went and snitched to Mary. One minute later their "private party" was officially canceled, and "mixed-sex twosomes" were banned for the duration of the shoot.

I asked Cooper if he was disappointed.

"Nothing was going to happen, Nick."

"Oh? Why not?"

"It was those gruesome braces. The experience of kissing her was discouraging to further intimacies."

I could see his point, but a horny straight guy might have soldiered on regardless.

SUNDAY, July 19 – I got an early a.m. phone call from Mrs. Chatzky, our next-door neighbor back in Terre Haute.

"Has anyone called you yet, Nick?" she asked.

"Called me about what?" I yawned.

"Did you hear about the accident?"

"What accident?" I asked, instantly alert.

"Your parents were in a wreck on the interstate. Your mother's in the hospital. So no one called you?"

"No! How is she?"

"The hospital says her condition is satisfactory. I have her number there if you want to call her."

I got the number and dialed it. My mother answered right away.

"Oh, hi, Nick," she said, sounding weak and far away. "I was going to phone you. I have some bad news. We were in a car wreck. Your fath–I mean Leonard–was killed. It happened yesterday. I hit an overpass abutment and he got thrown through the windshield."

"That's, uh, awful, Mom. But how are you? Are you OK?"

"I'm not so bad. The car hit mostly on Leonard's side. I got a bunch of bruises from the airbag and a broken ankle. I was wearing my seatbelt, but Leonard wasn't. You know how he was always complaining that they were too confining. His airbag didn't go off either. The nice highway patrolman said it was switched off. They say he died right away, so that's a comfort."

"I'm glad you're OK, Mom. How did it happen?"

"I was merging on the interstate, but there was a car in my blind spot. I didn't see it until the last second. I swerved to avoid it and lost control. After that, my mind's a blank. I don't even remember the airbag inflating."

"You want me come there, Mom? I could catch a plane this afternoon."

"No, I'm fine, Nick. I know you're busy there with your movie. And I wouldn't want you to see me with my face all swollen like it is. The doctor says I can go home today. No internal injuries. I can walk OK with my cast. Now I have to get busy on poor Leonard's funeral. Do you want to come out for that?"

Did I want to travel 2,000 miles to watch them plant my late stepfather in a hole? Not really.

"Uh, I think I'll be too busy."

"I'll let everyone know that you send your regrets. I'm sorry for the bad news, Nick dear."

"No problem, Mom. I'm just glad that you're OK."

Wow. The guy I used to think was my dad is now deceased.

I wonder what it's like to go through a windshield at freeway speeds. Do you have time to think, "What the fuck?" or is it all over super-quick?

At breakfast in the café everyone was shocked to hear my news. Cal remained silent until the others had expressed their sympathies. Then she leaned close to whisper in my ear.

"It was no accident, Nickie. Your mother is very brave. She had a problem and she dealt with it."

"You're saying my mother deliberately hit that concrete wall?" I whispered, shocked.

"It's obvious, Nick. And very inspiring to me as a woman."

Uh-oh, that was kind of scary.

"I don't know, Sheeni. That's just your conjecture."

"You know it's true, Nick. You know it's true in your heart. Your mother was in an intolerable situation and took the only way out. That's why we should be just as brave and deal with my brother."

"Not happening, Cal. Not happening at all."

"You'll come around, Nick. I know you will. Because you are your mother's son."

Dad said he hoped I didn't want to "go back there," because there was no room in his schedule for funeral leaves.

I said I was fine with missing it.

"Are you sure?" asked Mary. "I expect we could shoot around you, if you wish to take off a few days."

"How could we do that?" asked Dad. "He's in every scene."

"Show some compassion, Nick. There are more important things in life than our little movie."

"That's OK," I said. "I don't need to go to his funeral. I hate funerals."

"Spoken like a Twisp," said Dad. "We're livers, not dyers."

I felt bad all day. I felt bad because of what happened and because Cal thinks my mother is a murderer. I felt a little guilty too. I wanted Leonard Davidson to go away and leave me alone, but dying was kind of extreme. You'd think a guy whose parents croaked in a car wreck would see the point of buckling his seatbelt. And why was that airbag switched off?

Fortunately, we were too busy today for me to obsess over these matters. Brenda rented the office of the sole lawyer in town.

We filmed the scene where I show up in disguise and–flashing a big revolver–demand Sheeni's passport from her Pop. He opens his safe, then whirls around wielding a gun, so I blast him in the shoulder for his treachery. They used one of those special effects charges that very realistically blew a bloody bullet hole in Trent's shirt.

Brenda had procured a diverse selection of masks: the Easter Bunny, Shrek, E.T., George W. Bush, Mother Theresa, Elvis, Yoda, Quasimodo (from *The Hunchback of Notre Dame*), Alfred E. Neuman (of *Mad* magazine), and Marilyn Monroe. Trent and I preferred Quasimodo, but Dad decided Marilyn would be funnier. I had to speak my lines in a breathy falsetto, but I doubt I was sounding much like her. I pumped only one pretend bullet into Trent, but he hopped around in his leather executive chair like he was being riddled with lead a la Warren Beatty in "Bonnie and Clyde."

After I shot him, I dialed 911 on the office phone in a simulated panic and gasped, "There's been a shooting! Come quick!" I dropped the handset on the desk, rummaged around in the safe for Sheeni's passport, grabbed it, and fled. Meanwhile my victim was writhing away like he was doing the death scene from *Camille*. If they hand out an Academy Award for overacting, Trent's a cinch to win.

After lunch we shot two more scenes: My fleeing from Sheeni's trailer after the Thanksgiving confrontation with Trent. And the emotional departure scene where Nick, his family, and Albert the dog leave the RV park in Jerry's Lincoln (towing the derelict trailer). This was Nick's first separation from Sheeni, so I had to look mucho sad. I thought of my mother's accident and got misty-eyed right on cue.

"Jesus, Nick," said Dad after the scene ended. "Those are actual tears. That's some acting. You're a regular Margaret O'Brien."

Wow, sort of a compliment from my dad. The first one ever?

That was it for location shooting in Groveland. Tomorrow we head back to L.A. to film the rest of the movie.

We car-caravanned to Sonora to have a celebratory dinner at the only Chinese restaurant with decent Yelp reviews. Lefty ducked into the kitchen to confer with the chef, so we got their super-deluxe banquet with exotic dishes not on the menu. The manager went all out since Trent Preston was presiding at the table (and picking up the check). Another reason to become a film star: you get the royal treatment wherever you go. I think being fawned over incessantly could be a real ego booster. Everyone stuffed themselves except Cal, who said our excursion to rural California would go down as her all-time "Carb Overload Week from Hell."

I opened my cookie and read this fortune: "After tears you will find happiness with a Virgo."

"What's your sign, Cal?" I asked.

"Scorpio. Can't you tell?"

MONDAY, July 20 – Marooned in Bakersfield. Dad's cherry Lincoln broke down on the drive back. It and the trailer were towed separately to a service garage, where the mechanic found "evidence of leak sealer in the transmission." No bananas were seen. The viscous sealer plus towing the trailer in 100-degree heat combined to fry its internals. The rebuild is supposed to be finished tomorrow. Dad, Sheeni, and Cooper went on with Mary in her car. Cal, Arvin, Lauren, Megan, and I got left behind in a budget motel with Lefty. All bedded down in two rooms: guys in one, girls in the other. Neither Arvin nor I wished to cuddle with Lefty, so we're sharing one of the double beds.

God what a boring town. Totally abroil in the baking heat, so exploratory walks were out of the question. I don't see how my brother copes here. Some sadist had filled in the motel pool and planted a ratty cactus garden in its place. We had no car, so we hiked across the sizzling parking lot to a Denny's for dinner. Then it was back to our room and its laboring air conditioner.

"I see there's a beer bar across the highway," said Lefty. "I'm thinking of walking over there."

"Mention my brother's name," I said. "You might get some action."

"Can I rely on you not to raise hell?" Lefty asked.

"We're too enervated to raise hell," I replied.

"And no hanky-panky either, Nick," he added.

"We're too enervated for that too. Go and have some fun. Guzzle a beer for me while you're at it."

After Lefty left, we strolled over to the girls' room.

"Our adult supervision has departed and is unlikely to return for hours," I announced.

Arvin removed a deck of cards from his back pocket. "Anyone for strip poker?" he asked.

It was a very simple game: The person with the poorest hand had to remove one garment of their choice. The person with the winning hand got to don one garment. Since it was a hot night, no one started with that much on. Nudity–partial or full–was achieved fairly rapidly. I claimed my ZipPits counted individually as clothing items, but got voted down. The girls, in sandals, were handicapped by their lack of socks. Bras were soon shed, with Cal clearly winning in that sweepstakes. The Moran sisters, though, had nothing to be ashamed of, with Megan taking the prize for rosiest nipples.

Down to my tighty whities, I felt fairly safe with a pair of threes, but everyone beat me.

"OK, Nick," said Lauren, "let's see what you have to offer."

"Don't be shy," said Megan. "Anyway, we already got a peek at it on the video monitor."

Very reluctantly, I slowly worked my briefs down, one inch at a time.

"Boner!" bellowed Lauren, giggling. "Boner alert!"

"Hey, what did you expect," I said, red-faced.

"Circumcised," said Megan approvingly. "That's good."

"Why is it good that he's been mutilated?" asked Cal.

"I don't know," said Megan. "It just looks tidier. More stream-lined."

My streamlined boner settled in for the duration. Panties were shed, then Arvin's boxers. I think that guy should have his pitu-itary checked. He was sporting odd freckles down there and an intact foreskin, but no boner.

"God, what does it take to turn you on?" asked Megan, study-ing his limpidity.

"Come here and I'll show you," he leered.

But she didn't take him up on the offer. So we all put our clothes back on and called it a night.

TUESDAY, July 21 – After dropping off Arvin in Glendale and the Moran sisters in Westwood, we didn't roll into Venice until after 8 p.m. Big surprise: Cooper was ensconced in my bedroom.

"Shouldn't you be next door with your buddy Harvey?" I asked.

"Harvey says his bedroom is too small. I slept in his sister's room last night, but she's back now."

"Don't they have a guest room?"

"They don't even have a couch that makes into a bed. Mr. Haseltine says they're too close to Disneyland. If they had accommodations for guests, hordes of his relatives would be showing up to sponge off them."

"But I've only got the one narrow bed."

"I can't sleep on the floor, Nick. I hurt my back in gymnastics class."

I put the problem to Dad. His solution: Since Cooper was our guest, he sleeps on the bed; I sleep on the floor.

Damn!

And why is a blind kid doing gymnastics?

I texted Cal to meet me by the lap pool in five minutes.

"How come your damn brother isn't cuddling with Cooper?" I demanded when she showed up.

"It could be he wants to, but would rather inconvenience you."

"I continue not to believe Harvey is that devious."

"You underestimate my brother, Nick. Where will you be sleeping?"

"On the hard floor. Or I could sneak over and sleep with you."

"That's not happening, Nick. To oblige you to sleep on the floor, I'm sure my brother would be willing to delay sexual gratification."

"That seems to be a constant theme with your family."

"Don't complain. You got to see me naked yesterday."

"Looking without touching leaves a lot to be desired," I said, embracing her.

She gave me a long, slow goodnight kiss, then sprang away into the night like some startled nymph.

WEDNESDAY, July 22 – I didn't have to sleep on the floor. Lefty came to my rescue last night.

"Can't you read, Nick?" he asked, pointing to a small metal plate riveted to the foot of my bed.

I bent over to look at it. The label read: ACME PATENTED EX-PANDING HONEYMOON BED. CAUTION: KEEP FINGERS AWAY FROM MECHANISM.

Lefty flipped down a hinged panel and pulled out a compli-cated telescoping apparatus that elevated a concealed mattress, instantly doubling the size of the bed.

Cooper and I are now "honeymooning" in my queen-size bed. Both in flannel pajamas (he lent me his spare pair). So far, he's been staying on his side. Lounging in bed this morning, I told him about the strip-poker session he missed.

"I knew I should have stayed behind with you guys," he said. "It must have been tremendously exciting being in a room with three naked girls."

"Well, of course, it was," I affirmed. "But to tell you the truth, breasts actually look better in bikini tops. Starkly exposed, they're a bit utilitarian looking. Like babies might be sucking on them for nourishment. And below the waist there really isn't that much to see with girls."

"I suppose not," Cooper sighed. "Still it makes a fellow regret that he's sightless."

No time to meet Cal for coffee this morning. After breakfast we drove to a sound stage in Studio City to shoot a hospital scene. Cooper came along to observe. We used a standing set employed on that medical sitcom "Playing Doctor." The scene featured Lefty in bed after his penile operation. He's dopey from the pain meds, so it's Millie's job to excoriate Nick for talking him into the opera-tion and "ruining" her man.

It was nice to see Tiara Diamond again, even if we had to shoot the scene more than a dozen times because Dad didn't think she was projecting sufficient anger.

"Isn't there anything in this world that pisses you off?" Dad asked her at one point.

"I don't much care for the way Valerie treats your son," she replied.

"OK, then use that. I want some passion on display here!"

During a break I asked her if she wanted to have another date on Saturday.

"I'd love to Nick, but I already told Cooper I'd go out with him that night."

"How is that possible? You just met him."

"True, but Arvin's been phoning and telling me what a neat guy he is. Plus, he's about the cutest guy I ever saw. I could do Friday night, if you want."

"Uh, let me get back to you on that."

As Brenda might put it, ol' Cooper needs to sign up for a refresher course on Homosexuality 101.

I asked Tiara if she was a Scorpio.

"Of course not, Nick. I'm a Virgo. Can't you tell?"

"I got a fortune cookie last week that said I was going to find happiness with a Virgo."

"I'm not surprised, Nick. We Virgos are the best!"

To prove it she gave me a kiss on the lips. Rather nice and you just can't beat her cinnamony smell.

That afternoon the Gargoyle phoned me.

"I need you to take a photo of Desmond for me," she said.

"Why?"

"There's no record of his registering at the Pacific Palmetto Inn. But the fellow has dozens of aliases. He's very slippery. I need a photo to show the night manager."

"He's a famous author, Connie. There must be tons of photos of him on the Web."

"Not one, Nick. He's zealously camera shy."

"What about his wedding photos?"

"I've seen those, of course. He managed to duck out of every single one except the close-up of the wedding rings on the two intertwining hands. As if anyone wants to see his hairy fingers. I need his photo right away. You can email it to me. I understand you're sleeping with that Cooper boy."

"Not willingly. We need a bigger house."

"He was quite excellent as Trent. You can hardly tell he's blind. How's that Haseltine girl treating you?"

"OK. She's trying to enlist me in a conspiracy to murder her brother."

"Inspired no doubt by your resourceful mother. I suggest you consult with me before committing any major felonies."

"Will do, Connie. Thanks for calling."

Jesus, does everyone think my mother's a murderer?

When we got back from the studio, Cooper and I floated about in the lap pool. He still had that strip-poker game on his mind.

"When girls are naked, Nick, can't you see their pussies?"

"Not really. I mean if you got right down there and stared at it, there'd probably be plenty to see. But just in the normal course of events all you see is a patch of hair–assuming they haven't been shaving."

"Isn't that kind of disappointing?"

"No, it's quite stimulating. I could stare at a naked girl all day long and not get bored. So I guess you're not gay, huh?"

"Not in the least, Nick. How did you ever get that idea?"

"We thought you were in love with Harvey. You spoke so highly of him."

'You can like a guy, Nick, without being gay. For example, I also like you."

"Er, thanks. Did Harvey ever mention being gay to you?"

"No, we never discussed it."

"Then what is the big secret he has about Cooper at camp?"

"Oh, I know all about that, Nick."

"Really? What is it?"

"I can't tell you, of course. It's a secret."

A few minutes later Harvey came out in his yard to spy on us.

"Hello, Cooper," he called.

"Hi, Harvey!" said Cooper. "Come over and join us. This pool is great."

"If I did that, Cooper, the water would soon be running red with Nick's blood. I'd knock those cheap sunglasses off his nose and use the sharp edge of the shades to disembowel him."

"In your dreams, Harvey," I replied. "I'd trip you with Cooper's collapsible cane, then whip the drawstring out from my swim trunks and strangle you."

"While you're untying that difficult wet knot, Nick, I'd be stuffing your own flip-flops down your throat, blocking your windpipe."

"Isn't it time you two shook hands and buried the hatchet?" asked Cooper.

"I suppose it is," said Harvey. "But only if I get to bury the hatchet in Nick's skull."

After dinner I took his sister for a stroll along the canal. Cooper wanted to tag along, but I said the footing was too treacherous. I told her the news: No, Cooper wasn't gay, and yes, he knew Harvey's secret.

"Then it's your job to get it out of him," she said. "That shouldn't be hard. You're with him 24 hours a day."

"Don't remind me. Cooper's an honorable person, Cal. He doesn't go around blabbing secrets."

"It is in the nature of a secret that everyone is dying to blab it. You just have to employ the correct means for coercing it out of him."

"And what would that be?"

"Ingratiation, Nick. Be his pal. Win his confidence."

"OK, I'll try."

"You have to extract that secret, Nick. Or else I'll go after it myself. And you know what that will entail."

"What?"

"Sex."

"He might sleep with you and still not spill."

"I'm willing to take that chance. Cooper is a very attractive boy. Even more attractive now that I know he likes girls."

"He has a date with Tiara on Saturday."

"I knew that. That's why you want to take me out the same night. So you can see Tiara on Friday."

"How on earth did you know that?"

"Mentalism," she replied, tapping the side of her head. "I can read you like a book."

"So will you go out with me on Saturday?"

"I will if you have pried the secret out of Cooper by then."

Conditional love, thy name is Valerie Haseltine.

Later, as we settled into bed, I asked Cooper if he could give me a hint about Harvey's secret.

"I can tell you that the secret will be revealed sometime soon."

"Really? When?"

"That, naturally, is a secret."

"Will it be revealed before Saturday?" I asked hopefully.

"Sorry, no."

Damn!

THURSDAY, July 23 – Dad, being an optimist, announced at breakfast that he has emailed the seller of the Lincoln (nephew of the deceased little old lady) suggesting they split the cost of the transmission rebuild ($3,800). He requested that a check for

$1,900 be mailed to him "at your earliest convenience." Good luck with that. Since we were discussing financial matters, I hit him up for $100.

"Why such an exorbitant figure?" he asked.

"It's for the tears I shed the other day and for being compared to Margaret O'Brien."

"That was a compliment," he alleged, opening his threadbare wallet and forking over four twenties. "Little Margaret O'Brien used to terrify her fellow actors because they knew she was stealing the picture."

Cooper had seconds of the cheesy scrambled eggs and told Lefty he was a much better cook than his mother.

"Breakfast is easy," Lefty replied. "Hell, I sometimes have breakfast on the table before I'm even awake. My alarm clock goes off, and there I am buttering a biscuit." (His biscuits are light, flaky, and always fresh-baked from scratch.)

"Nick, do you want to go to Scott's high school?" asked Dad.

"I don't know," I replied. "Do I?"

"Scott liked it OK. It's a pricey private school for the pampered elite of L.A. Veeva went there too. You can check it out today. We're filming there."

The school was trying to look like a fancy college, but was hampered by its cramped campus and location in an industrial area. Today it was subbing for Sheeni and Trent's snooty French-speaking school in Santa Cruz. Originally, Dad drove there with two buddies from Ukiah, but to condense the story for the movie I was making the journey with Lefty. Since the school was closed for the summer, members of the French Club had been rounded up to serve as unpaid extras. All had been issued Dalton Academy blazers that Brenda scored from that defunct TV show "Glee."

Cooper donned his and had to break into a song ("Hey, Soul Sister") from the Warblers' repertoire. Not surprisingly, he sounded quite good, if you go for that sort of thing. Cal complimented him on his "perfect tenor voice," then nudged me to do the same. Oh right, I was supposed to be ingratiating.

"Didn't you just love 'Glee?'" asked Lauren, handing me a donut.

"It was OK," I replied. "Or at least the 10 minutes of it I saw."

Actually, I watched it every week (Mom loved it), but such indulgences could not be admitted casually.

First we shot the scene where Lefty and I arrive in a "borrowed" car and try to find Sheeni. We ask around and get increasingly frustrated as all the kids answer in French. At last we locate her, she kisses me, and immediately inquires about her "darling dog Albert."

The next scene had Sheeni introducing us to her roommate Taggarty, played by Lila Finster, the girl with the wandering eye, slight overbite, and enhanced chest whose website we had checked out all those weeks ago. She was cute, bubbly, and seemed quite nice. Cal, of course, took an immediate dislike to her. While Taggarty feigned severe menstrual cramps to distract the matron, Sheeni sneaked us into the building to spend the night. Opting to give Sheeni Saunders another chance, Dad drafted her to play the matron. She wasn't looking very matronly in her crisp uniform, but nobody could fault her French.

I ate my box lunch with a friendly girl named Alicia, the president of the school's Drama Club. Through a connection with Veeva, she got picked to play the shunned girl Bernice Lynch (who Nick enlists to sedate Taggarty). Alicia said if I enrolled at her school, she would take me around and introduce me to "the kids that matter."

I told her I also was planning to check out the school that Cal attends.

"Oh, you don't want to go there, Nick," she said. "It's full of misfits, scrabs, pankles, and zone-outs. Every year we send about four times more grads to the Ivy League. We also do well with Stanford, U.C.L.A., and U.C. Berkeley. I'm aiming for Yale Drama School, so this credit in your movie should be a big plus. I just wish the character I'm playing wasn't such a total loser."

After lunch we shot a scene that Dad added to beef up Cooper's part. This found him in a classroom surrounded by pretty girls. The dialogue was in French (to be shown with subtitles). Translated, it went something like this:

First girl: "Trent you are so handsome!"

Trent: "I know. For me humility is a trial."

Second girl: "Trent, my heart aches so for you! I can't stand it!"

Trent: "I can't love you alone, Margaux. It wouldn't be fair to the others."

Third girl: "Trent! I want to be your slave!"

Trent: "I'll let you wash my shirts. But, please, no starch."

Fourth girl: "Trent, darling! I want to have your babies!"

Trent: "I could pencil you in for four o'clock. But I might go wind-surfing instead."

Cooper's French sounded fine to me, but I heard Sheeni tell Dad that he sounded like "a rustic Quebecker transplanted to Manitoba." Those Frenchies are known for being snooty about their accents. I say just forget about it and speak English.

Next, we all trooped into the girls' restroom to shoot the scene where Lefty and I are brushing our teeth and encounter Bernice, who is vomiting in a stall. Assuming she's being friendly, we divulge that we are camping for the night in Sheeni's room.

The last scene of the day had us running down a hallway in our underwear after Bernice snitched on us to the matron. Sheeni Saunders did quite well chasing after us and shouting imprecations in French. I guess she can act, given the right part. Even Mary complimented her, which you know had to be a struggle.

Seeing that I wasn't getting anywhere with Cooper, Cal held his hand on the ride home.

I mouthed the words, "Stop that!"

She mouthed the reply, "Don't tell me what to do!"

But Cooper could tell something was going on and asked us what we were doing.

"Not a thing, honey," said Cal. "Nick is just jealous because I like you more."

"She's only trying to worm that secret out of you, Cooper," I warned.

"I know, Nick. But I'm enjoying the attention. Were those girls pretty who were saying such nice things to me today in French?"

"I'm sure Nick wouldn't kick them out of bed," said Cal. "But then, that's not saying much."

"They were all pretty, Cooper," I said. "I'm surprised you didn't ask any of them out."

"I thought about it. But I'm going out with Valerie tomorrow and Tiara on Saturday."

Not good news. Not good news at all.

FRIDAY, July 24 – A call from my mother woke me early this morning. Leonard Davidson's windshield-infused body has been planted in his native Indiana soil. Several mourners at the funeral home said they missed seeing me, but were looking forward to my movie. Too bad my ex-dad won't get to see it. All of his dry-cleaning locations were closed that day so employees could attend. Some of them even did.

"I'm selling the house and have listed the business with a broker," said Mom. "I have nothing to hold me here now."

"Where will you live, Mom?"

"Would you be terribly upset if I moved to Los Angeles?"

"Of course, not. I'd like that. I meant to ask you, Mom, about that lawyer he was going to hire. Did he give up on that idea?"

"Not entirely, Nick. He was talking about doing something, but only out of spite against your father. But we don't have to worry about that now."

"No, I guess we don't."

"Who, what, what's going on?" asked Cooper, waking up.

I told him I was on the phone with my mom.

"Who's that, Nick?" asked Mom. "Is someone in bed with you? It sounds like a boy."

"It's an actor in our movie, Mom. Our house is full up, so he's bunking with me."

"I'm fine if you're gay, Nick. I'm not narrow-minded like most people in Indiana."

"I'm not gay, Mom. It's only a temporary accommodation. Cooper here has two upcoming dates with my girlfriends."

"Sounds complicated, Nick. But then I guess that's L.A. for you. Leonard left you something in his will."

"What, Mom?" I asked, intrigued.

"His collection of matchbooks from Nevada casinos. It's quite extensive. I shipped it to you yesterday in a giant box."

"Gee, Mom, I can hardly wait."

Too bad he wasn't cremated. They could have used the matchbooks to light the fire.

Dad was looking nervous at breakfast. He was eating with one hand and squeezing his tennis ball with the other. Today is the day of the big auction in New York. Ada emailed him a link so he could watch the auction live as it happens, but he won't be tuning in. He said he doesn't need the stress. Nor was he willing to forward the link to me.

"It's a distraction we don't need," he said. "Fifty years from now no one will care what that damn painting sold for."

Especially him, since he'll be dead.

It was a struggle, but I managed to convince Cooper to amend his dating plans. We'll *both* be going out with Cal today and with Tiara tomorrow. I told him it wasn't fair to expect Lefty to transport four couples on four separate dates.

"And who will be kissing our dates goodnight?" he asked.

"I'll kiss Cal tonight, and you can make out with Tiara tomorrow."

"And what if both girls prefer me?"

"Then someone may be tripping over a mop bucket later."

"That's not nice, Nick. That's not nice at all!"

"True, but it's hardly fair for you to monopolize all the girls."

Just then the Gargoyle phoned demanding to know why she hadn't received a photo of her son-in-law. I told her I hadn't seen Desmond yet, but expected him here for the weekend.

"I should have photographed him myself," she said. "I had the chance, but I never expected my daughter's marriage to last this long. Children can be so exasperating in that respect."

I said I would nail him with my cellphone as soon as he showed up.

For today's shoot we returned to the Mar Vista house. "My bedroom" had been made over as Sheeni and Taggarty's Santa Cruz dorm room. French posters on the walls, a couple of battle-scarred desks, and a bunk bed replacing my single bed. A pair of sleeping bags had been unrolled on the floor for Lefty and me. Taggarty emerged from the bathroom in semi-revealing baby-doll pajamas, but Cal's charms were obscured in a long flannel nightgown. Felicity had Arvin and me in PG-rated boxer shorts, which neither of us wore in real life. And why would you? Your business just hangs down inside with a complete lack of vital support.

The script had me suggesting to Sheeni that we "go at it" in the bottom bunk while Lefty tackled Taggarty in the top bunk. But she replies, "Don't be silly, darling. Not with others in the room." So I bed down on the floor and go to sleep.

"Gee, Dad," I said. "Why am I being such a wimp? I drive all the way to Santa Cruz in a stolen car just to have a celibate night? Shouldn't my alter ego François Dillinger try a little salesmanship here?"

Dad thought it over. "OK, we'll shoot it both ways: As scripted and your way. I suppose you want to ad-lib that?"

I reminded him that film was a collaborative medium; he reminded me that he was paying my salary.

"So far that's only a rumor," I pointed out. "When exactly do I get paid?"

"That's all taken care of, Nick, per the Jackie Coogan Act."

Could be, but so far I'm feeling just as broke and exploited as poor Jackie.

Here's how we did the scene, when–with Lefty and Taggarty simulating the sex act above us–it was our turn to improvise:

Sheeni: "Nickie, darling, what are you doing?"

Nick: "Moving in with you."

Sheeni: "Is the floor too hard?"

Nick: "The floor and other things. Does this nightgown unbutton or are you sewed into it?"

Sheeni: "It's the deluxe chastity model. My mother ordered it from a Christian catalogue."

Nick: "Sheeni, darling, you appear to have three breasts."

Sheeni: "No, the third lump you're fondling is a toy stuffed dog. It's my substitute for darling Albert."

Nick: "I can't get this damn nightgown off. Where's the opening?"

Sheeni: "It's concealed against tampering. We could just cuddle."

Nick: "Cuddle, hell. Tonight I intend to make you a woman."

Sheeni: "Nature made me a woman, Nick. You're just making me uncomfortable."

Under the many layers my busy hand found a warm thigh and followed it to its apex. Cal gave a start.

Sheeni: "Good God, Nick! What do you think you're doing?!"

Right then the Matron and Bernice burst into the room; Cal gave a heave and threw me out of bed.

"Cut!" yelled Dad. "Not bad, but that seemed more like a rape than a seduction."

"I thought it was great," said Roland, chuckling. "It was François, the wild man, taking charge."

"Sorry, Cal," I whispered. "I was feeling the energy of the scene."

She was muttering about being "pawed like a piece of meat" when Dad's phone rang. He checked his screen.

"It's from Ada," he announced.

"Ne pas nous tenir en haleine!" said Sheeni the Matron.

"That goes double for me," added Brenda.

Dad answered the call, spoke briefly, then clicked off.

"Eight point four," he said, looking stunned.

"Eight point four what?" I demanded.

"Million, of course," he replied.

I did some quick math: seven percent of $4.2 million equals $294,000. Not a fortune, but it beats washing Town Cars for peanuts.

"When do we get paid, Dad?" I asked.

"I have no idea, Nick. But I expect these things take time."

"Congratulations, Nick," said Cal. "You just became marginally more attractive."

Sudden wealth is so great. I could feel the endorphins spilling into my brain all day. Naturally, I made a long list of all the things I would buy. Soon I will be dressing better and carrying state-of-the-art electronics. I may even procure a trinket or two for my loving girlfriends. And hire a thug to beat up Harvey. And find a budget motel room somewhere for Cooper. And have an Uber car permanently on call for my transportation needs. And so on!

Cal decided on "blind-friendly" activities for tonight's date. We rode the rides at the Santa Monica pier, then had dinner at that Mexican restaurant with the Korean chef. She held Cooper's hand to guide him and my hand because I was paying. My rival tried some blatant neck-nuzzling while waiting for a table, but desisted when I whispered "mop bucket." Cal told the waiter today was Cooper's birthday (even though it wasn't), so they brought him a free flan and everyone sang "Happy Birthday" to him.

Cooper blew out his candle, kissed Cal, and said it was his "best birthday" ever. The guy is not only blind, he's delusional.

After Lefty dropped us off in front of Cal's house, I suggested a group hug. Cal wasn't buying that. She gave Cooper the Number Nine Smoldering Kiss and me the Number Two Indifferent Peck. I told myself she was only playing up to him to extract that secret.

Oh well, at least I got to feel her up today. And there's the big pot of cash coming my way too. I mustn't forget about that.

SATURDAY, July 25 – Spotting Desmond's car in the driveway this morning, I went over there first thing.

"Desmond is still asleep," said Veeva, frying "clown face" pancakes for her kids. "Have you eaten?"

"I'm not hungry," I said, fending off Xenia's sticky embrace. "Can I go see him?"

"Uh, sure, I suppose," she replied. "Second doorway down the hall."

Desmond was snoring away nicely, but had a pillow over his head. I readied my phone, gave a sharp twist to his big toe, and snapped his photo as he reared up in surprise.

"What the hell!" he roared.

He may have said more, but I beat it out of there at a fast clip. I ran all the way down the block, hid behind some bushes, emailed the photo to Connie, then sauntered back home. I encountered the bathrobed author in his driveway.

"Let's have that photo, Nick," he said.

"Oh, sure," I said, handing him my phone. "I take photos of all my friends now. It's my new hobby. I like to take them by surprise."

Desmond erased the photo, then pocketed my phone.

"I'll get you a camera, Nick. And a new phone. But you can't take any photos of me."

"Why not?"

"Because I'm trying to protect my privacy."

"OK fine, Desmond. But I would like my phone back."

"Sorry, I can't do that. Your new phone will be delivered this afternoon."

"But what if I get some calls?"

"I'll let you know if you do. How's the movie going?"

"Uh, OK. Dad thinks it's going to put him on the Hollywood map."

"Good. And how's Valerie doing?"

"She's excellent. Her acting is amazing."

"Good. I'm not surprised."

Somehow I wasn't surprised that he wasn't surprised.

I went up to my bedroom and immediately emailed Connie not to call me because Desmond had confiscated my phone. Cooper returned from taking a shower and reported that there was no hot water and the bathroom smelled like perfume.

"Whose?" I asked.

"Either Mary's or Brenda's. They appear to use the same kind, have you noticed that?"

"Not really."

"Sighted people don't pay as much attention to their noses as they should. Right now I smell blueberry waffles, bacon, coffee, fresh-squeezed orange juice, and your discarded socks."

"Race you downstairs," I said.

I beat him as usual. Mary Moran was eating a waffle, but so was Brenda. Had Dad passed the night with the Big Blatt? Not very likely. Had Lefty? No, they weren't giving off any apparent love vibes.

Dad had been talking to Ada and had more intelligence to impart. The buyer of the painting was some deep-pockets art connoisseur in Dubai. So it's oil money that soon will be lining our pockets.

Dad also cancelled today's filming. He has an emergency meeting with his accountant to discuss the tax implications of his art windfall. I say just stash those millions in an overseas account like the rest of the Wall Street crowd.

After breakfast Cooper and I strolled to the coffee place, where we met Cal. Seated across the patio was her diabolical brother.

"Hello, Cooper," he called.

"Hi, Harvey," said Cooper. "Come join us."

"I'd like to," he replied. "But I'd feel the need to drag Nick inside and hold his head under the steam nozzle of the espresso machine."

"Not likely, old sport," I said. "I'd break your grip and run all your major appendages through the bagel slicer. Then I'd smear what was left of you with cream cheese and stake your carcass out for the buzzards to finish off."

"Before you even laid a mitt on me, Nick, I'd have you head-first in the coffee grinder being processed for the drip you are."

At that point a middle-aged lesbian couple at a nearby table got up and left in a huff.

"We're prying your secret out of Cooper," said Cal. "We're working on him day and night."

"Cooper is wise to your tricks, sister dear. I trust him completely."

"Shouldn't you be helping Dad open the store?" she asked.

"I'm on my way there now. Want to come over tonight, Coop, and hang out?"

"I'd like to, Harv, but I have a date with Tiara Diamond."

"Really? And what does my sister think of that?"

"I think you should butt out and drop dead," she replied. "Kiss me, Cooper dear."

He did so with an enthusiasm that was very painful to observe.

Desmond was true to his word. A van pulled up today and delivered two packages. One contained a cellphone many generations newer than my old one. In the other one was a fancy Japanese digital camera that fits in a pocket yet offers a 50-power zoom lens. Now I can snap photos of Desmond from way down the block. And what an asset this camera will be if Cal ever decides to undress in front of her window.

I knocked on the Uptons' back door, thanked Desmond profusely, and persuaded him to hand over my hostage SIM card so I could get connected. My first call was to the Gargoyle, but she wasn't answering. I asked her to phone me if she got anywhere with Desmond's photo.

I was downloading apps to my new phone when it rang.

"Hallo," said a juvenile voice. "Please to speak to Nick."

"This is Nick," I replied. "Who's this?"

"Tudor, your nephew."

"Who?"

"Your nephew in Argentina. My grandpa say I call you."

"Oh, OK. How old are you?"

"I have nine years. I perform trampoline at circus with my family. You like this?"

"I guess. I never gave it much thought. So do you talk to your grandpa very often?"

"Many do we speak. He say stories to me. I practice the English. I want to visit the U.S.A., but Mama say maybe next year only."

"When you talk to him, Tudor, does he sometimes remind you to speak English?'"

"Yes, he no do Spanish good. But I no remember the hard English words. You speak Spanish?"

"Not really. I studied it in school–for what that's worth."

"OK, 'bye, Nick. I say to Grandpa I call you. Bye-bye."

Geez, I have relatives who can barely speak English. So that's who Dad was phoning. It wasn't some foxy foreign girlfriend. His life was even more forlorn and wretched than I assumed.

In Encino tonight Tiara was having trouble wrapping her suburban mind around the concept of dating two guys simultaneously. When we arrived in Encino, she handed me a book titled *Anne of Green Gables*.

"What am I supposed to do with this?" I asked.

"It's my favorite novel, Nick. While I'm chatting with Cooper at the restaurant, you can read it."

"Why can't you chat with both of us?"

"That wouldn't be fair to Cooper, since he asked me out first. Nor would it be polite for us simply to ignore you. I'm sure you'll love the book!"

She chose an Indian restaurant on Ventura Boulevard that offered an extensive vegetarian menu. The handsome couple sat together on one side of the booth; I got the lonely guy's seat on the other side. She ordered a bunch of dishes with exotic names for us to share.

"I hope you like Indian food, Cooper," she said.

"Oh, sure. I've had it lots of times."

"There are quite a few Indian restaurants in Indiana," I remarked. "High-tech firms always have many Indian employees."

"Read your book, Nick," commanded Tiara. "I know you'll enjoy chapter one."

So I read the damn book. Page one was about some meandering brook and a guy sowing turnip seeds. Then we got mired in a flowery description of some house that I guess was going to figure prominently in the story. I was hoping a gunshot would ring out to provide some interest, but all we got was a couple of old dames having tea. Meanwhile, across the table the blonde and the blind kid were discussing our movie and edging into sharing their Life Stories.

"When does this Anne babe show up?" I asked.

"Just keep reading, Nick," said Tiara. "She shows up very soon."

"I hope so. I hope she's wanted in several states and has a price on her head."

Tiara and Cooper ignored that remark.

Eventually the food arrived and we all dug in. Most of it was recognizable and not that spicy. Even the fried okra went down without triggering my gag reflex. We were sharing the dishes, but not the conversation. I got excluded from theirs, so I returned to my book. Now we meet this Matthew Cuthbert dude, who was a strange-looking guy who "dreaded all women except Marilla and Mrs. Rachel." I know the feeling. I was starting to dread Tiara Diamond and her weird taste in literature. Now comes a major shock: Anne arrives and is an 11-year-old orphan girl. I stopped reading right there. No way was I going to read about some precocious preteen and her precious antics. So I put down the book and stared impassively at my tablemates until the bill arrived. I scrutinized the tab.

"Uh, my share with tip is $23," I said, extracting the cash from my wallet.

The others looked at me in surprise. It was all too apparent they had expected this pricey meal to be my treat.

I phoned Lefty to come pick us up while they were negotiating the balance of the payment. Somehow the rest of the cash got coughed up.

After kissing Cooper goodnight back at her house, Tiara asked if I wished to borrow her book.

"Not unless Anne gets sold into white slavery or becomes a heroin addict," I replied.

"It's a classic of literature, Nick. Not a tawdry paperback."

"I think I'll skip it just the same. Are you done here, Cooper?"

He wasn't. He had to kiss her again. And this time he got in a furtive grope.

SUNDAY, July 26 – I switched on my computer this morning, and found this email from the Gargoyle: "Your photo didn't come through. Please send it again."

Damn!

A few minutes later I sneaked out on the balcony with my new camera and snapped an extreme telephoto shot of Desmond leaving in his car on a bagel run. The screen displayed this message: "Install SD card."

Double damn!

I rummaged through the box, but found no memory card. Knowing Desmond would be returning within minutes, I shook Cooper awake and asked him if he had such an item.

"Fraid not, Nick. Blind people aren't usually into photography."

At breakfast Dad said he had many SD cards, but they were all in his storage locker. Lefty said he gave up picture-taking back when his Instamatic was stolen in 1986.

Dad asked me why Desmond gave me such an expensive phone and camera.

"He said it was to make up for all of my birthdays he missed," I lied. "A thoughtful gesture that others might consider emulating."

"My birthday is next Saturday," replied Dad. "That's something you may wish to keep in mind."

I can only hope that the Bulgarian candy is still on sale.

Today we returned to the pricey private school where I may (or may not) be matriculating (a word that sounds way dirtier than it is). This time the school was masquerading as Ukiah's Redwood High, Dad's fleeting alma mater. Members of the Drama Club had turned out dressed in their interpretations of small-town hicks. Brenda, however, made the guys remove the cigarette packs from their t-shirt sleeves. She also informed the girls that the manic gum-chewing and ratted hair would not be required.

Felicity had my "Mussolini Revival" costume ready and made me over as Carlotta Ulansky, a girl on the run who was obliged to dress like an elderly Italian widow. Dad said this would all be explained in a voice over.

My first time ever in a dress, long wig, panty hose, and padded bra. You do get nice ventilation up the thighs, should that be desired. Suddenly having prominent breasts gave one a new perspective as well. Who knew that one's view of the floor is impeded? Strap on high heels and then have to peer over your bust: it's no wonder gals were stumbling about.

I watched in a mirror as Felicity applied my rouge, eye shadow, and lipstick. Rhinestone-studded glasses completed my ensemble.

"What do you think, Nick?" she asked.

"I think I make a really, really ugly girl."

"Not at all," she laughed. "I think you're kind of cute. And don't forget your dad looked so good as Carlotta that Trent Preston asked him to a dance."

"Only guys with eyesight like Cooper would invite Nick anywhere," commented Cal.

"I wish I could see your transformation," said Cooper, who had to content himself with feeling up my enhanced bust line. This may be stimulating for girls, but did nothing for Carlotta.

The first scene of the day had Carlotta informing a guidance counselor named Miss Pomdreck (played by Uncle Jake's wife Lillian) that I had a rare disease and therefore had to be excused from girls' gym. She said she'd excuse me temporarily, but I had to provide a written note from "your family physician."

In the next scene I present her with a forged doctor's letter. Miss Pomdreck says I'm excused from the class, but will have to serve as assistant to the gym teacher.

"I can't go in the locker room, Miss Pomdreck," insists Carlotta. "I'm highly allergic to steam."

"Nonsense," she replies. "It's only water vapor. You'll do fine. Your job will be to make sure the girls don't linger in the shower. And to discourage horseplay and towel-snapping."

"I can't do it!" Carlotta protests. "I'll die in there!"

"Don't be a baby, Carlotta," she replies. "It's only the girls' locker room, not a foxhole in Iraq. Now get back to class."

We shot the next two scenes in the cafeteria. The first had Carlotta eating alone amid a sea of hostile students. (A nightmare I'll be facing in a few weeks.) In the next scene I surprise a table of girls by boldly taking a seat among them.

"Any of you girls need some birth control pills?" Carlotta asks brightly.

"What are you talking about?" demands a girl.

"Haven't you heard?" Carlotta replies. "Trent and Sheeni are smuggling them up from Santa Cruz. I can get you as many as you need. And cheap too!"

"Who dresses you, girl?" asks another girl. "Your granny? Or are you in mourning because your skinny butt died?"

"This is the Mussolini Revival look," Carlotta replies. "It's all the rage in L.A. That where I'm from. I'm sorry you rural girls are so desperately out of it."

"I never saw that look in any magazine," comments a third girl.

"Those magazines are produced months in advance," says Carlotta, fluffing her wig. "This awesome fashion revolution just swept up Rodeo Drive last week!"

At lunch I asked Cal if she had an SD card I could borrow. She didn't.

"Why do you need that?" she asked.

"It's for my new hobby. I've taken up photography in a big way. Shall I do some nude studies of you?"

"OK."

"Really? You're willing to do that?"

"Of course, Carlotta. Why not? I'll need some glossies to give to casting directors. You can strip down and photograph me fully clothed anytime you want."

Somehow I knew there'd be a catch to it.

The last scene of the day took place in a classroom. Kids are arriving for class and look surprised when Sheeni and Trent enter.

"Trent and Sheeni, you're back!" exclaims a boy.

"Not willingly," says Sheeni. "Our despotic parents made us return."

"Some criminal lowlife was spreading vicious rumors about us," says Trent.

A girl in the back screams, "Thank God, you're back, Trent! Life was hell without you!"

"Right on!" exclaims another girl. "Now I have a reason to live!"

Trent waves as all the girls applaud and cheer.

Then the camera pans over to where Carlotta is seated. She smiles in triumph. Sheeni walks over and takes a seat beside her.

"Do I know you?" asks Sheeni. "You look vaguely familiar."

"I'm Carlotta," I reply. "I'm told I look a bit like my mother, the famously obscure actress Bertha Ulansky."

"That must be it," says Sheeni, extending her hand. "Glad to meet you. I'm Sheeni Saunders."

"I know," I say, shaking her hand. "Your illustrious reputation precedes you."

"Want to drop by my house after school, Carlotta?" she asks.

"We can discuss your mother's film career. And try on some of my lavish jewelry collection. It will be just us girls."

"How nice, Sheeni. That sounds like tremendous fun."

If only my darling would invite me to do something tremendously fun in real life.

MONDAY, July 27 – A messenger dropped by early this morning with an envelope for me containing a 64GB memory card and this note from the Gargoyle: "I can only pray you are not this inept in other aspects of your life. Shape up, Nick! Remember you are a Twisp, the most resourceful of men. Don't disappoint me again!"

Geez, that woman is a ball-buster. I'm glad she's not my mother–or my mother-in-law. Desmond would have to be very foolish (and brave) to stray with her on his case.

We returned to the school to shoot the challenging girls' locker room scene. The problem facing Dad and Roland was to suggest a room full of naked girls without showing any nudity. You'd think if he can flash my butt like it's going out of style without risking his PG rating, he could show an undraped breast or two. Apparently not. Nor would the school authorities permit any disrobing to be filmed and filtered out later. That meant no students in bras and panties. Fortunately, Brenda came to the rescue with flesh-colored bikinis. The upper half snapped in the back and had no straps, permitting shoulders to be bare. The lower part was an unadorned spandex style designed to blend in with the body. Cal certainly looked semi-nude when she emerged from the dressing room to be ogled by me.

"Mind if I take your photo?" I asked, snapping away with my new camera. I had set it on burst mode to capture 15 shots with a single press.

"That's enough of that, Nick," she said. "This suit has absolutely no style. I look virtually naked."

"I think that's the idea," I replied.

"Mind if I look at it?" asked Cooper.

Naturally, she let him do just that with his hands, which was very painful to observe. Guys really don't like to watch their sweethearts being pawed by other men.

Next I snapped photos of Mary's daughters when they emerged. Lauren and Megan had decided this was their best chance to appear in the movie. I ogled them with pleasure even though recently I had seen them far more undressed. One really doesn't tire of gazing upon the female form.

Miss Arbulash, Dad's tyrannical gym teacher, was played by the school's actual gym teacher. She was an athletic-looking gal who decades ago had nearly made the U.S. Olympic swim team. I had no doubt she could beat me in any athletic endeavor, except perhaps competitive long-distance pissing.

First Roland took a lot of hand-held shots of the girls in street clothes pretending to undress. Then he shot them all in the showers until the hot water gave out. (Digitally created steam would be added later to obscure the bikinis.) Then he shot them toweling off. These were general shots for quick montage cuts.

Next, we filmed the scenes with dialogue. The first showed Carlotta, equipped with a whistle and clipboard, loitering reluctantly outside the locker room door.

"Carlotta, what are you doing?" demanded the gym teacher.

"Nothing, Miss Arbulash. I'm paralyzed with dread."

"Nonsense! You're the shower monitor! Get in there and do your duty!"

The next scene has Carlotta entering and being greeted by catcalls.

"What's the matter, Carlotta?" sneers Lauren. "Got your period?"

"Afraid you'd blind us if we saw your skinny bod?" asks Megan.

Carlotta blows her whistle.

"OK, let's hustle!" she commands. "Get those bras and panties off! I want to see some, er, showering–now!"

Cal sidles over wrapped in a towel. "Pervert!" she hisses. "You're going to burn in a lake of fire!"

"I tried to get out of it, Sheeni," I whisper. "Honest!"

"Hah! A likely story!" she replies.

The last scene had Cal and several other girls charging toward Carlotta, who blows her whistle, then abruptly turns and flees in panic.

All in all, kind of a fun day that probably reassured many members of the crew (especially Roland) that filmmaking was the right career choice for them.

On the drive home I asked Cooper if he had made up his mind which of my girlfriends he intended to pursue.

"Probably both for now, Nick. I like them equally. Although if I have sex with one, I may date her exclusively. We'll just have to see."

What he may not be seeing is my fist rocketing toward his nose. How much provocation must one endure before one is permitted to punch a blind guy?

After dinner I uploaded the photos to my computer. Considering all I did was push a button, they turned out surprisingly good. Everything came out in focus, including Cal's nipples faintly visible through her bikini top. If acting doesn't work out, I may consider photography as a career. Except these days every twit with a smart phone is snapping away. How can anyone make a living at it? The paying gigs seem limited to shooting weddings, posing babies at Sears, or hounding celebrities for candids. All of which sounds pretty tedious. Let's face it: the only job with any lasting appeal is staff photographer at *Playboy*. But the competition for that must be fierce.

TUESDAY, July 28 – When I got up this morning, Sheeni's leased Lexus was in the driveway. But she was gone by the time Cooper and I came down for breakfast. Guess she didn't want to eat with us peons. Or else she doesn't like showering in lukewarm water. The evidence cannot be denied: Dad is making it with two women. I wonder how different that feels. I mean physically. Do the sensations experienced during the sex act vary much from one woman to the next? There must be some reason he's going for variety here. I mean you'd think Mary's sizzling sexual offerings would be more than enough for an old guy like him. I really don't get it.

Speaking of which, I made love to Cal today.

Too bad it was only the pretend version on a movie set.

We went to the Mar Vista house again. I was surprised that the Chevy was still in the living room. Brenda says she's thinking of leaving it there as the ultimate movie collectible. She's having everyone in the cast and crew sign the exterior with a Sharpie pen. Here's what I wrote:

Brenda,

Thanks for rescuing me from that nuthouse. I hope I can do the same for you some day. Just kidding! Have a

Heath bar on me. . .

Your pal,

Nick Twisp II

Yeah, I'm ditching that Davidson name for good. The dude is deceased, so why should his moniker be adhered to me? And considering the circumstances of his death, I think he should be forgotten as soon as possible. Since I'm stuck with the Twisp DNA, I might as well have the name. Plus, it will help people understand why I'm the way I am.

Once again "my bedroom" had been made over, this time as Sheeni's Ukiah bedroom. All in white and decorated like the boudoir of some pretentious teen intellectual with an obsession for French culture. I hope moviegoers don't start wondering why all the bedrooms in our film sport the same windows, doors, ceiling light, plaster cracks, etc.

I got made up again as Carlotta; the scene was her after-school rendezvous with Sheeni. It opens with us seated together on the bed and trying on her jewelry.

Sheeni: "These garnet earrings will go nicely with your dingy brown eyes, Carlotta."

Carlotta: "They're lovely, Sheeni dear. But I don't have pierced ears."

Sheeni: "You don't? How is that possible?"

Carlotta: "Uh, there's a history of hemophilia in my family."

Sheeni: "Not to worry. That only affects males. Shall we pierce them right now? I'll go get an ice cube and pin."

Carlotta: "Please don't! My body is my temple. I intend to keep it intact."

Sheeni: "Really? And what about your hymen?"

Carlotta: "Er, what about it?"

Sheeni leans forward until her lips are just inches from mine.

Sheeni: "Do you intend to keep that intact as well?"

Not waiting for an answer, Sheeni surprises Carlotta by kissing her. Carlotta returns the kiss, then they break off.

Carlotta: "Goodness, Sheeni. Are you a . . . I mean . . . do you, uh, like girls?"

Sheeni: "No, Nick. I am not a lesbian."

Carlotta: "Sheeni! You know!"

Sheeni removes Carlotta's glasses and tosses them aside.

Sheeni: "Of course, I know, Nick. That silly wig, unbecoming makeup, and execrable wardrobe can't fool me."

Sheeni rips off Nick's wig and flings it away.

Sheeni: "Kiss me again, you weenie."

They kiss passionately until Sheeni pulls back.

Sheeni: "Oh, Nickie! I'm so upset!"

Nick: "Why, darling? Is it because I'm on the run and have to hide out from the cops dressed as a girl?"

Sheeni: "Of course not. It's dearest Trent. He's dumped me! I found out he's seeing some girl from India named Apurva."

Nick: "But, Sheeni darling, you broke up with Trent months ago. Remember? You ditched him to go out with me."

Sheeni: "Did I? Well, no matter. Je suis désolée!"

Sheeni gets up abruptly and locks her bedroom door.

Sheeni: "Dinner's not for another 45 minutes, Nick. Make love to me!"

Nick: "Really? Now? But what about your algebra homework?"

Sheeni: "That can wait. Take off that horrible dress! We'll pretend we're in Paris and make wild passionate love."

Nick starts to undress, then thinks of something.

Nick: "But, Sheeni, I don't have a condom."

Sheeni: "What does it matter? It will be fine. Nobody gets pregnant when it's the fellow's first time."

Nick: "Oh, Sheeni darling. Surrender yourself to me!"

Sheeni: "Never that, Nick. But I will have sex with you."

They fall into each other's arms and go at it hot and heavy. That is, we do so with as much enthusiasm (and groping) as can be shown while striving for a PG rating.

We did four takes of that scene, all of which I enjoyed. It was by far the most physical contact I'd ever had with Cal. Since the camera doesn't lie, she wasn't faking her enthusiasm (or so it seemed to me). Wildly overstimulated, I had a relentless boner most of the time, which fortunately wasn't showing under Carlotta's dress. Considering the anatomical issues at play, it seems to me fashion got it wrong: girls should be in pants and guys should be modeling the full skirts.

After lunch we changed into new outfits and shot the follow-up scene that takes place in Sheeni's bedroom a few weeks later. Carlotta enters and finds Sheeni looking glum on her bed.

Carlotta: "I just got waylaid by your mother. She's thrilled that I agreed to go to church with you on Sunday. What's the matter, darling?"

Sheeni: "Don't call me darling. My life is wrecked. Ruined by you!"

Carlotta: "OK, I scored higher than you on the physics test. Big deal. That's hardly a calamity."

Sheeni: "I'm late, you idiot!"

Carlotta: "Late for what? You were certainly on time for gym today. You skipped your shower and slapped me in the face with your bra, but I didn't blab to Arbulash."

Sheeni: "It's a disaster, Nick! I'm pregnant!"

Carlotta (staggering back): "What! Are you sure?"

Sheeni: "Of course, I'm sure. It's all your fault for not using a condom."

Carlotta: "But you said it would be OK!"

Sheeni: "Don't try to weasel out of it, Nick. You can't blame me. I have devout Christian parents. All I learned about birth control were the joys of abstinence."

Carlotta: "God, Sheeni! What are we going to do?"

Sheeni: "I've got it all figured out. You're going to steal my passport from my father. It's locked up in his office safe. Then we'll go to France."

Carlotta: "France! What will we do there?"

Sheeni: "Live there, of course. It is the historic haven for exiled intellectuals."

Sheeni opens a nightstand drawer, removes a handgun, and gives it to Carlotta.

Sheeni: "Here's my father's gun. You'll need it to retrieve my passport."

Carlotta: "You want me to hold up your father!?"

Sheeni: "It's the only way, Nick. The gun is fully loaded. Try not to shoot anyone."

Carlotta: "I, I can't go to France, Sheeni! I don't speak French."

Sheeni: "You'll learn, Nick. You've got to help me. You're the one responsible for my predicament. And you say you love me."

Carlotta: "I do, Sheeni! I'll do almost anything for you! But guns, I don't know . . ."

Sheeni: "It will be OK, Nickie. Wear a disguise. He won't know who you are. Just point the gun at him and look menacing. It will all be over in two minutes. Then we'll fly to Paris and start our new lives."

Carlotta: "Hey, I know, we'll get married!"

Sheeni: "Er, possibly. Just get my passport. And round up all your ready cash. Get packing because we leave tomorrow night."

Carlotta: "Wow, this is all happening so fast. I can't believe it."

Sheeni: "Be bold, Nick. Be the bold rebel that I know you are. Now kiss me and go do your duty!"

As I lean forward to embrace her, she swivels the barrel of the gun away from her stomach, and kisses me.

The metal gun looked real, but it was only a fake movie prop. Too bad. If it were real, I could borrow it and commit a major felony against Cal's brother.

Every night after dinner Cooper's been dragging me to the beach. He says it's a "very rich environment" for a blind person. We sit on the warm sand just up from the waves, and he has me describe every person passing by. In the case of girls, he wants to know if they're pretty, what they're wearing, and my rating of their shapeliness. It's like he wants to be a voyeur, but is not equipped for the task. When I crank off a shot with my new camera, he wants to know exactly what I've captured. Mostly it's girls in bikinis or people sporting extravagant tattoos. You see plenty of skin in Venice, and a lot of it is highly ornamented and/or pierced.

Walking back in the fading light, I spotted Desmond's car coming our way. My instincts kicked in and at the "decisive moment" I pressed the shutter button, capturing 15 rapid-fire images of his passing car. Only when I loaded the photos into my computer did I make out who was riding beside him in the front seat: my own true love. In none of the photos were they looking toward us, so they may not have noticed us. All the photos showed Desmond from the side, but I figured that would have to do. I cropped and enlarged the clearest shot, then emailed it to the Gargoyle.

Where do you suppose those two were going? For the sake of my sanity, I hope it was to her acting class.

WEDNESDAY, July 29 – No satiated women were in evidence, but Dad seemed oddly cheerful at breakfast. Suspecting something was up, I asked him for $100. Not cringing, he opened his wallet and handed over five crisp $20 bills.

"They paid you for that painting, didn't they?" I said.

"As a matter of fact, kid, they did. They wired the whole bundle into my account early this morning."

"In that case, Dad, you can fork over an additional $293,900."

"Don't you worry, Nick. It's all being taken care of. Your share will be transferred to an account that's supplemental to the one with your film earnings. My accountant tells me these moneys have to be kept separate."

Could be, but mostly it seemed like they were being kept separate from me. I told him I wanted to see written statements showing actual balances.

"All in good time, Nick. All in good time. I'll hand them over to you as soon as they arrive. No one's trying to cheat you. Here, you can have the last biscuit."

A cheap gesture, but I took him up on the offer. When you're dealing with Twisps, you have to get what you can when you can.

Just then the doorbell rang. It was UPS with a large package for me. I opened it eagerly. Oh right, my ex-dad's matchbook collection. His only legacy to me (besides all those rotten memories).

"Wow, that's a fantastic collection," said Lefty.

"You like it?" I said. "It's yours."

"Oh, I couldn't possibly accept it, Nick."

"Please do, Lefty. Think of it as a thank-you gift for transporting me on all those dates."

"Gee, thanks, Nick. You're the greatest!"

"We don't need any more stuff cluttering this place," said Dad.

"Don't you worry," replied Lefty. "I'll take it to my storage locker first thing."

So all of Lefty's worldly possessions are not contained in his two duffle bags. In some respects that's kind of a disappointment.

Today's movie location was the sidewalk in front of a certain pet store on Lincoln Boulevard. The line of shops was standing in for downtown Ukiah. This was a "day for night" shot where filters and digital-grading turn the bright sun into dim moonlight.

As the crew was setting up Harvey came out and asked to see our permit from the city. What an officious busybody. I told him if he took one step closer, I'd poke out his eyes with the microphone boom and stuff the "dead cat" (the furry cover that screens out wind noise) down his throat.

"Highly unlikely, Nick," he replied. "I'd grab that movie camera and shoot an in-depth documentary about the large colon–using yours as my subject."

"Not happening, old sport. While you were choosing an F-stop, I'd sling that tripod around your neck, close up the legs, and twist your head right off."

Fortunately for Harvey, his dad appeared and told him to go in and clean the hamster cages. Mr. Haseltine was thrilled to be selected to act as a passerby in the scene. He knows all the cops who patrol the west side and assured Dad that we would have no interference from them.

The scene opens with Sheeni waiting impatiently by the curb with her suitcase. She checks her watch, then looks up and down the street. She is surprised to see Trent approaching.

Trent: "Hi, Sheeni."

Sheeni: "Oh, hello, Trent."

Trent: "Going somewhere?"

Sheeni: "Uh, no."

Trent: "What's with the suitcase?"

Sheeni: "It's not mine. I'm watching it for a friend."

Trent: "It looks like the suitcase you had at school in Santa Cruz."

Sheeni: "I'm, uh, lending it. Shouldn't you be somewhere?"

Trent: "I'm meeting Apurva at the library. We're going to read poetry together."

Sheeni: "Sounds quite divine. Don't let me keep you."

Trent: "Apurva's really nice, Sheeni. I think you'd like her."

Sheeni: "Right. If you say so."

Trent: "Well, I'll see you tomorrow in English class."

Sheeni: "Very possibly."

Trent leaves, and a moment later Nick runs up laden with a large backpack.

Sheeni: "Finally, Nick. Where were you? Our bus leaves in five minutes. Did you get my passport?"

Nick (handing her the passport): "I got it, but there was a bit of a complication."

Sheeni: "Oh? What happened?"

Nick: "I, uh . . . that is the gun, uh . . . I shot your father."

Sheeni: "What!!!"

Nick: "I had no choice. He pulled a gun on me!"

They clam up as Mr. Haseltine walks by.

Sheeni: "So, what?!! Is he dead?!!"

Nick: "I don't think so. He was breathing when I left. I called 911."

Sheeni: "I heard the sirens! God, Nick, I can't believe it! You shot my father!"

Nick: "It was an accident, Sheeni. Honest!"

Sheeni: "Well, our trip is off. I've got to go to the hospital! I've got to find out if you have cruelly slain my father!"

Sheeni picks up her suitcase and hurries away.

Nick calls to her: "Hey, I didn't mean to do it!"

Nick kicks a fire hydrant.

Nick: "Damn! What'll I do now? I guess I should blow town. I hope he lives. At least now I don't have to learn French."

Nick sticks out his thumb in hopes of hitching a ride.

In between takes I asked Cal what she did last night. She said she watched a Netflix movie with her parents. Well, that was a massive lie. Not a good sign.

Since we were beginning to draw a crowd, we only shot two takes. Dad got nervous and said we needed to pack up everything right away. He shook Mr. Haseltine's hand and said his daughter was doing a "superb job." Behind him, Harvey peered out the store window and mouthed the words, "Your movie is going to bomb."

Of course, Harvey's problem is painfully obvious. The guy's got a severe case of MSE (Movie Stardom Envy).

The Gargoyle called me that night as Cooper and I were on bikini patrol at the beach.

"The night manager at the inn recognized him," she said. "It all sounds extraordinarily sordid."

I excused myself from Cooper and asked her what she found out.

"He goes there under the name Alfonso Scarnippini, as if any-one could believe he's Italian. He meets with a group of other degenerates monthly for lunch. Your Miss Haseltine has joined them there at least once."

"They got a room?" I asked.

"No, they only meet there in the private dining room. It's a group called L.A.T.B. Desmond is one of the younger members. All men, of course. They all drive expensive cars and pay with cash. No credit cards are used."

"What is that group?"

"I don't know. I never heard of it. I'm putting out feelers now. They drink expensive wines, have lavish meals, and pass around photos. The photos are always turned over when the waiters come in. And the conversation stops until they leave."

"That sounds bad."

"I know, Nick. And that man is sleeping nightly with my only daughter."

"What should we do, Connie?"

"You're going to find out from young Miss Haseltine what this is all about."

"She may not be willing to tell me."

"You're a Twisp, Nick. You will find a way to persuade her."

Fuck!

When you talk to Desmond, he seems so normal. Not really like a pervert at all.

Later, back in my room, I sent this text to Cal: "We need 2 talk re: L.A.T.B."

THURSDAY, July 30 – Big upheaval. We had to move. Veeva called Dad early and evicted us. She said we had to go today. She was most apologetic, but said Desmond was pitching a fit and in-sisting we leave. He claimed our presence was interfering with his writing–even though he lives most of the time on a hilltop miles away from Venice.

No response from Cal to my text; it appears she had an emer-gency chat with Desmond. What a mess.

We relocated to Sheeni's three-bedroom condo. Dad's in her room, I'm bunking with Cooper, and Lefty's been upgraded from the sofa to his own room, so at least he's happy. Expansive views from the windows, but if you open any, you hear the thrum of traffic from Wilshire and nearby freeways. Now miles from the beach and Cal. But we can walk to Westwood shops, which is great if you want to buy a pair of $500 shoes or a $2,000 dress.

Cooper's not happy being on the 14th floor. He says blind people have a history of walking into malfunctioning elevators and plummeting to their deaths. And now he has to find Sheeni's door on the corridor. If he gets it wrong, he may be shot by some burglar-phobic gun nut. Hotels sometime post room numbers in Braille, but not this building.

Sheeni took pains to point out that she was subletting the condo fully furnished from a professor in the French department at U.C.L.A. She stressed that its "neo-Algerian decor" did not reflect her tastes and that we should "do our best" not to break things. She was looking at Cooper when she said that, but he gave no indication that he was aware of being singled out.

Scott was in town and helped us haul our stuff. He likes the swimming pool on the roof and the well-equipped exercise room. He's not so happy that Dad's shacking with Sheeni. Too bad Mary's house is too small to accommodate us. If forced, though, I'd probably be willing to share a bedroom with Lauren and her bristling braces.

On the drive from Venice Dad asked if I'd done anything to offend Desmond. I denied it, of course. Dad suspects they've terminated his freeloading because of his windfall from the painting sale. I told him he should buy us a house, but specified that it had to be a short stroll from the beach. That was a must.

"The closer you are to the ocean," he replied, "the more they clip you. You want to chip in on the mortgage payments?"

"Gee, Dad, I'm just a kid."

"You're a kid with an impressive bankroll."

Could be, but you couldn't prove it by me.

"Barstow," he went on, "is a hundred miles from the beach and has very affordable houses."

"We can't live in Barstow, Dad. It's like living with roaches in L.A. It would stigmatize us and be very bad for our careers."

"Oh? You have a career now?"

"Haven't your heard? I'm starring in a movie."

"So am I," added Cooper from the back seat.

"You're co-starring," I pointed out. "That's different."

No filming today, but none was scheduled. Dad no longer has an ending for his movie. The latest version was supposed to end with Nick rescuing Sheeni from a home for unwed mothers, but she's decided she wants to keep that aspect of her past well buried. So now he has to cook up an alternative from the realm of fiction. He wants Mary to help, but she's not thrilled with his new living arrangements. He's under the gun because school starts in a couple of weeks. I'm so not ready for that. It looks like I'll be attending Scott's old school. Much as I'd like to, I can't really go to Cal's school because she'd find out that I'm a grade behind her. Being only 15 sucks more than I can say.

I've been phoning and texting Cal, but she's not answering. Deciding at last to man up, I texted her this ultimatum: "Call me 2day or I go 2 Veeva about L.A.T.B."

Lefty made a gourmet lunch which he served on Sheeni's balcony. She calls it her "terrace" even though it's clearly just a metal balcony suspended off the building. Wide enough for a table and some chairs. Not a place to eat if you're afraid of heights or mind a scruffy pigeon watching you dine.

Midway through the meal our hostess made a surprise announcement: She's buying a house in San Francisco.

"What!" said Dad, nearly choking on his grilled halibut. "You're moving?"

"In a month or two," she replied. "I tried this city and it's not for me."

She added that L.A. was OK if you wish to drive a fancy car, flaunt an opulent lifestyle, tan your brains out at the beach, indulge in frequent surgical makeovers, and lead a "totally barren" intellectual life.

Sounds fine to me except for number four. Where do I sign up?

Dad was impressed that Sheeni's buying a house in San Francisco's mega-ritzy Sea Cliff area.

"Are you on the ocean side of the street or the land side?" he asked.

"The ocean side, of course," she replied. "Why else would you live there?"

"That must have cost a few million," he said.

"Seven point three to be exact," she replied. "I have a splendid view of the Golden Gate from my back garden."

"Teaching French literature pays that well, huh?" he asked.

"My former husband did quite well in the wine business, Nickie. Under my savvy guidance, I should add."

Even if she is rich, Dad better not be thinking of marrying her. No way am I moving to San Francisco. Already I'm feeling the pain of separation from Cal, and we're only a few miles apart.

Later I received this text from her: "U r vile spy. B at coffee place in 20 min."

I got Lefty to haul me there through rush-hour traffic. Cooper was clamoring to go with me, but I suggested he take his cane and start learning his way around Wilshire.

No kiss from Cal when I arrived. She was back to looking at me like I was matter on the bottom of her shoe.

"It's not what you think it is," she said frostily.

"Then what is it?" I asked.

"I can't tell you. It's a secret."

"It's not going to stay a secret for long, Cal, because Veeva's mother knows about it. And she *always* gets to the bottom of things."

"That woman is so horrid. I can't believe you associate with her."

"So you have to tell me. But I promise to keep it a secret. I won't tell anyone, I swear."

"I wish I could believe you, Nick."

"I'm trustworthy, Cal. You're the one who's been doing all the lying. So what is this group? Are they sharing dirty photos or what?"

She sighed. "It's nothing like that, Nick. OK, I'll tell you. But if you blab to anyone, I'll never speak to you again."

"OK. Agreed. My lips are sealed. Cross my heart."

"What these men do—and they're mostly old guys—is collect tanks."

"What?"

"They collect tanks. Big deal, huh?"

"You mean like fish tanks?"

"No, moron. They collect army tanks. You know, those giant machines that roll on steel tracks."

"You mean Desmond owns a tank?"

"Hah! He owns a whole bunch of them."

"Why? Do they intend to overthrow the government?"

"Not at all. They're rich dudes and they like tanks, so they collect them. Some guys collect stamps, other guys collect art, Desmond collects army tanks. He's the president of L.A.T.B., which stands for the Los Angeles Tank Brigade."

"So what is your connection to this group?"

"Desmond's been having my picture painted on his gun turret. I went to a lunch meeting at that inn so their artist could sketch me. Having your picture on a gun turret is a great honor in the tank world."

"Why doesn't he have Veeva painted on his gun turret? She's his wife!"

"Well, her repellent mug is on one turret already. But he can't have that fat cow on all of his turrets, could he?"

"Veeva is not a fat cow. She's quite slim and trim."

"In your opinion, Nick. So the other night when you were spying on us, he took me to see my finished portrait. It's quite a nice likeness airbrushed in bold colors in the style of the 1940s."

"And where does he stash this tank collection?"

"He owns five acres way south of downtown that ages ago was a chicken farm. Very grungy neighborhood now. He has a giant metal building there. A retired army mechanic named Smitty works on them and lives in a camouflaged trailer to keep watch. Kind of a grizzled chap who's way overdue for a teeth checkup at the V.A. The whole place is surrounded by a tall cyclone fence topped with razor wire to keep out intruders. Vicious Rottweilers patrol the premises at night. I suggest you never go there because Desmond will talk your ear off about his tanks. It gets quite tiresome."

"Does Veeva know about his tank obsession?"

"No, he's never worked up the nerve to tell her. That's why it's such a top secret. Plus, owning all those tanks may not be exactly legal."

"So why did he tell you?"

"Because I listen to him and don't treat him like he's a nut. It's the least I can do since he's sponsoring my acting lessons."

"It's not because you're in love with him?"

"Get real, Nick. The guy is old! And kind of a nut."

"Did you take a photo of your gun turret picture?"

"I wanted to, but Desmond nixed it. He says photos have a way of leaking out. He also made me promise not to tell you any of this, so you can't let on to him that you know."

"Right. Of course."

"And you can't tell Veeva's nosy mom either."

"All right, but that woman is merciless in her probing."

"Well, Nick, you've got to resist. Stay zipped for once in your life. So what's this I hear about our movie not having an ending?"

FRIDAY, July 31 – Everyone took long hot showers in Sheeni's multiple bathrooms this morning. There's a giant boiler in the basement that is alleged to be inexhaustible. Now Dad is at Mary's, locked in a room with her, Brenda, Roland, and Monica Spall, who will be editing the movie if it ever gets finished. She came from Cleveland with Roland and was the DP on his hit film "Store Rage." Dad says no one will be released from the room until they've hammered out an acceptable ending.

At breakfast Dad observed that not having an ending for your movie is a common problem in Hollywood. He said some film critics, especially the ones in New York and France, prefer it if you leave things dangling and don't tie up all your loose ends. They think obscurity in your story implies intellectual depth. For example, I could terminate my journal at this point, but I think my future readers (assuming I have any) might feel they've been left in the lurch.

[Book critics can stop reading here.]

Two people phoned me this morning. The first was the Gargoyle, demanding to know what I found out. I said I had met with Valerie, but had promised not to divulge what she told me.

"Nonsense, Nick. You will tell me everything she said. At once!"

"Sorry, Connie. A promise is a promise."

"Not when it comes to perversion and law-breaking and corruption of minors!"

"It's not like we thought, Connie. They're not doing anything bad."

"Well, what are they doing?!"

"All I can tell you is that it falls under the category of 'boys and their toys.'"

"What's that mean?"

"Sorry, I can't say any more than that."

"You're only being coy with me, young Twisp, because you aspire to sleep with that girl. Or have you done that already?"

"Not yet, but it's definitely on my schedule."

"Truly remarkable. All right, I shall find out what's going on without your assistance. This is a grave disappointment, but I suppose one can only push a Twisp so far before one encounters the solid wall of his hormones. I shall interrogate you further at the wrap party."

"I'm looking forward to it," I lied.

The next call was from Cal.

"Sheeni's giving a birthday party for your father tomorrow," she said. "I've been invited. Have you?"

"Not formally, but I expect I'll show up."

"Did you get him a gift yet?"

"No, have you?"

She hadn't either. So we decided to shop for gifts together. It was a struggle, but I managed to persuade her to come here by bus so we can hit the upscale Westwood shops.

Dad's turning 54 tomorrow. That is so old! If you think about it, that's all the time from the year 1900, when people were riding in horse-drawn carriages and thinking wouldn't it be great if someday humans could fly, to the year 1954: a semi-modern era of jet airplanes, TV sitcoms, atomic bombs, Corvette sports cars, and bikinis at the beach. This puts me in a bind: What sort of gift do you get for an oldster who's practically in the grave?

Cal arrived at noon, so first I had to treat her to an expensive lunch at a salad place in Westwood. Cooper invited himself along to run up my bill. Having no shame, Cal pulled her birthday ploy again. This time Cooper got a free cupcake with a candle on top, a reprise of the festive song, and another congratulatory kiss from Cal. Once again he declared it was "the best birthday I ever had," and once again I felt like decking him.

You do get a little better service in shops when you arrive with a blind guy on your arm. Cal had to shop for two gifts and two cards. On Sunday her loathsome brother turns 16. She invited both of us to a small celebration in his honor at her house. It will be small because vile Harvey has virtually no friends.

"Are you sure Harvey wants me to come?" I asked. "We're rather on the outs."

"I should hope so," Cal replied. "As I expect you to kill him any day now. My brother must never live to see 17. No, he specifically requested your presence. And he expects a present from you as well."

Damn, that meant I had to scour the shops for something suitably cheap and offensive.

In the end we all decided on novelty socks. I proposed to get a pair for Harvey decorated with erect penises, but Cal said they'd offend her parents. Instead I got him vivid green socks with the word NERD all over them in contrasting orange. For Dad I got black socks with red martini glasses, and Cal got him the purple style covered with big golden stars. She bought her brother white socks with the message DOGS BITE HERE printed in red at ankle level. Cooper went with one style for both Harvey and my dad: yellow socks covered in lenticular eyeballs that blink when you move. Cal and I chipped in and bought Cooper a pair of those as well.

We moved on to a card store, but got expelled for having too much fun checking out their birthday selection. Not chastened, we went down the block to a drugstore and bought our six cards. In the kids' rack I found a card for Harvey that read "For a Good Little Boy Turning 6." I inked a "1" in front of the "6" and crossed out the word "Good" and wrote "Bad" above it. Cal got him a card with a buxom babe on the front. The message inside read: I HOPE YOUR BIRTHDAY GIFT IS A BIG BUST! Under that she wrote: "And I mean that sincerely. . . Your sibling, Valerie."

I wrote this in Harvey's card: "For a good time, scratch the sharp edge of this card across both wrists. Repeat until bleeding is achieved. – Your pal, Nick."

AUGUST

SATURDAY, August 1 – Dad and Sheeni slept-in this morning–although they may not have been sleeping the entire time. I
suspect she was giving him a birthday gift that only can be offered
by the female of our species.

When their door finally opened, Lefty served them a lavish
breakfast in bed. I don't know what Dad's paying him, but it's
probably not enough. Sheeni is threatening to lure him away to
be her cook/butler/chauffeur/handyman in Frisco. Or she could
marry him and get the whole Lefty package.

Despite being another year closer to the grave, Dad was pretty cheerful. A new ending for his movie has been achieved. And
this one will be cheaper to film. No new cast members will be
required, and Brenda won't have to rent all those strap-on fake
maternity abdomens.

Scott phoned me to ask what was the plan for Dad's birthday.
I said the festivities started here at four and didn't he get an invitation?

"No, I didn't, Nick. That woman has never liked me."

"Well, come anyway and bring Chloe."

"I intend to. What did you get him?"

"A card and novelty socks."

"I may get him an $80 bottle of single-malt Scotch."

"Do we want to encourage parental boozing?"

"Good point, bro'. Damn, he's so hard to buy for."

"The floor mats in his Town Car are looking threadbare."

"Good idea, Nick. I'll get him some nice ones. If I'd thought of
that before, I could have had them monogrammed."

"Did you hear? Sheeni's moving to San Francisco."

"Great, Nick! Best news I've heard all day!"

Cal arrived after lunch with Dad's wrapped gift and her bikini
and towel. We retired to the roof to check out the pool. I was look-

ing forward to some aquatic nuzzling, but Cooper tagged along to put the kibosh on that. He said if an earthquake struck, we'd probably be sloshed clear out of the pool and over the railing. Certainly an exciting way to go and in such a hip L.A. style.

Since it was the weekend, quite a few condo residents straggled in. Most over 30 and flaunting serious body flaws, but a few cute career gals arrayed themselves on chaises with their healthy tans on display. All described by Cal to Cooper in minute detail. Some tops were untied for back tanning, but no one rolled over to toast the other side. Cal said they likely were deterred by the leering teenage boys.

I got to hold her hand a bit and kissed her twice. She sort of kissed me back. I'm really in the deep end of the pool over that girl.

Dad's party was OK considering the high fogey factor. Lefty made the eats, which were excellent. Lots of bite-sized tidbits and savory morsels speared on toothpicks. The wine flowed freely, and some of it got diverted to us. The red stuff is rank, but the white is fairly drinkable. It kind of tastes like Seven-Up or Sprite gone flat. Tyler arrived with Uma, so I had to dodge her all night. I don't believe socializing with your shrink is high on anyone's agenda.

There were a few academic types speaking French that Sheeni must have invited. They mostly hung out on the balcony smoking Gauloises and swilling vino. None brought gifts or even a card.

Mary showed up looking glamorous in blue silk. Not gatecrashing, I think she'd been invited. Dad kissed her in front of Sheeni, which could have landed us all out on the street but didn't. I guess it's like my tolerating Cooper kissing Cal. We all have to be adult about these transgressions.

When Veeva and Desmond arrived, he made a beeline straight for me.

"Hi, Nick," he said. "I understand you took a photo of me even though I specifically asked you not to."

"It was a request from your mother-in-law, Desmond. She felt it was vital to have a picture of the guy married to her only daughter."

"I'd like to have that file turned over to me."

"I already erased it," I lied. "The Gargoyle has the only copy. You'll have to get it from her."

"You shouldn't poke your nose where it doesn't belong, Nick. That could be dangerous."

"Are you threatening me?" I asked, edging away from him.

"Not me, Nick. But some of my associates may not be so understanding. I suggest you drop all inquiries into my affairs."

"I already have, Desmond. I got warned off by Valerie."

"Good," he smiled. "Let's keep it that way."

"I intend to. And tanks for the warning."

"What did you say?"

"I said thanks for the warning."

If I wash up later in Santa Monica Bay, I hope someone finds my journal. Note to cops: interrogate Desmond Upton.

When Scott and Chloe showed, Sheeni smiled sweetly and said, "Oh, I meant to call and invite you both."

That woman is such a skank.

Scott told me his whiplash Montana marriage has been officially annulled. All those years of love and togetherness and friendship and sex have been flushed down the drain. Good thing he has Chloe to distract him. If it happened to me, I'm sure I'd be in a catatonic state.

Speaking of love challenges, I talked to Mary briefly. I told her to hang in there because her adversary will be moving north soon.

"So I heard, Nick. Did your father move in here because he loves her or because he's too cheap to pay rent?"

"Neither, Mary. He's busy trying to finish his movie and doesn't have time to look for a place."

"So you say."

"He's just confused. Please don't give up on him."

"If I he wants me back, Nick, extreme crawling will be required. You can tell him that if he asks."

Dad opened his gifts–all about as exciting as car mats and novelty socks. Sheeni gave him a book of her collected essays (in French). Mary gave him a can of tennis balls to (in her words) "help you cope with the stresses of your personal life." It's true that his old balls had been squeezed ragged. Then Lefty brought in his cake, we sang, Dad blew out the five-alarm blaze, and everyone applauded. Now he's only 364 days away from being 55, that milestone cut-off age for getting into senior-citizen retirement communities.

Other stuff happened after that, but I got a bit woozy from the wine. I think Scott drove Cal home, even though I explicitly invited her to spend the night. I do sort of recall some drunken snuggling in bed. God, I hope it wasn't with Cooper.

SUNDAY, August 2 – Dad wanted to haul us all to brunch at Tyler's, but Sheeni doesn't care for Uma. Nor is Uma wild about her. So Dad took her out for a pricey breakfast at the B.H. Hotel. Since Lefty was sleeping in, I phoned Lauren and invited her to bring over some donuts. She arrived with a large pink box and her sister Megan; both girls were eager to hear about the party and check out Sheeni's crib.

Cooper, who got first choice, selects his donuts by feel and smell, contaminating all the rejects with his cooties. He also claimed the sole maple bar, which is my particular favorite. I made a pot of coffee, but the girls preferred to pilfer from Sheeni's stash of herbal teas.

"Do you know what she pays for this place?" asked Megan.

"I have no idea," I replied. "Probably a lot."

"We could snoop around and find her checkbook," said Lauren.

"I've already looked," I said. "She must keep it in her purse."

"What else did you find?" asked Lauren. "Anything incriminating?"

"Well, she wears a push-up bra," I replied.

"I could have told you that," said Megan. "Women her age don't look like that without serious leverage."

"My mom wasn't going to come to her lousy party," said Lauren. "But we ganged up on her and told her she had to."

"Good for you," I said. "She can't give up without a fight."

"Not that your dad is worth the trouble," added Lauren. "He should be lined up and shot for the way he's been treating her."

"All those Twisps bear watching," said Cooper. "Nick tried to kiss me in bed last night."

"I did not!" I replied, blushing.

They all laughed at my indignant denials.

How embarrassing. More proof that we Twisps should lay off the booze.

Of course, the girls had to check out Sheeni's closet and sneer at her clothes. I cautioned them not to touch anything and to leave everything undisturbed.

"Sheeni is very perceptive," I warned. "She'll know we've been in here."

"Good," said Lauren. "What the fuck do I care? Oh, this scarf isn't bad."

Lauren rolled up a silk scarf and stuffed it in her pocket.

"What are you doing?" I demanded. "Put that back!"

"Sheeni owes me this scarf for all the grief she's caused my mother. Megan, you take one too."

"You'll get us kicked out of here!" I exclaimed.

"Good," said Lauren. "Isn't that what we want? To free your dad from her clutches?"

"Not until he finds a house," I said. "Otherwise, we'll wind up back in that slummy apartment with all the roaches."

The girls reluctantly handed over the scarves, which I folded as neatly as I could and returned to the shelf.

"I didn't want it anyway," sniffed Lauren. "The cheap thing reeks of her stinky perfume."

Harvey's birthday party started at two. Cooper and I arrived on the dot with our gifts indifferently wrapped (by me) in old newspapers tied with twine.

"How festive," said Mrs. Haseltine, eyeing them doubtfully. "Do you know Tiara Diamond?"

"Tiara!" I exclaimed, giving her a hug. "What are you doing here?"

"Oh, haven't you guys heard? Since you never call, I dropped you both and am now going out with Valerie's brother. He's very nice."

"Surely you jest," said Cooper. "We phone you all the time."

"Hardly ever," she replied. "I knew Valerie disliked her brother, so I figured he was a person worth knowing. I gave him a jingle and we totally hit it off. And, God, he's so cute!"

"You're deranged, Tiara," I replied. "You need professional help as soon as possible."

"That's not at all a nice thing to say, Nick," said Mrs. Haseltine. "Harvey and Tiara make a very sweet couple."

"Sweet as in gag me with a spoon," said Cal, arriving on the scene. She backed away and ducked as both Cooper and I approached with arms outstretched.

We all trooped to the back yard, where a table had been set up, and Cal's dad was busy grilling burgers and hotdogs. A trio of Harvey's nerdy friends were blowing up colorful balloons and fastening them to the shrubbery. We got introduced, but I immediately forgot their names. Nor were they saying much. All apparently were abashed by the presence of a famous star (Tiara, not me).

"Aren't we missing someone?" said Cooper. "Where's the birthday boy?"

"Harv had to go somewhere," said Tiara. "He said he'd be right back with a big surprise."

I hoped it wasn't a large club that he planned to use on me.

"It's just like my brother to duck out on his own party," said Cal. "Oh well, I'm sure it will be marginally less tiresome without him."

Nerd #1 pointed to the camera around my neck. "I considered getting that model. The long lens was a plus, but the tiny sensor puts it in the toy category. The resolution is a joke."

"Probably helpful, though, in blurring your zits," I replied, snapping his photo.

"Are you that dude who recently got sprung from a mental hospital?" asked Nerd #2, twisting a balloon into an obscene shape.

"That's me," I confirmed. "And I've gone totally off my meds."

"It was a facility for the criminally insane," added Cal. "So, please, no one provoke him."

They both backed away as Nerd #3 turned his attention to Cooper. "So can you be blind and like still play video games?" he inquired.

"No, but I understand stupidity is not a hindrance."

We all turned as an unfamiliar car pulled into the driveway. It was a dark blue and sporty compact. The driver door opened and Harvey climbed out.

"Where did you get that car, son?" asked Mr. Haseltine.

"I bought it, Dad," he replied. "It was my birthday present to myself."

"Where did you get the money?" asked his mother, shocked. "I hope you didn't raid your college fund!"

"Cooper, tell them where I got the money," said Harvey.

"He made a small fortune speculating in bitcoins," said Cooper. "He made enough to pay for college and had enough left over to buy his dream car: a Mini Cooper."

"And where did I buy it, Cooper?" Harvey asked.

"He bought it at Champ Motors, the only used-car lot in L.A. that accepts bitcoins."

"It wasn't Cooper at camp," exclaimed Cal. "It was Cooper at Champ!"

"Exactly, sister dear," said Harvey. "I needed to keep my purchase a secret until my 16th birthday. And now I'm old enough to get my license and have my own wheels."

"It's a fine-looking car," said Tiara, giving him a hug. "Is it new, honey?"

"No, it's three years old. But it has barely 10,000 miles on it."

"The style is OK," commented Nerd #1. "But a Mini Cooper is pretty useless in the fast lane. You won't be able to keep up."

"I don't want him speeding!" said Mrs. Haseltine. "I trust, dear, you'll be driving that car sensibly."

"Of course, Mother." Harvey turned to me. "Want a ride, Nick? You can leave your seatbelt unbuckled and I'll switch off the passenger-side airbag."

Was he prepared to wreck his new car just for the thrill of ejecting me through its windshield?

"Some other time, Harvey," I replied. "I never ride with unseasoned drivers."

Now it was all perfectly clear. In seeking out Cooper the camper we went down a totally unnecessary and blind alley. Had we not gone off on that wild tangent, I could be bunking alone and have no competition for Cal's affections. Clever Harvey Haseltine had played us like a violin.

When the eats were served, I spotted Desmond lurking up on my former balcony. Every time I pointed my camera in his direction, he ducked down out of sight. A camera to that guy is like Kryptonite to Superman.

As birthday gifts, our socks were somewhat anticlimactic. The Nerds got a chuckle over Sheeni's DOGS BITE HERE socks. They wanted to know where she got them, but she refused to say. Tiara gave her man a boxed DVD set containing all six seasons of

"Skateboard Park." He said he would treasure it always. Sarcasm? I couldn't really say.

No one except Tiara saw any reason to stick around after the cake was consumed. As we were leaving Cal kissed Cooper, but not me. I reminded her that since we now knew Harvey's secret, she no longer had to be nice to Cooper.

"Remind me, Nick," she replied, "why should I be nice to you?"

"Because I'm your boyfriend. We've been going steady all summer."

"Really? That's a memo I never got."

Nevertheless, she phoned me tonight as we were getting ready for bed.

"Nickie, honey, now that Harvey has a car, I need you to sabotage his brakes."

"I'm no mechanic, darling. I know nothing about cars."

"First we'll take out an insurance policy on him that pays double for car accidents."

"I saw that movie, Cal. Things didn't work out so well for Fred MacMurray and Joan Crawford."

"It was Barbara Stanwyck, you idiot."

"Oh, right."

"What a dismal party, Nick. It's just like my brother to have friends who are nearly as obnoxious as he is. Truly a turgid zit farm."

"A sorry lot," I agreed. "They were impressed, though, that he's dating Tiara."

"I know what that girl's up to. She's only seeing Harvey to get back at me for acing her out of the starring role in our movie."

"Speaking of which, the movie's almost done. You'll be paying me back soon for that tremendous favor I did you."

"Got to go, Nickie. See you tomorrow."

She can run, but she cannot hide.

MONDAY, August 3 – Sheeni was on the warpath at breakfast. She found a half-eaten crumb donut in a pocket of one of her expensive designer suits. It had left a nasty oil stain on the fabric. As a guy who grew up breathing dry-cleaning fumes, I assured her that the stain could be removed chemically.

"Were you eating donuts in my closet?" she demanded.

"Wasn't us, was it, Cooper?" I replied.

"Certainly not," he affirmed.

"I saw some of your friends in that closet during the party," I said. "They were jabbering in French and checking out your wardrobe."

"No donuts were served that night," she pointed out.

"True, but they might have brought in outside snacks," I replied.

"Lefty," said Sheeni, "have you bought any donuts lately?"

"None at all, Sheeni. I make my own breakfast confections."

Incontrovertibly true, but he didn't mention that yesterday he helped us finish Lauren's assortment.

"You always get a certain amount of damage at parties," said Cooper. "It really can't be helped."

"People are slobs," I sighed. "It's such a shame."

Today we returned to the "Playing Doctor" sound stage to shoot our revised ending on their hospital sets. To my surprise Trent Preston arrived accompanied by his daughter. Azura gave me a hug and apologized for ignoring my phone calls. I said "no problem" and added that I enjoyed being her brother-in-law for those few brief hours.

"It was the biggest disaster of my life, Nick, but I guess all that pain helped my performance in the movie."

"So you're all done?"

"Looks like it, except for a couple ADR sessions. How's your show coming along?"

"Great. Dad's hoping to finish today."

"Seen your brother lately?"

"At Dad's birthday party on Saturday. Scott got him floor mats for his car."

"Such a sentimental guy. I suppose he's still seeing his new friend."

"Seems like it. How are things in that department for you?"

"Sort of one nightmare after another. Last week I went up north to see Sheeni's son François."

"Not a happy reunion?"

"To say the least. He's a real chip off his mother's block. Don't tell Scott about that."

"I won't."

"Dad says you're stuck on your co-star."

"Yeah, kind of."

"Good luck with that, Nick. Try not to get in too deep."

"You know how we Twisps do things."

"Only too well. Have you booked your flight to Mississippi yet?"

"No, but it's on my mind."

Azura, Brenda, and Cal's mother were playing nurses today. They got dressed in aqua polyester and looked quite medical. By contrast, Felicity had me looking ultra unwashed and grungy. In the first scene Sheeni arrives with a box of chocolates for her father. I get her attention from where I've been lurking behind a door.

Sheeni: "Nick! Where have you been? I haven't seen you for days!"

Nick: "I've been hiding out in a drainage culvert."

Sheeni: "I can believe it. You smell like a sewage treatment plant on a hot day."

Nick: "Uh, sorry. How's your dad?"

Sheeni: "Much better. They may release him to go home tomorrow."

Nick: "I guess he's pretty pissed, huh?"

Sheeni: "No, that's the surprise. He's displaying remarkable equanimity. I told him about my predicament. He wasn't angry at all. He's promised to help me get it taken care of–at a clinic in Berkeley."

Nick: "We could get married instead."

Sheeni: "Not happening, Nick. We're too young. What are you going to do?"

Nick: "I guess I'll turn myself in to the cops. I'm on my way there now. But I wanted to see you first."

Sheeni: "Wait for me. I won't be long. I'll walk there with you."

Nick: "You'll tell the cops that you put me up to it?"

Sheeni: "Certainly not, Nick. There's no reason for both of us to get in trouble."

Nick. "Oh, right."

In the second scene Sheeni is about to enter her father's room, but stops when she sees that Trent is visiting him. She waits by the door and listens to their conversation.

Trent: "I can't believe it. Sheeni is pregnant!"

Mr. Saunders: "The news practically killed her mother. She refuses to say who the father is."

Trent: "I can assure you, Mr. Saunders, it wasn't me."

Mr. Saunders: "I never believed for a second it was, Trent. You are an outstanding and upright young man. No, I believe she's been traduced by that hoodlum Nick Twisp."

Trent: "I'll kill him if I see him!"

Mr. Saunders: "We'll let the law deal with him, son. The police have found his fingerprints on my gun. He won't get away."

Trent: "I'll do the honorable thing, Mr. Saunders. I'll marry Sheeni and be a father to her baby."

Mr. Saunders: "And subject our families to the next generation of evil Twisp blood? Not on your life."

Trent: "But what will you do?"

Mr. Saunders: "We're making arrangements with a home up north. Run by a respectable Christian couple. Sheeni will be confined there. Her baby will be put up for adoption. Preferably out of state."

Trent: "And what will happen to Sheeni?"

Mr. Saunders. "She will be sent away to a Christian boarding school. The strictest one we can find."

Sheeni (muttering to herself): "Like hell I will!"

Azura walks by and notices Sheeni.

Nurse Azura: "Can I help you, Miss?"

Sheeni: "That boy in there! I saw him tampering with my father's IV drip!"

Nurse Azura: "Oh, dear! We'll have to see about that!"

Azura hurries into the room as Sheeni turns and quickly leaves.

After lunch we shot the two final scenes. The first was a brief scene where Sheeni grabs Nick's arm and pulls him toward the elevator. In her haste they nearly collide with nurses Brenda and Mrs. Haseltine. Sheeni presses urgently on the DOWN button.

Nick: "That was a short visit. What's up?"

Sheeni: "We're getting out of here! Fast!"

Nick: "Are you that anxious to see me in jail?"

Sheeni: "You're not going to jail, Nick!"

Nick: "I'm not?"

The elevator door opens and Sheeni pushes him inside.

The last scene takes place in the elevator.

Nick: "Sheeni, you still have your candy. I haven't eaten anything in four days."

Sheeni (handing him the box): "Here. Be my guest."

Famished, Nick opens the box and starts manically stuffing in chocolates, paper and all.

Nick (with his mouth full): "So where are we going?"

Sheeni: "To France! Where else?"

Nick (swallowing with difficulty): "Really? We're going back to Plan A? But what about your father?"

Sheeni: "My father is a duplicitous traitor. A heinous fiend. And a reprehensible troglodyte. You should have killed him when you had the chance!"

Nick: "France, huh? I no speaka el lingo. Can we stop first in Mississippi and get married? That way our baby will be legitimate."

Sheeni: "Sure, why not? My life is lying in ruins. I might as well put the cherry on top!"

They embrace and kiss.

THE END.

We had to shoot that scene four times. I kept choking on Brenda's discount Bulgarian chocolates. I couldn't ease up because Dad wanted it to be an over-the-top parody of that movie cliché where famished victims madly gobble crusts of bread.

So I ate a bunch of chocolate and got a little sick, although the passionate necking with Cal made it all worthwhile.

I also received a compliment from the director.

"That was great, son," he said. "I liked your desperation."

First time ever he addressed me as "son." Always before it was "Nick," "kid," or "Hey, you."

TUESDAY, August 4 – School starts (for me) in exactly two weeks. Such a horror! And whose bright idea was it to move the start date up from September? That sadist should be assigned to teach macramé and finger-painting in a classroom of heavily armed Bloods and Crips. The good news is at some point Cooper will have to return to Sonora to resume his schooling. I'm seriously behind in my self-abuse due to a complete lack of privacy. I read on the Web that teens should give their prostate a strenuous daily workout to ward off future old-guy plumbing issues. Medical advice I can relate to!

Neither Dad nor Lefty was amenable this morning to hauling me to the coffee place to meet up with Cal. But to my amazement Sheeni volunteered. I guess she's over that donut incident. Of course, Cooper had to come along uninvited. He's like the handsome and personable brother I never wanted.

Kind of awkward sitting in the Lexus seat beside Sheeni. To make conversation I asked her why she married my dad at age 15.

"Good question, Nick. I'm not sure I have an answer. It was a long time ago."

"I suppose you loved him."

"He was certainly unique. I was pregnant with twins at the time. I had a lot on my mind. It could be that my hormones were screaming for a husband."

"You both lied about your ages to get a marriage license. Did you feel like you were really married?"

"I don't know. Perhaps for a time. Why do you ask?"

"Uh, no reason. Just curious."

"I don't think anyone should get married before they're 25, Nick. They're much too immature. Look what happened to your brother."

"Right. So why did you leave Dad like that? You know, when you were in France."

"Did he ask you to ask me that?"

"Not at all. He never discusses it."

"I left him because I was desperate to resolve my situation. He was too young to be of much help. He meant well, but he was hopeless. He wasn't fitting in and adapting to Parisian life. A friend helped me find a place to live and receive medical care. He also arranged for the adoption."

"So looking back on it, what would you change if you could?"

"Probably nothing, Nick."

"Really?"

"If I hadn't gotten pregnant, if your father hadn't helped me, I would have been stuck in Ukiah with my impossible parents. I might never have made it to France."

"So you're glad you spent all those years over there?"

"Of course. It was a dream come true."

"I want to go to Paris," said Cooper from the back seat.

"You should," said Sheeni. "It's the most liberating–and beautiful–city on the planet."

"But now you prefer San Francisco," I pointed out.

"Well, I do at the moment, Nick," she laughed. "We'll have to see how that works out."

I wanted to ask her if Dad was really the father of her twins, but I couldn't work up the nerve. Could it be that she got pregnant just so Dad would help her get to France? Had she played him for a patsy? The facts do sort of fit that interpretation.

Cal was waiting impatiently when we arrived. Across the patio Harvey and Tiara were toying with lattes and staring lovingly into each other's eyes. His socks, I noticed, were advertising for canine ankle bites.

Like the opportunist he is, Cooper immediately said, "Cal, will you be my date at the wrap party tonight?"

"I'd love to," she replied.

"Hey, wait a minute!" I said. "I was going to ask you."

"Sorry, Nickie," she said. "You're too late as usual."

Well that sucks. Aced out by a guy who can't even see.

"Hello, boys," called Tiara. "You'll be happy to know I've invited dear Harvey to the party."

"I wouldn't advise going in his car," replied Cal. "Nick is threatening to sabotage his brakes."

Harvey scowled at me. "Nick, if you get anywhere near my car, I'll remove the jack, insert it in your face, and crank until your jaw snaps off."

"Highly improbable, old chum. While you were reading the jacking instructions, I'd grab the crank, insert it in your zipper, and twist your puny package until your nine intact sperm were so dizzy they'd be attempting to impregnate you."

Tiara stifled a chuckle.

"You're delusional again, Nick," he replied. "By that point I'd have lighted an emergency flare and thrust the burning end down your pants. Your underpants would be burning brighter than Atlanta in the film 'Gone with the Wind.'"

"Not happening, dude. You're no Rhett Butler. You're not

even an Ashley Wilkes. While you were failing to ignite that flare, I'd have hot-wired your car and maneuvered it until your nose was decorated with the tread marks of all four tires."

At that point the owner came out and told us to knock it off because customers were complaining about the "violence of your rhetoric."

"They only threaten each other," noted Cooper. "It's just talk. Actually, they're stalwart pacifists."

"You mean wimps," said Cal.

"I think we should all try to get along," said Tiara. "Harvey honey, go shake hands with Nick. Remember he just gave you that nice birthday present and card."

The balding barista seconded her motion. "You two shake hands or I'm banning you from my place."

Faced with that ultimatum, we had no choice. We met in the middle of the patio, glared at each other, and shook hands. His cooties crawled up my arm like an inexorable scourge.

Dateless for my first Hollywood wrap party and I'm the star. Not even Tiara available as a backup. So I was obliged to phone Lauren and invite her.

"You should have asked me earlier, Nick. I'm going with Arvin."

"Damn. Is your sister there?"

"Megan's bringing some creep she met on a street corner somewhere. I told her he's probably a serial rapist."

Fuck!

Desperate, I called Azura Preston.

"I'm not going to the party, Nick. I only had two lines in the movie, and I don't want to run into you-know-who and his little blond friend."

"Won't you do it for me, Azura? You'll have to face him sometime."

"On the contrary, Nick. I fully intend to avoid him for the rest of my life. In fact, I'm hoping to get a TV that can be programmed to explode if anyone tries to watch an episode of 'Wildcatter.'"

I finally scrounged up a date: Cooper's mum and dad. They were happy to hear that the filming was over. Unaccountably, they've been missing their boy. They're zooming down to make the party and tomorrow they're dragging him back home. I didn't tell Cooper that I'd phoned them. The sudden appearance of parents should always come as a nasty shock.

Skinflint Dad wanted to have the party at Mary's or Sheeni's, but Trent Preston only cavorts at A-level venues. So Dad is renting the entire premises of a trendy bar in Santa Monica called Bzzzzzz. According to Brenda, the building originally housed a firm that manufactured toy airplane motors. There's still a large industrial milling machine behind the bar that is used to mix margaritas and other frothy drinks.

Both Cooper and I got moderately dressed up for the event. He donned his eyeball socks and put mousse in his hair. Why this is considered sexy I don't know. He also had Sheeni highlight his handsome but unseeing eyes with eyeliner and blue eye shadow. She offered to do the same for me, but I declined, being from Indiana. Sheeni, of course, went all out in the full French Regal Couture Style. No donut stains marred her slinky silver gown.

Dad drove the four of us in his Town Car. Lefty went separately in his Jeep in case he got lucky. The bar was a cavernous dark space with concrete floors and furnishings rescued from abandoned factories in Poland. Staffed by a crew of sexy waitresses in skintight black tops showing dazzling cleavage. Unfortunately, recent run-ins with the Liquor Board necessitated their extra vigilance in checking IDs. We youths made do with grapefruit juice into which Cal dribbled a soupcon of vodka from her flask. Tastier than wine, but providing no detectible buzz.

Cooper's date looked awesome in diaphanous layers that appeared to have been rent and flayed in some industrial mishap. Holes here and there offered tantalizing glimpses of her delectable flesh. Similarly, her hair was swept about in cascades as if she arrived here after a high-speed police chase in an open sports car.

I complimented her on her stunning appearance. Cal thanked me and said I looked like I had dressed for a meeting of Math Nerds for Jesus. Then she clutched her escort, kissed him passionately, and told him he was the "sexiest man alive."

Soon the band fired up. They were Trent's pick, so no rap, punk, or hard rock. Four elderly black men on a small stage in a corner played funky jazz tunes. They swung a driving beat that was surprisingly danceable. Even Harvey and I–guys who couldn't get any whiter if we tried–were dragged to the dance floor, where we gyrated and spasmed to rhythms alien to our souls.

Dad, oiled by alcohol, hardly did any better. I was pleased to see that he danced more with Mary than Sheeni, who kept endeavoring to pry Trent away from Apurva without much success.

My brother and Chloe also graced the dance floor for the slower tunes. Mary commented that they're still at the stage where they can barely let go of each other. Scott said he's been hearing "nothing but good things" about our movie. He added that Dad hopes to get the editing finished in time to enter it this fall in the prestigious Toronto Film Festival. The title is still "Nick Twisp's Youth in Rebellion," but everyone is pestering him to drop the extraneous name.

Lauren, looking pretty in flaming orange, neglected her date to hang with me. I chastised her for the prank with the crumb donut.

"Oh, she found it, huh?" she snickered. "I bet her nose led her right to it."

"It was an expensive suit, Lauren."

"That's why I picked it. Ooo-eee, the devil made me do it!"

Lauren introduced me to her white-haired grandmother–a Mrs. Jean Moran (visiting from up north)–who told me that my father was a legend in Ukiah. She said that he still held the record there for the number of police jurisdictions that once were after him.

I also met Megan's date, a owlish-looking fellow who's a grad student in film history at U.C.L.A. Somehow we got on the topic of Jackie Coogan. He declaimed at length on the curious parallels between former child stars Jackie Coogan and Jackie Cooper. I didn't catch all of them as I was absorbed in watching another Cooper manhandle my love. Fortunately, that mostly tapered off after his parents arrived.

Brenda was fashionably late, arriving with a studly guy sporting a shaved head and extravagant tattoos. I never did get catch his name. They sat at a table with Roland and his date, our film editor Monica Spall. She was dressed inoffensively and didn't say much, being from Ohio. Roland coordinated his moth-eaten white tux with red tennis shoes. He got roaring drunk and told Sheeni Saunders that she was "tighter wound than London's Big Ben." Very true, but she let down her hair sufficiently to toss her drink in his face.

Orbiting in Harvey's exclusionary zone, I only got to talk to Tiara once, when her date was grazing at the catered buffet. She told me she recently ran into Denman Turnbull.

"Is that what Denny's calling himself these days?" I asked.

"Yes, he's settled on Denman."

"A den man is a guy who lives in a den, like a bear," I noted.

"Well, Denny likes it. He thinks it's very distinguished. Did you hear he had to get plastic surgery on his nose?"

"How's it look?

"Rather dainty actually. Denny's thinking of suing his surgeon. He did some research and discovered that he now has exactly the same nose as Shirley Temple at age six."

"He should sue," I said. "The publicity would do wonders for his career."

I tried ducking the Gargoyle–scalding the eyes in a gown fashioned from the feathers of some rare tropical bird–but eventually she tracked me down.

"Nick, why have you allowed that blind youth to usurp your presumptive girlfriend?" she asked.

"It's his last night in town, Connie. I thought I'd do him the favor."

"Your dating habits continue to astound. You were superfluous to my needs as well. I found out about Desmond and his clandestine armory."

"Really? How did you do that?"

"I asked his wife. She knew all about it. Desmond, you see, talks in his sleep. Plus, he has several thousand books on those rolling death machines."

"Veeva doesn't mind?"

"She says she would rather he devote his time, money, and energy to tanks than to running after starlets. Rather astute, but then she is my daughter. Her only real mistake was marrying him in the first place. So how does your Miss Haseltine fit into his obsession?"

"He had her portrait painted on one of his gun turrets."

"Her visage on a large steel phallus. That's entirely appropriate, I'm sure. Speaking of low carnality, has your scheduled love-making taken place?"

"Not yet. But please excuse me, I'm about to arrange it."

I had Lauren drag Cooper onto the dance floor, then waylaid Cal. "How's your evening going so far?" I asked.

"OK until now. What's up with you?"

"I found out my dad is going away for a few days. It should be easy to get some privacy for our hook-up."

"You know where he's going, don't you? He's flying with Sheeni up to San Francisco to look at her house."

"Really? Well, I'm not moving up there. He can forget that!"

"You wish. I just had an interesting chat with your aunt Joan in the ladies room."

"Did she say what starving, third-world country donated her dress?" I asked.

"No, Nick. She divulged something disquieting about you."

"What?"

"She says you're only 15. You're a mere child!"

"That's a lie. I'm 16."

"So you've been claiming. So you led me to believe. There's a place they send people who have sex with children. It's called prison. So you can forget about that favor I supposedly owe you."

"But, Cal, be reasonable. We're nearly the same age. There's only a few months difference. And no one will find out. Come on!"

"Not happening, Nickie dear. You show me a birth certificate proving you're of age and we might get together. Otherwise, forget it."

Fuck!

She had more bad news. She was leaving tomorrow with her parents for a family reunion in Seattle. Then they were continuing on to Banff and Lake Louise to gaze at scenic mountains and awe-inspiring glaciers.

"Why?" I demanded.

"Beats me, Nick. But my mother's hot for it. Lucky Harvey gets to stay home and mind the store. He'll probably be having torrid sex with Tiara every night."

"Don't rub it in."

"Now do you see why you should have killed him when he was so conveniently next door?"

"When will you be back?"

"The day before school starts."

"What? You'll be gone for two weeks?"

"That's right, bunky. A two-week car trip with my parents. My descent into hell begins tomorrow at dawn. Now I have to get back to my man. Some deluded girl in bright orange has him confused with her Halloween date."

All in all, it was by far the worst wrap party (and night) of my life.

WEDNESDAY, August 5 – I helped Cooper pack this morning. He was most disconsolate about leaving. I imagine small-town Sonora will seem quite dull after the bright lights of Hollywood. We promised to stay in touch; he even may have been sincere. He's coming down for the premiere, but with any luck that won't be for months. Cal may have forgotten all about him by then.

His parents, who had bunked at Brenda's, were hot to get an early start. Everyone exchanged hugs and off they went. No more blind people in my life. Once again I was free to leave mop buckets strewn about.

While Sheeni was packing for their trip, I asked Dad what was up with that.

"It's a short holiday to relax," he replied, squeezing his new tennis ball. "It's very stressful directing a major motion picture."

"You're checking out her new house?"

"That's on the agenda. I'm curious to see what you get for all those millions."

"I don't want to live in it," I said. "I don't want to move."

"Hey, I didn't want to live in a camel truck in France, but I did it. You do what life hands you and make the best of it."

"So you're thinking of moving there?"

"I'm not thinking of anything, Nick. My brain is entirely on vacation. So get off my back."

Not very communicative, but I could tell he was hung over. He probably had about five brain cells awake and on duty.

"So are you officially divorced?" I asked.

"I will be shortly."

"You're not getting married up in Frisco are you?"

"No, I'm not."

"That's good, Dad."

"Of course, the argument could be made that I'm already married. Sheeni and I never did get divorced after our Mississippi wedding."

"I vote you marry Mary Moran instead."

"My love life is not a democracy, Nick. You get no vote."

He reared back and threw a strike right at my head. I caught the ball an inch from my nose.

"Good catch, son," he said. "You got those fast Twisp reflexes. Want to learn to juggle?"

"Why would I want to do that?"

"Well, for one thing, over the years I've impressed a lot of babes with my juggling."

Something to consider.

"OK, Dad, I'll give it some thought."

Mary phoned right then to say they needed him to commit to a movie title.

"Oh, what the hell," he replied. "Let's make it 'Youth in Rebellion.'"

"Rebellion is such a clunky word," I pointed out.

"I know," he sighed. "We need some word that's shorter and more to the point."

"How about insurrection?" suggested Sheeni, rolling her suitcase out from the bedroom.

"How is insurrection shorter than rebellion?" asked Lefty.

Mary nixed insurrection because she said it would make our film sound like a war movie.

Since no one could come up with anything better, they settled on "Youth in Rebellion." Not great, but not revolting either.

Lefty took them to the airport. Suddenly, there I was alone on the 14th floor. I thought of all the fun things I could do unsupervised, then went back to bed and took a long nap.

Lauren called me as I was sitting on the balcony and watching a guy mow the grass in a military cemetery across Veteran Avenue.

"Hi, Nick," she said. "Great party, huh?"

"The best. What are you up to?"

"Hanging out here. Want to come over? There's something I need to show you."

"I have no transportation. Lefty went to the beach with a catering gal he met at Bzzzzzz."

"You could walk, Nick. It's only five blocks."

"Oh, OK. I'll be right over."

She was vacuuming the living room when I arrived. No one answered my knock, so I let myself in.

"I'm glad you're not a rapist," she said, switching off the Hoover.

"Don't make any wild assumptions," I replied. "Where's the rest of your crew?"

"Gone shopping for Megan's fall wardrobe. What did you think of her guy?"

"He seemed OK. What's with his goofy round glasses?"

"It's a common affectation among grad students. He's trying to look intellectual. I hear your co-star flew the coop."

"Off on a two-week vacation. Kidnapped by her parents."

"Her brother Harvey is awesomely cute. I can see why Tiara grabbed him."

"He's mentally deranged. I may be forced to waste him soon. What did you want to show me?"

"It's around the block. Let me get my keys and we'll go."

Around the block was a two-story stucco house with a FOR SALE sign posted in front.

"You know what's special about this house, Nick?" she asked.

"Ricky Nelson lost his virginity in it at age 12?" I replied.

"No, its back yard backs up against ours. We could tear down the fence and be one big happy family."

"It looks expensive. What are they asking for it?"

"Only $1.8 million. It's been on the market for a while. The kitchen needs a remodel and the pool is sort of funky. Your dad could buy it with his Hopper money and still have a big pile left over."

"It's nice, Lauren, but we want to be closer to the beach."

"You mean you want to be closer to Valerie. Listen, Nick, if your father doesn't buy this house, it's off to San Francisco for you. Do you want that?"

"Not at all, Lauren. I want him to stick with your mom."

"So getting him to buy this house is the best way to assure that."

She did have a point. I took out my phone and snapped a photo of the info on the sign. It was a much nicer place than my old house in Terre Haute. And it would beat living on the 14th floor with Sheeni.

We went back to Lauren's house and had some ice tea and lemon bars that her mother had baked.

"So what do you think, Nick?" she asked.

"It could work. You guys could live here and we could live there. Your mom could make dinner one night and Lefty the next. Dad could sleep over here any time he wanted to get laid, but would have a place to retreat to when they have arguments."

"Let's hope they don't have too many of those. And what about us?"

"I guess you'd be my stepsister. I expect the incest taboo would be kicking in."

Wrong answer. She leaned over and kissed me.

Rather nice. We embraced and kissed again. This went on for some time and was quite inflaming to the nerves.

The braces weren't bad.

Not that lacerating, if you didn't press too hard.

Later, back on the 14th floor, I got a call from Cal. They had just had a late lunch at a restaurant on Interstate 5 next to a feed-lot containing 10,000 smelly cows.

"What are you doing, Nick?" she asked.

"Writing in my journal. If in 40 years they make a movie of it, you could play Sheeni Saunders again."

"That would be too twisted even for Twisps. Oh, I'm so bored, Nickie!"

"I'm told the scenery improves in Oregon."

"I'm not interested in scenery, I'm interested in life."

"Yeah, me too."

"I suppose you're vastly pissed at me."

"Always, Cal. That's nothing new."

"You could dump me."

"Probably not going to happen. We Twisps got that masochism gene."

"Glad to hear it. Do you think our movie will be a success?"

"I hope so. You were great."

"You were not entirely incompetent. Oops, my father just emerged from the men's room. Got to go. Try not to forget me."

"Right, darling. I'll try not to."

As if I could if I tried.